GAME

SHIRLEY DAY

PUBLISHED WITH
PASSION

Print ISBN: 978-1-7392091-3-1

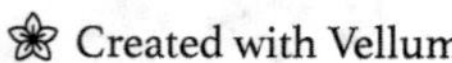 Created with Vellum

To Caroline
Remembering all the stories we told
The endless summers
And the sheer joy of being young.

AND SO IT WAS

'You said it was going to be the Caribbean.' Becca found herself wondering if she should pop the safety lock on the old car and jump out.

'Beccs, it was you who said a weekend in the Caribbean couldn't be done.'

She glanced over at her husband—the unshaved stubble, the cheeky crinkled face, the sheer joy of life painted over his features. At thirty-eight, Scratch was still a man who loved life, even when the sunny Caribbean wasn't a possibility.

'Teach you to be a smart arse.' He laughed.

'You didn't tell Finn I said the Caribbean was too far for his stag do?'

Scratch's eyes glinted. He loved a prank. Scratch always claimed humour was his biggest asset. He was your original GSH—good sense of humour—guy, always walking around with a few one-liners stuck up his shirtsleeves sure as the pop-up flowers magicians carry. Whatever shite life threw at him, Scratch might not be able to turn it into gold, but he could sure as hell turn it into something with a punchline.

He should have done stand-up. Missed his calling. That's what he said. Scratch had an elephant's graveyard of things he should have...could have...done.

'Besides...' she pulled her slim olive hands wearily through her dark bobbed hair, with its silver-grey streaks, '...there's a long way between the Caribbean and Falham. Like a whole different planet of "*way*".'

'Come on now, a weekend without kids, wherever we go, it is going to be perfect.' He took his hands from the wheel and squeezed her fingers gently between his, and Becca knew he meant every word. Scratch was an easy man to love. She'd never known him to be down. He could always find the bright side of a disaster. Even though he was driving, she kissed him on the side of his stubbled cheek. 'Not the two of us, though. Finn will be there.'

'We can let him off just this once. It is his stag. Besides, whatever that man wants, that man gets.'

Despite herself, Becca felt the bile rising in her throat; wasn't that the truth—Finn wanted, Finn got. The three of them had been friends since forever. Blood brothers with a sister in the mix, wandering the moors till way after dark. Telling ghost stories. Playing knock-out-ginger on the lost and the lonely. In short, they were the perfect pranksters for a stag. Though Finn had left it all a little late in the day. Becca and Scratch currently had twenty-three years of marriage under their belts.

She watched the squashed streets of Manchester slip past her rusted car window. They'd become urbanites, city dwellers. She couldn't quite work out when that had happened or even if she liked it. Though there were bene-fits. Some. 'There's no way I'd let any of our kids get up to what we used to, any of it. Any of them.' Becca and Scratch had enough kids. Five in total. The kid thing had gotten out of control. Family was important to both of them, but Becca had vowed to herself that whatever Scratch said to her, the little one—Ryan—four years old, would be their last.

'It was a different world when we were growing up,' Scratch mumbled. Changing the gear up, giving the car that little extra encouragement to run quicker. 'We were practically feral. That's what comes from having crap parents—absolute freedom. No one gives a fuck.' He took time to shoot her a wry smile. 'We're better than that, Beccs.'

In truth, the *parents* hadn't all been crap. Becca's mum had been sweet, but...then again, her mum had walked out, leaving Becca to cope with an alcoholic father. So, maybe not so *sweet,* then.

'Beccs. The weekend will be fun.'

Fun. She glanced over at her husband, his ready smile, that slightly off-centre face. The face she had spent most of her life loving. And she wished she could tell him that not wanting to go back home was so much more than not fancying the mud and the rain and the wind. She should have told him the truth years ago. Now the only thing she could do was keep trying to bury it and hope it would stay six feet under.

When Finn had rung to tell them where they were going for the stag, unluckily, he'd got hold of Scratch. If he'd got through to Becca, if she'd have had any say in it, they seriously would have been packing shorts in the case rather than wellies and jumpers.

'Scratch, did Finn say why?'

'Why?'

'The house. Why hire Old Man Byrde's house?'

Scratch shook his head. 'I mean, seriously, I couldn't believe it.' He laughed. 'Who'd have thought?'

'But it was horrible.' Even the thought of the old place sent a shiver down her spine.

'It's all changed now. I couldn't believe it. So smart. Absolute luxury. And that's what we need, Beccs. Seriously, these days it's not creepy at all.'

SHE STARED out of the window, wondering how it was that time had changed things so much. Did time change things? Or was it people that altered? As a kid, she'd have jumped at the chance to go stay at Old Man Byrde's. They used to love to scare themselves back in the day. Scared themselves shitless and then laughed till they could barely stand straight, but that was decades ago. Now, all Becca had been after was a weekend away somewhere nice. Ideally, with a sauna and a steam room. She wasn't sure anymore why they'd ever loved being frightened. After she had the kids, she didn't want to hear any stories that didn't have the Disney treatment. She certainly wouldn't want to go knocking on some poor unsuspecting bastard's door in the middle of the night with a knock-out-ginger surprise—which is what they'd done to poor old Byrde.

OLD MAN BYRDE'S had been their world beyond. The place where they could test themselves—face it, and they could face anything. The only way to get there was to follow a long winding path up the cliff face, and all the while, Scratch would be spinning his stories about lost legions and Rock Babies—spirits that crawled out of the earth and cuckooed themselves into other people's lives. Then, when they got to the top of the escarpment, jumpy as Jack and breathless from the climb, they'd surface about a hundred yards from Byrde's lonely old farmhouse. Only just before the ground flattened out, they'd have to go past this twisted dead tree, burnt and black, standing right up close to the edge. There was no way of avoiding it. You had to move, skin on tree, past the blessed thing. You needed to reach out and grab it just to steady yourself for that last step onto the escarpment.

LUCKILY, Becca's balance had always been good as a kid. She had kept her hands in her pockets. She'd touched the dead tree once and hadn't liked what she'd felt. It was as if the stump was just the tip of the iceberg, leading down through the earth to something older, nastier. Becca had always had this uncomfortable feeling as she got closer to the stump; the skin on her neck would start to pucker and crawl. It was as if one day that thing would throw out one of those blackened limbs, grab hold of her and hurl her rag doll body back down the rock face, cracking her skull on the granite below. She had even given the tree a name: The Watchman. She hadn't told the others. Tell Scratch a thing once, and he'd regurgitate it for the rest of your natural.

Besides, it was stupid to be afraid of a dead tree; even as a child, Becca knew that, but it didn't stop the fear. So, instead of dwelling on the crippled shape of the stump, she'd keep her eyes fixed on Byrde's kitchen window, which was forever spilling its warm orange halo of light out into the darkness. All the other windows in the house were permanently dark as coal pits, set into a wash of white plaster, giving the house the unnerving look of wearing a ghostly shroud. Even at night, the old house lurked like a death threat in the darkness, apart from that one kitchen window lit like a lighthouse, with Byrde always there framed in its centre, writing in his little book, always writing, until that night when he stopped.

So, no. Even if the ghost and devils had only been in their heads. Only plot points in Scratch's made-up stories. Even if the place had changed and was steeped in luxury, she wasn't looking forward to going back.

2

THE STAG DO – (RISK)

(RISK: A board game for 2 to 6 players. The goal: to occupy territory. Players form and dissolve alliances during the course of the game.)

Despite the overhaul, if you stood and looked out of the kitchen window, not much had changed. The smell was different. The house used to smell of wet tea towels and inch-thick dust, but not now, twenty-odd years on, it smelt of... Becca tilted her head and held her nose in the air, trying to catch a drift of some fresh waft as it filtered past—expensive clothes shops. That was it. Promises of a different life, maybe, but mostly, clean. The smart surfaces sparkled. The place smelt clean. Other people clean, perfect people clean. There was a note stuck to the fridge. *Irish Wolfhound LOST. Answers to the name of Trouble* and a phone number. So not everything worked out well in Planet Perfect. The date on the note was two weeks gone. Surely the dog couldn't still be lost? Then again...what kind of space cadet of an idiot would go calling a dog Trouble?

In the quiet, before the men tumbled through the front door, Becca gave herself a moment to take in the room. These days the farmhouse was all spotless white. Not a trace of dog, dirt or life. Who'd have thought some flash bugger would have given Old Man Byrde's place the twenty-first-century makeover. She remembered there had been a curtain under the sink. That had gone. Now there was a fitted cupboard. Byrde's kitchen had been a botch job, like everything else in their once-upon-a-crime world. It was all magazine smart now: fitted units, a long island, all the lighting hidden away. Not one wire was left dangling from the ceiling. The place gleamed as white and bright as an operating theatre. Becca wondered how much a kitchen like this would set you back, but she didn't have to think far to come up with an answer—too much. Despite the fact Scratch worked at a builders' merchant, he had always been crap with a screwdriver and worse with a budget. He'd made this hideous shelving unit over their bed, which they'd had to keep because he'd done it himself. He was proud as punch about the gangling, ugly thing even though the doors wouldn't shut properly. He had photos of it in his wallet that he showed around to his mates at work. Thankfully, that was the extent of his DIY endeavours. Becca was convinced he worked at B&Q solely for the banter. So, a kitchen like this one at Byrde's was out of their league.

Despite the luxury, she couldn't help feeling that it was stupid, coming back here after all these years. Some misplaced sense of childhood nostalgia. Every inch Finn's idea, which didn't stop it from being daft as shit. She pulled open the door under the sink. She couldn't help herself. It was all proper these days with its own hardwood panel and little safety catch. Despite the twenty-three-year gap, Becca half expected to see her sixteen-year-old self stuffed in there. All folded up and hiding like a Chinese gymnast. She bent down and had a good peer under the basin. It was just the usual: cleaning stuff. Storefront tidy, though. Not the usual skirmish of cloths and bleaches stashed away in a mouldering heap like she had back home. All the bottles in Byrde's rental were lined up and proud. Nozzles switched to off. Dusters washed, folded and smelling of laundry powder.

She stared, once again, out of the window. None of the glitz made any difference: all that smart lighting, the kitchen overhaul, the smell of money. It was neither here nor there because of that bad feeling that the house oozed like sweat. Stand at the window and look outside, and it was the same old eyesore. The large empty barns that should have come down years ago, they were still out there crouching, restless as a pack of wolves. Waiting. The iron struts poking out like bare bones, quivering and chattering in the wind. Asbestos, Becca thought. She'd be willing to bet that was what the roof was made of. That would be why the barns were still skulking at the edge of the yard. Even with a fortune to spend, it would take a fortune to pull the buggers down.

This was the view Byrde must have had when he sat there hour after hour scribbling away in his battered brown notebook. According to Scratch, Byrde had been making a list of everything he wanted. Scratch claimed it was the Devil's book Byrde was writing in, and the deal was—everything Byrde wrote in that book of his would come to pass. Everything. Only according to Scratch, when the last page was written, the Devil would come tap, tap, tapping for Old Man Byrde's soul. That was why the game of knock-out-ginger worked so well—Byrde lived his life permanently on the edge. Until, one day, the edge got too close.

To the right side of the house, the ground still disappeared off over the escarpment, just like it always had. An easy hundred-and-fifty-foot drop. Becca shivered at the thought. Why did she have to go thinking things like that? She'd told herself she wouldn't. It was such a long time ago now. An accident. She didn't even see the bugger go over. And yet, in her head, she always sees him. His windmilling arms. The look of sheer terror over his large ruddy face. Imagine a thing enough times, and it starts feeling real.

Becca had managed to convince herself, in the warmth of her own kitchen, in the mess of daily life, in the swell of chatter from the kids, that if she went back for Finn's stag, she could put the whole sorry incident of Byrde to bed. She'd half expected, half hoped, the old place might have changed beyond recognition: had such a dramatic overhaul that she wouldn't be able to fit the past into the present. But no. It was the fact that the tree was still there, which really took the biscuit, standing at the edge of the escarpment. That was what surprised her most. Why would anyone leave the tree? The Watcher. Ridiculous. How much did it cost to hire a chainsaw? The tree had been dead since forever, yet there it stood, still on the horizon, ugly as sin. Black and charred like the burnt body of something, someone, you caught sight of in the Sundays and wished you'd flipped the last glossy magazine page just that little bit quicker.

Closure: that was what Mr Phillips, the therapist she'd been seeing, had said. Not that she'd told him the whole story—Mr R Phillips. She'd toyed with what might be lurking under the 'R'. Scratch said maybe it was Roger. He'd told her if the bugger tried to hypnotise her, she was to run for the door. It was one of Scratch's jokes. Although it didn't really hold up because Becca couldn't remember the last time a man had looked at her like he wanted to make a move, well apart from Scratch. Becca had been wearing an invisibility cloak for years.

It had been Phillips who had put forward the only argument that worked as to why the stag in Falham might be good for Becca. Phillips had said how revisiting a place that held bad memories could help *move a person on*. And she knew that was part of the problem—letting things lie. Because none of it lay still in her brain. It was all very active, very alive. Phillips had explained how going back to the town where she grew up might show her that there was nothing to scare her anymore. It made sense. She needed to make peace with the past because she was the only one who knew exactly what had happened, and it was all too much for one person to carry.

She glanced again out of the window. Finn's car was parked up close to the barns. The only bit of colour in that dismal grey yard: a bright red Lotus. Some people had the devil's own luck—from poverty-street to flash-with-cash. Becca wasn't good with cars. She didn't have much of an interest, but Scratch had told her what Finn was driving. She supposed they must have had a conversation: *'Hi, Finn, I'm thinking of taking the rust-brown Skoda to the shindig, and yourself?'*

A smile crept up over Becca's lips. They'd had the Skoda since the nineties, and it was old then. More rust on it now than metal. Scratch had always wanted a Lotus, so he said. So he'd told her today on the drive up—when he'd told her that Finn would be driving one. That was the thing with Scratch. Sometimes it took Finn telling him what Finn had, for Scratch to realise just how much Scratch wanted that exact same bit of whatever. Yet, looking out at that chunk of bright red metal, Becca couldn't help feeling that Finn's car was far too shouty, embarrassing, too expensive and frankly —a bit daft. It should have been basking on a racetrack, not parked up some godforsaken escarpment. Besides, if she was Finn, she wouldn't have parked it so close to those barns: some bit of something loose could easily fly off and remodel that bodywork. It was always windy up on the escarpment. It wasn't supposed to be blowing a gale today. She'd checked. "Fine and dry," that's what the report had said, but up here on the scab of the world, the weather seemed to follow its own rules. Then again, if something did hit the car, no doubt Finn would be insured. Accidents for people like Finn never turned out to be much of a problem.

3

MARCO POLO

(A game for multiple players. Players are confined to a set space and must locate each other using auditory signals.)

Becca filled the kettle, not worried about the gender stereotyping, just glad to have something to do. They'd be wanting a brew when they got in. The men were supposed to be unloading the cars, but it was taking forever. Finn had bought enough food for them to set up their own supermarket. She glanced out of the window just in time to see a toilet roll go flying over the top of the Lotus, pulling a stream of white paper behind it. Becca had brought loo rolls from home; the holiday places she'd stayed in before often forgot the basics. She needn't have bothered. This wasn't that kind of a holiday place. In fact, this trip, she'd be taking stuff home. She wondered if Finn still did that, still had those light fingers of his. She knew that money didn't make much of a difference on that front. Once you've had the thrill of re-appropriating stuff that isn't yours, a new kind of need takes up residence in your soul. Besides, it was hardly the worst of his crimes.

Becca banged on the window. It didn't make a blind bit of difference. The lads continued dicking around oblivious. In answer to Scratch's toilet roll, Finn had gone for a bag of oranges. They'd broken free from their tight little net and were rolling like Mexican jumping beans all over the yard.

She banged again. 'Oi!'

The wind must have lulled because Finn glanced up. He was bent double, but he caught her look. The serious one she used on the kids: the *not-funny* scowl. He held up his hands as if to say, *okay, okay, we'll calm it down.*

Only just at that moment, some kind of high-dairy-content flan went flying from off-side and into his face.

Becca couldn't help herself. She laughed too. In a straightforward head-to-head fight, Finn would always have the upper hand, but Scratch was the sort of threat that came from the wings, unseen. The cheesecake made a satisfying impact.

Becca set to work rummaging in the cupboards looking for mugs. Each cupboard, each shelf, was neat and bland as a lifestyle store. Why would anyone even need all those plates, all those gadgets? People were only ever here for a week at most. Who spent their holiday stood over a Kenwood? Eventually, last cupboard! She found the mugs nestling beside the coffee, the tea, and a pack of on-the-house biscuits. Now she wouldn't have to wait till the lads got in with the groceries before making the brew, which, considering the pace they were going at, was just as well.

They hadn't seen each other for what? Eight...twelve months even? It was harmless enough: all that taking the piss with the groceries, a little light relief. Despite Scratch's all-pervading sense of humour, Scratch and Becca's lives had become a bit head-down-serious of late. So many bills. Rainforests were being carved up so those bills could keep flying through their letterbox. Why hadn't they paid more interest to the interest? One of Scratch's jokes. Which would have been funny if it wasn't so tragic.

Watching the money, that was Finn's deal, and this weekend might be a good time to see if he could give some advice or maybe even a swag bag full of help. He'd said he'd help with Ella's uni fees, but they needed more. It wouldn't hurt to ask. Besides, Becca had always thought he owed her one. She glanced back out of the window. Scratch was "helping" clear Finn up. Wiping cream from his face. The two men couldn't stand straight for laughing, and for a moment, she could see that this trip had been worth it. She couldn't remember the last time she'd seen Scratch laughing like that. There was white curd all over Finn's coat, and Becca was willing to bet both the curd and the coat were expensive. It didn't matter. The lads were oblivious. Because suddenly, cheesecake was the funniest joke on the planet.

On the looks front, Scratch came off short and dumpy compared to Finn. But Scratch wasn't a bad-looking guy. Kind eyes and a ready laugh, what more could a woman want? Her husband must have picked up on her watching because he turned and smiled. That was Scratch's medium —smiling. No one's face quite came together in the way Scratch's did when it had a little joy behind it. He'd put up with a lot from her over the years. But that was going to change. There would be no more children, no more exhaustion. They were going to get on with their own lives. They probably wouldn't even need Finn and his finances because they'd get their money under control themselves. With the youngest out from under her feet, Becca could pick up a bit of part-time work.

She heard the front door rattle open in the wind and the men tumble through.

'How long did you say we were staying?' Scratch's voice came from the hallway.

He'd gone more Northern, Becca noticed. He always did that with Finn, as if Scratch were a dog marking its territory. Up here at Byrde's, the accent was even more obvious because it had a kind of echo attached: that hollow reverb that big hallways, unused to life, seem to hold on to. It might have been over twenty years ago, but Becca didn't need to concentrate hard to conjure up Byrde's voice; that same echo, those same Northern tones shouting out from the past.

'What the hell do you think...' The memory from the past called out to her.

She shook her head, wanting to dislodge the noise. Two nights, she thought. What can happen in two nights?

'Got carried away in the deli section.' Finn's arms were weighed down as though with bags of evidence.

There was more food stacking up on the front porch than Becca and Scratch got through in a month, and they were a family of seven. She dug her nails hard into her palms. So hard the skin puckered into small luminous crescents. She had to rein herself in, stop falling into the hard-done-by trap. It was boring, predictable and worse than that, ugly. What did it matter if Finn was loaded? She had something priceless with Scratch. Money couldn't buy you that.

'Stick the bubbly in the cellar, mate,' Scratch called out, navigating his body around the bags piling up on the floor. 'That'll keep it cold. It's frosty as Hell down there.'

'Thought Hell was hot?' Finn tried the house keys in the cellar door, but nothing budged.

'It's fine to leave it up here. There's plenty of room.'

Becca threw open the fridge door, wishing they'd stop fiddling with the cellar. '*What the hell do you think...*' Byrde shouted from the past. That was the last place she'd seen him standing, just at the top of those cellar stairs, and those were the last words that came out of his mouth. Is that why Finn had brought her back here? Was he going to confess? Had it all proved too much for him as well?

'You seen this pile of food, Beccs.' Oblivious, Scratch laughed again.

And still, Finn kept turning those keys in the cellar door, worrying them again and again in the lock.

Becca glanced down at her hands. She'd circled them around her hot mug. They were shaking. Carefully, she balanced the cup on the side of the long kitchen unit, afraid the hot liquid would spill. 'Put it in the fridge, Finn. There's enough room.' Her voice sounded too high.

'No. I'll get it.' Finn continued worrying the keys.

Despite being close to that cellar door, Finn was still sounding bright and breezy. Had he forgotten?

The door swung open, letting out a low, hollow sound. Eerie as a small human gasp, as a cold sliver of pure frozen past dug its fingers deep into the nape of Becca's neck. She wanted to scream.

Finn didn't move. Instead, he stood like a statue in the dark shadow of the door.

'What, mate?' Scratch came up beside him, staring down into the darkness.

'Maybe, I will stick the bubbly in the fridge.' Finn hovered there, not taking one step forward.

'I told you...' She was trying so hard to keep her voice level, but all the time, she kept thinking, *shut the frigging door. Shut the door. Shut the door before It gets out.*

But Becca had no idea what *It* was. But there were a few

things for sure *It* wasn't. It wasn't some Stephen King clown from the imagination, something she could fold back into the covers of a book. No, this *It* was all too real.

'Finn,' Scratch laid a hand on his friend's back. 'Put the bubbly in the cellar, mate.' He tapped some of the bags with the toe of his trainer. 'There's too much stuff. Bubbly in the cellar will save room in the fridge.' He leaned forward, pushing his body out into the darkness. 'It's freezing down there.'

But Finn still didn't move, just stood staring into the dark well of the basement room, and Becca knew deep down in her gut—knew that even if they shut the door over now, they would be too late—*It* was out.

'Ha!' Scratch's voice boomed loud, clear and amused. Wallowing in delight about something else, something that was so not important. Because all Becca could hear was that voice from the past. Only now, it had new words. Words she couldn't get, not yet, but the buzz of them felt like a swarm of bees at the base of her spine, one that spread out over her nervous system, so her whole body trembled.

'Finn's scared, Beccs,' Scratch teased, oblivious. 'Finn's scared. Course he is... Big city players like Finnbow can't be doing with cobwebs. Cobwebs mean spiders.' Scratch arched his fingers and ran them over Finn's shoulders.

'Don't be stupid.' Finn hit the lights, brushing off Scratch's hands and disappearing down into the cellar with a case of champagne.

'He's always hated spiders. You remember that, Beccs?'

She didn't, not really. She wasn't sure how much more she could take of this. She wanted to scream. Instead, she looked up out of the window, and there was that tree again, standing on the horizon. The Watcher.

4

SCRUPLES

(A card game for three or more players based on ethical dilemmas. Object: to make players sweat as they ask each other how they would act in a variety of moral predicaments. The group then vote as to whether the player sitting in the hot seat is telling the truth or simply has an inflated opinion of their own moral standing.)

I t didn't take long for the lads to haul themselves up into what the vacation website called "the sunroom". Although, the sun had well and truly gone, slipping over the edge of the escarpment, pulled by its ankles from the world and not putting up an ounce of a fight. Becca had taken twenty minutes of peace and quiet away from the men. Scratch had been right about the overhaul; their bedroom was amazing. Finn had given Scratch and Becca the master. It was so big. Bigger than their entire ground floor at home. You could navigate all the way around the bed without even a hint of a shuffle, and the room was pure white, soft and clean as a snowflake. The dressing table, the chair, the bedspread, everything looked brand new. She put on a fresh coat of lippy and did a quick change into one of her evening outfits. She hadn't brought much, and this wasn't the kind of change that would invite comment.

Not that Scratch would comment anyway. Scratch had lots of positives but being fast on compliments was not one of them. Although she couldn't complain. In all the years they'd been together, he'd never once looked at another woman. Well, maybe if it was to crack a joke, but he had never looked like he wanted anyone else. Becca knew she was Scratch's everything, and oddly enough, sometimes that made her feel a little lost because that's a lot of weight for one person to carry. She wasn't sure she was up to it.

Most parents prioritise their kids, but Becca wasn't convinced Scratch did. If the family found themselves in a burning building, Scratch would be lifting her out first. He was smitten, whatever she did, whatever she wore. That's why this trip, she'd decided to keep the dress code simple. She couldn't bear Finn feeling as though he was being prompted into having to say something...something nice. She was creeping towards forty. She didn't need to see a picture of Finn's bride-to-be, Daisy, to know that everything about the girl would be perfect. Finn had the kind of looks, the kind of money, the kind of life that ended up with *perfect*. That man could get away with murder. She glanced at the roses he'd bought for her, the ones she'd stuck in a vase and carried upstairs. And she realised with a sickening hollow feel at the base of her gut that, most times, her price tag was way too low. A smile for a rose. It was all too cheap.

Another loud laugh exploded into the air from down-stairs and she knew that she should get down there too. But as Becca went to switch out the lights in the bedroom, the security light on the barns flickered on. She stood there for a moment, looking out at the yard, waiting for signs of movement. Half expecting to see three kids, their hands outstretched, ready to knock at the front door and run away, but there was nothing. Of course there was nothing.

She switched off the light in the bedroom, but she didn't move. Instead, Becca stood, a dark statue in the master suite, watching from the darkened window. Outside not a breath of air stirred as though someone had put a pause on the world. Not a thing moved. Not even the shadows, and yet still the hairs on the back of her neck began to stand on end because she had the curious uncomfortable sensation that the landscape outside was waiting. Waiting as it always had for hundreds of years. Soaking up tragedy and violence. The place was under no rush. It had time. And she shivered.

IN THE SUNROOM, the lads had lit themselves a fire using the chopped, neatly piled logs stacked by the back door. Everything in the house had been thought of by their absentee "host". All was at hand. You wanted a coaster. It was there. You wanted a blanket for your legs. Look at the end of the couch. By the time Becca arrived in the sunroom, the flames were roaring in the grate like a friendly spirit that the lads had caught out on the moors and dragged home for their entertainment. Even though the radiators worked a treat without even a protest or a gurgle, Becca was pleased to have the living warmth of the flames in the wood burner.

She'd shovelled a few handfuls of nuts into her mouth on her way through the house. It hadn't done the trick; she was still hungry, but Becca knew the score: admitting she wanted something to eat would see the chef's job landing itself neatly in her lap. She'd had years of that. Twenty-three, give or take the odd weekend off for good behaviour.

She wasn't even that good at it. So now she figured it was somebody else's turn. This was supposed to be a holiday, and that was exactly how she intended to play it. Let Finn fix the food. He'd bought enough.

'What did I miss?' She threw herself down on the over-large sofa, sinking into the duck-egg blue cushions, and took a swig from her second bottle of beer. She'd never liked the taste, but it was one of those things you just had to do if you were in with the lads.

'Lies and deception.' Finn smiled. 'Your husband at the centre.'

Becca snorted. 'Well, that can't be right.'

Scratch reached out and ruffled her hair affectionately.

Then she caught sight of the cards laid out and primed across the coffee table and let out a groan. 'Not Scruples.'

'Sweetheart, it's a brilliant game.' Scratch was always over-enthusiastic.

Brilliant. Was it really brilliant? It was an okay game. *Brilliant* for losing mates, burning bridges and rubbing everyone up the wrong way. Maybe. They'd stopped playing it years ago. It must have been Finn's game, or maybe the house had a set. She'd hide it tomorrow. A thing like that could only ever cause a meltdown.

'You are just in time.' Scratch gave Finn his best evil-eye look. Pure melodrama. 'Because this man here, my supposed best friend, he just called me out.'

'Too right.' Finn flicked the slim game card clutched loosely in his slim hands. 'Scratch said he'd fix something—structural stuff.' He glanced down at the text before reading it out loud. '*You are about to close the deal on your house sale when a disused well caves in, causing potential danger. Do you a) Cover it up hastily with a bit of hardboard—say nothing. Or b) Get it fixed, an expensive job.*'

'Hardboard!' Becca laughed. 'More like bloody cardboard.'

'What!' Scratch threw a hand across his chest as though his heart had been skewered. 'I swear, if it was dangerous, I would fix it. The keyword here is *danger*.'

'Scratch, how long have we been married? If there was a gaping hole leading directly to Hell from our bedroom, and you thought a bit of gaffer tape would do the trick...'

'Guilty.' Finn smiled.

The word struck Becca as odd under the circumstances.

'Beccs?' Finn leant towards her. 'Verdict?'

It was a game. Only a game.

'Absolutely.' She shot Scratch a conciliatory look. 'Babe, I love you, but...guilty as hell.' She sighed, stretching her limbs out like a cat into the warmth of the fire. 'Anyway...the next question is the important question.' She made sure she was looking comfortable. The sort of *comfortable* nobody likes to move. 'What are we having for supper?'

'You can't be hungry!' Sadly, Scratch had always been able to survive on a liquid diet.

Becca constantly had to remind him to eat. These days, the scales were inching up heavier on the overweight side of the checks and balances for Scratch, but it wasn't due to overeating. When there was beer and alcohol supplying the appetiser, Scratch would often skip the food element altogether. Becca, on the other hand, was after something to soak up the bubbly.

'One more game,' Scratch's voice sounded pitiful and small, like a child begging for five minutes more. 'You scoffed all those kettle chips, Beccs. And remember Finn's had a whole lemon cheesecake all to himself.'

'Actually, it was a New York Cheesecake I was wearing.

Your loss, guys. That cost me over twenty quid at the local deli. It's legendary on the wharf.'

'Wharf!' Scratch snorted. Spewing the word out with disgust. 'Twenty quid! For cream and biscuits. What have I always told you, Beccs?'

'Bet long enough, and your number comes up?' She smiled cheekily.

'Yeah, but...not what I was after. More money than sense these people.'

She threw a pointed finger into the air. 'Yup.'

Finn glanced down awkwardly, a flush of red hitting his cheeks.

'Not *these people*, Scratch.' It was Finn's turn to adopt the hurt look, only this time it was genuine. 'I'm your people.'

Scratch nodded. 'Course. Sorry. But one more game, mate, got to be done. Need to get my own back on the old character assassination front.'

'If we're going out...' Becca sighed, 'someone needs to stop drinking.' She hated this—being pushed into the role of sensible sister. Only somebody had to state the obvious.

The guys looked down at the beers in their hands, the movement as synchronised as if someone had counted them in—*one, two, three, go*. No one was driving anywhere.

Scratch laughed, putting on his best pinched and proper voice. 'Sorry, how many bottles of champagne can you have before you are over the limit, Officer?'

'Maybe a taxi,' Becca said. She wouldn't usually suggest it, but this was Finn's stag, and he had the deepest pockets of anyone she knew.

'One more game, guys,' Scratch continued. He loved games. Was never so happy as when he had a dice or a pack of cards in his hands. 'Think of this weekend as a liquid diet.'

Becca sighed. 'More like an experiment in pickling.'

'There was a time, my love, when we could have taken Sarson's on with just a few deep breaths. Fiery.' Scratch filled his lungs, before huffing a full stream of hot, beery air out into the room. 'The games have only just started. More.' His voice pleaded. 'We can't break it up so soon.'

'Okay...' Becca smoothed her hands over her thighs as if fixing her thoughts. 'One more round of Scruples, but that is it.'

Finn shuffled the cards. 'Your turn in the hot seat, Beccs.'

'Why not you?' She hated this game. It always ended in a fight.

'We've done Finn. Took you bloody ages getting changed, and know what—you still look exactly the same.'

Becca felt herself deflate, sure as a balloon that's had all the air sucked out; some bright bit of celebration that thought it was pretty, but no, in truth, it was just a wrinkled bit of nothing special.

'I thought you looked nice,' Finn said into the small silence.

Becca wasn't so sure the compliment was genuine. Finn was a man so crippled with manners that he couldn't be trusted. In fact, Finn couldn't be trusted with anything.

'She always looks great,' Scratch said, grinning ear to ear. 'No improvement necessary,' and he threaded one proud arm across her shoulder.

'Maybe.' She eased his arm off with a small shrug. 'But we'll need to eat.' There's always something comforting for a mother in that line. Despite the picky eating, the day, however bad it gets, is soon anchored in place by three ports of call: breakfast, lunch, dinner—safe havens.

Finn nodded, leaning forward to offer Becca the pack of cards so she could pick.

The sooner this was done, the sooner they could move on. She leaned towards Finn, extending her arm across the coffee table and picked out a single white rectangular card. Holding it up before her face, she squinted her eyes at the small, tightly packed text.

'Beccs! One of us has to read it.' Scratch sighed. 'You know the rules: no fudging your own Scruples card.'

'Would I?' In truth, she probably would. Knowing how and when to *fudge* was part of the whole "game" thing. Fudging was fine, only to be expected. Not fudging was wet-blanket territory. She doubted Daisy would fudge. Wanting it over, Becca handed the card back to Finn. 'Go for it then.'

'Okay.' Finn cleared his throat before starting to read, '*Your marriage is going through a rough patch*.' This seemed to amuse him. 'Can't say I didn't warn you.'

'Too late now, mate.' Scratch smiled. 'I had the market cornered. If you're an ugly bastard living in the Yorkshire wilds, best bet—marry a pretty girl quick before she disappears off into the big blue yonder.'

'Scratch!'

'Pretty girl…small pond…mine, mine, mine.'

'You know there's something deeply disturbing about that, don't you? You smug git,' she added, giving Scratch a flick on the leg for good measure.

His grin just got wider. 'Smug git? Crafty sod, mi amore, I go by many names.'

Becca's eyes shot to the heavens. 'My question, please. I haven't even had the bloody question yet! Scratch, why do you always have to be the one dancing in the spotlight?'

'What can I say.' Scratch smirked. 'The spotlight just loves old Scratch.' He extended one leg out across the floor and kicked Finn playfully on the foot. 'Like the lady said— keep up, mate. She's waiting.'

Finn glanced down at the card. '*Your marriage is going through a rough patch.*'

Scratch raised his eyes as though losing patience. 'You've said that once, mate. Get a move on.'

Finn smiled, his turn to look smug.

Cheeky bugger, Becca thought. Finn knew exactly what he was doing—savouring that phrase about their marriage in trouble. There was nothing wrong with their marriage.

'*You meet someone you were in love with and still have feelings for,*' Finn read. '*Do you... a) Say hello but get away quick. b) Act on this long-term passion.*'

'No question.' Becca didn't even bother to mull it over. 'Say hello but get away quick.'

Scratch's brow furrowed. 'Isn't there an option where she doesn't say hello?'

'Scratch! I can be trusted to say hello.'

'But what about passion, Beccs?' Finn appeared to be having a problem computing. 'I mean, if this weren't you and Scratch. If this were you and someone else. Say you weren't even married to Scratch. Don't you think passion is important?'

'Twenty-three years,' Scratch said, oblivious to the mounting tension. 'That's what me and Beccs have got between us, and that's just the love and sex. Before that, we had friendship.'

'Yeah.' She nodded, pleased for once that Scratch was letting his thoughts spill, though wishing he hadn't said S.E.X. Love would have been enough. She took his hand gently between hers. 'It's monogamy, all the way. Marriage... well, you'll find out soon enough, Finn, it's all about belief.'

'And shit hot sex.'

Becca refused to even pick that one up and run with it. 'Actually, Finn,' she said. 'Know what the secret of marriage is? I'll tell you this one for free. It really is belief that counts. Without that, everything crumbles. Besides...' She drew her hand gently across Scratch's unshaven jaw. The thin layer of stubble on a younger man would have looked trendy. Even though trendy was a long time behind them, rugged still worked. She smiled and planted a kiss on his familiar, rough cheek.

'Besides?' Finn prompted.

'The sex is alright.' She had meant it as a compliment. She genuinely did...but...

Finn burst out laughing.

'Alright!' Scratch was looking pissed off.

Mock pissed off? Becca wasn't sure, but the expression was writ large.

'Cheers.' He grunted.

Well, what did he expect after twenty-three years! Surely *Alright* was enough.

5

____

VILLAGERS & WEREWOLVES

(A card game for multiple players. Each player is dealt a card with a character on it. Most players will receive a villager card. One or more players will have a werewolf card. The aim of the game is to discover who holds the werewolf cards before they destroy the village.)

As Finn had packed away the Scruples, Becca felt an overwhelming sense of relief. It looked as if they'd escaped with minimal damage. Most egos remained undented. Though, come to think of it, Scratch never had a problem with a dent in the ego. Even so, maybe two rounds of Scruples were all most people could reasonably be expected to cope with before having to pick themselves up from full-scale nuclear fallout. The box should carry a warning.

'Talking of shit hot sex,' Scratch said, and Becca realised that there was another problem with the game: it left scars of conversation open, ones that could be picked over all night.

'Where's your woman then, Finn...this Daisy?'

Daisy, even right up on that scab of the world that was Byrde's old place, Daisy was clawing her way in.

'I haven't even seen a picture.' Becca managed to sound curious. 'Have you got one on your phone?' Becca hadn't wanted to know anything about Daisy when the woman first appeared on the scene. She'd felt there was a good chance that the whole Daisy thing would wither on its chain. Life loves a good irony. And now, Becca still didn't want to see because there was one thing for sure: Daisy was going to be gorgeous and younger and brighter and teeth whiter. Although at some point in time, Becca knew she was going to have to take a look. And maybe it was best to be forewarned before having to gawp over a woman dressed like a million dollars. Standing at the altar in a swirl of diamonds and white lace pretty as the happy ending of a fairy tale.

'Later,' Finn said dismissively.

'Don't tell me...' Scratch laughed, 'she's ugly as sin. I think he's embarrassed, Beccs.'

'Scratch! Daisy's not going to be ugly as sin. Finn's a looker, always was.' She could give him that, but only that. Her eyes narrowed as she shot Finn a wry glance. 'It's just the man's personality that's so disastrously flawed.'

Finn smiled; it was mostly teasing. It had always been this way: barbs hidden in compliments. It was the only kind of endearment any of them knew how to deliver. 'Who needs enemies, hey?'

'Why didn't she come then?' Suddenly Becca was burning with curiosity. This might be Finn's stag, but it was more weekend away than old school boys only. Maybe this wariness Becca felt, maybe it worked both ways: who knew what Daisy thought about Becca?

But no, Finn's face was pure innocence. 'She had to do some urgent spending.'

Becca laughed. 'Is that like a hobby now, an activity?'

'More like an Olympic sport—the amount of time Daisy puts in.'

'Know what, Scratch.' Becca let her eyes rustle up a grain of a sparkle. 'I fancy a bit of that myself. When we get back home can you diary me in a bit of *urgent spending time*?'

'You can *urgent spend*, my love, around Aldi to your heart's content.'

Becca pulled one of the soft velvet cushions from the armrest and crashed it playfully across Scratch's head.

'Oi! You weren't always so bloody tight.'

'Can't be called tight if you don't have any money,' Scratch returned, smug as if he was talking with the wisdom of Solomon flowing through his veins. 'Then it's called being careful.'

'Yeah, but sometimes you were seriously flush back in the day, and it didn't stop you from being tight. Scratch cards, remember?' Finn laughed as if even the idea was oh-so-funny. 'Scratch was always winning on those damn things.'

The memory brought a smile to Becca's face. 'He had... Do you remember? He used to have silver foil under his nails? That was why we called him Scratch.'

'Long time ago. I was a lucky bastard in those days. Alas, the Gods have forsaken me. Gotta work for a crust these days.'

Outside, the wind howled as though pitching in with some mournful soundtrack: the working man and his troubles, and despite the fire and the fact that the sunroom was now all new-built and fancy, Becca couldn't help but remember where they were: sitting at the edge of the escarpment with its sheer drop back down to earth.

'We shouldn't have come back,' she said. It was out of her mouth before she had time to stop it.

Finn looked hurt. 'You don't like it?'

'Too many memories.' She felt her molars clamp together in her jaw fighting the impulse to grind them together so the truth couldn't spill out into the room.

'But it's a different story now.' Scratch squeezed her hand, reassuringly. No one wanted a trip back into the past, but everything had changed for Scratch. The present was filled with excitement. He glanced greedily around the room, drinking it all in. 'It's barely recognisable anymore. Such a high spec. Luxury. The taps in the bathroom weigh a ton.'

'Scratch! You're not supposed to lift them off. You're supposed to turn the bloody things.'

'Odd to think, all that time growing up haunting the place, and we never once came inside.' Scratch threw one arm over the back of the sofa and took in the room. 'I bet even Old Man Byrde wouldn't recognise the place these days.'

Becca wasn't so sure. She could still feel the old man's presence. Besides, 'Those barns are still an eyesore.'

'And the tree!' Finn laughed. 'Who'd have thought that would still be standing. You can see it from here.'

A cold shudder passed down Becca's spine. 'I don't think so. We're too far around.'

'No.' Finn jumped up keen as a puppy, his slim arm pointing out through the long windows into the shiny darkness that lurked just past his reflection. 'Just there.'

Becca squinted out into the night. 'No, you're wrong, Finn. Like I said, this sunroom's too far around.'

'There. Look just over there.'

He pulled her from the sofa, taking her thin shoulders

into his wide palms, shifting her slightly into position. And despite the fire in the stove, a cold gripped Becca's insides as her stomach turned because, sure enough, she could see it. Not exactly the tree, but a patch of night. A slit, darker than all the rest, a shadowy black shape.

'We seriously shouldn't have come back,' Becca mumbled, unable to turn away from the tree now she knew it was there. Because it seemed to Becca that if she turned her back on it, the thing would creep-mouse right up to the glass and smash its hard boney arms against the window.

'Remember that time...' Oblivious, Finn's face lit up with some warm memory as though someone had switched a memory projector on in his brain, and he was basking in its flickering sepia light. 'Remember when Old Man Byrde almost caught us. We must have been about fourteen. You got something in your foot, Beccs?'

She shook her head, pretending she couldn't recall, not wanting to go back. What was the point? There was only forward, that's what Phillips, the therapist, said, but Finn wasn't stopping.

'Scratch ran on, he was way ahead of us, and you...you must have stepped on something?'

'I don't remember.'

'You must remember, Beccs! I realised you weren't with us and came back for you. It was...shit, I think it was a piece of glass cut straight through your trainers.'

'No.' She shook her head. It was sandals, not trainers, yet she didn't want to fix the old details too firmly in her head. She didn't want to think about Byrde. *Speak my name.* Isn't that what all the horror films say? Becca knew she couldn't afford to go dredging up their childhood. Yet she could see Finn reflected in the glass beside her. It was her, the tree and Finn. Just like that night with Byrde.

'Beccs?' A crater of a frown cut through Finn's smooth forehead. 'You can't have forgotten? I came back. I realised you must have gone into one of the barns, that you were hidden in there, and that Old Man Byrde must be in there too.'

'You sure?' Scratch stopped for a moment, looking up from the spliff he was rolling.

'Yeah.' Finn nodded.

'I don't remember that. This is before Byrde went flying?'

'Scratch!'

'Way before. We were fourteen or so. You don't remember, mate, because you'd run off down the bloody escarpment. You didn't wait. Byrde cornered Becca in the barn. I knew he was in there because the front door to the house was standing wide open where he'd run out after us, and then I could hear voices. A voice. His voice.'

'No.' She tried to shake her head dismissively as though she really couldn't recall. What good would it do?

'And I picked up this boulder.' Finn lifted his arm as if replaying some muscle memory. 'Put the window in to try and flush him out—get him away from Becca.'

'You're lying.' Scratch stuck out his pointed tongue as though in charge of a precision instrument and licked the paper before rolling it into a neat sausage.

Becca was glad of the pause. Sadly, it didn't last.

'Like I'd run off and leave her. Sir Galahad at your service.' Scratch laughed, adding some kind of half-bow. 'You saying you rescued her, Finn?'

'No. I... You don't remember, Beccs?'

'It was such a long time ago.' She shuddered. 'Point is, we shouldn't have come back here. Now. Never mind the overhaul. This place was always trouble.'

'Nah.' Scratch laughed. 'That was the dog.'

She looked blank.

'Irish bloody wolfhound, lost.'

The dog had gone clear out of her mind. 'I just think...'

'Becca! Give it a rest, love. You're just tired, sweetheart. Finn, mate, she appreciates it. Seriously, she does. I mean, apart from the no smoking rule, which it has been my absolute pleasure and honour to break.' Scratch took a toke. The breath in seeming over-large, exaggerated. 'The place is amazing, and we should start as we mean to go on, eh? And who'd have thought that one day we'd end up on the inside. So, not such a bad idea, really. Hey, Beccs?'

She'd never told Scratch that she'd been in the house before. In fairness, it had only happened once. Not the night when Finn had broken the glass to distract Byrde. The other time, when Byrde had picked her up in his car after her dad had gone loopy. The time that Byrde had wound up dead.

Scratch smiled his all-contented smile. 'First time for everything, eh? Top of the world.' He leaned forward, passing the joint to Finn. 'So then, Finn mate, what about the A-list party? Will that be in the big smoke?'

'A list? You are the A list, you and Beccs.'

Scratch pumped Finn's fist in the way they always had. 'Well met, sir. Shit, the parents we had. Apart from Beccs' mum, obviously...'

Finn nodded. 'Yeah.'

'While she lasted.'

'Scratch.' Becca didn't want to talk about her mum. Even after all these years, that cut still bled. How could her mother just walk out and leave her?

'Sorry, Beccs. But we managed. It was always us, stick together through thick and thin.'

Becca stared out of the long glass windows at the shadow of the tree, and suddenly, the noises in the room, the chatter, seemed to fade away. Because when she blinked her eyes, she was sure the tree lurched forward. The shape dancing just a little, closing the distance between them.

'There's going to be the party at the Groucho club,' Finn said as if the world was still turning. 'I told you this?'

It's a tree, Becca thought, and a dead one at that. It can't move. Can't even wave its arms in the wind. Any movement would just be shadows catching the light, playing tricks with her eyes.

'Nah.' Scratch shook his head. 'Don't think you did mention any party, mate... Groucho what?'

Her heart suddenly leapt. She could swear the tree had jumped. This time she'd seen it. One foot, two. The thing was closer. Becca peered anxiously into the darkness.

'A club on Dean Street. Soho. Private members.'

'Members,' Scratch drew out the word, making it sound perverse. 'What like dicks? Members means dicks. Private dicks!'

'Whatever, Scratch.' Finn was refusing to react. Instead he drew in on the joint. 'It's two weeks tomorrow. I told you already. Daisy sent you the invite.'

Becca focused on her breathing. In and out, that's all she had to do. That's what the therapist said.

'If you and Beccs want to come, you're welcome. You know that.'

In out, regular and calm. The tree was going nowhere. Trees only walk in fairytales, and that Shakespeare thing she read with Ella when Ella had been doing her A levels—Macbeth. She needed to stop this and stop it now. So she did. She pulled herself from the window, wrapping her cardi tighter across her shoulders, and turned her back on the outside. The Watcher was under control. It had to be just a trick of the light. Trees don't move.

'But Finn,' she had to ask, 'why this place?'

He shrugged as if the decision wasn't important. She wondered how he could be so cool, how even if the tree didn't strike terror into him, how could he avoid feeling that the ghost of Old Man Byrde was still rattling around the house?

'It was a pure fluke how I found the place. I was looking through this rental website around this kind of area, and there it was. And when I saw the house, and I thought... Well, why wouldn't we?'

Becca could think of a shedload of good reasons why they wouldn't, but like always, she said nothing.

'Old Man Byrde.' Scratch snorted. 'You remember? Selling his soul to the Devil.'

The wind moaned a low predatory howl as it prowled full circle around the house. Did it ever stop pacing?

'Scribbling away in that little brown book.'

'For Christ's sake, Scratch,' she snapped, and the bite hung awkwardly in the silence it carved. 'Sorry, love, but the man's dead.'

They stared at her in that embarrassed way people do when they realise someone's losing it. They shine the spotlight on you, and whether they mean to or not, they make you squirm.

'Anyway,' she said just as though everything was normal. 'I'm starving. I'm going to stick something in the oven.' Somebody had to. 'We've been boozing like teenagers home alone with the drinks cabinet. Can't stomach it anymore.'

Finn nodded. 'Sure. We could get a taxi into town.'

'Take forever to get here,' Scratch said, still sunk into the sofa. 'Why don't we walk?' Suddenly his face was all illumination. He was even shifting on the sofa as though he seriously might pull himself up. 'It'll be like old times. I can tell stories about ghosts and Rock Babies.'

Another howl from outside.

'We can't walk.' There was no way Becca was taking a night-time hike down that escarpment. 'We've got a fridge full of food, and I'm hungry now.' She couldn't help herself. She could hear her voice, too whiny, too high-pitched. 'I can put a pizza in the oven. Finn, you did buy pizzas?' That was just snip and unpack. She figured a pizza wouldn't null and void her no-domestics vow.

Finn looked blank. 'No. I mean...a lot of people...women don't eat wheat anymore.'

'I like wheat.'

'Sorry. I didn't know. But what the hell, Beccs? This is a celebration. Scratch is right. We should go out. I can foot the bill.'

Another howl from outside.

'Shit!' Scratch laughed. 'What is going on out there? It's like the Arctic.'

'Check the weather report.'

Scratch glanced at his phone. 'No signal. What network are you on?'

'EE. Phone's in the bag.' Finn pointed to the tan leather case propped up at the edge of the sofa. Angled beside Scratch's legs.

'Shall I just put the oven on?' She didn't want to be doing this, but she had to get some kind of food inside her to soak up the booze. The alcohol was making her edgy. 'There's gotta be something easy we can eat? Pasta?'

'No pasta, Beccs. Didn't buy any.' Finn was looking sheepish again, realising he'd made an A-one blunder on the food front.

'Where did you get this rubbish about women not eating wheat?'

'Daisy doesn't.'

'Well, most of us do.'

Finn shifted awkwardly. 'Scratch, grab my phone, will you?'

Scratch reached down to get Finn's case.

'My vote is,' Finn announced, like a Guardian of the Galaxy, 'if the weather's alright, I say we take a walk into town. There's a couple of restaurants down there. The wind always sounds worse up here.'

Scratch unzipped the bag. 'Walk?'

Finn nodded. 'Has to be feet. We'll just check. If there's no storm forecast...'

Becca could scream. Why was no one listening? It was such a bad idea. 'The report'll say it's fine, but it won't be. Guys, if we're all too pissed to drive a car, we're too pissed to walk down that escarpment. Chips? Have you got any sodding chips?'

'Sodding chips and ketchup.' Scratch laughed. 'In a fancy joint like this. All that food we've got.' Suddenly, his face dropped. 'Fuck!' And instantly, there was silence. Even the wind appeared to have caught on to the idea that something monumentally bad had just reared its ugly head. Even the elements wanted to listen in. Because Scratch wasn't holding Finn's shiny new mobile up in his hands, no. Clutched between Scratch's large rough fingers was a small leather book—Byrde's book.

In a split-second, Finn jumped him, pulling the book from Scratch's hands and scuttling off halfway across the room.

'Guys?' Becca looked from one to the other, confused.

'It's the book.' Scratch laughed. 'Finn's got Byrde's bloody book.'

'I...I...' Finn stammered, but he wasn't trying to deny it.

'It is Beccs, I swear.' Scratch's voice sounded triumphant. 'Where the hell did you get it?'

Finn kept the book held tight: hands clasped around it, the colour leaching from his fingers till they were luminous white.

'Spill, Finnbow, my mate.'

Oh, shit. Becca thought. It was all going to come out! That was why they were here. Finn wanted this. He was going to tell everything, and in a way, that was good because if Finn told, Becca could pretend she knew nothing about it. It would be Scratch's problem. Scratch would have to decide what to do with her memory of Byrde's body and the way it went spiralling off the edge. Maybe Becca could finally bury it.

'Finn, I'm waiting?'

Finn swallowed hard as though there was something physical wedged deep inside his throat. 'Okay, so after Byrde did himself in...'

'You mean after he died.' She couldn't help herself. Becca was itching to have Finn tell all, but she needed him to tell it right.

Finn looked pale, washed out. He didn't have the energy to quibble over semantics. 'After Byrde went over the cliff, I just came up one day and...the house was empty, the door was open.'

And it hit Becca hard, an eternal sense of disappointment and weariness—this wasn't the right story. But Finn wasn't stopping. He just carried right on dealing out the lies, as processed as packaged meat spewing out of a sausage factory.

'I didn't mean to do anything wrong. I was just curious.'

'Those light fingers,' Scratch teased.

'Scratch, shut up.' She couldn't help herself. 'Finn, you need to tell the truth. It's best, seriously. The first time you came into the house. Tell us. No judgment. Tell it all.'

Becca could hear that odd buzzing at the base of her skull. The bees knew Finn was coming for them, going to put them to rest once and for all.

Finn took a deep breath as if hoping it would support his words through the worst. 'I came back after Byrde's funeral.'

No, she felt the scream rattle around her head. This was wrong, all wrong.

'I saw the book. It was on top of one of the cabinets, and I...I took the damn thing.'

Becca couldn't help herself. Tears pricked at her eyes. 'Finn!' Byrde wasn't a bad man. He didn't deserve what happened. He had been kind to her once, talked to her about her mum. Talked like he cared, and then...Finn pushed the guy to the brink before stealing his sodding money and his bloody book.

'The man was dead,' Finn said simply, as if that would put an end to it. 'Come on, loads of people write in journals. Scratch, you used to.'

Scratch's eyes widened in disbelief. 'Diary, mate. I had a diary because I was behind at school, and they thought it would help me catch up. But you! Byrde and that book, man they were both cursed.'

'Scratch!' Becca felt the irritation rising in her voice. 'This is not the time.'

'*Cursed* was just kids' stories, Scratch.' Finn's voice was so quiet. It was as if he was slipping into mouse mode, trying to hold on to reality as though everything would smash if he spoke too loud. 'Your stories, Scratch.'

Scratch shot him a wry look. 'But if the cursed book is just *my story*, mate, why in hell would you keep it?'

Becca stared at Finn, trying to work out where this was all going. 'Are you writing in the book?'

Scratch snorted. 'Finn? I mean, what can Finn want for? It can't be money. You got that coming out of your ears faster than wax.'

'It's just a…' Finn shrugged. 'It's kind of like a bad habit. Like not walking on the cracks in the pavement.'

'So, what do you write in it?'

'It's just like a journal. You used to have a journal, Scratch,' Finn pleaded.

But Scratch was stonewalling his friend; that explanation wasn't going to wash however many times Finn tried to rephrase it. And so, Finn lowered his head, avoiding eye contact. His voice slipping down low in his throat as though he was trying to hide the words. 'Everything I want, I write it in the book.'

Scratch nodded as if this was all so predictable. 'Just like Old bloody Man Byrde.'

'That was a story.' Finn and Becca spoke together, at the exact same time, and Becca felt a glow of relief: at least they were on the same page about something.

'Does it say things about us, Finn?' She couldn't help herself. She needed to know. 'Have you written things about me and Scratch?'

'Some. When Scratch was ill.'

Scratch looked puzzled but kind of touched. 'You wrote that in there?'

'I wanted you to be okay again.'

'But, mate, after what we'd said about that book, you wrote...?'

'You were at death's door.'

'How many pages have you got left?'

There was a silence, awkward and full, as though someone had shot it through with an electrical current.

Finn lowered his eyes once again. 'Two.'

Scratch threw back his head and roared. Becca wasn't sure why. All she knew was that she wanted to get out. She couldn't stay in that room any longer with Scratch not knowing the full story and Finn clutching for explanations that didn't make sense. She had to go somewhere quiet.

'Becca?' Scratch called after her, as she walked from the room. 'Come back. The fun's only just started.'

But for Becca, it was finished. Finn could have told all; his moment had come and gone. She was still stuck with the guilt, with Byrde. With his voice, *'Why didn't you tell?'* And that buzz at the base of her skull. Like a hum. Like permanent tinnitus haunting her.

Becca went to the kitchen and stuck two slices of toast in the toaster—wasn't toast wheat? To make matters worse, the toaster was one of those fancy ones: Dualit. She'd seen them in John Lewis. Heavy as buggery, with some old-fashioned mechanism you'd need an engineering degree to figure out. Everything in this place was set against her. Becca scrutinised the dials. How difficult could it be? Bread in—easy. Lever on the side—toast down. Only, her fingers were shaking. She was on edge, and the hunger wouldn't be helping. The book. What was Finn doing with the book!

The bread disappeared down into the wide metal slots, but nothing happened on the action front. There were two large knobs on the side. She flicked one around, and instantly the toaster began ticking sure as a time bomb. Sorted. She would master this place if it was the last bloody thing she did, and Finn would end up telling the truth. He had to.

Outside, the yard lights were on. They must have been new ones. They were way more powerful than the old versions. Giving out full coverage in a piercing white LED scream. There'd be no hiding from anything now. Even the front door had a light over it these days. A light over the front door, how simple was that? Why hadn't Byrde put a light in? That would have stopped them. Probably.

Course she remembered it: the night Finn was talking about when they were fourteen. Way before Byrde fell to his death. Finn had put a brick right through this very same window she was looking out of now. It must have cost a fortune to repair. It takes being a homeowner to help you work that kind of thing out. So why hadn't she said? When Finn kept asking her *do you remember*...why hadn't she confessed? She didn't know. It was just another secret to add to the pile. Or maybe...maybe she wanted to punish Finn in some way for letting her down because that night, that night when they were just fourteen, up here alone with Byrde on their tail, that should have been the first night of their lives. Everything was laid out in front of them. No choices had been made. No blunders stitched into the personal history of their world.

Standing in Byrde's kitchen all those years later, looking out at the front doorstep, Becca got the unnerving feeling that if she looked hard enough, she would be able to see the three kids standing there on that stone slab of a doorstep, huddled together: a group of up-to-no-good and nothing-special fourteen-years-olds, egging each other on and up and finally over the point of no return.

6

———

KNOCK-OUT-GINGER

(A prank game for multiple players. Goes under many different names, including Knock, Knock, Ginger and Ding, Dong, Ditch. It involves knocking on the front door of the victim, then running away before the door can be answered.)

As kids, they had played knock-out-ginger maybe every month or so through the winter. Scratch said it had to be winter because *the darkness was their friend.* Unsurprisingly, he used his voice-over voice to deliver this little nugget of wisdom.

By season three of the fun and games, Byrde had put in an arc light over one of the barns, but instead of spoiling things, it just made the whole song and dance even more fun. Because when they went past the orange beam from the industrial-style light, it threw grotesque shadows onto the walls. They spent hours trying to hold in belly laughs as they twisted their bodies into ridiculous shapes, striding like monsters or cowering like victims. Well, maybe not hours, but a fun-filled five minutes—they had short attention spans, a fact everyone seemed more than happy to keep telling them.

Becca wasn't sure if Old Man Byrde ever saw their shadow show. She thought probably not, leastways he never came out for it. After their improv light performance was done and dusted, they would crouch down low and sneak past the kitchen window. Byrde would be inside, pen in hand, scribbling, scribbling, bald head facing out for all the world to see like a polished brown egg, never looking up.

The night Becca got caught had started off as a total riot. They had been pissing themselves laughing even before they'd got to the big barn. Byrde's bald egghead had been practically glowing luminously in the kitchen. It was so bright. Scratch said it was a shame not to use him as a lighthouse. Funny the bits of a person you see. Bits that they'll never catch a look at themselves. The three friends were still laughing when they slipped into the barns. They'd decided they were going to explore. Finn figured that maybe Byrde was storing something in there. Something worth nicking? Nothing really valuable; they weren't criminals, just your average young hooligans out for a laugh. At least, that's what Scratch said. When you were young, you needed to milk the experience because the powers that be couldn't lock you up, so playing a bit dirty here and there, what did it matter?

But when they shone the beams of their torches over the barn, they were disappointed. Whatever had been stored in there had long since gone. There were some massive blue plastic barrels, all empty. The only things left were dank air and echoes.

'What even is this place?' Finn aimed a corridor of light at the strips of clear swinging plastic that were strung from the ceiling like massive shower curtains. The light from his torch went mental, bouncing off everything it touched, so you had no idea as to depth.

Becca tripped over a heavy link of chain and fell flat on her face.

'Beccs!' Scratch laughed, even though it wasn't funny. 'You alright?'

'Stupid question.' She eased the chain away from her ankles. 'That thing is seriously heavy.' She could barely lift it off the floor.

'You'll live,' Finn said because they all knew that was the bottom line. 'So what the hell is this place?'

'Used to be an abattoir.' Scratch ran his torch into the corners, always the expert. Even when he knew diddly-squat about a thing, he'd still manage to fish you up an answer. Only this time, maybe his answer wasn't make-believe. Maybe this time, he'd hit true because there was something odd about the place, a faint metallic stench.

Becca made her breath go shallow, squeezing her nostrils shut from the inside and walking back towards the entrance so she could stick her head out of the iron door. The one that rattled along rails like some train to nowhere. The wind was bad outside. Byrde was still there, though, sitting in the window. That bald head shining.

'What's he doing now?' Scratch had asked.

She shrugged. 'The usual.'

'Writing his name in the Devil's book.' Scratch's Hammer House of Horror voice was doing the rounds again. Though it sounded maybe a tad more game show host, a curious mixture, but one he took relish in delivering. 'And when all the pages are written,' Scratch said, 'the Devil's gonna come walking across the escarpment, with those heavy boots and that long scythe, knock, knock, knocking for Old Man Byrde's soul.' Scratch threw back his head and started howling like a wolf.

In the window, Becca saw Byrde's head tilt slightly. 'Shhh!'

'Howww hooo.' Scratch continued. Though the sound soon caved into laughter.

Byrde must have heard. He'd switched from egg profile and was staring right out into the night.

She pulled back behind the door. 'Scratch!'

'He won't hear,' Scratch howled again. 'The man's away with the fairies. Probably wishing Britney Spears into existence as we speak. That's why he always sits so still at that table. Britney's under it, giving him a blow job.'

'In your fucking dreams, Scratch.' Becca was in no way being left out of the action. When it got too dirty, too male, she felt she had to overcompensate. Besides, being a girl gave her insider knowledge on the ins and outs of the female smut front. 'Britney wouldn't do a blow job on an old man like that, not even with the Devil at her back. She'll have taken him upstairs and shoved her face in the pillow for a bit of get-it-over-with-quick. PLEASE, PLEASE, PLEASE.'

Finn laughed. 'Should have called Scratch in. Isn't that your speciality, mate? Over in five. Seconds that is?'

Scratch gave Finn the evil eye. 'You have been warned.'

'Guys, are we gonna do this?' Becca pulled the litre of cider out of her bag. 'I can't be arsed to carry the bloody thing back down that cliff face.'

'You...' Scratch said, taking her jaw gently in his hands, 'are a little star. What is she, Finn?'

'A little star.'

'Dad bought his stash for the weekend.' Becca handed the bottle to Scratch. 'Just lucky timing.'

Finn shot Becca a concerned look. 'Will this get you in trouble, Beccs?'

'Nah.' She shook her head. 'Can't count when he's sober. Doesn't stand a chance now.'

Scratch took a long, hard drink before handing the bottle on. 'So, whose turn is it this time, Finn?'

'It was me last time.'

Scratch's jaw dropped as though he'd just heard some wild audacious pigs-might-fly of a whopper. 'It was me last time.'

'Guys, it was me,' Becca said, knowing full well it wasn't. But if there's a bandwagon going, as every playful young hooligan knows, you've just got to jump right on.

'If there are no volunteers then, Beccs?' Scratch fixed her with his no-joking eye, which was similar to his joking eye, only harder. He had her number, like always. Despite all the messing, Scratch knew for sure it was her turn.

She wimped her arms in front of her body. 'Scratch! You know he's a runner.'

'And he's got a gun,' Finn added. 'Bloody farmers.'

They smirked, one and all, because this was the kick-off point for a whole song and dance routine. In truth, they were like some zombie version of stage school kids. The smiles were mawkish; the anarchy choreographed in their souls, not paced out by some Lycra-clad teacher. They made this kind of thing up all on their ownsome. 'Run rabbit run rabbit...' they sang, every note out of tune.

∼

'You have to stand up on the top step.' Scratch pushed Becca forward.

'He's got a gun.' She sank back into Scratch's fingers,

laughing quietly, not sure if she should be scared shitless or just savour the adrenaline coursing through her veins. It was cold, and she felt like a greyhound, anxious for the run.

'It always takes him ages to get the gun,' Finn offered helpfully.

'Like that's supposed to make a difference when he puts a round of shots into my arse.'

'Closer.' Scratch pushed again. 'And keep the bloody noise down,' he hissed.

With her bottom lip clenched firmly between her teeth, Becca stepped up, hand raised, knuckles balled in a fist. Why the fuck was she doing this?

'Now,' Scratch hissed in her ear. And she knocked. Three times, just like they always did. BANG. BANG. BANG. Third knock released, Becca turned, keen to run.

But Scratch was right behind her, holding her firm on that top step. 'You know the rule. You have to wait so they see the soles of your feet.'

Even above the wind, she could hear the chair in the kitchen scraping back across the cold tiled floor—Byrde was on his way.

'Scratch!'

'Knock again,' Finn whispered.

Like she was seriously going to do that! Luckily, Scratch shook his head: there was no point—the Byrde had been flushed. Scratch was still holding Becca fast, though, only suddenly she got the feeling that there was something curiously comforting in it; like a dog in a trap, as soon as he let go, she would be off. As the light inside the hallway flicked on through the glass door panel, they saw a shadow hunched and blurred right at the end of the corridor. Still, Scratch held Becca tight.

'Who's there?' There was a slight reverb on the voice.

Even though they were on the outside, they could still hear it—that echo in the passageway.

Scratch suppressed a laugh before hissing... 'Like we're seriously gonna tell him, names, addresses, telephone numbers. Anything else you'd like, sir?'

They all sniggered quietly, just the sound of their bodies shaking.

'I'm calling the police.'

They didn't move. Becca pressing her body against its gate—Scratch's arms. Understanding it not so much as a trap but a bridge out. They said nothing. Where bluffing was concerned, they were a class act.

Byrde could threaten police as much as he liked; by the time the blue lights got all the way up that hill, they would be long gone. Then they heard the sound from inside, the inevitable shoe-shuffle coming step by step down the long corridor. Becca wanted to run. They'd done their bit. It made no difference how close they let him get. Only Scratch was still not letting her go, pushing her forward even. Suddenly, she'd had enough. A ball of panic rose up inside her. It was no longer comforting. She had to break free.

'Soles of our feet,' Scratch hissed. 'That's the deal. He's got to see them.'

She glanced down at her toes because they were bare. It was winter. She was wearing sandals. She should have been wearing running shoes. She knew that... But... Glimpsed through the door panel, the shadow inside was no longer blurred. The edges were taking on shape, hard block lines. It was reaching forward, one long fat arm elongated and stretching out towards the door. There was the sound of the doorknob turning.

'Run!' Scratch's voice exploded in their ears.

Suddenly the hand on her back was gone. She turned

sharply and could hear Scratch whooping and laughing as he high-tailed it towards the edge, and then... Then everything started to go slow for Becca. Slow when it should be going fast. Before she'd even stepped down off that blasted top step, Scratch's body disappearing into the night in front of her, her foot slamming down, she heard it. The sound first; a high-pitched tinkle. It was a sweet noise, like fairy bells ringing away into the night, but Becca knew that sound all too well. It wasn't fairy bells. She was not a kid anymore. Sodding fairies! It was glass: the bloody milk bottles. The ones Byrde always left out on the step. How many times had they kicked the damn things over? Only tonight, it was different. Tonight, there were shards of broken glass, and they were underneath her left foot, wedged inside her open shoe. The pain was unbelievable. The splinters sank deep into her flesh. Agony shot up her leg as though carried on a red-hot wire.

She looked up and around in blind panic, searching the black night. Scratch had gone. He was safe on the other side of the arc lights. Finn's shadow was also slipping away, streaking off into the darkness. They'd left her! There was no time for self-pity. Becca knew she had to move. She couldn't get caught. She threw herself forward, taking the pain in her foot as a given. She had to get away from that front door. Becca was down the steps as Byrde pulled open that last hardwood barrier between them, and off she stumbled headlong into the darkness, making for the barns. She'd never make it to the escarpment, but the barns, well maybe...maybe there would be someplace for her to hide. At least in there she stood a chance.

'Bloody kids. I've got a gun,' Byrde shouted from somewhere back by the door.

Becca didn't look. She just dived straight for the metal

slab of the barn door, pulling it back on its wheels. The thing rattled into the night like a ghost train. She glanced behind her. The doorway to the house was open, hanging like a burnt rectangle in the night, perfectly cut and empty. She stared frantically around her into the shadows, the lights from the house blinding her for a moment. Was Byrde there? Was he following? Why hadn't the others waited? Then she saw Byrde framed in the doorway; he'd gone back to get the gun. She eased the barn door back quietly and dived into the dark interior. Her breath was so loud it sounded as if it was giving the wind a run for its money, and her heart banged in her chest like a trapped, frightened bird. He would hear. He would catch her. She had to crouch down and shut up. She sank behind a pile of empty plastic barrels and put her hand over her mouth. *Nothing was a given. Bluff to the end.* Isn't that what Scratch always said? Maybe Byrde hadn't seen her dip into the barns. Maybe even now, he was heading over the escarpment for those *pesky* boys.

But no, even as that thought was edging through her brain, the train's metal door rattled back on its rails.

'I know you're here,' Byrde called out, moving into the barn.

Bluffing, she thought. He could be bluffing. She closed her eyes tight shut. Squashing the lids together as though if she couldn't see Byrde, he wouldn't be able to see her.

She could hear the footsteps, though. His flat feet, his leather boots hitting the packed mud floor. Shuffle, shuffle, moving forward.

Becca opened her eyes, staring out from behind the barrel; the stink of old plastic filling her nostrils so bad she wanted to gag. Byrde's torch was flashing around like a demented lightsaber, casting beams in the air, splitting motes of dust and dank. Lighting up the plastic curtains into misty streaks. Becca held her breath, scared it would betray her. Then the light fixed on the barrels, and she shrank back into the shadows. He wasn't waving the beam anymore. The light had come to rest. He'd got her.

'Rebecca.'

That's when her heart really hit her mouth. He knew her name.

'Rebecca Nilsen?'

There is magic in a name. The storybooks aren't wrong. When someone speaks your name, it holds a kind of power over you. It's not just the fact they can dob you in effectively to the police. No, the power a name holds is something deeper, something way more elemental. Despite her own best instincts, Becca poked her head around the barrel, blinking into the light.

'I thought it was you,' Byrde said, but he didn't sound mad. Nothing like it. He sounded gentle. It was the kind of voice you use on a scared animal.

'I knew your mum, Rebecca.'

Tears pricked her eyes. This man knew all the magic words and the right order to say them. Rebecca; no one had called her that for years.

'Your mother was a lovely woman,' Byrde had said. Which was different from the lies that her dad threw around. 'You're the image of her, Rebecca.'

Her name again. She said nothing, but she was staring at him now. Her eyes caught and glittering in the beam of the man's torch as though he was the Pied Piper and she was one of his rats. He could lead her anywhere. The old man dipped the beam of the torch slightly so it wouldn't shine too harshly into her eyes.

'Know your dad too.'

Bugger, she thought. Now she was in trouble.

But then Byrde snorted. 'Rotten bastard.'

Well, he'd got that right.

'You know you shouldn't be up here, don't you?'

Only his voice, it wasn't angry like it should have been. They'd been tormenting Byrde for years, and yet Byrde's voice was gentle, caring even. 'That escarpment's dangerous at night.'

She just stared at him, saying nothing.

'Here.' He leant forward, offering her his hand. 'I'll run you back home in the car.'

She stared at the hand. Stared at the face. He looked genuine enough. But where were the lads? She'd heard all the stories: don't travel with strangers. Don't take sweets. Watch out for kind words and promises, and yet Byrde seemed so...genuine. Becca reached her hand forward. Her fingers almost touched his, and she got the feeling he was offering her something, maybe something more than just a lift down into the village. Maybe a way out—he knew her mother. It was then that she heard it: glass, again, but this time she was willing to bet it was more than a milk bottle with a crack in.

'Bloody Hell!' Byrde turned sharply towards the open door that his patience appeared to have escaped out of. 'Hey!' he shouted again, running back into the night, all anger and hate.

The boys, she thought, triumphant; they'd come to save her. She had to go, quick. Byrde would be back, and this time there would be no gentleness. She'd known from the sound of that glass that someone had done something which was going to cost, but before she could move, she had to get the bits of bottle out of her foot.

'Becca?'

She looked up. A tall slim shadow stood framed in the doorway—Finn.

'Here,' she moaned. Her voice sounded more like a wounded animal than she felt comfortable with. 'Where's Scratch?'

'Don't think he realised you were missing.' Within seconds Finn was beside her, hand out, trying to pull her up. 'Come on, we don't have much...'

'Finn, my foot. I can't...'

They could hear Byrde outside, prowling and shouting, but Finn flicked on his torch anyway and shone it at the offending foot. It was a mess, blood all over and a piece of glass sticking an inch and a half out of her skin.

'We need to get it out. You can't walk like that.'

She knew he was right.

He went to tug it. Becca winced, but the glass wouldn't budge.

Finn sighed. 'I reckon it's barbed on the edge. Beccs. It's gonna hurt.'

'Just do it.'

'Here.' He thrust his shoulder forward. 'Bite into me. You scream, Byrde'll come back.'

She did as she was told.

'I'm gonna count to three.'

Her teeth gently pierced his sweatshirt. She wished he'd just get on with it.

'One, two...'

At two, Finn pulled. The pain shot through her body, and she bit down hard enough to draw blood. It was sheer agony, but the glass was out. For a moment, they crouched there, hugging each other. Clinging to one another as silent sobs racked her body. She didn't want to do this anymore.

She was suddenly tired of this game. She was tired of all the games.

Finn took her face into his hands, moved her eyes up to his. 'Alright?'

She nodded. He leant forward. Her eyes glittered up into his. There was a moment when neither of them moved. For the second time that night, the world slowed. Her lips parted; he was about to... He moved in just that inch more... Then kissed her on the forehead and pulled away. She felt as though she'd just had cold water poured over her from top to toe. With the iciest bit saved for her heart.

'Sorry...I... We need to go.' Finn pulled her to her feet.

What just happened? Or what just didn't happen? Becca didn't know. She felt so confused. She wanted to ask him, but an angry voice rang out above the wind.

'I know you're there.' Byrde's words were carried in on the cold Yorkshire air, flapping around the barn like a mad crow.

'I'll cover you,' Finn whispered. 'There's a window at the back, boarded up, but the planks are rotten-through.'

'No.'

'Yes.'

And he was gone, running out the front screaming like a banshee.

Yes, of course, she remembered it all. Even that look when he should have lowered his face just a fraction towards her lips, lowering it rather than raising his mouth up to the top of her head. Even if you didn't fully understand why something had happened, you didn't forget rejection like that.

7

TENNIS

(A racket sport for two or four players. The object of the game is to manoeuvre the ball in such a way that the opponent is unable to play a valid return.)

It was gone twelve before Scratch made it upstairs. Becca had only come up ten minutes earlier. There was a small part of her that would have liked a little longer. A bit more time to inhale it all. Never mind the roses. It was the bed, the sheets, the linen, just that delicious idea of solitude she wanted to bathe in. She'd pulled her best nightdress out of the case. It looked tacky and cheap laid out on the bed, its body twisted as if it were about to take itself off for a dance.

'Love that one,' Scratch said, pulling on the shoestring strap.

'It's really old.'

He grabbed her arm, nibbled her ear, and ran his bristled jaw over her cheeks.

'I'm tired, Scratch.' She grabbed the nightdress up into her hands, keen to get the lights off.

'No problem. I can do most of the work,' he whispered.

Becca laughed. 'You.'

'Me.'

'No more kids, Scratch.' She entwined her fingers through his.

'Beccs!' his voice was all hurt indignation.

'I mean it. Nine months. It's like a bloody prison sentence, and then there's the nappies and the crying and the broken nights.'

'I can help. I like helping.'

She stroked her fingers through his sandy hair. 'You're a brilliant dad, Scratch. Seriously you are, but even if I didn't feel that we'd done our time, we can barely make ends meet as it is. That loan...'

'I know, I know.' Scratch stared up at the ceiling. 'Shouldn't have taken it out. But we needed more room.'

'We didn't get much.'

'The extension is not finished yet, Beccs. Patience.' He implored his blue eyes to do that thing that cats do, the big-open-cutesy-implore. 'When it's done, it'll be brilliant. This house won't be able to hold a candle to it.'

She smiled. 'I love our place. Okay, so it's small, but it's home. Our home. It's just the loan. If we have to sell it because...'

'Beccs.' He threw his arms around her. 'Never. I'm not going to let that happen.'

She rested her head against his shoulder. Inhaling him, that familiar smell of cotton shirts and the shampoo they bought in bulk. 'Maybe, but Scratch, can't you see, the last thing we want to go doing now is filling that newfound space that we haven't even paid for up with babies.'

'Sure.' He brushed the top of her arm as she pulled away. 'They do move out quick enough, though.'

She shook her head but couldn't wipe the smile off her face. He always, *always* had to have the last word. 'Eighteen years minimum, Scratch, and don't count your chickens; they bounce back.'

He sighed, grabbing her arm, pulling her close, tracing her face with his fingertips. 'Then I guess we must be doing something right.'

'Yeah. But when Ryan starts school, I get a job...'

'You don't need to get a job. I've put in for manager. That's an extra...'

'Scratch, love, I do need a job.' The words hung in the room for an age. Becca knew Scratch wanted to be the provider, even if he wasn't much good in the role. He wanted to think he could bring home the bacon and fight off the wolves. Only life wasn't like that. Life was about bills and basics, not muscle. Besides, there were no big predators left to fight in the UK.

'Okay.' He nodded. 'I'm listening, Beccs. No more kids.' He paused, glancing down at the nightdress once more. 'Unless I win the lottery.'

'Scratch!'

'Alright, alright. I've just got this feeling, love. It's coming in. That job...'

'Scratch, every year you go for the manager's job. You've been there five years. If they were going to promote you, it would have happened.'

'Yeah, well, it's going to be different, you just wait and see.'

They'd gone over the same ground time and time again, him always talking about *different*, and neither of them seeing any reality of it. They were caught in groundhog country, only this time things were going to change because in September Ryan would be at school. Becca would find something, anything. She'd sell her soul for a minimum wage, zero-hours contract if she had to. Because maybe that's all she was worth. In the past twenty-three years, she'd managed to upskill herself at loading a dishwasher, changing a nappy, and knowing when a kid had a fever. Not exactly the kind of thing that gets you a job in corporate banking.

It didn't matter; she'd start at the bottom, put a little food on the table. Help with the bills. She could at least do that. Besides, a job to Becca was more than simply a wage packet. She'd talk to people, get out of the house, meet other adults who weren't trying to squeeze in a pinched conversation before the next nappy change or sore-gum scream. Being a cog in somebody else's corporate machine was all that she wanted; a system to place herself in that had nothing to do with family. She just wanted a bit of "out". Not an easy thing to tell your cave-man-husband, so she didn't.

'You seen the bath?' Becca loosened herself from Scratch's grip. Taking her nightdress, she pushed open the door to the en suite. It was like walking into her own personal pocket of peace.

'How the other half lives, Beccs,' Scratch called from the other room, throwing himself down onto the mattress with his habitual sit-down-grunt before pulling off his socks.

'It's bigger than our Megan's bedroom. The bath, not the room. You could drown someone in that tub.' She set one of the taps running. Hot water gushed out like a hydraulic fountain.

'Hot, straight from the tap. No warm-up. Could drown a whole family in that tub. Or boil them.'

'Becca, don't,' Scratch warned from next door.

Her forehead creased into its mummy frown—the don't-do-that line she'd tried hard to shake off. 'What?'

'Don't wallow.'

'Not funny, Scratch. Should have seen that one coming.' Wallow—bath.

'But you didn't.' He let out a sigh, with just a touch of the smug about it.

No, she hadn't seen it coming. Maybe after a lifetime of cracks, she was too jaded with comedy to care.

From the other room, she heard a sniff.

'You pack me any clean socks?'

Like he had to ask. 'Yes.'

Becca put her wash bag under the mirror. The washstand had its own little light and everything. It even had one of those shaving mirrors that pull out on a concertinaed metal arm, the ones that make your skin look like a lunar landscape. Becca turned it in, so it faced the wall; she didn't need that kind of help. Taking her Nivea face cream out of her bag, she turned to grab a wadge of loo roll and saw the cotton buds angled towards her in a conch shell as if offering themselves up in sacrifice. 'There's even free cotton wool balls.'

'Anything not nailed down'll be joining us on the ride home.'

She couldn't help herself. She laughed. 'Scratch! I can afford cotton wool balls. I just…'

Becca stared at her face in the mirror, not even the magnifying one. She was looking old, tired. Those dark eyes that once had so much laughter wrapped up in them, well, now they were dull, ditch-water ponds rather than pools of possibility. She had to get some energy back into them. Inject a little bit of joy before she keeled over dead with overwork and boredom: that classic combination.

'Know what, Scratch, I was thinking…when did Finn say they were going to have that party? The one in London. Two weeks, was that it? Reckon I might just go.' She could find something on eBay. Get it as a joint Christmas / New Year party frock.

'Really?' Scratch's voice came back flat as a brick wall.

She figured he hadn't taken in what she'd said. He was probably still staring at his socks.

'Finn's party.' She mulled it over again. Maybe it would do her good, do them good. 'Why not?'

'Beccs, you know what those things are like.' Scratch's voice was resigned, as if he was about to state some self-evident truth.

She heard his weight shuffle from the bed, the floor-boards creaked, and he appeared in the doorway, vest, boxers and two days' worth of unshaved, all of it hanging in the doorframe. 'You'd hate it, princess.'

'Would I, though? I mean it's years since we've been to London. We wouldn't even have to ask Nan to look after the kids. Our Ella could sit for us. She wouldn't mind if it was just a one-off.'

Scratch wandered into the room, nodding his head as if chewing the thought over. The door had been open. There were no boundaries when you'd been married as long as they had.

He plonked himself down on the closed toilet lid. 'Remember that last time.'

'Scratch!' Becca laughed. 'That was years ago. Finn had only just gone to that fancy college. We were kids.'

Scratch shook his head. 'Kids or not, Beccs, we didn't fit. You were wearing that cap. You remember? That brown one you had. I loved that, but some idiot, some woman said…

what did she say?' He stopped, head tilted as if searching his brain back through time.

He needn't have bothered. Becca knew what he was talking about. She could even do the accent. Got it to a T. 'I just love the way you Northerners dress.' That was it. 'You'd have thought I was wearing a flat cap and a pair of bleeding clogs. In town for the weekend with the Tetley tea folk and the Hovis kid.'

'Talked yourself out of it?' Scratch stood up again, letting his hand rest for just a moment on her shoulder before he wandered back into the bedroom.

'Talked myself out of it.'

She grabbed her pill bottle from her wash bag and threw a couple of Seroxat into her mouth. Becca had stopped the Prozac two months ago; they were buggering up her sleep. The Seroxat were similar—serotonin something inhibitors. She guessed they did the trick. What she'd really like was a pill to turn back time, give her another shot at the future. It wasn't that things were bad. She loved Scratch, loved the kids. It was just...she stared at her sad face in the mirror. She couldn't help feeling that somehow things could have been different. Becca pulled her cheeks up a little. The lines around her mouth disappeared. All she'd need would be a couple of bulldog clips, and the wrinkles would be sorted. But no, the flesh sprang back down, pulled by gravity into familiar creases. She was looking old. 'Why did we have to come back here?'

'I thought you liked the luxury.'

'I liked the free cotton wool balls and the bath.'

'And I like a woman that's easily pleased.'

Becca pulled the snowflake of cotton across her face, watching as it took with it the last traces of something that had promised on the packet a *years younger glow*.

'You ever wonder, Beccs, why he's marrying her?'

'Daisy? What kind of a stupid question is that? He loves her.'

It went quiet next door. Becca began packing away her creams.

'Loves her? You think?'

'Scratch, course he does.'

'I'm not so sure. His heart's not in it.'

It was gone twelve, and Becca was tired. 'Can we leave this till morning?' Since she'd got to the house, her head had been buzzing. Those bloody bees. She needed to shut them up before she lay down on her pillow, but Scratch kept poking the nest. 'You're being daft, Scratch. Why would he marry her if he didn't...'

'Hey, don't have a go at me! How would I know why? All I'm saying is his heart's not in it.'

'Scratch.' Becca sighed. 'You are about as perceptive as a lump of granite. It's late. You've picked a fine time to go deep and meaningful on me.'

'I'm a man of many parts. You just watch him though, Beccs, when he mentions her name, nothing.'

'You asked him about this?'

Another silence. 'Not in so many words.'

'You mean, no.'

'Yes.'

Becca switched off the light in the bathroom. The extractor fan must have been on some kind of timer. It went on regardless. At home, they had to open the window after a shower, let the condensation out. Even in the winter, that window had to be open to the world. People with money have all the simple things sorted without even realising it.

Back in the room, she found Scratch sitting his side of the bed. Just sitting there, staring out of the darkened window. Becca picked up his socks, the ones he'd left on the floor, put them on the chair and pulled the curtains. He didn't move, just carried on sitting, staring, as though he could see right through the heavy fabric drapes. It was late. Whatever was on his mind could wait till morning. The priority for Becca was shut-eye. She moved around the room to her side.

'You should ask him, you know,' he said.

Still! He was still on that same track! 'Don't be daft, Scratch.' Becca took herself a pump of the house hand cream from the dispenser that had been left thoughtfully within reach on the bedside table. Rubbing it into her fingers and palms. It smelt of fresh citrus. 'Daisy will be beautiful and clever and all those things that those women always are. Why wouldn't he be bowled over?'

Scratch shook his head. 'Like I said, not sure, but mark my words, the whole thing'll end up a mess.'

Becca slid herself under the clean white sheets, enjoying the cool of them against her skin, and hit the lights. 'Scratch, shut up.'

The bed was so comfortable. It was as if she was reclining into a sea of clouds, and the smell! They needed to get a new mattress, and maybe switching their laundry powder would do...something? She'd check the utility room in the morning, see what they were working with at the house. Laundry powder was not going to break the bank. 'Did you call the kids?'

Silence.

'Scratch, did you...?'

A strange, muffled noise came from the other side of the bed as if Scratch had gaffer tape over his mouth. 'Hmm, hmmm.'

She was so tired! But she manoeuvred her body into a

hefty three-point turn, so it was facing his way. He was still sitting there, staring at the curtains as if sitting at the Hippodrome, waiting for a show to start.

'You daft bugger.' She reached out a hand and stroked his back, the cotton of his vest feeling so worn, so familiar under her fingers. 'I didn't mean shut up. I just meant...shut up.'

'Oh, right. Sorry, got confused there. Yes, I called the kids. The house burnt down. Nan Harris has run off with some Taliban tout from the takeaway. Ella's ditched all plans of college. Caitlin's knocked up, and our Ryan's turned the small bedroom into a lab. Started cooking up crystal meth. Not bad for a four-year-old.'

Becca buried her face in the pillow and let out a long sigh. 'I'm going to sleep.'

'I'll be here when you wake up.'

'Do you think this used to be Byrde's room?' she asked. There was a pause.

'Nah. No. Guest room, I reckon.'

Becca felt a sense of relief. To be sleeping in the same place as the old man slept, that felt like a step too far.

From the bathroom, the extractor continued to hum. Was it the extractor or that noise in her head? Becca was dog-tired. The pills and booze had her all over the place. She wondered what it would be like if life had a reset button. How comforting it would be to know that when you'd messed your body up with crap for years and years, you could just reset. That was what she needed. She rolled over in bed, expecting to see Scratch lying next to her, bulking up the sheets. But no, Scratch still hadn't got in! She opened her eyes wide. He was sitting there. The exact same position. Sitting staring at the curtains.

'Scratch?'

Only she realised that his shoulders were shaking. 'Scratch? What, love?'

'Sorry.' He sniffed. 'It's just...' And finally, he lay his heavy body down next to her, and she realised that she found an overwhelming sense of comfort in it, just having his depression beside her. As if they were kings and queens of old, their monument fenced and sheltered in a village church. Laying sleeping beside each other for eternity.

Scratch rolled over so his face was close to hers. She could feel his gentle breath against her cheek. 'I just wanted to tell you that...' He reached for her, balled her hand into a fist and brought it to his lips. Holding on to it for dear life. 'I love you, Becca.'

'Scratch, that's really sweet, and...'

'No, wait, you don't get it. I know it could have all worked out differently. I'm under no illusions that I'm the luckiest bastard alive. And maybe I don't buy you flowers...'

'I don't need flowers.'

She could smell the scent of the flowers Finn had bought for her filling the night air.

'Or tell you that you're beautiful.'

'Scratch, I'm hardly...'

'Shhh, it's true. I don't make enough of you, enough of us. But you are my life, Beccs. Without you I'm nothing.'

She leaned towards him, took his face into her hands, and kissed his dry, cracked lips.

The unnerving thing was she knew he wasn't taking the piss. She knew there would be no punchline coming, no joke rattling along in the wake of the showstopper reveal.

'I know, Scratch,' she said. 'I'm tired, love. Let's go to sleep, eh?'

It was only after she heard him snoring that she realised she hadn't returned the love. She'd taken his face and kissed him on the lips, only it was the same kiss she would have given a child, and she hadn't sent the love back to him. Not finished the serve properly, done a return: like a game of tennis, a compliment is supposed to have a return. Then again, he probably wouldn't have noticed anyway. After all, he was pissed out of his head.

8

———

HIDE AND SEEK

(A game for multiple players. One player closes their eyes and counts to ten. The other players hide. When the first player finishes counting, they announce: 'coming ready or not,' then proceed to find all other players. The first player found is IT.)

The image had a sluggish quality to it, the colours washed out, the edges of the room fading into a murky grey as though someone couldn't be arsed to fill out the detail. Becca was sitting on a hard chair in Byrde's kitchen. Only it wasn't the new kitchen. The one with the clean marble surfaces and fitted units. It was the old one. The craped-out one from the craped-out world of days gone by. Her legs had fresh-from-the-shop bruises, and her skirt kept riding high over her pale teenage knees. She couldn't see her eyes, but they felt crusty. Creaking when she moved them side to side. She figured her mascara must have leaked out and dried.

Somewhere, there was a kettle boiling, and yet there was nothing comforting about the sound. It was far-off-persistent like the whistle of something large and nasty working its inevitable way down the track. Becca got the feeling there was probably a scream hiding under it somewhere. A moment where the whistle opened its mouth full-throttle and gave out all it had. The low hiss was stringing her nerves, pulling them taught as catgut till there would be no give.

She noticed Byrde was there too. Casting a shadow over her as he moved around the room. He was all in one piece, nothing broken, nothing bent. The old guy was stooped slightly, focusing on making tea, oblivious to the kettle or maybe just determined to ignore it. She could feel the bees beginning to buzz at the back of her brain. He shouldn't be focusing on sorting her out. He should be barricading the door. Becca had this sickening feeling in the pit of her stomach. The kind you get when you see something out of control but inevitable, like a car hurtling towards a small kid, standing smiling in the road. The kid might have no idea what's coming up behind, and maybe there was no way to stop it because you were too far away. All you could do was watch everything play out. Watch and wish that you couldn't see the threat, either. Wish that the only thing you had in your eyeline was the kid in the street, with the smile.

Byrde was mumbling something, only Becca couldn't catch his words. She could hear fine, but it was like being in some Charlie Brown cartoon where the adults couldn't talk properly. They're just legs and torsos and meaningless sounds. Byrde handed her the mug of tea. It didn't stop the kettle boiling, boiling, and there was something wrong with his arms. They were way too long, like comedy arms or Stretch Armstrong sausages.

When she heard the glass panel in the door cave in, Becca knew it was all happening again. This was when the teenagers came to tea, and people failed to get out alive.

There was a roar of air whooshing through the corridor as if they were in a spaceship, and someone had broken the airlock. Then the sound of heavy footsteps, running, sprinting across the hard-tiled floor. Byrde looked scared shitless. Every inch of life draining from his face till he was white as a lump of lard.

'It's coming for you.' She heard the words slipping out of her mouth. 'They said it would.'

Byrde turned back towards the door. You couldn't paint any more fear on that face without the man dropping down dead on the spot. She knew she had to get out. They both have to get out. BANG.

Becca sat bolt upright in bed. A lump of fear caught in her throat. It took her a moment to figure out where she was, and what had just happened. Her breathing was all over the shop, and the room was different: odd. Bathed in streaks of shadowy blue. The moon must be out? Or maybe something or someone had triggered those LED lights outside. The lost dog? She wasn't sure.

The only thing she knew for certain was that the same always-and-forever depression was right beside her on the mattress: Scratch, laying there like a guard dog, unconscious, but there. Breathing in, breathing out loud and rhythmic as a walrus. It was just a dream. She'd had dreams like it before. Too many over the years. This one was different, though, more vivid. Then again, what did she expect? It was bound to be worse. In coming back to Byrde's house, Becca was feeding the memory. Stirring things up. She had to make sure not to do that. The past couldn't have new bits added to it. It was a closed loop.

Suddenly a noise. Loud. She jumped out of her skin. Laughter. A hacking splurge of mirth. Her heart smashed inside her rib cage, galloping so fast, so sudden.

'Ha ha ha...' Scratch. He was laughing.

He was fast asleep beside her but laughing into the silence as though he'd lost the plot. She sighed, relief flooding out from her smooth as a wave drawn across the sand.

Silly bugger. Becca sat there in the darkness, taking a moment to gather herself. Her heart rate slipping back to speed. Then she kicked him. 'Scratch.' She didn't kick him hard, just enough to jolt him out of whatever joke he'd found himself enjoying.

He'd always done it: sleep laughing, even when they were kids. Becca had never heard of anyone else having that particular habit; sleepwalking, sleep talking, but laughing in your sleep? He really was one of a kind. Thank God, none of the kids had inherited whatever warped gene was responsible for that little party trick.

Becca was wide awake now—no chance of getting back to sleep. She picked up the clock by the bedside, focusing her eyes on the red square numbers dancing over its rectangular face. Holding it tight till the edges stopped shimmering for just a moment. Four o'clock. Four in the morning. Too early to get up, but there was always a problem with those early AM hours. Four, five, they were difficult times to get back to sleep. Her mind would start racing. She could spend an hour easily, thinking about lunchboxes and school uniforms. Wondering if the sports kits were clean. Sometimes she'd just have to get up and check, and then before she knew it, the day would have started and been pulling her along with it.

BANG.

'Bloody Hell.' The expletive spilled out into the muggy, sleep-filled air of the room, causing Scratch to mumble and turn in his sleep. Not that she cared because there was something downstairs, something banging in the wind.

'Scratch?' Becca nudged his warm slumbering body, but he'd sunk back into the mattress and just grunted. Turning up the decibels on the snoring front before continuing with his guzzling of night air as if he was a buffalo come to drink at a waterhole.

'Scratch!' She tried again.

But no. There was no moving him. He was like the rock in the garden of Gethsemane; it would take a miracle to move him when he was under.

She threw back the covers, the cold nipping into her skin, and shuffled to the door.

BANG.

There was no mistaking the noise this time. It was real and coming from downstairs. They must have left a window open before they went to bed. Becca could have kicked herself. She shouldn't have trusted the men to lock up. She'd just thought...but they were worse than five-year-olds. They needed constant watching.

THE LANDING WAS quiet as a graveyard, bathed in the same shadowy blue light as the bedroom. Finn must have been away with the fairies too. Because there was no noise from his room. How could they sleep through?

BANG.

The kitchen—it was coming from the kitchen.

The thick-pile carpet crunched under her toes, soft as moss. The house felt dead, but no, that wasn't it. It was more as though the house was waiting, the silence before the tiger's pounce. Time was on hold. It was just Becca and this place, this house, that had unfinished business.

'Bricks and mortar...' she said calmly, her voice just audible, 'do not have unfinished business.'

The past was in the past. She wouldn't scare herself with...with nothing. The demons might have taken up residence in Becca's head a long time ago, but she knew they couldn't get out unless she let them. Giving them airtime was the only way for them to live, and she wouldn't do that. It was just a window banging in the wind. That was all. Just more of the pedestrian everyday.

At the bottom of the stairs, she stopped feeling so confident. She should have woken Scratch. Say it wasn't just a window left open? Becca was continually spooking herself with things from the past, but that didn't mean to say horrors didn't happen ten-to-the-dozen in the present. You only had to read the papers to know that some poor bugger somewhere was having their head stoved in, their wallet nicked, their wife raped. This area was okay, as far as she knew, not worse than the city, but there was unemployment. Rural areas didn't have a lot to offer. Desperate people take desperate measures. Nobody knew who Scratch and Becca were—their personal circumstances. They were just rich people from the city who had booked a holiday home that cost a small fortune every night. That's what an outsider would think: easy pickings.

BANG.

This was stupid. Her fingers were holding on tight to the newel, numb where she was squeezing so hard that the blood had stopped, and it was cold too. Seriously cold. There was wind coming from somewhere, slipping around the house like an eel. Fear was so much worse than reality. The imagination had a high budget on that front; no expense spared. Best not to let it pitch you a horror story. Becca sighed deeply, muscling up her self-control. She needed to keep a grip on reality. If they were all going to be murdered in their beds, then maybe it was best to get it over with quick or shut the bloody window and get some sleep. She started off towards the kitchen but then stopped. She was going to have to walk past the cellar, and somebody—no doubt somebody needing an emergency bottle of bubbly—had left the door ajar. Becca stood for a moment, letting the ingrained cold of the tiled floor in the hallway seep through her feet, crucifying her toes.

When they were kids, there had been a house on her street with a dog. The animal used to sit at the gate quietly as a stone lion, but every time she had walked past, it would jump up, claws catching on the cement pavement. Its jaw juicing with growls, hackles standing on end like a dark stain, giving out this low rumble that seemed to shake the ground. It couldn't reach Becca on the street. The chain wouldn't let it out of the gate. Becca couldn't always see the chain, and so would imagine there was an invisible barrier between her and the "monster". Even so, she hated walking past.

Before she got to the gate, her heart would start to race. She'd try to clear her mind, think nice thoughts because the bugger didn't bark at everyone, not Finn. It chose its victims, knew if you were scared. The only good thing about it, or at least the only thing that was in any way amusing, was that it loathed Scratch even more than it hated Becca. She swore that was part of the reason he never came around to call. It was as if the dog could sense fear, sense that there was something not quite right about her, something different. But there was always that invisible barrier; formed by the chain. In her head, she imagined this giant force-field of a dome, the dog on the inside, Becca and the world just through the membrane. Only, she couldn't help worrying because invisible membranes, well, who knows what's holding them up. How would you even know if it was in place? Besides, membranes are the kind of thing that burst.

Becca felt the same way about the cellar. Something was down there; jaws salivating and hackles up. Even before they'd opened the door when they arrived, Becca had felt uneasy walking past, and the bees in her head, well, they started to buzz just that little bit quicker when she stood near the door. Of course, the cellar was where they threw Byrde before...before he ran, and she couldn't help feeling that there was something of him still down there. A little bit of panic. A little bit of fear. A lot of anger. *'Why didn't you tell?'*

BANG.

If Becca kept her distance from the dark cellar pit, maybe two feet, maybe three, would she be alright? The light from the lamp above the front door was spilling in through the glass panel and over the tiles. At least she didn't have to cope with darkness. That would have been worse, although none of the switches illuminated the part of the hallway she was walking into.

BANG.

Bloody Hell, why didn't they wake up? There was nothing but silence from upstairs. Silence from downstairs, too, just the occasional bang and those bees that she was always carrying with her. There was no intruder, no one after Finn's fancy tech. She knew that now. The business in the house, it was between her and the old place.

Quick, Becca thought, just like she used to with the dog, get past it quick. She walked fast to the end of the hall where the cellar door stood wide open, yawning cold air into the hallway like a death rattle. Becca took a deep breath, the buzzing filling her brain just a little harder, a little more insistent. But she didn't listen. Instead, she leaned in over the stairs, over the dark yawning hole of the basement into the cold, and blind groping, grabbed the blessed door handle. She'd done it. What a fool, she thought, when the door was pulled tight shut. Did she honestly think something was going to reach out and grab her from the dark? Yet her skin was still puckered into goosebumps, scaly as a dead chicken, and the bees, even though they'd stopped agitating, Becca could feel the bruises where they'd been, where they'd bumped up angrily against the sides of her brain. No amount of 'rational' made the thought of that black pit lying on the other side of the door seem better.

She went through to the kitchen, switched on the lights, any lights, every light—running her fingers across the controls till everything jumped on. Becca had been right. The men had left the window open. The kitchen counters were strewn with empty cups, glasses, bits of toast. There was a fridge full of food. A kitchen Gordon Ramsay would be happy to have a party in, and toast and tortillas had been all any of them could rustle up for supper!

Tired and cold, Becca pulled the window shut. She knew it wasn't good for her: this night wandering, night waking. She needed sleep. She needed to get back upstairs, and under those covers, but as she passed back through the hallway, her back to the illuminated glass window in the front door, she felt it, a sudden dip in the light. Turning to face the door, she saw a shadow on the other side. There was someone there. No, that was stupid. Why would anyone be up here at this time of night? It must be a shadow from one of the barns thrown up against the building. She had to stay rational.

But suddenly, her heart filled her throat as the panel of

light thrown through the door onto the tiled floor, cut in half, moved, snuffed out. The shadow gone. And the whispering, whispering, but this time it had a different tune. Something new and fresh. *'It's come for you. They said it would.'* The words rose like ghostly spectres from Becca's dream. Rose like a swarm of bees in full flight. The thing, *It*, wasn't after Byrde anymore. Whatever *It* was had turned its sights. She was the one it was after now. Becca flew up the stairs, taking them two at a time, before hurling herself back under the covers. Every inch of her body hidden. Her breath came in short, sharp frightened gasps because the future was getting drowned in the past. Phillips had said it would be alright, that there would be closure, but that's not how these things work. Sometimes the past doesn't want to be closed.

9

———

ARTICULATE

(A fast-talking game for multiple players. Describe a word or situation on a card without naming that word or situation using descriptive powers only: no rhymes or 'sounds like' allowed.)

Becca's dad had been what Scratch would have described as an 'absolute and utter cunt'. Even Becca's mum high-tailed it out the door as soon as she got the opportunity. Her dad was fine when he was legless, but if he wasn't drunk enough to see double, if he still had the power to move, he was a problem. He was a problem the night Byrde died. That was when it all started. That was how she knew more about Byrde and his cliff dive than she liked to let on.

Sixteen, barely that, and her dad had been shouting the street down yet again. It felt like the walls would crumble. Becca had managed to get out of her house, face bruised and dress torn. She knew straight off where she was heading —Finn's. He lived closest; only Finn wasn't in.

It had been Old Man Byrde who found her, nearly ran

right over her when he drove around the corner too fast. He offered to take her to the hospital, but she wasn't having any of that. So, the old guy drove her up to his farmhouse. He took the road, the one no one ever used but him. The one that wound up high, over the potholes. Up and up so far, it felt like he was driving straight into a brooding bank of storm clouds. She'd said nothing. Just fiddled with the hem of her skirt, trying not to feel sorry for herself.

Inside Byrde's house, it was warm, which had struck Becca as odd. She'd always thought it would be cold as an icebox inside as well as out. All the rooms smelt of dust like nobody cared, but Byrde had bathed her cuts and made her tea. The sharp smell of TCP filling the kitchen. It had felt nice—being looked after.

The book, the Devil's book, the one that Byrde was always writing in, had been lying there on the kitchen table. So she had just come right out and asked him what was in it? How could she not? She'd thought it would be accounts, or something boring, something domestic. Something that would put an end to Scratch's story about the Devil coming for Byrde's soul. They were getting too old for all that ghost rubbish. Only, Byrde's explanation hadn't silenced her questions. Instead, it had just given her a few more. He had told her how one day after his wife died, he had awakened one morning feeling as if he was at the bottom of a black hole. He'd lost the will to live, but that very same morning, the book had just appeared on the doorstep. No note, nothing, and every page was blank. That night he'd started writing in it. The next morning, he felt a little bit better and so he didn't stop.

He had been about to tell her more, but then they'd both heard the great glass window in the front door smash and the wind roar angrily as it ripped a hole into the hallway.

Byrde went out to see what was up. When Becca heard his voice rising in panic, she'd known not to hang about—she'd had enough trouble for one night. There was that curtain under the sink. She'd squashed herself up just as small as a fist, and under the pipes she went. She'd seen legs and bodies and shoes but no face—the intruder was wearing a black balaclava: just a kid, not sent from the Devil, more likely off the estate.

'In the cellar,' one of the lads had told Byrde, and she'd heard the door to the cellar rattle open as a second blast of cold air whipped into the kitchen. Becca wasn't sure if it was from the cellar or the front door, but she could hear Byrde struggling. Then there was a THUMP, THUMP, THUMP, something heavy falling down the stairs. Byrde?

The lad in the kitchen grunted but said nothing. Instead, he picked the book up off the table and kind of snorted as though it was a piece of rubbish. He'd flicked it with his fingers before taking off his gloves. And her heart stopped. Because that was when she'd seen Finn's ring. The ring Finn had shown to her the day before. He'd bought it at the market, and now there it was again, sitting proud as a peacock on his hand. Finn had always been light-fingered. But coming into Byrde's house was a long way from shoplifting at the market. It was brutal.

Suddenly all hell broke loose. Byrde must have got out of a window in the cellar. He was free and running off towards the escarpment. Becca didn't hear the scream but could tell that something had gone belly up, or back up, or whichever way it was that Byrde dived off the edge because suddenly the house went dead quiet as though all the life had been sucked out through those dark silent windows.

She had waited two hours before making her way down the escarpment. She'd thought if she stayed there much longer, crouching under the kitchen sink, she'd freeze into a block of ice. No one had shut the door. The house had been cold as a freezer when she picked her way through it. The book had gone, and the door to Byrde's safe was yawning open.

IN THE DARK of the night, Becca had shimmied deeper and deeper down the path through the wind, through the rain. Putting those stories Scratch told them about ghostly legions and demon Rock Babies out of her head because she didn't care. The living were as scary as the dead. Even when you thought you knew someone well, you could be wrong. Besides, she was worried about stumbling over Byrde's broken body. Maybe he wasn't dead? Maybe he'd make a grab for her? She was Finn's friend, after all. She was part of this now. And all the while, that blackened dead tree stood sentry at the top of the escarpment, watching her go down, deeper and deeper. It stood there like a dark angel, waiting and watching and judging.

10

———

WHO AM I?

(A game for multiple players. All players are assigned a character but are unable to see who they have been assigned. They must use character traits, questioning the other players, to try and work out which character they have been allocated. The winner is the person who discovers 'their own' identity.)

The next morning, Becca didn't wake when Scratch got out of bed. She was dog-tired. The monsters of last night, the moving shadow, the open cellar door, they seemed overblown when day came up over the escarpment. Nothing but the conjuring of an overactive imagination and too much mixing of booze and pills. She had to keep a grip on reality. Besides, a lie-in was a luxury. Back home, it was difficult, bordering on impossible, to stay sleeping with the kids always pulling and poking, and if Scratch left the bed to try and give her a break, she'd roll into the depression he'd made in the mattress and wake up with a bump, but here, the mattress held her firm. She only woke later when the smells of a cooked breakfast started to creep up the stairs.

From the train of clothes scattered from bathroom to bedroom, Becca figured Scratch had already showered. Even in a big room, Scratch could draw the walls in a little closer with his mess. She could hear him from downstairs, clattering pans and humming some joy-of-the-world tune. Becca had never known him to miss a beat on the optimism front, and he rarely suffered from a headache after a skinful. Sadly, she didn't share the same story; her own head felt as if someone had rammed it into a vice and turned the screws until they would turn no more. She looked at the clock, squinting at the disturbingly red digits that lasered straight through her retinas. Seven-thirty. First time away from the kids in years, and they were up at half-seven! The smell of bacon wasn't exactly helping to settle the hangover. Becca pulled the sheet over her head and tried to snuffle back into some deep pocket of sleep, one that had maybe got left over in the warm under-the-covers air. Why did he have to hum? The fact that Scratch was such a happy bugger only made it all so much worse. Becca was continually measuring herself up to a yardstick that was off the scale. Couldn't Scratch see the cracks in their life? Didn't he realise she was trying to hold every single day together with prayers and pixie dust?

'Oi, oi.' Even under the downy, she could hear Scratch's chipper tones from the kitchen. 'Morning, morning.'

Finn must be up. Suddenly Becca didn't feel sleepy. She wanted to hear what they said, fly-on-the-wall style. It was a bad habit, Becca knew that, but she'd always done it, amazed at what you could pick up by sitting just outside the circle. Once, when she was eight, she'd heard her dad on the downstairs phone talking about the Christmas present he was going to buy her: a dollhouse so big it would take up one whole side of her room. She had been beside-herself-excited about that blessed house. She was going to buy three dolls. One would be Finn, one for Scratch and one that was all her. There was a shop in Manchester that had dollhouse figures, even sunburnt brown ones like Becca. She would act their lives out in that house. There'd be no dog on the street. No dead-weight adults. Becca would be in control of that little house, and everything would be perfect. Only when Christmas came the money and the good intention had fallen by the wayside: her dad bought her a Furby. There had been no explanation about the dollhouse. Her dad didn't know that she'd overhead the conversation. So, there'd been no need for him to go into explanations when it failed to materialise, but there had been no hiding her face when she walked into the front room on Christmas Day and saw a fat, squat six inches of crinkled wrapping paper sitting under the tree. Her dad had accused her of being ungrateful. The Furby had gone evil by Boxing Day. Becca never got it back on the right side.

Eventually, her dad put it out in the snow. The thing carried on bleating and garbling for a few days till the damp got into the batteries, and it gave up the ghost. It was all a bit shit, really, but for the two months between earwigging herself into that phone conversation and the major-league disappointment at Christmas, Becca had a dollhouse. She'd played with it in her head. She'd actually bought the three dolls from the shop in Manchester out of her pocket money. One for Finn, one for Scratch, and the sunburnt brown one that was Becca.

Without anywhere to house them, the dolls soon got lost beneath everyday living. The plan had gone tits up at point of delivery, but there had still been two months of joy: two months of planning out a rosy future for the pocket people. And Becca learnt a valuable lesson from the whole dollhouse experience—when life is liable to deal you a crock of shit, you have to bite off a bit of joy wherever you can.

So even though Becca was nearing forty and should really know better, she was still a great believer in fly-on-the-wall tactics. She grabbed a blanket from the bottom of the bed and pulled herself up a ringside seat standing by the door to the bedroom.

'You're bright and early.' Scratch's voice came out of the kitchen, cut staccato by exertion: washing the pan in the sink? Holding a kettle over a cup?

'Sleep...ask me, it's overrated.'

At the sound of Finn's voice, Becca snuggled down, pulling the blanket around her shoulders—this was prime time.

'Not for me. Love my bed. If I could, I'd conduct my entire life from under a duvet. Just the missus for extra warmth. Maybe not an option for you though, 'spect Old Nick would be pulling at your bedclothes.'

She'd forgotten about that. Of course—last night, they'd found Byrde's old book.

Becca edged closer into the hallway, waiting, listening, because surely now Finn would spill the whole story. Maybe he wouldn't let on to Becca. He probably wouldn't want to burden her with it—he didn't know she'd been there that night, but Scratch? Finn's best mate. Maybe that's why they'd come back—Finn wanted to tell someone about Byrde and how he'd flown off the escarpment. The whispering inside her head went up a notch.

'Can't believe I told you that,' Finn's voice came from downstairs.

'You didn't, mate. We rumbled you. That's a secret and a half. If I'd have known... Can you imagine the mileage I could have got out of that one?'

Yeah, Becca thought. Actually, maybe, if you did have a secret, maybe Scratch wasn't the person you would tell. You might be able to trust him not to go to the police, but he'd rip the shit out of you for the rest of your natural. So, what did that mean? If Finn wouldn't confess to Scratch, at some point, Becca was going to have to get Finn to talk. It would have to be the two of them, and they were going to have to decide what to do. It wasn't murder. They couldn't prosecute Finn, surely? He didn't intend to kill Byrde. It was just an accident. Most likely, the police wouldn't even be interested. It was a long time ago. But that didn't matter. *Why didn't you tell?*' To shut Byrde up, Becca had to get this thing out in the open.

'Yeah, well...' Finn sounded uncomfortable. 'Breakfast looks good.'

'Like the table arrangement? Flowers for you...well, pansies. Ha!' Scratch laughed. 'Fitting! Found them in one of the tubs outside and a fresh tablecloth.'

'Quite the homemaker.'

'Try my best. Tea, sir?'

'Just a drop.'

'Already in the pot. The Scratchmeister thinks of everything. Can't get you out of your little predicament with the king of the underworld, though. That one's all on you.'

'It's just a story.'

'Just a story. Yup. Course. No point fretting. Everyone loves a spooky tale. Think it's because the mind, it likes to feel like it's done something, overcome some kind of major achievement. And with a spooky tale, you're kind of out there, mentally at least, battling the odds for survival. Remember that time... There was a screening of The Exorcist. Probably Halloween or something. I was doing that live-in waiter job, some spooky old country house out in the middle of nowhere. Near Rotherham. We had to walk all down those scary dark lanes...get the bus to the pictures... get the bus back. Walk all down those lanes again into that spooky old house. You decided to go up to bed early, but me, I'm one step ahead. I'm already under the bed. You, Finn, get yourself in. Turn out the lights. I give it a moment, pause for effect. Timing is everything with a joke—you ask any comedian—everything. Then I start rattling that bed hard as buggery.'

Becca hadn't heard the story before, but it didn't surprise her. It was Scratch all over.

She could hear him laughing from downstairs like he was fit to burst.

'Chased you right out of the house before I caught up with you. Your face! White as a sheet. Fuck me, we used to have some fun.'

You had to have a strong stomach to be in Scratch's inner circle, to appreciate his sense of *fun*. They all knew that.

'Always the joker,' Finn said, getting the gist of the story from the get-go because it wasn't really about Finn. The story was only ever about Scratch and the lengths that his never-ending sense of humour could stretch to.

'You gotta laugh, mate. Keeps the world turning. Speaking of which, your marriage, when do we get to meet her?'

Becca couldn't help herself; a smile creased her face. Scratch, what was he like? Turning Finn's wedding into a joke. Not saying the words but leaving them threading through the air. Finn, for his part, appeared to be blissfully unaware.

'Best if you come to the party in London.'

'Yeah. Yeah. Must admit, thought you'd never get around to it. Confirmed bachelor. That's what me and Beccs had you down for. What was it then? The final shove? Wanting to sow your seed, get a foothold on eternity?'

'Never wanted kids.'

'You told Daisy that? Oh, sorry, she is a kid anyway.'

'Scratch!'

'My advice...if you don't want the buggers, check yourself into a clinic for some fancy scissor work. I only have to look at Becca, and she's up the duff. First time we had sex...'

Becca wished he wouldn't. Finn knew all of it anyway. Did Scratch seriously have to go projectile-vomiting their entire sordid history out just for the sake of shooting the breeze?

'First time, and I used a bloody condom. We were bloody seventeen when the kid arrived. Not sure who was the biggest baby, me or our Ella.'

There was a pause. Finn's voice, when it came back, was level. But Becca couldn't help but get the feeling there was something more to that studied resolve. Something she couldn't quite put her finger on.

'Would you have it any other way?'

'Nah, mate, nah. Becca's my world.'

Bless him. Becca glanced at her face in the hall mirror; her dishevelled hair; her skin marked with frown lines, and the fungus-brown circles under her eyes. You couldn't fault Scratch for his loyalty.

'Absolutely my world. I mean...I see you, Finn...all the ladies, all the glitz and sparkle, but know what? I think I was the lucky one, really lucky. My whole life's built around her, always has been. Remember how she was? Her dark hair so black it shone like you could almost see your reflection in it, and her skin sunburnt from being outside. She was like some kind of wild creature that didn't belong indoors. Her sheer passion for life.'

Scratch paused, his voice dropping down a tone, although if he did it out of secrecy, it fell flat: Becca could still hear.

'I mean...'

Becca edged closer till she was standing on the top step. If they came out of the kitchen, they'd catch her, only she couldn't not listen.

'I have to say, she's lost a bit of that now. A bit, but... Last night.' Becca could hear the smile in his voice. 'Her arguing away about monogamy and passion. She's always got an opinion. Got life all worked out. One of the lads. That's what Beccs has always been. I mean, the kids are beautiful, don't get me wrong, but they're just pale imitations of the original. Nothing can hold a candle to Becca. Nothing.'

Tears pricked her eyes. Yet, Scratch wasn't stopping.

'You can have yourself all the Daisies you like...'

'It's not like they're factory produced.'

'Course not, mate. But that's not the thing... The thing is, when I look at Becca...every time I look at Becca, I still see that young girl. Even though...'

Tears poured silently down Becca's face. She was glad she couldn't see the mirror from where she was standing. That would have just finished her off. The disconnect between how Scratch saw her and the reality was just too painful.

'Then...' Scratch's voice faltered, uncertain, as though there was something that he didn't want to spell out.

'What?' Finn asked.

'Nah, mate.'

'Scratch?'

'You wanna eat your breakfast. It'll get cold.'

'What were you going to...?'

'Stupid. Just eat up.'

'Scratch, what were you going to say?'

She couldn't help herself; she was hoping Scratch would spill whatever it was he was struggling over. In truth, Becca was curious as hell. Although at the same time, scared to death about what she'd hear. It was more than a kid's doll-house at stake now.

'After the last kid...'

'Ryan?'

'Yeah, the little one. After the little one...she got...well, it was just a bit down.'

A *bit* bloody down. Why would he tell Finn this? This was her business. Becca's business. Maybe, at a push, their business. But there was one thing for sure—it was nobody else's beeswax.

'It's nothing major,' Scratch said easily, as if he was talking about a dent on the car, a minor inconvenience. 'Nothing life-destroying. She's fine now.'

Bloody Scratch, why plant that seed and then brush it under the carpet? If he wanted to describe what she'd been through, why didn't he lay it all out bare on the table? *'A bit down,'* like it was all just a bit of a bad day.

'Only sometimes...' Scratch lowered his voice again, so she had to push her head around the banister. So she had to step out and down one stair on that thick mossy staircase.

'When I catch her off guard... Sometimes, I think she's not really in there anymore.'

Becca pulled back as if she'd been stung. Standing straight, coming face to face with that mirror again, catching her reflection. The last thing she needed. Scratch was right, of course. Who'd have thought a joker like Scratch would have so much intuition in him? Who'd have thought the comedian could pick past the surface and see the truth?

'Fuck.' Scratch laughed. 'Postnatal depression and vasectomies all before you've touched your bacon and eggs.'

'You were lucky.'

Finn must be saying it to be nice. She knew that. How could anyone but Scratch call Scratch *lucky*—a depressed wife, a house packed to bursting with kids, a job he loathed. But if Finn was just being polite, it went supersonic over Scratch's head.

'Like I said, I'm a lucky bastard. What do they say? Lucky in money or lucky in love. Maybe you can't have both.'

She heard the back door rattle.

'Where you going?' Finn called.

'Skoda's knackered. Gonna take it to the garage. Tell her ladyship where I am, will you?'

'Shall I call Becca? Get her to help me eat this?'

'Nah...she finds mornings a...a struggle these days. You fill your belly. Leave a plate for her.'

She heard the kitchen door open and Scratch laughing again as he stepped out into the world before mumbling to himself. 'Fucking underneath the bed! Classic.'

Becca went back into the bathroom, took a handful of pills, a glass of water, then hit the sack. She wondered if it would be possible to just sleep the next few days away. Would they even notice? Probably not—*'a bit down'*.

11

―――――

SNAKES AND LADDERS

(A board game for two or more players. A series of 'snakes' and 'ladders' connect squares on a board. If the player lands on a ladder, they move up the board. If they land on a snake, they slide back down.)

By the time Becca woke again, the smell of breakfast had disappeared, chased away by an army of unseen air-fresheners that were set to pump automatically into the house. The light in the bedroom had also shifted from harsh morning sunlight to a kind of muddy all-inclusive washing-up-bowl grey. The house was utterly silent. The radiators must have run their course. There were no radios on, no people walking room to room. Becca got the odd empty feeling that it was just her and the ghosts left abandoned up on the escarpment.

When she glanced from the window, she could see the Skoda was gone, although Finn's Lotus was still parked up, still shiny red and shouty. Still sitting too close to the barns to be any kind of sensible. She had a bath and washed her hair, making sure to rub her scalp hard with her hands as if she were willing herself back into existence. The pills took the edge off sensations. You had to push a little harder to make anything feel like real life.

Then again, that was kind of what they were supposed to do. Shame there was no way of turning down the dial or allowing for subtleties. There were things that she missed about not feeling, a sensitivity in the skin, the tingle of hot water from a shower when it ran over her body. Sometimes Becca felt that maybe the medication was a high price to pay for being...being...what did Phillips call it: 'level'. Only there didn't seem to be much of a choice. So, she rubbed her follicles harder with the soft towel, hoping to wake up some kind of energy in her brain. Good energy, energy left over from a different place.

When she got downstairs, Becca could tell no one had been in the house for a while. The empty rooms had a hungry hollow feel. She walked through each one picking up the odd sock (how many feet did Scratch have!), a T-shirt, an empty packet of tortilla chips. Maybe Finn had gone with Scratch down to the village? She thought Scratch had gone off on his own, but she didn't know. Becca glanced out of the sunroom window. Finn was right. You could most definitely see the tree. It was just a tree. Suddenly her skin puckered cold as the trunk of the gnarled old beast appeared to split, allowing a large dark shadow to leak out. She stepped back from the window, trying to catch her breath, catch her thoughts.

Then she realised. What an idiot! The tree hadn't split. That was no shadow. Finn! It was Finn. He must have been standing right by the damn thing so that when he stepped away, it had looked as if the tree had pulled itself in two. Becca let out a small bitter laugh. The eye was always more than willing to play tricks if the mind had taken to working overtime and her mind was always on overtime. She seriously did have to get a grip. Jumping at shadows like a school kid was daft, bordering on embarrassing. Only, she couldn't figure out for the life of her what Finn was doing out there. Peering through the long glass pane, Becca could just make out that he was right on the edge. Walking along the precipice, arms outstretched, as though offering himself up to the gods.

'Finn, Finn!' The wind ripped her voice from her mouth, chasing it away and across the moors.

It was pointless. He couldn't hear.

Becca was wrapped up in her coat, scarf, boots. Even to her own eyes, as she'd bundled out of the warm house, she'd looked a mess. Like some kind of Cold War refugee, a woollen blob—not how she wanted to look in front of Finn.

'Finn!'

Arms still outstretched, he turned and caught sight of her, a smile creasing his finely chiselled face. How could he not feel the cold?

'Finn, you crazy bastard.'

He was right out on the edge.

'Can see why he jumped,' Finn said, glancing down. 'It feels like you could fly away.'

Becca couldn't help it. Her face dropped because they both knew for absolute certain that the man hadn't jumped. 'Maybe he didn't have much of a choice.'

Finn shrugged, not bothering to agree or disagree. He wasn't going to come clean on his own, that was for sure. She was going to have to coax it out.

'It's not safe, Finn,' she said—short and sweet and every

inch true. 'The wind could push you off. You might not mean it, but over you'd go anyway. You, of all people, should know that.'

Finn let her last line linger. Just stood there smiling, not taking one step closer to her. This would be the perfect time, Becca thought, for him to come clean. Yet he said nothing.

'Finn!' she shouted. She'd got her permanently maternal angry voice on. She wished she didn't, but it was the only one she could muster up at short notice. 'I said it's not safe.'

'No.' He smiled back. 'And maybe that's what I like about it.'

The wind slapped her hard, causing her to unwittingly gulp in a slug of cold air. Making her hair waterfall over her face in a series of crazy unwanted tentacles. It seemed like yesterday when she'd been up there, standing just where Finn stood, the world at her feet. In fact, what was it that she used to say as a kid? *It's not safe. That's what I like about it.* She had good balance back then. Fuck knows why, perhaps it was something you were born with. She was walking at nine months. Her gran used to joke that she was pushed into that. Had to walk if she wanted to show everyone she was still there and needed feeding.

Maybe that was true, maybe not, but at school, Becca always walked the beam every sports day. And there was the old hospital in town. Its rafters and roof open to the sky. She was always down there practising. Even when the fence went up and the NOT SAFE signs got plastered all over the barriers. It was only when the beams rotted through that she gave the stunt up as a bad idea. Becca couldn't understand the fuss about balance. You just stick your arms out straight and focus on something ahead. That's what she used to do at the old hospital, and up here on the edge of the world, you were even higher.

Maybe it was riskier, maybe not. It's the last few feet that kill you. Instead of rotten beams, here you had playful winds. The lads weren't half so brave as Becca. Scratch was always hanging back, watching in admiration as Becca walked a line so close to the edge, she could feel the soil crumbling from under her feet. Didn't bother her. She was nimble-footed as a goat. Forward and backward she'd go along the edge. Sometimes she'd even dance, raising one leg to stick it out behind her straight as an arrow. How things changed.

'Come on...' Finn's lips creased into that half-held-up smile, the one that was all challenge and goading you on. 'It's fun. You used to be brave. You used to be really brave.'

He held out his hand. The left one she noticed. The one that used to have the ring sitting on it like a bird ready to fly. Now there was nothing, just a cool white band of flesh where the ring had once been.

'That was a long time ago,' Becca said, trying to tear her eyes away from those long pale fingers. 'Now I'm just safe, boringly safe.'

'Nah?' He offered his hand again. 'You were brave and fearless and fun. Come on, Beccs!'

'Fun?' She glanced at the edge with its sheer drop. 'Finn, that was a different lifetime. I've had all the fun squeezed out of me.'

'Don't believe it. You'd have to be a completely different person. A replica. The Beccs we all know, she had fun running through her veins.'

'I'm friggin' forty, Finn.'

'Not yet. At least another year.'

She shot him a wry look. 'Yeah, and that's seriously making a difference.' She scraped her hands through her hair, trying to hold it tight away from the wind. 'Point is, we've all changed, Finn. Maybe some more than others, but...'

'Not you.'

'Yes, me.' She sighed. 'You think it won't happen because...' She laughed but not with any shred of delight as she stood staring up at the wide powder-blue sky. There was too much bitterness in her for that. 'Everyone likes to think they're different. That they'll never get the fun squeezed out of them. But no, believe me, I've been well and truly juiced. It sets in slowly, builds over time. All those years of being at home, of wiping bottoms, of checking baths with your elbow. Of being afraid that someone might just step in front of a car, or stop breathing, just stop. I've had twenty-three years of having kids, Finn, of putting everybody else first. See how brave that makes a person. Five children and I love them, every single one. Wouldn't change it. But...' And the cold air caught in her throat—*but* is such a big word, such a keyword. 'God knows how many pairs of socks balled that is. How many washes put on. How many heads searched for lice and kissed goodnight. And sooner or later...you just forget how it's done—being brave, having fun, living.'

'But none of that stops you being who you were, Beccs.'

'No?' Her eyes had started to water. It must be the wind, which was stinging, feeling so much sharper than a chopping board full of onions. None of it helped. The tears just made her feel even madder: at herself, at the world. Even mother nature was up in arms against her. Becca took a deep breath, filled her lungs. Why not tell him, then? Hadn't Scratch already spilt half the beans, made her look like a lost-cause-looney? Why not give Finn the whole story?

'It's like being one of those Egyptian mummies,' Becca said, letting her hair loose, letting it spiral out of control around her face as the wind toyed with it. 'That's what happens to women. You know the things—wrapped up in bandages, forgotten in museums. You have kids...and then it's like you stop moving, stop living, stop being in your own right. You're just somebody's mother; a bloody dispensary system; a nurse; a taxi. And so that first layer of bandages goes on. And all through the years, all through the years, we just carry right on—willingly wrapping ourselves up in those bandages. Thinking...fuck knows... Fuck knows what we think! Thinking it's going to preserve us. Winding those bandages around tighter and tighter. Until eventually, the person inside just disappears. There's nothing in there anymore. It's just bandages standing up, walking around, functioning, living some kind of half-life.'

For a moment, Finn didn't say anything. He just stared at her as if it was the first time he'd seen her, really seen her, in years. He just stood there looking as the wind thumped into their bodies, boisterous as a yuppie mother bashing them out of the way with her double-buggy carrycot combination. Their bodies pushed and swayed on the escarpment as if they were caught in some kind of obscure interpretive dance routine.

Then Finn raised his head up to the heavens and drew in one long, wet, heather-soaked breath of air. 'And now? Deep breath, Beccs. How is it now, up here?'

God, why wouldn't her eyes stop bloody watering? She sighed, filling her lungs with cold air, just as Finn had done. She could feel it pushing out the corners of her body, running through her veins. A firecracker of life, trying to goad the rest of her into action. 'Is that why you're marrying Daisy?' She could barely say the woman's name. It felt like a stone in her mouth, one that made her want to spit. 'Because you want to feel?'

Finn laughed. 'No.'

There was another pause in which, she noticed, he didn't say the obvious: *I'm marrying Daisy because I love her.* Mercifully that remained like an unpicked scab somewhere in a different conversation.

'So why now then, Finn? Why, after all this time?' Scratch's words had got her curious.

Becca had just assumed that Finn would be marrying for love. She'd never thought to ask, not before, but now the cold Yorkshire air was working its magic, and she was feeling brave.

Finn lowered his eyes to the ground. Not half so cocky anymore. 'Because...' he shrugged, 'maybe I don't want to be alone anymore. Maybe I want someone to come home to...' He laughed. 'Maybe I want a home! I'm tired too, Becca— tired of standing at square one and never moving forward.'

'Snakes and ladders?'

'I'll watch out for the snakes.'

'But you do love Daisy?' She knew the score, had worked on it for her entire life: if you have a direct question, don't sugar-coat the bugger. Euphemisms only lead to years of dead ends.

Finn suddenly looked lost, and despite herself, somewhere in her body, Becca felt a little kindle of life, a little spark of relief.

'She's the closest I've got.'

'Closest? That kind of means, no.'

'For Christ's sake, Becca. Would that make you feel good? Is that what you want?' His eyes flashed a siren of blue towards her. Sparked a mixture of, what was it? Bitterness, and what? A little bit of hate?

'No, I...'

'Do you get some kind of smug satisfaction out of it? There's you and Scratch twenty-three years of married bloody bliss... Decades of whoopee cushions and electric-buzzer-handshakes.'

'It's hardly...'

'You're rubbing salt into wounds. Can't you see that? I find a woman who...a woman who makes me feel halfway normal, and you...you shit all over it.'

'It wasn't like that. I didn't mean...'

'No?'

She pulled her coat tighter around her. Well, she'd made a mess of that.

'Scratch went into the village,' Finn said, taking comfort in the normal. 'The car was playing up.'

'Nothing new there. We're on a hill. Switch the engine off, we can coast all the way back into town. Come to think of it,' she twisted her mouth in distaste, 'I could fuel the bloody thing with my breath.'

Finn smiled, a small one, but they were out of the woods for a bit. 'How much did we put away last night?'

'It was impressive.'

They were back on safe ground, maybe not geographically, but conversationally at least.

'So, the book then, Finn? You want to talk about that?'

'Nothing to say.'

'That's rich.'

'I told you, I found it.'

She wasn't even going to pick him up on that. They could play his game, see how far it got them. 'But, Finn, what's in it? That's what I'd like to know.'

He snorted as though she'd said something funny and only he was in on the joke, but he didn't answer, not straight off. Instead, he stood staring out over the escarpment and the world below laid out like a regurgitated mess of browns and greens and bare open rock. 'Tell you what...' He turned his blue eyes back on her. 'You take a step closer, and I'll tell. One wish for every step.'

'My God, do you ever stop!'

He looked blank.

'Games. Always games with you and Scratch.'

Dismissively Finn turned back towards the sky, which was shifting from blue to grey. 'Please yourself.'

'Okay.' She clenched her bottom lip under her teeth, knowing she might live to regret this. They had a lot to play for.

Finn nodded as if he'd been expecting nothing less. 'Every time you take a step closer, I'll tell you one thing that I've written in the book. One step for every entry you take. But they've got to be big steps mind, not small ones.'

'You're on.' She pushed the hair back out of her eyes. Fastened it with her right hand. 'First wish. What was the first wish you ever made?'

'Step.'

'Seriously?'

He said nothing, so she tilted her body forward.

'Big step mind, that was the deal.'

Becca shook her head in irritation. Games, games and more games. Resigned, she threw her leg out in front of her in an exaggerated arc. It was a big step. There was no arguing with that.

Finn smiled, oh so pleased to have her playing. 'That's an easy one. Scratch. I wished he'd get better.'

'You told us that last night.' Becca felt cheated. She was looking for more information, the sort that could only be shared with herself and Finn.

'So...you're the one that's asking. Scratch caught pneumonia. I'd never seen anyone so ill. Not even old people.'

Finn was right. She could still recall how thin Scratch

had been. He'd never had much weight on him back then, but the pneumonia had left all his bones poking out through his skin. Becca had always found it hard to believe that the skeleton in the biology department was really the tent poles they were all of them strung together over until pneumonia hit Scratch; then the human framework became painfully obvious.

'I'd just got the book, so I wished that he'd live. That he'd have a long, happy life and...that he'd have the thing his heart most desired.'

'That was all one wish?'

Finn smirked. 'Gotta milk it when the Devil's after your soul.'

She nodded thoughtfully. He had a point. 'Wish two. The second thing you put in the book, but nothing to do with Scratch. What did you wish for, for yourself?'

'You have to step, Becca.'

Once again, she threw her leg out in front, wide as if she were a mime artist on stage. 'You know this is seriously weird, don't you?'

'We're talking about some book that you and Scratch are convinced has a hotline to the Devil. You honestly think anything about this is not going to be weird?'

'Okay. Spill.'

'Career success.'

She snorted. 'Well, you got that.'

'Not all at once. I was only sixteen remember, difficult to take over the trading floor.'

'So, it was just the start of the upward trend.' She couldn't help it, *upward trend* sounded bitter when it came out of her mouth.

'I guess.'

'Some of us never got on that.'

'I was lucky.'

'You got all that money from that *aunt* you'd never heard of?' It was impossible to hide the ironic tone in her voice because she remembered Byrde's safe standing open. She'd closed it over with her own two hands.

'Why didn't you tell?' Even out there with the wind filling her eardrums, she could still hear Byrde rumbling, grumbling underneath it all.

'Yeah. That's right...long lost aunt.'

Lying bastard. But she didn't say that. Instead... 'Isn't that a bit...' Becca wondered how far she wanted to lean on this. Everything could, should, come unravelled this weekend. Then again, she knew Finn too well. He wasn't going to tell unless he was ready. Unless it was his idea. 'Wasn't it a bit...odd, didn't you think?'

'Course I *didn't think*, Becca. We all wanted to get out. I saw the opportunity. I got the money. I wasn't going to hang around and ask questions?'

But there had been something too eager about the way Finn had snapped back. He was protesting too much, as that clever bugger, Shakespeare, would say.

'So...it was university, and then, well after uni, the banks snapped me up. Barely had time for my feet to hit the ground.'

'No.' She stared down the escarpment which was falling away beneath her. From where she was standing, she could see the little path snaking this way and that all the way down to the bottom.

'Almost there,' he said, and he was right.

It would be just like old times: her wandering along the edge with her perfect balance. Did she have the nerve? Becca took a deep breath and stepped forward, reaching for his hand, letting Finn lace his fingers through hers. Letting that creep of sensation, of life, fire up her heart like an old boiler coaxed back into action.

'Brave again,' he said. Slipping his other arm around her waist, and she laughed.

Maybe the first laugh she'd felt come bubbling up through her body, bubbling up of its own volition, in years. Becca was kind of surprised to hear it. She'd forgotten it could do that. 'It feels good.'

'Doesn't it? You can be too safe, Beccs. You can smother yourself in the everyday.'

'Don't I know? Only here...here it feels like I'm king of the world,' she shouted out for the whole bloody county to hear.

They stood for a moment, neither of them talking, just the sound of her words triumphant, echoing off the rock, looking out at the pale forever sky. 'Why did you do it?'

'What?'

'Why'd you bring us back, Finn?'

'It's just a holiday. My stag do.'

'But here? Finn, I know things. I know more than you think.'

He looked surprised, curious, but above all, she realised as he unthreaded his fingers, laughed and pulled away, he looked wary.

'Finn!'

'We should go back in.'

'What! Hey. I've still got my third wish!'

'You moved forward.' He was walking backward to the house, leaving her stranded out there on the edge.

'What?'

'You moved forward. You didn't ask for the wish.'

'Finn!'

'No.'

'That's cheating. The third wish...was it about me?'

'Becca, it's just a book. Just a daft book.'

'One wish for Scratch, one for you. What was the third wish? It was about me, wasn't it? Finn, you promised, and I took the sodding step.'

'That last step was small. We had a deal. The steps had to be big.'

'I'd be off the bloody edge! Tell me, what did you wish for me?'

'Becca, it was stupid.' The wind tore his voice from his mouth, scuttling it away before it got to her. She could barely hear. 'It doesn't matter. It didn't come true.'

'What?'

'Tell you this for nothing, Byrde wrote about you.'

Her whole body felt as if it had been plunged into ice. 'Sorry?'

'Byrde, one of his last entries. It said, Keep Rebecca Nilsen.'

'What?'

He shrugged. 'I think there may have been more, but it was scribbled out.'

Keep Rebecca Nilsen. The words flooded her brain with panic. Byrde had wanted her. Why?

Suddenly Finn pulled his phone from his pocket and glanced at the screen. 'Scratch,' Finn shouted towards her above the wind. 'He wants me to pick him up.'

Then he turned his back on her and walked off, leaving Becca standing there alone, exposed to the raw Yorkshire air, feeling sick to the soul.

12

CANASTA

(A card game for two or more players with four jokers. Players attempt to make melds of cards of the same rank. Players go 'out' by playing all the cards in their hand.)

As Becca got closer to the house, she could practically feel the steam coming out of her ears; her mind was feeling as disturbed as a mound of fire ants trapped under the weight of some giant's boot. She kicked off her boots by the back door, not even bothering to set them straight. The rubber heels leaving a thin, curiously satisfying curve of muck across the perfect white of the wall. If Finn broke his neck coming through the door, tripping over the boots, Becca wouldn't care, not in the mood she was in.

What had Finn meant about Byrde writing her name in his book? Byrde barely knew her. *Keep Rebecca Nilsen.* What did that even mean? She wanted to see it. Needed to hear more. But that wasn't going to happen for hours. Becca knew how the "trip to the garage" would go. The lads would stop for a pint because how could they not? And one pint would leach into two; sod the fact that two pints consumed, this fine winter morning, would sonic-boom the two friends sky-high over the limit and that they were already silo-ing more than enough fermented liquid from last night to stock a microbrewery.

Then there would be the jaunt to the bookies. Scratch had promised, how many times she couldn't remember, that the bookies was a no-go. A bad habit he'd ring-fenced and archived in Scratch's museum of idiot ideas. It was a *mug's game*. His words, not hers and yet still, there would be a bet. Probably three. Scratch liked doing things in threes. And when Scratch got back, she knew there would be the inevitable furtive listening to the race on his phone. He'd be spending just that bit too long in the toilet with the door closed. Sometimes he'd pull the flush one too many times, forgetting he'd already done it twice. Occasionally he'd cry out in frustration, the tiled bathroom walls giving his howls that added extra reverberation of despair. Did Scratch seriously think she didn't know? Then, on top of it all, there'd be that brief irritation when the dog finished OOP: out of picture, which Scratch's dog always managed to do.

Yup, the man had a talent for picking a loser. Although the mood never held him down for long because that big win was always just around the next corner. Stood to reason, according to his warped logic, that if you lose that many times—at some point, you've got to win. For Scratch, it was a case of sound mathematics—odds and statistics. Since it was only Finn that had managed to pass his math GCSE, Becca wasn't sure she or Scratch should be larging it on the computational odds front.

Though, Scratch managed to keep the family boat just above the Plimsoll line of sinking. His pockets might be lighter, but thankfully the bets never annihilated the housekeeping life raft permanently. No, it was the extension that was doing that. But you can't send bricks and double-glazing back, not once they've been planted, watered and grown. Not once the plastered walls of an extension are smothered liberally with potato print pictures. It hadn't even been finished. There was still electrics and painting to go, but once the roof was on, the artwork had gone up.

They'd been in trouble before. Most people, normal people, were. Interest rates had been low. The country had been diving merrily into trouble for years as if trouble was an open-air lido with the sun shining. Provided interest rates didn't get greedy...they should be okay, and Scratch whittling away a few pounds on the dogs—did it really hurt? Times had shifted, but the gambling habit hadn't. No, Becca knew the men wouldn't be back for a long time.

Keep Rebecca Nilsen. It didn't make sense. Why would Byrde write that? She needed to see it. Finn had said he thought there was more. The book must be here some-where. She'd take a look when the lads were out. It wasn't prying. Finn had said he'd tell her, only there was a bit miss-ing. A bit she needed to see for herself.

She walked through the house, running her hand along the cold, clean paint of the hallway. A small part of Becca couldn't help feeling thankful that Scratch didn't realise quite how shit their life was. They may have sold their souls to the bank with a smile on their faces and a Bic biro in their hands, but there was no point in both of them hitting the antidepressants. Besides, Scratch would never need that kind of medication because Scratch, leaving debt to one side, Scratch's world had everything he always wanted in it —her and the kids. If that big win ever did come in, well, it would only ever be icing on the cake material.

Finn had been right about one thing, though, she

thought as she rounded the thick newel and placed her socked toes on the carpet. Scratch used to be one lucky bastard when they were kids. Scratch cards. That was where it all started: a life in gambling. Though, of course, it was Scratch's fake dad, Tod Harris, that had whittled away the housekeeping on the dogs. He'd taught Scratch how. Becca had always felt that maybe that was why Scratch liked to keep his flutters secret: Scratch hated Old Man Harris. The idea that he'd mentored Scratch in anything, any habit whatsoever, would have turned Scratch's stomach contents into projectile vomit material.

Mr Harris had his dogs. Mrs Harris had her bingo. So initially, Scratch had settled on specialising in short bets you could buy through the newsagent—mainly scratch cards. Scratch cards were to Scratch what shoplifting was to Finn. Everybody had their vice. Becca could name the vices of the whole town they grew up in if she were called on to take the stand. It was pretty much the same old story: coveting wives, small-time thieving, gambling, drinking, badly fitting tempers, and drugs. The stories never changed. It was only the players that switched around.

In comparison to Finn, who had been forever shoving stuff up his coat sleeves and under his jacket, Scratch's small-time gambling vice was pretty innocent. You couldn't get nicked for it, even when you were under-age. He must have started when he was about ten. He'd stand outside the shop waiting for the older kids to come by, offering them a cut if he got lucky, and funny thing was, he often did. By the time he was sixteen, and it was all legal, Scratch was lending a helping hand to the little-ies, bets and cigarettes. Scratch never asked for anything upfront. He said he just did it to be helpful, but if there was a win... (and he'd often stand over them so he could see the foil come off), if there was a win, they always saw that Scratch was alright. They liked him. You couldn't help it; with his ready smile and open ears he was a likeable guy.

The betting, Scratch claimed, was not an addiction, nothing so fun-of-the-mill. According to Scratch, it was built into his DNA. Not from the Harrises. In fact, Scratch claimed that the Harrises had never had a flutter until Scratch arrived on the scene. Scratch had been the Harris' gateway to gambling, so Scratch said. Because it was Scratch that provided a means to it—through the foster money. He used to have this story, yet another one! He claimed he exuded some kind of primaeval force over the Harrises. An irresistible influence people just couldn't help buying into, based on a gut feeling, a kind of premonition, that time was running out.

Nothing was ever simple with Scratch. If it was true, if Scratch did exude some sort of force over people that made them want to throw caution to the wind and take a bet, it failed on Becca. She could not see the attraction of taking a flutter. The only thing she was sure of as far as betting went was that it was dogs that had become Scratch's chosen brand of weakness. Which was odd, not only because of Tod Harris but also on account of the fact that Scratch hated dogs. She'd go as far as saying that he was actually scared of them. According to Scratch, there was only one type of dog that was ever any good in the whole damn world—a dog that was running. And for a track-running dog, Scratch was a lost cause.

It could be worse. Casinos left him cold, and there were only so many races a dog could run. That was his take on it too. If Becca got him in a tight corner, he'd tell her that greyhound racing had limited outlets as far as gambling went. Though she knew there was more than one dog and more than one track. The good thing was Scratch didn't blow the housekeeping money like people did at casinos.

When life is tough, everyone needs a little something in their corner. She knew that. So, Scratch had his dogs, his secret bets, and Becca? Well, Becca had her secrets too. She'd never told him about the break-in at Byrde's or about Finn, but that wasn't all. Sometimes she'd fantasise about the life she could have had. There are no criminal charges on that one. But dreaming is still the kind of thing that can wreck lives. It was wrecking hers, inch by inch. And, of course, her secret got bigger and nastier. The fact that she wasn't going to spill the beans about their "best friend" and the manslaughter; that little secret could see her banged up behind bars if she told all these years later. If she said anything, she could be in trouble.

Keep Rebecca Nilsen. What on earth did it mean? Why write her name in the Devil's book. She shook her head, trying to clear the thought as she came to the top of the landing. It wasn't the Devil's book. It was a notebook. The whole Devil thing was Scratch's idea. Scratch's story.

Back at the house, the heating was off. The old place was getting cooler, and she had no idea how to kick-start the boiler. She didn't even know where the blessed thing was. The cold from outside had begun to seep through the thick stone walls. They hadn't meant to abandon her there. It was just how things had turned out. They'd be back soon enough, louder than life, soused again and delivering a brand-new string of one-liners: a little something for the weekend that Scratch had coined on the boys-only trip out. She wasn't sure how long she had, but she knew she had to find that book. Becca pushed open the door to Finn's room.

13
———

GAMEBOOK

(A gamebook is a work of printed fiction that allows the reader to participate in the story by making choices.)

Finn's room was a good deal smaller than the master bedroom he'd generously put Becca and Scratch in. The curtains were still drawn, trapping the tea-coloured air in a tonal womb-like state. It smelt of him; the expensive aftershave, the soap, the deodorant, a heavy leathery taint layered finely in an aromatic strata through the still air. There were no clothes on the floor. The sheets on the bed had been pulled across tightly as if by a house-keeping expert. The line of the pillows eased silky straight by the flat of a hand. The man was a bachelor, used to looking after himself. Becca hesitated there for a moment, not wanting to violate the room, but only a moment. People had been writing her name in a book. Not once but twice, first Byrde, then Finn. She had a right to know what was being said about her. All that *'step forward, and I'll tell you a wish'* stuff. Who did Finn think he was? To Becca's mind, three was an awkward number. She'd always struggled with it. Three meant someone was left on the outside. This morning, it appeared to be her turn. Well, sod that. She entered the room and started to open the drawers.

The bag was not there, the book nowhere to be found. In hindsight, Finn probably had the thing in his car. Becca sat down heavily at the end of his bed. A dull aching, throbbing, hammering at the inside of her brain. If Scratch hadn't called Finn away, then she probably would have gotten to the bottom of this. Most likely, Byrde had written her name in his book after he'd seen her in the barns. The full sentence would no doubt read, '*Keep Rebecca Nilsen and her no good mates off the property.*'

Byrde hadn't known the others' names, only hers. Perhaps he'd jotted her name into his book so he could report her to the police if needed. They'd smashed his window. Well Finn had. That was vandalism. Only the idea of her name sitting there in that book for all those years made her feel an overwhelming sense of dread.

As she moved out of the room, Becca took the sleeve of Finn's dressing gown, the one that was hanging up on the back of the drawer, passing the soft material through her fingers and draping it idly around her waist for just a second. It was grey, soft. Cashmere. She found herself wishing it wasn't quite so soft. So expensive. Wishing that somehow the gap between them all hadn't grown so wide over the years.

The house outside Finn's room was growing colder as though soaking up the icy granite rocks that it stood on. If the temperature continued to drop, she'd have to find that blessed boiler. In the meantime, though, she was hungry. She could stick the leftover breakfast in the oven. That would kill two birds with one stone; hunger and a little warmth in the kitchen. Only as Becca rounded the newel on the stairs she caught sight of the glass panel in the door and her entire body appeared to cave. Her heart dropped, her arms suddenly fell boneless at her sides, and her breath caught in a rasp in her throat because there was someone outside. Someone was standing on the doorstep. A shadow. For a moment, she couldn't move. Cold fear laced through her body. Had it seen her? She wasn't sure. Becca stared at the glass rectangle, her eyes dry where she failed to blink. She wouldn't move. Wouldn't breathe. Wouldn't let it know she was here. It couldn't be Scratch or Finn. It was too soon, surely, and yet there it was, a shadow at the door.

Keep Rebecca Nilsen. The ghostly words repeated once again in her head. *Keep.* Her life was trapped between the pages of a cursed book. Written in ink for all eternity. Was that why she couldn't move on?

Suddenly the shadow fractured and disappeared. It must have been thrown from one of the barns. Not a person at all, just a shape. Yet, despite trying to grab herself a slug of rationale, Becca noticed her hands were shaking.

From the kitchen window, Becca stared out over the yard. It was empty. Not a soul, just the wind stalking around like a bad-tempered four-year-old. She took one cold sausage from the hastily packed breakfast containers and tucked in. Turning the knob on the oven so she could reheat the plate Finn had left for her. It would be hours before they were back. She'd have to find that boiler, too, or she'd be frozen like an icicle by the time they sauntered back in. Besides, the cold, that was pushing in from the edges of the house, was creepy. With the lights on, and the heating blasting out with no thoughts of climate change, the upmarket refurb of Byrde's house could just about chase away any ghosts from the past, but once that death-cold grip got a hold, there was no hope for the rational mind. It would be terror all the way.

The boiler wasn't in the kitchen, so Becca tried the hall. Avoiding the pocket of space in front of the cellar. There was a broom cupboard under the stairs. She opened the wooden panelled door, and sure enough, there it was. A large rectangular white block, tubes extending out of its top: the boiler. Opening the casing was easy enough, but she wasn't sure where to go from there. There were switches and a pre-set timer. She just needed to find the override button. It wasn't their fuel bill that the thing would be eating into. Only the controls weren't easy to navigate. There had to be an instruction booklet somewhere. Becca leaned into the cupboard, sticking her arm towards the back, feeling along the shelves arched over the boiler till her fingers clutched on a large A4 book and a mass of paper. Pulling it into the light, she felt relieved to see that, yes, the bundle of papers did indeed contain the instructions.

Within seconds, the boiler was growling. About to put the paper back into the cupboard, she glanced down and realised that the A4 book was, in fact, the house guest book. Odd that it hadn't been in the kitchen. Someone must have stashed it there by accident. Becca blew a little dust off the cover before opening the front page. The date was two years ago. It must be from when the house first had its refurb. Someone must have forgotten to move it back into the kitchen.

Taking the book, Becca closed the cupboard door and headed to the kitchen. It would help pass a few minutes while the breakfast warmed up. Besides, she was curious about what holidaymakers had made of the place. Byrde's house was so ingrained in her own life that it was impossible to gain any sense of neutrality, and she felt it would be amusing to come at it from a fresh perspective.

The Davidsons in 2016 loved it.

The house is immaculate. Had a lovely weekend with extended family. Great walks. Although footpath precarious.

The Critchleys in the same year but a few weeks later.

Comfortable house for family and friends. Kitchen very high spec. More wine glasses, please!

The Kents were not so keen on the area.

House lovely, which was lucky as weather stank. Spent entire week housebound.

BECCA FLIPPED on through eulogies about the bathtub, the laundry room, the one decent café in Falham, finding herself surprised that there was, in fact, one decent café in the old town. Then something caught her eye. It was spring 2018. The change of heart started with the Mitchells.

Initially bowled over by the house, but problems with faulty security light outside meant we had to move to back bedrooms. Needs to be fixed.

Then following hot on the heels of the Mitchells, the Smiths arrived. April 2018.

Security light still faulty. Took bulbs out. However, we heard someone prowling outside on three occasions. Not sure what the answer is. Best to lock doors when leaving house. Keep valuables out of sight. Wouldn't come again.

Becca felt a cold shiver pass over her body. So, there was someone outside.

She glanced out of the window. They'd done it as kids, climbed up the escarpment looking for stuff they could nick or people they could terrify. Maybe the game was still going on. Different kids, same story. Despite the warmth from the radiators, Becca found herself pulling her cardigan tighter around her body as she continued to read.

The Thomases found that the house was:

Not for us. Maybe there's too much of the "city dweller" in our family. Odd noises kept us awake most nights.

The Browns had a slightly different tone:

This place is crying out for a remake of The Exorcist. And Mrs Hennings! What the hell! Feels like those old Rock Babies of old could be living in that creepy old cellar.

Rock Babies? Becca remembered the story that Scratch used to tell, about the creatures born at the centre of the earth. The things that went searching, crawling crablike over the moors. In search of innocent families to creep into and rot from the inside out. Unable to stop herself she glanced towards the cellar. Its dark closed rectangle of wood sitting between her and whatever was down there. So, it wasn't just her then, that felt there was something wrong. The Browns had felt it too. Slowly she moved towards the cellar as if drawn by a magnetic pulse older than time. At the knock on the front door, Becca jumped out of her skin.

There was a woman standing on the other side of the door. Not on the step, she was standing back from the house as if reluctant to come in. Her hair was grey, cut short. Her face pale and sickly looking, like sun-bleached leather.

'I'm looking for trouble.'

Becca stared awkwardly from the doorway. Squinting into the light. The cold moorland air biting into her skin.

'Sorry?'

'Trouble,' the woman said, her face remaining hard and expressionless. 'Dog. Irish Wolfhound.'

'Oh, of course.' Becca laughed. 'I thought you meant...'

But the words dried on her lips. The woman wasn't smiling. 'There was a note.' Becca indicated back through the door towards the kitchen. 'We saw...only no. There's been no sign of the dog.'

The older woman nodded thoughtfully as though this was only to be expected.

'Were you staying here?' Becca asked, brightly.

The woman scoffed. 'No.' The word came out sharp as a slap. 'Cleaner.'

'Oh right.' An awkward pause hung in the air. 'It's beautifully clean.'

'Yes.'

'There was um...' again Becca indicated back through the door, 'something in the guest book about security lights?'

'Guest book?'

'Yes, it had been pushed in with the boiler.' Becca knew she should invite the woman in, but something about her awkward stance made Becca reluctant to offer the invitation. The woman's body was crinkled into an odd shape. A shape Becca found familiar somehow yet couldn't quite place.

'Stupid people.' The woman's thick lips curled into a snarl. 'They write stupid things.'

'You wouldn't be...Mrs Hennings, by any chance?'

The woman nodded. Becca felt a rush of amusement. The old bird had hidden the book because of the veiled insult.

But the amusement barely had time to land, because the woman fixed Becca with her hard flinty eyes. 'And I know you.'

Becca suddenly felt uncomfortable. She glanced over the woman's shoulder. They were completely alone.

'I saw the name on the booking form.' The woman continued, in her humourless tone. 'Thick as thieves, you lot. If it was my place, you wouldn't be here.'

'I...' Confusion spread through Becca's brain.

'Never mind the bloody dog, they're trouble those boys. Both of them.'

She found irritation welling up inside of her. 'They're not boys anymore. And we weren't...'

'I know what happened.' Mrs Hennings scowled. 'And as soon as that booking came in, the old place, it started to grumble.' She looked up at the house, skimming her cold eyes across the plaster as though examining a familiar face as Becca's mind reeled like a spinning top.

This woman couldn't know what happened about Byrde, surely? 'Grumbled?'

Hennings returned her eyes to Becca, eyeing her shrewdly.

'It's just a house,' Becca said defensively.

'Maybe. Point is, nothing about those two lads of yours is in any way good.'

Her lads? Becca couldn't help but smile. Were they still really that tight in their friendship? Was it so obvious to everyone outside of their triangle?

But Hennings wasn't giving her any chance to wallow. 'And,' the woman's tone was hard and unforgiving, 'you being with them, that makes you guilty too.'

'Guilty?'

'You should have stayed away.' The woman was backing towards the escarpment.

'What the hell!'

'You see that dog, you give me a call.' Hennings called over her shoulder as she continued shuffling away from the farmhouse on her path towards the cliff edge, her gait awkward and bent. And as she moved forward step by step her hard silhouette flitted across the shadow of the tree. It was then that Becca realised, with a sickening lurch in her gut, that was it: that was the shape that the old woman was twisted into—The Watcher.

14

———

TROUBLE

(Trouble, also known as Frustration, is a board game in which players compete to be the first to send all their pieces around the board. A similar game called Headache was produced by MBC.)

'Looking for Trouble?' Finn laughed. It was Finn who had picked up the phone, though she could hear Scratch laughing in the background.

'I know.' But something was bothering Becca, something that she was itching to get out. 'Do you think she saw...' She hesitated. 'Anything?'

'Plenty.' Scratch laughed.

'We were just kids.' Finn's voice sounded so casual. 'Kids doing normal kid things.'

Becca wasn't so sure that what they got up to was normal, certainly not all of it.

'Hennings,' Finn mumbled. 'Didn't she have a daughter?'

Becca searched her memory. Now that Finn mentioned it, the name did ring a bell. 'Yes, you're right. Year above us.'

'Below,' Finn said. 'Remember, Scratch?'

Scratch's voice came muffled from the background. 'Hennings. No.'

'Yeah, Francis? Fiona?'

'Freya.' Suddenly it all came back. 'Yes, year below. What happened to her?'

Becca hears Finn draw in a deep breath. 'Don't know. But, have to say, don't know what happened to anyone from back then.'

'She left town,' Scratch called from the driver's seat. 'Wow, this thing goes fast.'

'Watch the bend,' Finn's voice sounded a little tense.

'When will you be back?'

'Not sure,' Finn said. 'They're just checking on a part.'

'Won't be long, love. Don't you worry,' Scratch called. 'And Becca, sweetheart?' His voice came too loud through the handset, full of the morning's laughter and jokes; things he carried on his person as effortlessly as Becca carried tablets and tissues.

'Yeah?'

'You should just see how this thing moves.'

She could hear Finn's, so-much-smaller, voice transported over time and space. 'It's a Lotus, not a fucking Tardis.'

'Warp factor three!' Scratch shouted. In the background, the engine stepped up its growl.

'Scratch, go careful.' The last thing Becca needed to add to that playlist in her head was the crunch of her husband and best friend as they folded up neatly against some wall.

'Careful is my middle name. We thought we might stop off for a bevvy, you know...while we're down here.'

'Scratch! Don't you think maybe you had enough last night to see you through? You shouldn't even be driving.'

'Hey, look at that.' She caught Finn's voice. It had a

faraway quality, as if he'd been pushed into the back seat and given a packet of crisps and a Coke to keep him quiet.

'Means diddley squat,' Scratch mumbled.

'What?' Becca felt the irritation rising in her. Nothing is guaranteed to get up a person's nose quite so quick as standing half out of a conversation. 'Scratch, I'm still here?'

'Right, sorry, love. The old hospital in town, well the wreck of it. Some property developer's stuck signs up. Planning permission stuff. But they've been doing that for years.'

She could picture the old place in her mind. It had been a shell since they were kids. Best thing for it would have been to flatten the site once and for all. Maybe that would have happened, but the council hadn't been quick enough. They'd sold it on for a song in the late eighties, and then it sat there like a beached whale waiting for property prices to hit sky-high. Or at least raise back up. Becca figured there would be a tad more waiting on that front. No one wanted houses here; jobs first, then the houses would look after themselves.

'Nothing changes fast in this place,' Scratch announced, as if he had a direct tap to her brain.

'Just get back, will you.' She glanced around the kitchen. It felt empty without the others close. All that white, it was almost surgical. Like a morgue waiting patiently for a body so the autopsy could be done and dusted. The autopsy on her? Cut her open. Find all the secrets bubbling under her skin. She couldn't help it. She shivered. 'I don't want to be stuck up here on my own,' she said, flicking her nail across the long white countertop. 'It gives me the creeps. Get back quick as you can.'

'Sure. Sure.' Which Becca knew, in Scratch speak, meant sweet Fanny Adams.

Freya Hennings. That was it. Becca just about remembered her. Quiet girl. When the call went down, Becca looked at the guest book laid out on the table. She hadn't told them about that. It made her feel uneasy. What had Hennings said: as soon as their *booking came in, the old place, it started to grumble'*.

But houses didn't grumble. She wished the lads would get back. Well, at least Finn. Scratch would go all out spooky on the entries in the book. Taking relish in the possibility of a haunting. Finn, despite his faults, or maybe because of them, he would take things slower; work out some rational explanation.

15

CONNECT

(Also known as The Captain's Mistress. A two-player connection game. The aim: for players to get four counters in a row. The player who succeeds in lining up their counters wins the game.)

Geographically, when they were kids, Becca had been slightly closer to Finn. He lived on the next street, so that kind of bought them an intimacy she didn't really have with Scratch. She snorted, almost choking on the cold pork that she'd pulled from the fridge. She was married to Scratch, for Christ's sake; how much more intimate did she want? Becca wiped her greasy fingers on a tea towel and ran herself a glass of water. What did intimate even mean? Not just sex. No, she didn't mean that. She meant like soulmates. A person you can be with, that you don't need to talk to. Like a person who knows you as well as they know themselves. With Scratch, there was always a punchline. Always something funny, sure as a full stop at the end of a sentence.

But she and Finn, they didn't need words. Not then, back

when they were kids. She'd always call for Finn first, or he'd call for her. Was it just geography? Or maybe a dislike of the Harrises? Tod Harris was scarier than that chained dog. Tod Harris could bark too. In truth, she wasn't sure why it was always Finn she had called on; the whole thing had got so messed up over the years. Even though they had counted themselves as a dyed-in-the-wool threesome, sometimes it would just be the two of them: her and Finn, and she'd liked it. That quiet pocket of peace. No jokes. And as a teenager she couldn't help feeling a little swell of pride walking beside Finn. His limbs had been so long, so easy, and that floppy swell of hair swayed into his deep blue eyes. He was a good-looking guy. Some things never changed, but back then, in a world of grunge and grey skies, Finn had stood out as something just that little bit special. He could have been a model in one of the magazines or lead singer in a band if he could sing. Maybe even if he couldn't sing? People always stared at him when he walked past, followed the both of them with their eyes. But none of that went to Finn's head. In fact, he seemed oblivious.

So, because of the geography thing, they'd always manage a snatched five minutes before they got to Scratch's, and if Becca was upset. If her dad had been pulling one of his blinders, she'd either go straight to Finn's or sometimes Finn would come find her. It was as though he had this sixth sense for when trouble kicked off. Or maybe he could actually hear her dad shouting; her dad liked things loud when he was totalled. Around six months before Byrde went flying, her dad had been letting loose with his fists, this way and that. He hadn't hit her. People always used to ask her that question—*does he hit you?* Like if he did, that would be stepping over the mark, and something could be done. But without the actual hit, everything must be A-okay. Business as usual. No, there was never any skin against skin. Sometimes she fell, but genuinely fell. It was always best to get out of his way, and accidents were accidents. Probably, somebody should have done something anyway. He may not have hit her, but he was bloody scary when he got going. It had taken her years to realise that abuse didn't just mean a black eye and broken bones. If you ended up cowering in your own house, well, abuse must be sniffing around the place somewhere. There were a couple of times when her dad did a classic. Once it was over, a bloody fried egg! She couldn't remember what about the egg, just that it had been fried and that a lot of china saw its last.

It kind of felt as though he was warming up over the years because the aggression, the anger, the volume, it all kept creeping up a notch. In retrospect, she saw it all in the context of that fateful night, her with her grazed knees and Byrde going off the edge. But maybe she just linked the fried egg and Finn with Byrde six months later because those two nights stood out like mountains standing high in the landscape of her past. They were the footstones in her life that saw everything going wrong, then right, then finally belly-up and beyond recovery.

The pan had been in the sink, still steaming. The fried egg had hit the bin, half in, half out, the yoke broken and bleeding to the floor. Her dad had started on the dinner service. The one he'd got as a wedding present. Royal Doulton. You can still buy the same set on eBay: white bone china with a thin gold band at the edge, a strip of grey, then a repeat of the thin trace of gold, like two gold wedding bands set against a slug of mist. It was a miracle it had lasted so long. Her dad liked to smash stuff, but her nan had boxed it up and put it in the dresser.

After the everyday plates had hit the wall, he'd started

hunting around for the dinner service, and that was her cue. Becca didn't wait. She was off out the door. She'd taken her school bag. God knows why. It was heavy with books but nothing useful. She hadn't had time to get to the bedroom. She had a fiver in her purse. There was more in her room, but she couldn't risk going upstairs or coming back down again. No, she had to get out. A fiver would have to be enough. She didn't care where she was going. *Out* was the best she could do at short notice. The noise of her dad's anger was so loud it was taking up her whole brain. There was no room left for thinking. He'd gone too far. One day, maybe one day soon, it wouldn't be the wall that was taking the brunt of the plates. She'd have a ready answer for them then when they asked their question, 'Does he hit you?' But why wait like a sitting duck? Why bother? She was sixteen. She needed to get out.

When she got to the bottom of the road, she heard Finn's voice calling her back.

'Becca, hey...what's up?'

Finn's footsteps came from behind her thundering down the street, trying to catch her up. 'Where's the bleeding fire?' He'd pulled her back, his hand on her arm. His touch carrying that small electric current it always did. His face dropped as he took in her swollen eyes, the bitten, bloody lips.

'The fire's...' Her words came out a mix of spit, anger and frustration. 'It's in my friggin' head. That bloody man.'

'Hey.' Finn pulled her around, their bodies facing each other, a gulf between them which seemed unbridgeable, hopeless. He leant towards her wiping her tears with his long fingers.

'You should hear the messed-up crap that comes out of his mouth.'

'Your dad?'

She stifled a sob. 'Who else.'

'He's drunk, Becca. He doesn't mean it.'

She knew all this, but it didn't make any of it any better. Why couldn't her dad just keep his gob shut? Why wasn't he one of those quiet drunks, the ones that fall asleep snoring in front of the TV?

'I can't stay there anymore.' She'd scuffed the heel of her toe across the tarmac. 'One day, I'll swing for him. I swear I will.'

Finn pulled her closer, so her head rested into his chest, and the fit felt so right. He was warm and smelt of soap and Blue Stratos.

'Seventeen,' he said, running his hands gently across the top of her head. 'We wait till we're seventeen, got that deposit, then we're all on that bus.'

They'd been saving, working part-time jobs. Finn had even stopped nicking things—couldn't afford the criminal record, so he said. By the time Becca turned seventeen, they would be out. They'd have the deposit for a little flat in Manchester. One bedroom would do. They'd put three single mattresses in the bedroom, and they'd be sorted. Only, seventeen suddenly felt so far, far away.

'I can't wait any longer.' Her voice was barely audible. 'I had to leave my friggin' money. It's in my room.'

'Let him sleep it off, Beccs. Then we'll go back in. I'll come with you. You know what he's like. Just a bit longer, then we're all out.'

She didn't reply.

'Come on.' He took her hand. 'You can stop the night at mine. Let your dad knock himself out. He doesn't need an audience.'

A fiver was never going to get her far; besides, she liked

holding Finn's hand, liked being close to him. Her skin felt more alive when it was up close near to his. Becca didn't want to leave Finn or Scratch, not really, not ever. That was the one thing she could pick clean out of all this mess: the lads made everything better.

Finn had carried her bag slung over his shoulder as he led her down his street. A street identical to hers apart from curtains and rubbish bins and the odd splash of bright paint, a blue windowsill, a red door, the sole statement of someone's spirit of individuality. There wasn't much room to shine, not in a town like Falham. Finn's house was at the end of the terrace. Despite the odd splash of paint, all the houses were the same, biscuit-coloured and bleak. With a little alleyway between each pair, standing just back from the pavement like a surprised dark mouth. Black tunnels that smelt of rainwater and cement. Some people stacked bikes in the arches. Mostly, they were all choked up with rubbish, things that people had wanted so bad they could bust, then forgot they had.

Before they even got to Finn's place, a spray of Gremlin laughter hit the air. Their footsteps slowed.

'She's got company,' he said, the words so sour in his mouth they made his chin twist as though he'd bitten hard into a lemon.

Becca didn't comment. She just nodded. *She*, Tina, was Finn's problem. Just as awful as Becca's dad, but in her own special way. There was an entire spectrum of ways it was possible to be awful on the parenting front. Neither of their parents was winning. Instead, there was a lot of level pegging.

Finn opened the gate into the tunnel that ran down the side of his house. Becca knew the score, mother in the front room—they'd have to go around the back. It wasn't easy. The bins were overflowing and stinking rotten as a corpse.

'Robert...' Finn's mum could be heard from inside the house, her voice all sugar-coated and trying its hardest to hit sexy. 'You are such a bad...bad man.'

Finn didn't catch Becca's eye. They both chose to go deaf. Finn's mum often said the kind of thing that made toes curl so sharp and inward if you listened you'd be in danger of never walking again. But hey, they both knew the score. Tina was bad enough when she didn't have company, the excitement of entertaining tended to push that woman over the edge.

'You've been away so long...' Each of Tina's words was drawn out and savoured. 'I should give you a piece of my mind.'

'Think maybe...' Robert's voice was all gravel and beer, setting Tina laughing expectantly: no doubt he'd hooked her closer. 'Maybe it's a piece of something else that's on my mind.'

Finn said nothing, just squeezed Becca's hand between his, and she knew they were on the same page. He couldn't help Tina, just like she couldn't help her dad. There was no turning the adults around, making them better. The only solution was to leave them behind. For now, Finn was right. They had to bide their time. When they got out, there would be no coming back.

Finn found it easy enough to scale the back wall, using the outside kitchen windowsill to give him a lever up and in. He'd been doing it for years. Besides, these days he was six foot one and had the upper body strength needed to heave himself through the bedroom window like a pro. For Becca, it wasn't quite the same story. Her trainers slipped off the decayed wooden ledge. The action had to be fast.

You needed to just dab it with your foot before you leapt. That day, it didn't seem to want to work. Maybe it was because she was scared shitless that any minute Tina would come through the house and catch Becca's legs dangling outside the window. Disaster seemed only a hop, skip and a jump away with Finn leaning out over her head so far it was a miracle he didn't drop right back past her. Luckily, a cup of tea was the last thing on Robert's mind. The kitchen was mercifully quiet. In the end, Becca had to lean a broken bike up against the wall and hurl herself up at the window, her foot just grazing the saddle. Her trainers scraping madly against the hard, gristly wall trying to get purchase. Finn remained half inside his bedroom window, arms dangling, grabbing out as she flew up, and the bike went clattering to the floor. They waited for a moment, thinking the noise might draw attention. Then the record player had gone on downstairs. No one was interested. Finn held on tight to both of Becca's thin arms. So tight she felt her muscles stretching away from their sockets as her jumper sagged around her body. The two teenagers hung there for what felt like a lifetime, Becca just dangling on the outside of the house, her feet trying to get some kind of grip.

'One last go,' Finn called down, and she knew if this didn't work, he was going to have to let her drop. He kind of shifted down below the window, got his feet planted firm and yanked good and hard just as her toes braced against the wall, and she slithered up and over the windowsill, scraping her boobs back to pre-puberty as she fell to the floor, ending up flat on top of him. They couldn't help themselves; they cracked up laughing.

'Shh, shh.' He placed his hand across her lips. 'Quiet.'

Becca nodded. Pulling herself off him and onto the bed.

Her eyes shining brilliantly, bright with excitement. Full of escape.

'Mad,' she said, loving the word. Loving the world.

It was dark by the time they woke. They'd fallen asleep fully clothed, lying on top of the covers. His arm looped around her waist. It was a single bed; he didn't want her falling off, he'd said. They were so comfortable; they probably would have slept through. Becca felt warm and safe in Finn's room. It felt as if this was the one place in the universe she was supposed to be, not realising that on the street that ran parallel, her father had woken himself up with a killer dose of dehydration and set himself on the warpath. It didn't take long for him to figure out she was gone. He probably blamed her for the smashed dinner service. That was the way his mind worked, drunk or not. There was always a bit of blame to be dished out. It was forever and always somebody else's fault. Becca figured even if her dad shot someone, he'd argue they shouldn't have been standing in front of the barrel.

At about nine-thirty, he'd managed to drink himself silly enough once again to stumble uninhibited out of the house and traipse the short distance to Finn's. He wouldn't have made it to Scratch's. That would have been a step too far for a man half-pickled. Besides, Tod Harris never needed any encouragement to partake in a quick brawl, specially not when it was home-delivered, and even though Becca's dad was more than happy to beat up a few inanimate objects, a sixteen-stone human being was a different ball game. Maybe he knew where she was, maybe he didn't, but the sound that woke her with a gasp was her dad standing on Finn's doorstep, banging on the front door for the whole town to hear. Becca's eyelids shot up as though they were attached to a trip-wire.

'Becca! Becca! Where the bleeding hell are you, girl!' There was a plaintive note in his voice, a whiff of the injured lone parent about it. She was always amazed that he had the nerve to pull that one out of the bag. It wouldn't wash with her. It wouldn't wash with the rest of the town either. At some point or other, the whole of Falham had come up against the sharp side of her dad's tongue.

Becca and Finn remained perfectly still on the bed. The room seeming somehow very far away, a place outside of time. Becca had never known two people could be awake and yet so still. She stared up at the tea-brown ceiling of Finn's bedroom, almost as if her spirit was up there looking down. It was like that feeling people say they sometimes get when their heart stops—out of body. She and Finn were floating somewhere safe in another dimension, hearing all the crap of life, the battles, being acted out somewhere far below.

'Hey...' Tina was saying, from somewhere far off, far under. 'It's bloody Nilsen,' she mumbled. 'Bloody drunk.'

They heard the sound of shuffling through the rooms downstairs and the front door rattling open on its hinges.

'She's not here.' Tina's voice sounded irritated and dry, snappy as a Pringle, with not a note of the playfulness they'd heard earlier—she had no time for this. No time for the waster that was Becca's dad.

'She must be.' Her dad was still going for plaintive and hurt. He'd only just started. No way was he going to give up that easy. 'She's always hanging around.'

'Well, she's not.' Tina's voice was bitter now, hard as nails. 'And he's not either.'

'So, where are they?'

'How the fuck would I know!'

'He's in there...I know it. And I reckon...'

Suddenly a different voice, deep and resonant: Robert cut through the forward-backward. 'Leave it, mate. I've been here all afternoon. No one's come in or out.'

Upstairs in the safety of the bedroom, Finn turned to Becca, and they both smiled, thanking God they went for the window.

'She's my little girl. She's just…'

Becca's face filled with hatred at her dad's words. 'Shit face,' she hissed, which kind of blasted the heavenly float the teenagers had been experiencing out of its orbit. Anger ties a person to the terrestrial even more neatly than gravity.

'She's just…' and suddenly her dad's soppy turned to snide in an instant, 'messing me around.'

'Jekyll and Hyde of the bottle.' Becca sighed. She knew the story well.

'Bloody dirty stop out, that's what she is.'

'Ey, watch it.' Robert came back swiftly from the hallway, ever the knight in shining armour. 'Ladies present.'

'It's hard, see.' Her dad had switched tack again. Now he was going for snivelling peasant. If he ever took up acting, the man could get an Oscar for his emotional versatility. 'Bringing up a kid on your own. Rebecca don't appreciate it, the pressure. You tell her, you see her, you tell her…s'not right, leading her old dad on a dance. She can't just…'

'Uggh.' Becca groaned, not wanting to hear more, shoving her head under a pillow.

'It's late.' Tina's voice was seen-it-all-done-it-all tried and tested. 'Go home.'

For a moment, there was silence, then the sound of staggering footsteps moving into the street and Becca's father muttering something before the inevitable crash as he collided with the bin, and yawned its contents over the pavement.

'Hey!' Robert snapped. He'd still got the energy for a fight if needed, but then he was from out of town, just blown in like some bit of tumbleweed.

'Leave it,' Finn's mother said gently. 'The man can be a right bastard when he's drunk.'

The door closed over below them, the letterbox rattling once more like chattering teeth.

'Robert...' Finn's mother giggled. 'Now you stop that!' She might have been saying 'stop' but her voice was definitely meaning please, please, please. Then, thank God, Robert must have pulled her into the living room and shut the door because all went mercifully quiet. Finn's room wasn't above the living room, so they were spared the interaction. Instead, Finn and Becca both stared back up at the ceiling. Just stared and stared till the lines morphed and melted around them.

It was Becca that finally broke the silence and brought them back down to earth. 'Seriously, we have got to get out of this place. You know, sometimes I think Scratch's lucky not having parents.'

Finn rolled over on his side, staring at her in the darkness. His clear blue eyes flitted across her face trying to take it all in. 'You reckon? He's got a pretty shitty deal with the stand-ins.'

It seemed like there was no way of winning, not for them anyway. They both lay there in the new-found quiet, listening to the night. Only suddenly, the night, the world felt big and sad and empty: hopeless.

'Becca?'

She turned to him, her body cocooned in shadow, but her eyes sparkling like diamonds in the spill of light from the street outside.

'I've been wanting to tell you something...' Silence. The

words failed him, but he leaned in towards her anyway; looked deep into those wide brown eyes.

And she knew exactly what he was thinking, what was going through his head because it was doing the rounds through her own brain as well. What about Scratch? What about the three of them? What about their plans to get out? That single room in Manchester with the three charity-bought mattresses. How would those three single mattresses work? She didn't know what to say, but she knew what to do. Becca leant in towards Finn, feeling the delicious warmth from his body, taking his face in her slim olive fingers, and kissed him.

'That it?'

He nodded, tears pricking his eyes, and she could see it all now. How did she ever miss it? This had been tearing him up inside for so long. When they were fourteen, it had almost happened outside Byrde's when Finn had come back. It wasn't indifference that had stopped him from kissing her then, she realised, it was fear, fear at not reading the situation right. Now there was no mistaking it. Every-thing seemed to slide into place. Finn put his arms around her, pulling her towards him. He was about to kiss her, sink into her soft lips again...but...

'What about Scratch?' he had to ask.

She didn't look into Finn's eyes, didn't have to. She knew the answer. 'He's not part of this.'

16

SOLITAIRE

(Any tabletop game played by one player. Most solitaire games function as a puzzle which, due to a variety of starting positions, may (or may not) be solved differently every time.)

Becca stared out of the window at the empty yard. The concrete space, hard and unforgiving without cars, lay there bold and angry as a scream. She could go down the escarpment, head the lads off at the garage. That would give them a surprise. She caught sight of the tree waiting at the edge where the ground fell away, waiting like it was daring her. Maybe not. No, that would be inviting disaster. The phone in her pocket dragged her attention back, vibrating with quick movements persistent as a fly dancing its death throes. Becca raised her mobile into the light from the window and stared at the display: Nothing.

At least he'd called. At least she had a phone. If the creeped-out sensation of being alone in the house got worse, she could ring him. It was daylight outside. What could happen in the broad, grim light of day? The phone was her own private umbilical cord. She could even ring the kids. Becca hesitated. She could, but no, she put the phone back in her pocket. She'd ring in the evening. They'd be doing things now, too busy to speak. She'd be the outsider, the interloper, and Becca didn't want to feel that way, not with her own kids.

Becca dropped a teabag into a mug and poured boiling water over it.

It was a joke—Scratch saying he'd go see her dad. Becca's dad was six feet under. Ten years ago the old guy's heart had stopped. Scratch had gone into shock claiming it was *a medical impossibility*—he hadn't realised her dad had a heart. It was cardiomyopathy. Years of alcohol abuse thinned the old bastard's heart muscle till it no longer had the arse-over-whereabouts to pump. That was the last time they'd been back, the funeral, and Scratch had been right about the hospital; there had been talk of selling the old site off then as well. Time turned slow in Falham.

Becca took her tea and went to the sunroom. As she walked through the hallway, she got a faint whiff of something off. Something like rotting veg or...she wasn't sure, but that aspirational hired-house smell, well, that appeared to have vanished. Becca glanced around. The hallway was stone-cold empty. Nothing dropped and forgotten in the corner. Nothing rotting away quietly to itself, just her boots, and she knew for a fact that they didn't smell, not like that— rotting flesh. To get to the sunroom, Becca had to pass the cellar, but the door was shut. She flipped the latch as she went past, just to hold whatever it was firmly beyond the door. Stupid really. What did she do with the kids if they were scared of a half-open door—she'd open the damn thing, take them through it and give them a poke around with the lights on. Show them that there was nothing there.

She had no intention of doing that for herself. Because… because actually, she was damn sure that there was something down there.

If there are no monsters in the world, people just invent their own, and maybe that was alright. Only a part of human nature. Maybe Byrde was the monster she had to cart around with her. If so, best to keep him on the other side of the door. Every time Becca passed that opening to the cellar, the hairs on the back of her neck prickled, and she could definitely smell something going rank. It was getting stronger. Becca turned the plug-in diffuser up a notch. It was probably just damp. Old places always had a spot of dampness.

She liked the sunroom—it might have been decked out mid-century retro, but it was right of the moment, which couldn't be a bad thing. Even though there wasn't a trace of Byrde in this part of the house, she found herself pulling the curtains slightly on the kitchen side: so she couldn't see that tree.

She could light a fire, get herself all cosy, but she didn't. Instead, she just stared at the empty grate like it was some dead curiosity the cat had dragged in. The house was beginning to get cold, the radiators hiccup clanking as the water cooled, and the wind raced round and round the house carrying bits showers of leaves with it. The cold blasts worked the escarpment so relentlessly as she watched, that she felt the eyeballs in her head would wear out. There was no peace in this place. She pulled one of the throws from the sofa, draped it over her legs and lay back into the soft blue velvet cushions. They'd be back soon. All she had to do was wait and make sure she didn't lose her mind in the next couple of hours.

When she woke, the light had shifted from one side of

the room to the next, as if the dull winter sun had taken a weary jaunt across the room, highlighting an abandoned shoe and illuminating the dust. Becca glanced at her phone. No messages. What did she expect—out of sight, out of mind. She texted, intending to give Scratch a prod.

When are you back?

The text stuck stubbornly. She had no bars. She glanced at the display; it was one-thirty in the afternoon. Sleeping in the day! That was a sure sign they'd be shovelling soil on her soon. She sighed, got to her feet and grabbed her mug from the table. It felt ice-cold to the touch. Life had leached out of the house while she had slept. Becca needed to get a little spark back.

There was nothing for it. She might as well chop an onion: knock up a chilli. At least cooking would keep her busy. As she pulled herself away from the couch, she couldn't help but catch the shadow behind the curtain: long and thin. A deep dark slit of black—the tree. It was as though it was moving slightly, swaying a bit from right to left, as though waddling forward towards the house. The wind was still racing outside, but it wasn't possible for the tree to be swaying. The thing was straight and stiff as Lot's wife. It must have been the sun, the way it was slanted, or possibly the movement of a cloud making the shadows shift and change? Hennings would have been long gone. Becca couldn't believe the old woman would have seriously stayed out there for the last few hours. She'd be back down in the town, peeping through her net curtains and finding things wrong with the world. Yet still, a shadow on the curtain swayed. Could it be the tree? Rocking, rocking up towards the house. Reminding Becca of those trees in Ella's story-book: Macbeth and Birnam Wood—trees hunting down the guilty. *'Why didn't you tell?'*

Maybe Becca should have turned her back on the shadow. Gone to the kitchen and started on that chilli. Out of sight, out of mind, taking a leaf from Scratch's book, only the saying didn't work as well for haunted landmarks and people stuffed to bursting with guilty secrets. *Out of sight* continued festering till brain overload was achieved. No, she had to pull that bloody curtain open, see what was out there. Why had she pulled it across in the first place? *Face your fears.* That's what Phillips, her therapist, was forever banging on about.

Her breathing was coming faster now, as if her lungs had withered to half capacity. Still, that shadow outside kept flickering across the drapes, moving forward step by step. Her breath caught in her throat like a lump of dried bread, and her heart beat so hard against her ribs that she couldn't help but think of her dad. All those years, everything had been winding up faster and faster. His little heart pumping quicker and quicker. Trying its damnedest to get the same old job done. Till...

Maybe it was congenital, what her dad had? Nothing to do with the alcohol. Maybe... Her palms began to sweat, melting like lumps of lard in a hot pan. She needed to get a grip. What would Phillips say? Breathe, breathe. So, she did, long and low, over-exaggerated breaths filling her rib cage. Taking her time. If the kids were here, she'd pull back the curtain. Tell them to take a look. Say, *'There's nothing out there, you big daft nutter. That tree can't move.'* Yet still, the shadow twitched and stepped and inched towards the house. It was dead as stone. It was all a trick of the light. All Becca had to do to stop the fear was pull the blessed curtain back, and the threat would evaporate, like the wicked witch of the north dissolving under a bowl of water. She stepped one step closer to the window. Not the big steps Finn had been so insistent on. These were baby shuffles. Her body leaning back as though she just might have to run in the opposite direction.

Brave, she thought. Get a grip. Be brave, and with that, Becca lurched forward fast, grabbed the curtain firmly between her hands and tugged. The tree stood silent and watchful right at the very edge, just like always. She let go of her breath; she hadn't even noticed she'd been holding it. Stupid.

BANG.

Her lungs collapsed; her heart stopped. The noise was behind her. The curtain still clutched in her hand, she turned sharply. The noise had been real and loud and angry, and Becca knew immediately that there was someone else in the house. Scratch. It could be Scratch and Finn?

'Hello?' she called out hopefully into the cold, empty corridor, her voice ricocheting off the fancy clean surfaces like a bird that can't find anywhere safe to land. 'Hello?'

Silence. But she'd heard it. She'd heard something move.

Slowly, slowly she traced her footsteps back through the hall. Her ears listening out into all that stillness till the air around her buzzed with quiet. When she reached the cellar door, she was met by that same stench from earlier. Only now, it was worse. It filled her nose till she was sure she'd gag. There was a bruised echo clinging to the air in the hall-way, an emptiness where some kind of sound had punched through. The catch on the door was still rammed down, just as she'd left it. Then again, maybe somebody/something was already down there? And that smell! Becca reached out and hesitated, her clammy fingers hovering just above the latch. Then she noticed her whole hand was shaking, vibrating to a tune all of its own. Seeing it flutter uncontrollably only made her feel fifty times worse. Her knees felt as if they were about to give.

She could run upstairs, take another one of her tablets, forget what was going on down here, and maybe, just maybe, *it* would forget her. Although…maybe that wouldn't work. Besides, she needed her wits about her. She was trying so hard to think rationally. Rational was good. Rational was the kind of thinking that kept a person sane. Phillips liked rational. Rational told her—no one could have got in. So, what had made that banging noise; it had been so real. Byrde's hilltop house was not some impenetrable castle. She'd seen people get in before. Besides, she'd been outside on the escarpment with Finn. Anyone and his uncle could have walked in through the front door: anyone, anything, and that smell.

Nose crumpled, Becca sniffed the air: it smelt like matted hair and blood—animal, something wild and dirty and half rotting. Trouble. The ridiculous dog with the stupid name, had it come in from the cold? Two weeks out on the escarpment, and the thing would have gone feral. The stench was like decaying flesh, dead tissue, some wound that won't heal. If the dog had been out on its own for a couple of weeks, it could easily have some cut festering away.

Finn and Becca wouldn't have seen the animal moving into the house when they'd been outside by the escarp-ment. They had their backs to the door. When she'd come in she hadn't locked the door behind her, but the dog would have had to push open the door? It didn't make sense. Maybe the latch was dodgy. She'd been asleep on the sofa. The dog could have just wandered on through. Anything could have wandered in. Why hadn't she locked the blessed back door! Her mind raced, sped around like a rat on a wheel: recrimination, fear, memories. '*Why didn't you tell?*'

Then again, just because someone could have got in, she kick-started the rational side of her brain. It didn't mean they had. She'd heard a noise, but... She needed to take a step back. If the kids were there, what would she do? She'd tell them something must have fallen over in the cellar. Maybe a mop or a broom...or... She didn't know, and it didn't matter because open the cellar door, and she'd find out. It was—*switch the light on and show everyone the Bogeyman's not crouching under the bed*—time.

Becca leaned forward, more confident now, grabbing the door handle, then, suddenly, stopped. There had been people in the house before: men dressed in black with balaclavas, men with fists. Men with energy and bad intentions. She couldn't risk that.

She went to the kitchen. For once, the house appeared to be offering her a break: the first drawer she slid open held the knives. A gleaming row of chef's blades offering up the possibility of every kind of cut and amputation. Becca settled on a long meat knife with a black plastic handle. If there was someone down there, or if Trouble had found his way in from the cold, long forgotten and fancying an afternoon snack, at least Becca would be able to protect herself. She was too old to hide under the sink. She glanced one more time at her phone, still no signal. Useless.

Knife in hand, Becca turned the handle on the cellar but felt a sinking sensation at the pit of her stomach when she remembered—the door didn't open out towards her. No, it fell away into the darkness leaving a gapping empty hole of black washing up against her feet, and the cold blast that seeped out of the doorway felt like some hideous ghostly sigh. It was as if the room backed onto another world, and that other world was colder than death. Even if the cellar wasn't heated, surely it would absorb a little warmth from the building, at best—a little insulation? Only this place was more frigid than a morgue, and the smell was stronger now; the rotting dead flesh that surrounded a cankerous wound. Roadkill when you pass it on a hot day. Trouble, she thought. Didn't it have to be him? She put her free hand over her nose. 'You in there?' Becca called out, feeling like an idiot; she needn't have bothered; it was only silence that came back to her. There were no noises, no whining, no scraping, no padded paws or claws on concrete.

'It's just a cellar,' she mumbled, still clutching the knife. Talking to herself just as she would to a child. 'Hello? Trouble?' she said, suddenly feeling like a fool. What kind of a person names a dog Trouble? The thought died in her head because she was sure something was moving down the stairs and to the left of her, something hidden deep in the shadows. Steadying her voice and speaking louder for good measure, Becca punched into the silence again. 'I know you're there.'

She could hear something, a small high hiss like a snake coming from the belly of the darkness. But that was stupid; there would be no snakes here. Certainly not this time of year. 'Hello?' she called again, her fingers sweating, slipping on the plastic handle of the kitchen blade. Becca would be useless in a fight, but then, deep in her brain, she knew the fight wasn't happening there and then. It was something from the past that had carried on punching its weight into the future. She needed to call time on it. Turn the light on and chase away the monsters.

She flipped the light switch. Her heart sinking when it clicked dead under her fingers. She felt a small wave of panic rise in her gut. It was so black down there, no windows; anything could be hiding. 'It's just a cellar,' Becca reminded herself, so there was no getting away from it. She could wait till they got back; ask Scratch to go down and check it out. Ask him to go down with her, just like she was the kid. No. That wasn't going to happen because she was a grown woman. *Face your fears*, Phillips said. Becca went back to the kitchen, grabbed the phone, still no signal. She flipped it to torch mode. Standing at the top of the steps, Becca shone the thin beam down into the cellar.

The shadows pulled themselves lazy as opium addicts out of the darkness, slipping like liquid as the light passed over them: stringy people, long arms and legs, stretching this way, that way. There was a lamp in the hallway. Becca turned her back on the gaping doorway for just a moment, and as she did, the bees welled up in her head, as if they'd suddenly woken up. She had to get them quiet. Had to get the light to the door, the shadows put to bed. She lifted the lamp gently from its table, carrying it to the top of the dark well. If she put the lamp at the top of the stairs, it would keep the shadows in check.

For a moment, Becca felt insanely proud of herself. She didn't like stepping out of her comfort zone, not anymore. Over the years, she'd shrunk to barely living mode. She couldn't keep doing that. It wasn't working out because it wasn't really living. It was just ticking off the minutes till she died.

Carefully Becca reached out for the handrail, a thick wooden pole set into the cold wall, and put one foot on the top step. It was like sinking into a cold bath. The temperature slowly but surely crawled up her skin and over her heart. Only the temperature wasn't the only thing to crawl. Each step she took down into the basement, the bees in her head buzzed just that little bit louder.

Face your fear—isn't that the reason she'd come back? Byrde had only been in the cellar for a few minutes. He didn't die here, and yet the cold, the buzz, the smell— getting stronger with each and every step. As she moved slowly down the stairs, all of a sudden, her body blocked the light behind her, holding her in inky darkness for a moment till she swayed away. She didn't want to do that again, so she edged her body closer to the cold, clammy wall, letting the beam from the hallway upstairs shine down bright. When she stepped wrong, got too close to the house, it felt like icy ghost fingers clawing at her skin. Is that what he felt? What Byrde felt when he got thrown down here all those years ago, pushed by rough hands? Becca could almost feel his presence, a bulky man, his body wheezing with short beats of panic when that firm young hand had pushed up against his back. His feet slipping, unsure on the tight, close steps.

Face your fear—Phillips said. Look under the bed for the monsters, and they disappear. Look in the wardrobe for the killer clowns, and there are none. Shine the torch into every corner of your world to chase those shadow men, and you'll see it's only your own clothes piled in a heap on the chair.

She could do this. When Becca reached the bottom step, her hand on the rail was shaking so hard and so fast that her wedding ring kept bang, banging against the wood. She stopped, listening in to the darkness. The hissing was still there, a persistent sound. Not a snake, maybe a radiator? The stench as well. It was stronger now and all around. It couldn't be the dog. The dog wouldn't be able to keep quiet. She'd have heard it scratching or whimpering, and it was so cold down here.

Becca turned her head back towards the hallway and the small rectangle of light at the top of the stairs. It seemed such a long way, not just physical distance but maybe in time as well, as if she was back at the house all those years ago, that fateful night. Did Byrde stare up at that same cutout shape far above? Did he lie at the bottom of these very stairs, scared and alone? He should have stayed here. If he'd stayed put in the cellar, not tried to break free, life could have had a whole different story.

Suddenly she realised, as she stared up at the slab of light from the hallway, she should have wedged something between that door and the outside. If it banged shut, she'd be trapped. Then again, why would it bang shut? There was no wind in the cellar, not a breath. It was more like every inch of air had been sucked from it. She glanced around, peering into the darkness: into the black space jam-packed with awkward dark shadows. The detritus of someone's forgotten life covered in dustsheets; work benches piled high with cans of paints, unwanted colours dribbling like worms down their sides. There was nothing more, nothing mysterious. No young men come to rob or maim. No half-starved hound. No Trouble.

Becca's grip on the knife loosened—*face your fears*. She'd done it, part of it. Then she noticed something odd: the floor was wet, covered in a pool of liquid. Cautiously, she moved towards it. As she did, the hissing noise swelled. Something was leaking across the floor.

Suddenly there was an almighty POP, and an impenetrable blanket of inky darkness rushed out, smothering her, pushing her breath back into her chest with a thump. The knife clattered to the floor, its silver blade cutting through the air, slicing a hundred images as it fell. Becca squealed like a trapped pig up for slaughter as the room, and the cold, and the fear closed in, and the bees, those blessed bees, started to swarm in her head till their constant hum separated out into fragments of words—*coming, for*.

She couldn't catch it all. There was no need to panic, she told herself. A light must have blown. Becca stumbled forward, trying all the while to conjure up Mr Phillips in her head. The flat practical tones: the no-emotion, no-messing party line—*just a bulb popped*. Rational. She had to use her head. But her head was so full of bees, and she could barely breathe.

She needed to get to the staircase, get to the handrail. She fumbled across the floor, feeling a wave of nausea shoot through her body as her bare toes encountered something on the floor, sticky and wet. Blood, is it blood? Could it be? The bees called out again, finding their voice: *it's coming for*. Becca stumbled, the knife skittering across the floor kicked by her feet, its blade pulling the last fragments of light into its sharp edges as it twisted.

There's nothing to be afraid of, Mr Phillips said from somewhere far away, in a world where people didn't murder and lie and steal. She closed her eyes and thought of his office, trying to think of his flat, unemotional counsellor's face. Hold on, Becca, she told herself. Hold on to Phillips.

Opening her eyes, she stepped forward again through the wet floor, through the blood? Through the piss? Through the spilt life? Then...BANG. The sound ripped into the air like a gunshot as something streaked passed her. It was all too much. Becca screamed, falling to her knees, the knife cutting into her flesh as the bees swarmed. She forced her hands flat over her ears and screamed and screamed and screamed, but she could still hear the bees because they'd found her now, taken up home at the front of her brain, and they wouldn't ever leave her alone. 'It's coming for you,' they buzzed and droned and shouted with delight. 'It's coming for you. They said it would.'

17

DUNGEONS & DRAGONS

(A role-playing game for multiple players. Each player constructs their own character. These characters embark on adventures within a fantasy setting. The Dungeon Master acts as the game's referee and storyteller.)

'You ever feel guilty about Byrde?' Becca was standing in the kitchen, exhausted, staring out of the window. It was dark out. Dark enough for her bedraggled reflection to fuse with the world outside as if the landscape beyond Byrde's kitchen had been built into her just as surely as her blood and bones.

'Guilty?' Scratch didn't even bother looking up. His large, heavy frame was crouched over the kitchen table, intent on a one-man gameathon with a Jenga tower. Becca couldn't help noticing how his voice was blank, so...innocent, so lucky. 'Why would I feel guilty?'

She shrugged, turning to look at him as he slid a finger of wood out from the tower. 'All those times we were up here knocking on his door.'

'Beccs, that's just kids. It's just part of growing up.'

'But did Byrde know it was always only ever us—*just kids*, or did he really think the Devil had come for him?'

Scratch laughed, stopping what he was doing for just enough time to pass her an indulgent smile as though she was one of the kids and had travelled way off track. 'Beccs! It was just a story. He didn't even know us. He didn't even know the story.' Amused, Scratch turned back to the tower, 'Guilty.'

She stared back out at the barns, looking past her image this time and feeling a little more settled. It was always good to hear Scratch's take on things. Sure, he might be a clown most of the time, but there were worse things; he had his feet grounded. As always, she could tie herself to his anchor.

'Yeah.' Becca sighed. 'Sometimes I forget where the stories stop, and the truth starts. You remember that one about Rock Babies?'

'What?' He didn't bother to look up.

'You used to say there were these spirits under the moors. Gremlin kind of things. Kind of creatures. They'd come out through the cracks in the stone, looking for someone to sink into, carry them through life.'

'There were a lot of stories.'

'You said you were one.'

'What?'

'A rock baby.'

He laughed. Still not taking his eyes off the tower. 'No. Adopted. That's me. Some kid of some far-off prince. Probably set to inherit millions. Finn. I reckon Finn's your rock baby.'

Perhaps. Had that story all been about Finn?

A cold blast of air curled up and around her ankles.

Becca knew that the door to the cellar was standing open. Finn was down there. It wasn't bothering her, though, not now. She'd taken two tablets. She felt calm as a rock. Dead as a rock. Scratch and Finn had found her in the cellar when they got back, kneeling in a puddle of her own piss, blood, with a pool of ginger beer thrown in for good measure—very Enid Blyton twenty-first-century style. The mystery of the smell was soon wrapped up: it was designer cheese doing the stinking. Finn had bought it at some fancy deli. It cost fifty quid a shot. They all agreed the price wasn't important. The cheese was now sitting in the bin outside the back door, double-bagged.

Scratch had picked her up, cleaned her off. She wouldn't let him do it in the kitchen. That would have been too déjà vu. He'd taken her to the bathroom off their bedroom and washed her cuts in that drown-your-sorrows tub. She'd scared Finn a bit. Becca hadn't noticed the fear on his face when the men had first got back. She'd been too beside herself to care. Now she'd calmed down and could see he was avoiding her, giving her that little bit of "extra room" in case she went into meltdown mode again, but what did it matter? What did any of it matter?

Becca couldn't hear the bees anymore. The drugs worked like cotton wool in her ears. Take enough of the damn things, and she could build a wall between her and the outside, which felt like a good idea when she'd started taking them years ago, but now she wasn't sure. How did it work in the long term? Could be she'd end up trapped with herself on the wrong side of her own head. That didn't seem like a good idea.

From the gaping cellar hole, Becca heard footsteps. Finn emerged carrying a dustpan and brush.

'Got most of it.'

'It's the cheese that did the real damage, mate. I can still feel the stuff like half-inch plugs in my nostrils. Fifty quid, they saw you coming.'

Finn paused by the door, wondering whether to shut it or not.

'Funny,' Becca said, although her voice held not one ounce of amusement in it, 'seeing you coming up out of that cellar.' It reminded her of all those years ago. She wondered if he would pick up on it, wondered if he would be catapulted back into the past. Searching Finn's fine blue eyes, Becca realised that he just looked lost.

'What?'

But then, of course, Finn didn't know what she had seen or heard all those years ago.

She shook her head. 'Doesn't matter.'

'You alright?'

Becca wished she hadn't spoken. He was staring at her now, chock-full of concern. A good-sized part of her wanted to scream—*No, of course I'm not alright! You killed a man, Finn. I helped you keep it quiet. He won't leave me be.* But that would just start a whole landslide of questions, the most crucial being—why the hell wasn't Byrde after Finn? Or maybe he was. Finn was just better at absorbing the old guy. If you were a killer, maybe that's what you had to do —move on.

'Life...' Becca said stoically, wishing that tears were pressing up against her eyeballs because they should be. It was only the drugs keeping emotion at bay. 'Life isn't fair.'

Scratch gave a snort of amusement. 'Amen to that one,' he confirmed, still not looking up.

Finn emptied the wet shards of glass into the bin. 'It was the ginger beer. I must have shaken it up when I was down there yesterday. The stuff just exploded everywhere. I fixed the light.'

'Quite the handyman,' Scratch said quietly, easing out another finger of wood. 'That city job doesn't work out for you, buy yourself a white van, and you'll be sorted.'

'You okay now, Beccs?'

She nodded. She was fully up for brushing a mini-mega-breakdown under the carpet.

'Course she's okay,' Scratch said dismissively. 'You're fine, aren't you, Beccs?'

'Absolutely fine.' Wasn't that what they all wanted?

Scratch stopped for a moment, just enough time to give her a kind that's-my-girl nod. 'It's coming back here, Beccs, brings lots of memories out of the woodwork. Your dad... Messes with your head a bit. Even mine, and mine...' Scratch informed them laconically '...mine is on pretty tight. I mean, it wasn't all happy days. In fact, last time we came back was your dad's funeral, Beccs. Okay, so that was a happy day. Wanted to do a bit of dancing on the old bastard's grave, but the Anglican church, they don't really go for that kind of malarky.'

'Scratch!'

'You're right, Beccs, totally uncalled for. The comment was out of order. That man deserved a whole bloody rave, not just one lone tap dancer.'

'He's dead,' Becca said, her words coming out flat and tired. So flat they could have all been steam-pressed by an iron. 'That's enough.'

The Jenga tower tumbled, the wooden pieces clattering to the floor. Scratch gave no reaction, just sat there for a moment in the rubble, his thoughts far away. 'You know the bastard didn't even want me to marry Beccs?' This had been a sore point for their entire married life. 'There she was six months pregnant, and he's saying I'm not good enough for her.'

'Scratch.' She'd heard this all before, so had Finn.

'You believe that!'

'It was a long time ago, love. You need to let it drop.'

'The man never had a good word for anyone, Scratch,' Finn added helpfully. 'No point in taking it personally.'

Scratch nodded as he began to place the wooden shafts of the tower back into a pile. He knew it all, but somehow it didn't take the sting out.

Becca ran one hand gently over her husband's shoulders. In the end, it turned out that marrying Scratch was the best thing she could have done. He'd been her rock. 'Phillips says it's no good living in the past.'

'Phillips?' Finn looked curious.

'Oh, this guy I'm seeing.'

'Beccs!' Scratch milked the moment, dishing out a mock show of indignation.

'Not seeing as in seeing. He's just a counsellor. Helps me sort out a few things in my head. Like therapy.'

'Only cheaper,' Scratch laughed.

Becca glanced into the hallway because even though the pharmaceutical barrier in her head was up, running and working on full power, she could still feel the chill from the open door. 'Can you close that, Finn?'

He looked blank.

'The cellar.'

'Sure. Sorry.'

He went out into the hallway, switching off the light, leaning right out and over that great crevasse of darkness in the cellar as he fetched the door back. He didn't even blink. God, she thought, he was a cold one. How can that be? He was the one with the biggest secret buried, and yet it didn't appear to haunt him, not one bit. He really was a lucky bugger.

Then suddenly, she noticed the empty corner in the hallway. 'Hey? Where's my boots?' They'd gone. They were by the back door, but now there was nothing, just that brown skid mark on the wall where she'd kicked the things off.

'Boots?' Finn looked blank.

'Scratch!'

'Not me.' He pulled the pile of Jenga chaos towards him, ready to set up for another game.

'Scratch! What have you done with my boots?'

'What is this, the Spanish Inquisition? Why would I go moving your boots?'

'They were by the back door. Now they've gone. It's got your prank-style hallmark stamped all over it.'

The pills must have been wearing off because she was beginning to care.

'Not me,' he said, concentrating hard, stacking a row of wooden fingers into the pile. 'Can't pin that one on me. Got to be your man, Finn. Seems like he's the joker in the pack these days: shaking up the ginger beer, hiding your boots.'

'What?' Finn looked baffled.

'Stuffing them with food,' Scratch continued, on a roll now he'd got started.

Finn laughed. 'It wasn't me, but…'

'You remember?' Scratch glanced up, that old twinkle in his eye. 'Any woman taking her shoes off at a dance, well, she's just asking to have them stuffed. Custard. You remember the custard?' He laughed. 'That was best.'

'And that squirty cream,' Finn added, getting into the spirit.

'The good thing about squirty cream…' Scratch said, as

though he was the resident expert, and this was his chosen speciality on a quiz show. 'It's portable.'

'I wasn't at a dance.' Their little cameo was beginning to irritate her.

'Rest my case...' Scratch said with a shrug. 'Not my style.' Overconfident, Scratch went for a rod at the bottom of the stack. The Jenga pile clattered into pieces once again. He pulled his large hands through his sandy hair. 'This is seriously not my night.'

'Fancy the pub?' Finn was trying for a subject change.

Scratch laughed. 'You think? Who's gonna drive? Same old same old. Why don't we stay in, eh? We've got enough booze to stun a rhinoceros. You got Tortillas as well.'

Becca sighed wearily. 'How can it get better.' Seems like she'd spent the best part of her life *staying in*.

'You fancy a game of pool, Finn?'

'Sure.'

And they were gone, leaving the Jenga in pieces strewn across the table. Becca fought the urge to do the clear-up. Boys might be boys, but no way was she going to end up keeping house. Not on the only weekend she'd had away for the past twenty years. Well, that was what it felt like. She glanced out of the window, and suddenly she saw—the side door to the barn had swung open. It was banging like a dying fish, mouth opening wide in the wind.

'Bloody Scratch.' That was where the boots would be.

Becca crossed the yard barefoot. It was cold outside, the wind not so much howling that night as moaning, a long low persistent bellyache of a groan. Behind her stood the house, the white plaster making it look curiously like a head wrapped in bandages rising out of the escarpment. She shivered. Two more nights, and then they'd be gone. She just had to keep it together a bit longer. Today had been a setback, going mad as a hatter in the basement. Well, that was a pretty big setback. Although, hadn't it proved beyond doubt that all of the mess, the sounds, the ghosts were all in her head. Scary? Damn right, but really, actually able to harm her? No. When they all drove away on Monday morning, Becca was going to be able to leave everything behind, just like that poor sod of a dog, Trouble.

She wondered, would it ever turn up? Maybe she'd take the note back out of the bin. Give the people a ring. She'd kind of like to know how the Trouble story ended. Then again, the phone number might belong to Hennings, and no way was Becca going to tangle with that woman again. Cheeky old bat. Becca stared down at her soaked feet. She should have borrowed someone else's shoes. Her toes were freezing into blocks of ice on the hard concrete of the yard. She hadn't been thinking straight; she'd seen the door banging open in the wind, pulled on her coat and struck out into the night. She had to start looking after herself, she thought as she strode across the yard, the bitter wind scouring her face. The sooner this interlude was done, the better; it was such an old joke. They'd played it out when they were kids, and Scratch had done it again to all five of their own children. There were different variations along the same theme. The stuffed shoe was Scratch's all-time favourite. Becca hoped to God she wouldn't get to the barn and find her boots stuffed with beef bourguignon. She was pretty sure there'd been no custard in the fridge, but anything sloppy worked as far as Scratch was concerned. He hadn't played this particular prank on her for years. She racked her brains, trying to think when he'd last tried it. The wind moaned a little louder as though it was warning her not to go back to the past. Live in the present, that's what Phillips said, but this kind of reverie didn't matter: it was just a game, just a prank.

The first time Scratch had pranked her with it had been after the party: the night they went to London when the woman got Becca muddled with the Tetley Tea Folk. She'd felt so down. They both had. They'd gone down to Finn's digs. It wasn't called that anymore. Ask Ella what her digs were going to be like, and she'd laugh you out of the century, but that's what people used to say. As though you were shovelling into the coalface for the long run. Digs just meant accommodation. Student accommodation. Finn's place hadn't been that special, really, dank and dark. It smelt of mouldy fabric, and there was dust piled so high in the corners it could have stood up and walked out all on its own. Despite the squalor, she'd still been envious. Because Finn had his own front door. The Great Escape hadn't exactly gone so well for the three friends, not when Finn found himself a quicker route. So much for solidarity. Scratch and Becca ended up short on one-third of the down payment. Instead, they'd found themselves doing the same dead-end pick-up jobs, walking the same old streets, waiting for just a bit more top-up on the money front so they could prise open their own cage.

Having your own front door was something Becca dreamt of. Climbing through windows had lost its attraction. But that night in London hadn't gone well. It was the first time she realised there had been a complete shift of orbit: that there was a world of difference between her and Finn now. It wasn't just the M1. They didn't even speak the same language anymore. Someone had been polishing up his vowels, drip-feeding him a whole dictionary of new words and "better" ways of saying the old ones. Becca's own words had sounded heavy and unnatural. Forget communication. Every syllable that came out of her mouth sounded as bulky and awkward as lead.

They had caught the coach back. Scratch had wrapped her in his parka, the one with the snorkel hood. She'd actually zipped the blessed thing right up to the top. She must have looked a right idiot, and Scratch? Well, he must have been freezing. It was cold on the bus. A bargain ticket didn't seem to run into hot air. Condensation ran down the inside windows giving a continuous curtain of tears to the world outside. They said nothing all the way back: that was four hours and a bit extra. Then, when he got to her street, Scratch had asked her all casually if she wanted to come around to his. The dog had been dead for years, the one that pulled on its chain, but even as they walked past the gate, they could feel its presence, and they shot each other a look. It was good having people who didn't need words: having friends you could just shoot a smile to, and they'd know exactly where you were coming from.

Scratch made her a mug of tea when they got to his house. The Harrises were out. There must have been a race on, or maybe they had friends? She didn't know. Stranger things happened. Becca was glad for Scratch's company. She was still getting used to Finn not being around and hadn't wanted to go home. Her dad would be there. Becca didn't want to deal with small talk to the man as she picked across her highway to nowhere—the front door thing again. She desperately needed her own.

They had taken their tea. The milk must have been off. The Harris' sell-by dates were stuff-of-legend. Whatever it was, something had turned her stomach. Becca had been dog-tired after the trip. It wasn't late by the time they got in, but they were tired. The streets were dark. It felt as if the world had closed up shop and left her and Scratch on the outside.

After the tea, Scratch poured her something stronger. He took the gin from the Harris' drinks cabinet. They had a little bar shaped like a ship, with mirrors and portholes down the side. It was wedged in the corner of the room as though it had stuck its prow through the wall one stormy night. The drink was good: shaken, not stirred. Scratch even put a maraschino cherry on top and an umbrella before topping the old bottle up with a couple of slugs of the finest Yorkshire tap. The gin must have been two parts H2O by the time Becca's shot had come out, but it still hit her hard. She wasn't used to spirits.

Then, when she had tried to go home, her shoes had "vanished". He'd laughed and laughed, and she was glad at least for that; it felt welcome; a bit of normality poking through, and yet despite the fact that Scratch thought his joke was so good he could have sold it to Comic Relief, he hadn't let her have the shoes back. Instead, they'd had another drink. A second cherry, another umbrella, and it had just happened. He'd stopped laughing, looked deep into her eyes, and that was it. Right there in the Harris' sitting room, with the prow of the ship bar in the corner, earwigging on all the sounds, sticking its nose through the wall while it waited for them to finish.

Losing your virginity stories are rarely an as-good-as-it-gets type deal. Which Becca supposed was how it should be —there was always a strong element of *room-for-improvement*. Only *her story* somehow seemed like defeat. As though instead of moving on to a new phase, she'd lost the one thing she wanted in the world. It wasn't even Finn, not after she'd seen what he was capable of; how ruthless, how disloyal, what a snake in the grass, two-faced lying prick the man could be. No, what she really wanted, the one thing was—a chance. When she woke that night in the darkness of the Harris' sitting room, Scratch had been mouth-breathing like a caveman next to her, squeezed into the crack of the sofa. She had found the shoes placed neatly by the back door, all ready to go, stuffed with a slice of lemon and an umbrella.

When Becca thought of the shoe trick, when she saw it played out again and again over the years, Becca always remembered herself standing at the Harris' back door, cleaning out the shoes before hobbling home through Falham's dark, sleeping streets.

There were two doors on the barn. The big one was intended to slide like a train on rails. The smaller one was cut into the iron. That's the one that was left banging. No doubt the big one had rusted over. Becca pulled her cardigan tighter over her chest. It was so cold her breath came in puffs of steam like she was a dragon, and her bare feet had lost all feeling.

She couldn't help herself wondering how long it had taken Trouble to die, but that was stupid. She didn't even know if the animal was dead. Although, she reasoned it wouldn't take long; if you got stuck out on those moors for long, something bigger than bad was sure to swallow you up.

Suddenly the light above the front door popped on. It must have been on a timer. Instinctively, Becca turned back towards the house. The place sat there, crouched in the shadows behind her, like a giant white rabbit. Most of its eyes were dark blanks, just like always. Only the kitchen and the sunroom continued to throw sad orange streamers into the night. The pool room was around the back. The men must be tucked somewhere out of sight, in the stomach of the beast. Because the house did look like a beast. It wasn't just her imagination. The white-painted stone glinted hard in the inflexible light from the moon, and Becca had the uneasy feeling that she was being watched. By the house? She wasn't sure.

The hairs at the back of her neck pulled to attention. Whatever it was, it was playing the long game, but that was stupid. She shook her head, trying to dislodge the thought. It was because the windows looked like eyes. The wind whispered to her angrily as it passed, '*Why? Why?*' Becca cupped her palms over her ears. The sound stilled a little, only now it was like being on the inside of a shell. The voice muffled, '*Why?*' Becca pressed her palms tighter till her eardrums stung. She could run back, only she was closer to the barns now. Besides, the house felt like some kind of prowling beast stalking her, and suddenly she had an uneasy feeling that there was something, someone staring right at her, its eyes boring into her soul.

Then she saw it, standing at the edge of the escarpment —the tree. The warm orange light of the kitchen seemed like a tiny flower in a dark ocean: inadequate and floating out of reach. She should go back, get Scratch to come out and get the blessed boots. Only, curiously the tree looked like it was standing closer to her now than the house. If she had her boots on, she could run faster. Her feet were so cold they were painful. Becca needed to move, to make a decision one way or the other. She thought of the scare she had given herself earlier in the day, the pointless waste of time and energy. You couldn't keep living, terrified of your own shadow. Becca let go of her ears. The wind had dropped to a gentle murmur, carrying no words, no accusations. She pushed on, reaching out for the metal door of the barn, which was wagging like a witch's tongue in the wind. It stopped wagging when she held it tight, and she allowed herself one snort of relief. You had to be active in your own story. She knew that from all the chats she'd had with Phillips. Be active in your present, not just pushed around storing up resentment and fear. Her imagination, Becca knew, was on the overactive side of the spectrum. Reality was what she needed to keep hold of.

Suddenly she remembered that the barns might not have a light. That wasn't good on the imagination front; dark shadows are fertile ground. She was going to have to step into the darkness and grope for a light that might not even be working. Stupid. Becca should have left this till the morning. She didn't even need the boots, but she'd been cross with Scratch. She'd wanted to pull the power back. In the cold night air, she wished she hadn't bothered, and still, she felt that boring sensation at the back of her neck. Something was watching, watching. *But it's just a tree!* Becca thought, irritated with herself. 'You're the one giving it power,' she mumbled, barely audible. She switched on the torch. A white beam shot out in front, cutting through the darkness of her as she stepped into the barn.

After all these years, it still smelt just the same, though maybe a little mustier now. The air had been trapped, stagnating in this giant tin can while she'd been living her life, having babies and making mistakes. Was that tannin taste that lay heavy in the air, blood? She sniffed. Probably not. There must be minerals leaching up through the bare mud floor and wet iron—blood smells like that sometimes. There were metal walls standing rusting in the barn to support her on that one. It felt as though she was stepping back through time. Everything was in the exact same place—the plastic sheets, even the barrels at the end, the ones she'd hidden behind. And rotten planks piling up at the broken windows.

There was just one thing different—sitting in the very centre of the floor were Becca's boots.

'*I know you're here.*' She could almost hear Byrde's voice drifting up from the past. Becca must be standing exactly where he'd stood when he'd come searching for her. She'd like to have said sorry, would dearly love to be able to apologise for all those years of taunting him.

'*I knew your mother,*' he'd said.

Her blood cooled in her veins. Physically cooled as if a part of her was dying. No one talked about her mother, not then and certainly not now. It was odd because the boys knew her mum before she ran off. They were about eight years old when it happened. Even so, Scratch never mentioned her mum's name. Maybe it was because they all felt Becca's mother had been the only proper one, the one who could have pulled them all out, but then the woman appeared to think better of it all and decided to take off by herself. What a legacy. Becca sometimes wondered if her own kids would be better off without her. When did it get to the stage when you committed to something like that? What would have to happen? But no, she shook her head as if trying to dislodge the thought; she couldn't think like that. If Phillips were to crawl in through a window in her head right now, he'd be having her committed. Suicidal thoughts were a no-no.

She walked towards the boots. They looked curiously lost. As though someone had been wearing them only minutes before and then rocketed right up, through the metal ceiling to the moon. If they had food in them, Becca vowed to herself, it would be Scratch clearing it out. She needed to get this over with. She lurched forward through the darkness into the cold. The boots were almost within reach when suddenly, the door behind her banged shut. Its metal ridges clanking sharp as skeleton teeth. It was only shut for a moment before it rattled back open, and she had the light. Only the bees didn't like it, not one bit. They started to buzz.

'*WHY? WHY? WHY?*' they screamed as Becca grabbed up her boots and ran.

18

BLIND MAN'S BUFF

(Also called Dead Man's Bluff. A variant of Tag. One player is blindfolded. The other players give the seeker a push. The blindfolded player must find the others and, by feeling the contours of their face, identify who that player is.)

When Becca arrived back at the house, breathless and trembling, she went straight upstairs—heading for another shake of pills and a shower. Anything to warm her up and wash away those voices from the past. Cocooned in the impersonal luxury of her room Becca turned the hot water tap hard, pushing it to max till it ran so hot that the water scalded, making her skin blossom in red patches down her back and over her frail arms. The marks looked like someone had squeezed her hard. Is that what Byrde wanted to do?

'It's coming for you.' That's what she'd said to Byrde all those years ago, sitting in his kitchen the night she'd heard the glass panel in the door cave in and seen the men in black bundling through the house like rogue atoms in a hadron collider, and yet now the whole Byrde thing seemed

flipped around and stood on its head. There was something at Byrde's old farm, a presence, not just her imagination. Becca could feel it. Hear it. Only now, it wasn't coming for Byrde. No, it was coming for Finn, and she kept getting the uncomfortable feeling that she might just be the thing standing in the way.

'Just a book. It's just a book. Just a book,' Becca mumbled as water pooled around her luminous white feet into the porcelain tray, till her toes flushed red and itched. She was half waiting for the tank to empty. It's what she did at home, the cold water giving her a prompt to step out and towel down. When the cold water failed to arrive, she leant out of the walk-in doors and started to dry herself off with one of the giant fluffy white towels that were folded neatly and waiting on the rack. The towel should have felt soft on her skin. Becca's small thin frame should have sunk into the cloud-like material as if sinking into angel arms, only she couldn't feel anything now; the pills had worked their magic. She had entered that familiar zombie-like state: without any emotional appetite. As she moved around the bedroom, Becca could hear the scatter of balls on the pool table, chink after chink, and the murmur of voices punctuated by Scratch's loud triumphant guffaws. As always, life was going on without her.

Something smelt too. She wasn't sure what, but the oven must have been on. Some smell from a home she'd never had—a like-mother-makes stew—appeared to be wandering through the house, doing its best to tempt her down. The smell was pretending that this place was a home, and they were all in it together. She sighed, sinking down onto the white bed, pulling her towel up a little over her bare chest. They were certainly all in something together.

Becca tied her hair out of her face and put on a bit of the

face cream that appeared to be included in the rental. It smelt of somebody else. Someone fresher, newer, not so messed up. She threw the tub into her suitcase, so she wouldn't forget to take it with her when they left.

It was still early. She'd have to go back down, small-talk her way through a couple of rounds with the lads. Do her best to eat some of that stew. She pulled on her clean jeans and a skinny white top. It worked. It all looked fine, good enough. Clean. Who cared anyway? Of course, she did a little. Not that she'd let on.

Becca grabbed her phone. It had a couple of bars. She'd promised Scratch that she wouldn't call home. He knew what she was like. Speak to one of the kids, and she'd want to be wrapped up in her dressing gown, small sticky hands pressed into her own, sitting watching TV. Then again, she didn't need to talk to them to want that. She'd shoot off like a hare out of a trap, given half a chance, but that wasn't going to happen. *Face your fears.* This whole thing needed to be played out, despite the fact that what she needed now more than anything was a shot of normality, and kids had that in buckets. Glancing at her phone, she saw it was six o'clock. They'd have had their tea. Becca pressed Home. A couple of rings, then the voice came over loud and clear.

'They're all busy.'

Not even a *Hello*. It was Megs. Bless her. None of the others could be bothered to pick up. The thing would ring out till it gave the whole street tinnitus before anyone could be arsed to answer. But Megs was different. Eight years old and going on thirty. She was the sensible one, head in a book, never bothered with TV or screen-style games. She was doing well at school too. Ella had managed to get into uni, but then it felt like everyone had *managed* that now. It had taken her a couple of years extra. There had been special dispensations for the fact Ella's school had been crap. Eventually, all of that had bumped her up a grade, but Megs wouldn't need the extra help. Even at eight, you didn't need a crystal ball to see that the girl would go far. Sometimes, Becca couldn't help but think, but wonder—she could have been like Megs: the world at her feet. She was bright enough, well bright enough back then.

Becca reckoned her "happy pills" had killed off around eighty-five per cent of her brain cells. Or maybe it was not having to use the said "brain cells"? Inactivity had to get rid of a whole stack of neural pathways. Could it have ended up differently? If her mum hadn't run for the hills; if her dad was the kind of dad that gave a shit. Well, perhaps Becca could have been something "proper", had some kind of career. A nurse, maybe? Something, anything that told everyone, easy-peasy, who you were. Being a mother told no one anything. It just said loud and clear how you were living two steps out of the picture.

'Hello?' Megs asked in a sarcastic voice, throwing the greeting away like an accusation down the empty line.

Becca bumped back to the twenty-first century. 'Sorry, love, got distracted.'

'Mum. They're all busy. Nan Harris has got some chips in the oven.'

That was about the size of Nan Harris' culinary skills: fridge, to oven, to plate. The fact that she was looking after the kids didn't mean bridges had been built. Scratch's foster mother was still a hand-for-hire. As always, the transaction was financial.

'Don't bother her then, love. I just wanted to check everything was alright.'

'Yeah.' Megan's voice was steeped in that vague wash of disinterest. She was offering no details, just a few bland coveralls. That was what being eight was like. Kids of eight thought that you could take the top off their brains and scan the internals. See all the memories and events, and exactly just how *alright* everything was—no need to explain. 'How's Uncle Finn?'

'He's good.'

'Did you ask him if I could be a bridesmaid?'

Becca hadn't. She shouldn't have to. Finn should have seen that one coming. The kids rarely got a chance to dress up, and Megs was itching for some pretty taffeta snowball to dance around in. Becca didn't know all the details on the wedding front. She hadn't asked. She knew Daisy had cousins. Becca also knew Scratch had told Finn not to bother inviting their kids. He'd said they needed more time as a couple. She hoped that didn't mean what she thought it meant. There could be no more babies. Surely, he knew that? The days of building your own army or football team were long gone.

Megs was going to be disappointed. Becca went for safe ground. 'I don't think he's having bridesmaids.'

'Oh?'

'It's kind of an adult do.'

'Sounds boring.'

'Yeah.'

Becca caught some muffled call from off the handset.

'Mum, I've got to go.'

Tea must be on the table.

'Course.'

'Big hugs to you and dad.'

'Big hugs.'

The line went dead. It was odd. It felt kind of empty. The silence in the room clamoured suddenly as if they'd forgotten something—the important bit. To talk? They'd forgotten how to do that because Becca was, well she was just part of life's functioning, and back home, everything was all still functioning just fine without her.

'BEEF STEW AND DUMPLINGS.' Finn slid the metal tray into the oven.

'Smells great.' Becca smiled, trying to work up an appetite.

'Be ready in fifteen. It's a Waitrose one. Homemade straight from the factory.'

'Just the ticket then.' She pulled up a chair and sat at the table.

'You okay?'

'Not really. I didn't like what you did to me out on the escarpment.'

He looked blank.

'Getting me to walk right up to the edge then backing out of your promise.'

Finn shrugged. 'It was just a bit of fun.'

'I wasn't laughing. And that thing about Byrde. My name in his book?'

Finn started fishing in the cutlery drawer as if it had all the answers. 'I know. Keep Rebecca Nilsen. Yeah, I always thought that was odd. You want garlic bread?'

'With beef stew?'

'Scratch likes garlic.'

'Do him a favour, leave it out. The amount he's drinking, the garlic might just land us in divorce territory.'

Finn laughed. 'I've got to go back, finish the game. You found your boots?' Finn glanced out into the hallway where the boots were standing innocently, toes pointed out—ready to walk.

'*Somebody* put them in the barns.' She thought of her walk over the cold concrete yard, of the way the tree watched, of the buzzing bees at the back of her head.

'Sounds like Scratch. Filled with food?'

'No.' She sighed. 'Not the food. Not this time. I wish he wouldn't, always messing. He's like a kid.'

'It's part of who he is.'

'Maybe I'd like him to have other parts.'

It was a bit of a conversation killer, entering the room like some kind of silent bomb. Becca knew she shouldn't have said it. It's not cool to slag off your husband. No brownie points for loyalty.

Finn stared awkwardly at his hands.

It could have all been so different, she thought, if only Finn hadn't been so...greedy. Becca sighed. It was now or never. 'Look, Finn, I wanted to talk about what happened— what happened here.'

If he intended to answer, he didn't get the chance.

'Finnbow, I am waiting...' Scratch's head appeared around the door frame. 'I've got the pool table all set up.' He glanced out towards the hall. 'Found your boots then, Beccs.'

'No thanks to you.'

A frown crossed Scratch's face. 'Seriously. Not me.'

'Well, who?' Becca felt her temper begin to fray.

Finn looked thoughtful. 'I just don't see how Scratch could have done it.'

Scratch smiled his appreciation. 'Thanks, mate.'

Becca eyed her husband. 'It's his MO.'

'Sure, but Scratch was with me.' Finn rubbed his fore-head, as if trying to ease the thoughts into place.

'Okay. Mrs Hennings,' Scratch said, nodding slowly.

'What?'

'Housekeeper. You said she didn't like us.'

'She probably had a good reason.' Becca toyed with the edge of her place setting. 'If she knew us when we were kids.'

'Don't take it personally, Beccs,' Scratch said gently. 'She always was a sour old biddy. I bet she took your boots. Probably wrote that entry in the book as well. The one that was talking about those Rock Baby things.'

Becca had showed them the book when they'd returned.

'She wanted to creep you out.'

'That is so elaborate.' Finn was looking bemused.

Scratch shrugged. 'Why not. Anyway, it doesn't matter. Bolt the back door tonight, keep the old dragon out, and you've got your boots. Result. Finn…' He turned his focus on his old friend. 'Game. Prepare to meet your destiny.' And off Scratch swaggered down the hall.

'I thought you'd finished one game.'

'We're on another.'

'Is he winning?'

Finn shook his head. 'No, but I get the feeling the thing won't be over till he has. I'll give him one more round. That's it. You want crisps?' he said, grabbing a party-size bag from a cupboard and emptying them into a bowl. He seemed to know where everything was. Everything with Finn was effortless. 'Cheese and onion?'

'With the garlic and the booze?' She shook her head. 'I'll wait.'

He picked up the two beers, hooking long fingers into the rims, and tried the same with the crisp bowl.

'You manage?'

'Like an octopus.'

'There's no hiding from the Scratchmeister,' came the far-off voice yet again. 'Prepare to meet your fate.'

'I'll shout when the food's done.' She would even plate it. There was bugger all else to do. Becca felt curiously lost without the routine of home.

'Great,' Finn called back as he left. But it didn't take long before she heard the inevitable crash. It came from somewhere down the hallway.

'Shit!'

'Don't worry,' she said, her voice resigned. 'I'll get it. You go do what you've got to do.'

'Thanks, Beccs.'

Becca heard the door shut behind him, and Scratch's voice raised in a muddled wash of male camaraderie.

She looked around for the dustpan and brush, then realised—there was only one place it would be: under the sink. She pulled open the drawer and stared inside. No bees, no buzzing. No creeping up the back of her skull. Byrde wasn't there, only the brush.

The downstairs hallway looped around away from the entrance, taking you towards the sunroom to the left and the Billiard's Room (was it pool or billiards? she could never remember) to the right. The crisp catastrophe was straddled between the two rooms, an impressive spew of china from the bowl mixed in with a mound of wafer-thin potatoes, salt, and whatever powdered flavour was passing for cheese and onion.

'Oh, nice shot,' Scratch's voice came from behind the closed door. At least he'd given up on goading Finn. 'You'll need to line the next one up carefully, though.' He'd slipped into advice mode.

Becca bent to her knees and began to sweep.

'I was going to ask you.' She heard Scratch's voice, and

something about it made her stop. It was a little too languid, too effortless, as though he was trying too hard on the casual front. 'Did you hear anything last night?'

Becca heard a cue snap against a ball and the steady roll as one of the colours eased down the green baize.

'How do you mean?'

She was listening again. Bad habit, but it wasn't as if she was looking for it this time. Besides, Becca was curious.

'Did you hear anything?' Scratch's voice sounded overly innocent.

What was he up to? If one of them had heard the window banging, she swallowed down a shard of irritation. Why didn't they get up and shut the damn thing?

'There was a window banging,' Finn said, as if in answer to her thoughts. 'But then someone got up? You?'

'No, mate. No. Didn't hear that. It must have been later on, early morning, I'd have said. If you bounce it off that side, you might stand a chance.'

Becca heard the sound of bodies shuffling around the table. Becca, on the other hand, had stopped dead in her tracks. She wasn't even pretending to sweep up the crisps because something wasn't right. Scratch sounded...edgy.

'It was still dark,' he said as if he were setting the picture.

'What are you getting at, Scratch?'

'Oh stupid, just stupid... But this noise.'

'Well, we are out in the middle of nowhere.'

'It was just after reading those entries in the guest book. You read them?'

She heard the cue breaking a row of balls.

'Nah.'

'Hmm.'

'This is the country, Scratch. You're not used to it anymore. Just like all those others in the guest book with their spooky stories. Your townies. It could easily have been an animal: deer, foxes. That dog.'

'Trouble?'

'Stupid name. So, what did you hear?'

For a brief moment, Scratch failed to reply. But Scratch had always been a man who liked a story. He took himself a long, deep, thoughtful breath, then continued on. 'Know what, it was really odd?'

'Scratch, don't keep me hanging.'

'You remember knock-out-ginger?'

Becca felt a cold fist grip her inside: that game always appeared to be following them around.

'Yeah.'

'You remember the sound?'

'Well, yeah...'

Becca couldn't help herself, she looked instinctively back to the front door, and there it stood: the glass panel fully illuminated. She didn't want Scratch talking about it. She felt as if he mentioned their little game, he just might conjure something back up. Something that was all too keen to get itself on constant replay; the three of them standing forever on that doorstep in the cold and the rain, her freezing hand held high, ready to knock. And as if on cue...

'Knock, knock, knock,' Finn said, tapping the edge of the table on the other side of the door.

Becca's breath caught in her throat. How stupid was that! To get scared by someone knocking on a table! She glanced back again towards the door, sharp this time. Expecting to see three shadowy shapes. But the glass panel remained empty behind her. The kids weren't there. Then with a sickening thud in the pit of her stomach, she realised: no, of course they weren't, because this time the kids weren't outside. No, they were standing on the inside. The positions had all changed, and Becca couldn't help feeling that maybe that wasn't such a good thing.

Finn rapped his knuckles once again on the table. 'That was the sound. Three knocks, and we were off.'

'Maybe, mate, maybe... But...' Scratch had adopted his armchair-by-the-fireside voice. He was working his way through his story. Enjoying the delivery like he always did. 'When I think of it, it's not just the knocking sound I remember. In fact, I can't really remember the actual knocking at all. There was always something else. Think on it. We'd walk up to the door, bold as brass. We'd knock. Give the door a good rap. Then there would be the sounds from inside the house... Someone beginning to stir, pushing back the chair in the kitchen. The scrape of it on the tiled floor, before the pad pad pad of someone dragging themselves from the armchair, heaving their body to the door like the living dead. That was all part of the fun, the anticipation. And we'd wait, wait till the very last minute. That was the game. The insiders had to see the soles of your feet as you buggered off down the road. We'd wait, wait, wait. Door open—we'd scoot. And just as we took that first step—that noise. Remember?'

'Scratch, I have no idea what you're...'

'Someone would kick over the bloody milk bottle.'

Instinctively, Becca reached down to her left foot as though the glass was still in it.

'Always happened.' Scratch laughed. 'However careful you were, a milk bottle always went down. And that was it.'

'Sorry, mate. You've lost me.'

'See, that was what I heard last night. That small, high-pitched sound of glass hitting the stone step then rolling, rolling, backward, forward, backward and forward.'

'The wind, Scratch.' The flatness of Finn's tone made it

sound as if he was trying hard to inject a dose of reality. 'It probably just blew a milk bottle over. Or maybe, like I said, a fox clipped it.'

'Yeah, yeah...' Scratch shuffled slightly, lining up another shot. There was a pause, then the sound of a cue hitting the ball and that soft inevitable roll, roll, roll. 'But trouble is...' Scratch continued, 'when was the last time you saw a milk bottle on a doorstep?'

From inside the room, someone took another shot. Becca heard the balls split and scatter, just like her thoughts, which were bouncing all over her brain. Because it looked as if it wasn't just Becca who was finding this whole trip down memory lane odd. Scratch sensed something, too; something leaking out from the past, wanting to pull them back down.

It was then that she saw it—Finn's case, angled by the window. Propped up against the wall, standing innocent as you please. Becca couldn't help herself. The thought just popped right up there in her brain: was Byrde's book still in it? The bees in her head began to stir as if they were just waking up, as though they so wanted to get to work. The secret was out now. They all knew Finn had the book. And Becca knew something more—he owed her a last wish. He'd promised her three, and she'd stepped up just as she'd been asked. Two could play dirty. Becca left the dustpan in the hall and stole her way into the sunroom.

THE WINDOWS WEREN'T QUITE AS dark as last night. A cloudless sky and the dreg-ends of a moon meant the escarpment was lit by a sliver of silver light. The tree was there, just where it should be, dead as a skeleton's finger, but waiting, watching, goading her forward. *Go on,* it said, *that third wish it's yours. I heard him. I saw him make the deal. Open the book and find out what that Finnbow's hiding.*

What damage could it do? Becca grabbed the case. But before opening it, before committing, she tilted her head just to catch the sounds from next door and see where the land lay. They were still playing. She could hear the muffled growls of male voices, cut short now and then with the occasional sound of the cue. No signs that they were about to stop playing.

Becca unbuckled the case and peered inside. It was so organised. Everything lined up as though Finn was working for the military. A row of expensive-looking pens, colour-coded and all hooked into the lining: like soldiers standing to attention. A small flat pocket inside contained a narrow wallet. Becca drew it out and opened it. A smiling young woman stared back at her. The eyes were dark, but they had caught a glint of light, giving the woman an active, excited-about-life look. Her hair was dark. Black like Becca's. Black like Becca's used to be before it went dull with the odd snake of white. The woman's skin in the photo was sun-kissed: olive. Suddenly, Becca let out a gasp because it all began to fall into place. The likeness was unnerving. She could be holding up a mirror, one that knocked twenty years off and gave free makeovers into the bargain, yet still a mirror of sorts. No wonder Finn hadn't been bandying photos of Daisy about. She wondered if Scratch knew. This photo was Becca, younger, fresher, better educated, better dressed, but Becca.

She sat down heavily on the soft, blue sofa. If Scratch didn't know, would he notice when it came to the big day? Then again, what was there to notice? So, the woman looked a bit like a younger version of Becca. Did that matter? There were no rules to say that all women bearing similarities to

Scratch's wife were out of bounds. She traced her finger over the woman's heart-shaped jaw. The exact same shape as her own face. Some kind of loss hit her in the base of her stomach, an indescribable emptiness, sharp and physical as a thump. It could have been Becca who was *urgent spending* in the big smoke. It could have all been her if... If she'd just kept her moral compass out of the picture. She'd have her hair done every six weeks before the grey had time to slither out of her skull. She'd have facials, body massages. Drinks of ice-cold white wine in restaurants with all glass windows, aquariums for the wealthy. She would be one of them.

Women, like the face in the picture, did that kind of thing. She'd join a yoga group or Pilates. She'd fret over things like maybe some of her stretches weren't as good as they used to be. Then, yoga mat rolled, Lycra still on, she'd grab a coffee with the "girls". Who were not girls at all but women that had been frozen in their youth. They'd all chat over skinny coffees about how their spending was going: holidays in exotic places, new cars, private schools for the kids. She wondered how many kids she'd have. Five seemed excessive. People like that. They didn't work according to the fumble-fuck and foetus guide to family planning. There would probably only be two kids.

Which two would she take? And that was where the whole crock of shit fell to pieces. Her little head trip to a different life came tumbling down Jenga-tower style because this was the kind of choice that couldn't be made. She couldn't reverse back out of her kids' lives. Not even reverse back out of her marriage. Finn was slippery. She knew that. He was the kind of man who could backtrack on promises: one out, all out. That had been a promise they had all made to each other. But now, she was after her third wish. Her moral compass had seen her alright. She was a damn sight better off than a lot of women she knew. No one was giving Daisy a happiness guarantee, not even with all the rich trimmings. Especially not since it looked like Daisy had been cloned rather than picked fresh.

Becca slipped the photo back into the bag. Scratch, bless him, wouldn't notice that Finn was marrying an improved version of an old model. Scratch was not exactly observant on the female front. If she'd asked Scratch what she'd been wearing yesterday, he'd have a job to remember. As far as he was concerned, there was only one Becca.

Becca buckled the case and was about to stash it again by the wall but then she noticed a thin pocket at the back. The leather was pushed out slightly, into a rectangle. The book!

Quickly, she unzipped and pulled it out, not even listening to check the coast was clear. Something was goading her on. She didn't care anymore. Didn't care if they all walked in. This was her wish, and she was going to have it.

The leather felt curiously soft, more like skin than any other leather she'd held before. It felt warm in her hands. Almost as if there was still a pulse running through it, but that was just stupid; it was just a book. It didn't take her long to find Byrde's curious entry. What did it mean?—*Keep Rebecca Nilsen.* The rest had been scrubbed out as if someone had been angry at the thought, the meaning lost. But there was so much in this small book. Hours and hours of scribblings. The pages fell open in front of her like lost autumn leaves, cascading a waterfall of snatched words across her retinas: *Scratch – get well. Money for study* and near the back of the book, *Daisy.*

Only Becca didn't bother looking back there or at least didn't read because that wasn't her wish. She wanted the one that she had asked for—the third wish Finn had made. Her wish. Each wish was dated like a diary entry and numbered. Even though Becca wasn't stopping to read, she could see that the writing in the book changed over time, from the scrawl of a young man to the neat cursive hand of someone older, someone smarter: an industry leader. The writing got smaller as well as the book progressed. The first pages, the letters were over large, as if Finn had all the space in the world, but towards the end, the words got tighter and closer together.

Only two pages were left blank. He was running out of time. She saw Scratch's wish right at the front. Finn had even started it, *Dear Book*. Just as though he was in some English class and writing a letter for a youth opportunity scheme. She didn't read further. She knew what it said. Scratch had been so bloody ill that spring. They'd all thought he was going to die. But it was easy for Becca to find wish three. At first, Finn had written them all one wish to a page. He probably regretted that kind of generosity after twenty-three years, but there was no going back. Anxiously, Becca turned to page three, and as she read, tears stung her eyes. Bastard, she thought. What an utter bastard.

19

———

HISTORY LESSONS

When they had found Byrde, neck broken at the bottom of the escarpment, the sun was full-on shining. As though God was strutting about with his trumpet—*behold the new day*! A couple had been out walking their dog, and there was Byrde sunbathing; legs bent, head twisted like a corkscrew. Fucked up in a way that all the king's men would not have been able to fathom.

When the storm had eventually rolled over, the storm that Byrde had decided to go flying in, those large grey clouds had pulled a heatwave in their wake, a listless swelter, sticky as quicksand. A summer that turned out to be hot as buggery. Record temperatures. Forty in the shade. Ice melting, and not just in people's drinks. It was as though the planet had gone menopausal.

They'd buried Byrde's body extra quick, so Scratch thought. True, Scratch didn't have a great deal of knowledge on six-feet-under protocol, but it seemed like those in charge weren't keen on having anything languishing away in the freezers. Which was maybe just as well because as soon as the weather had shifted to hot, old people started dropping like flies: *move 'em on, move 'em out.* There had been a coroner's inquest, but there was nothing to say—the old guy had fallen. Could have been suicide. Could have been an ill-advised wander after lights out. However, it happened, and the result had been a broken neck for Byrde. He'd also picked himself up a few choice bruises on the way down. Scratch couldn't see that it mattered. Who was there left to care? Byrde's wife was dead. The old man didn't have kids and luckily, he didn't fall on anyone when he came down. So, case closed.

You'd have thought no one would have been interested in the bon voyage send off. Byrde had always kept himself to himself, but a death in Falham was as good as a street party, and since there'd been no royal wedding for a while, most people over thirty went and hung around in the shadowy graveyard. Shoulder to shoulder, they stood, hemmed in by rows of burnt, black headstones that looked more like broken teeth than a celebration of anybody's life. Some Falham residents made an effort, wearing suits. Most people didn't bother going to the trouble. Despite the shade from the escarpment, it was still too hot. They'd only had a week of sun, but the grass was already parched dry as a dead man's cough. So funeral attire was a bit pick-and-mix. A couple of women were even in sundresses, as though this was one of those funerals where some hippy Christian had told them to *come bright and colourful as a Mardi Gras.*

Truth was, no one made a real effort. People were wearing whatever was easy and half-clean because no one seriously gave a toss. It was curiosity hemming them all in tight like sheep in a pen. They weren't interested in the past-his-best dead guy lying in the box. They came to see the living: the stories that were still rolling out on a weekly basis. Like all small towns, Falham living contained more sleaze than daytime TV. *How close was Mr Smith standing next to Madeline Crass?* Because rumour was, they were banging every time Mr Crass set his Nissan on the road to work. *Was that a bonanza-pack of Mars Bars in Jennifer Thomas's stomach, or something more long-term?* Small towns like theirs thrived on gossip, bartered it more than any other single commodity. A northern town without gossip, according to Scratch, was like a man without a cock—missing the point.

Good thing was, at least everyone's motivation was out in the open. No one bothered to fake cry. It was dry eyes all around, and the fact that nobody read for Byrde came as no surprise. There wasn't anyone to do the "personal". Becca said she thought that was sad. In fact, for some odd reason, it was Becca that appeared to take it worst. She kept banging on about how somebody needed to get up and say something nice. She seemed to have developed a soft spot for the bugger after he took a dive. Scratch felt this was all a bit —*after the horse had bolted.*

But to jolly her along, he offered to tell the gathered how Byrde had always kept a light on in the window for them. How he'd often run out to meet them when they went visiting. How, on many treasured occasions, Byrde had tried his hardest to make their parties go with a bang. Only Becca hadn't been in the mood for jokes. She'd been sullen for a while, brewing something that was beyond the boys. Any funnies Scratch delivered dropped like seeds on a desert floor.

Instead of a few personal words, the vicar had trundled through the service as if he was on zero hours and had to be somewhere else getting on with the next item on his checklist before he lost interest. In short—seven days after the man "fell", everything was sewn up by one-thirty. A great full stop had been slammed up against Byrde's name. Rolled at the end like the stone across Golgotha. But, although it's easy enough to put a body in the ground, you can't stop it from sprouting. Ask any good gardener, and they'll tell you —you can't always tell where a plant's going to come up. Bury it in one place, and it throws out roots, sprouts, tendrils to wherever it feels the ground is fresh, clean and ripe for the picking. Byrde's corpse was no different. It came crashing through their lives like old Jack's beanstalk. Finding odd ways of elbowing everything out of sorts.

For six whole weeks after Byrde died, there was not a drop of rain. The world felt parched, as though it had something to say, but the words just wouldn't come, only a dry, rasping death croak. It wasn't just the weather that shifted. Scratch couldn't help but notice that Becca wasn't so tight with Finn anymore. The attraction between them, the excitement that had been brewing up steadily, morphed into something ugly. No one mentioned the Becca/Finn thing, but everyone knew how they felt. If the grid had gone down, Scratch reckoned he could have plugged both of them in and grabbed some juice. The attraction had been that strong, only after Byrde's death, the physics shifted big time. All of a sudden, it was like there was an angry storm cloud sitting over Becca's shoulders. She seemed irritated with Finn, resentful, maybe? And it didn't take long for Finn to get right-back-angry at her. Scratch knew something was up, but whatever it was, he found himself on the outside of it. So, what was new there?

Oh yeah, he knew all about Finn and Becca. He knew how they'd always stop for a while at Finn's place before coming over to him. He knew that maybe they were having conversations that he wasn't a part of. He sometimes worried, when he wasn't playing the fool, that if that flat did turn into reality, there was a strong chance that Scratch would be on the sofa, the odd one out. It hurt him a bit. Being absolutely upfront and honest, Scratch would have liked Becca to call for him first. He could see that geographically that wouldn't have been so neat, but he still wished she'd stop by his doorstep on her own.

Scratch had always carried a torch for Becca, not just because she was beautiful, no. Though that would have been reason enough, he just loved the way Becca was so wild. Energy coursed through that girl's veins like she could draw it up through the ley lines riddling the country. Like she was not just standing on this world, but part of it—feet growing out of the soil. Only after Byrde died Becca's energy went all wrong. You don't need a degree in psychiatry to know that energy's best channel. If it's not pegged down doing something useful, it'll sure as hell be buggering something up.

Scratch read somewhere about something called the doldrums: something that happens at sea—a period when everything stops. No one and nothing is going anywhere. Which sounds alright, only it's not. Underneath all that going nowhere, there's this brooding sense that something is on its way. Because people aren't meant to stop. Energy/people, they have to keep going: making plans every day, moving forward, moving back, doing jumping-jacks on the spot if need be. Point is, people don't like it when the air goes stagnant, and everything seems deadlocked. It makes them feel uncomfortable, restless, as if they're waiting, waiting for something big and bad to give them a push off. Any direction will do, but off they need to go.

Maybe it wasn't just Byrde's death or the soaring temperatures that were making Scratch, Becca, and Finn feel out in the Pacific without an oar. Maybe, probably, it was because, after all those years of hoping, of watching, of waiting, school was finally out: over and done with, done and dusted, and they had scrimped, saved and...okay, so maybe even stolen. But by whatever means, the money to get them a deposit was squirrelled away under three different beds, all within half a square mile. Oddly, no one was suggesting going looking for a place. Scratch mentioned it once, just once on the way back from Byrde's do. And Becca shot him down faster than he was a clay pigeon. He dropped it after that because he could tell there was something deep going on there, and he needed to tread carefully.

Everyone's temper was frayed that summer. It wasn't just the musketeers. The tarmac on the roads started to go soft. You could hear the playlist of the world and his wife since windows on cars, pubs, houses were left down. The North had gone ratty. No one was getting a good night's sleep anymore, and people needed sleep. It was common to see a person sticking their head in the freezer at the supermarket, spending just that little bit longer than strictly necessary in the frozen foods aisle. Even the dog on Becca's street, the jowly monster that always barked when Scratch walked past, had given up. It lay listless as a sleeping lion. Its great stupid head drooling thick and chunky over its giant paws. So, in a summer of wall-to-wall scorch, where two days hit the hottest UK temperatures on record, Scratch wasn't sure if it was odd, crap luck, karma, or fate that he came down with pneumonia.

It was Scratch that suggested swimming in the quarry. He thought it would be fun. Finn had been away for a couple of weeks, just got back. So, Scratch said they should go for a dip; a cheap day out. Spithy Common was always a favourite haunt, but too crowded when the sun shone. If you hitched out of the town for a bit, there was an old quarry.

You had to trek uphill through some woods, which always put people off, and it was dangerous. Every summer, the newspapers were filled with kids drowning in wild-water haunts. This always alienated a fair few more would-be bathers. Becca hadn't been keen at first, but Scratch managed to talk her round, and once Becca was going, even though Finn appeared to have his nose out of joint where Becca was concerned, the boy still couldn't bring himself to opt out.

The hitch had gone alright; a straight ride in some farmer's four-by-four. The guy kept rattling on about how when he was a kid, *they did this, they did that.* Scratch just sat in the seat nodding away like one of those dogs people have on the dash, adding the odd bit of banter here and there to make it seem like what the guy said was more interesting than it was. Scratch was good at that. Sit him next to the most boring person in the world, and Scratch could add pixie dust to the conversation. Becca and Finn were in the back. Scratch kept catching sight of them in the mirror. Becca had her head jammed right up against the window as if she was an overheated bloodhound. Scratch just could not work out what was going on. There must have been some kind of fallout. He could have asked Finn, but he couldn't help thinking, somewhere deep down inside him, that maybe it didn't matter what had happened. Maybe the good thing about it all was—that *happen* it had. If Finn and Becca were no longer heading for joined-at-the-hip futures, then maybe all of a sudden, there was a little room for a quick Scratch.

The farmer dropped them off at the track. He told them to stick to the path. It would take them around an hour to get to the quarry. He said there were adders up there. *'Don't go poking under any rocks,'* he told them. If an adder wasn't slithering, it was hiding. So best not to look.

Scratch wasn't worried. Snakes didn't scare him.

The ground was hard underfoot, packed tight as cement after all that sun. Even under the trees, the earth felt hard and unforgiving when trainers hit it. Scratch wasn't used to that. He was used to walking over the soft soil of the moors. Seemed like the weather was changing everything: the world, his friendships. They should have been laughing about their bright new future: that little flat for three. Only the future appeared to be coalface hard. Becca and Finn said nothing to each other as they climbed. Not one word. Scratch cracked a few jokes, but the others didn't even humour him with the usual groans. He was just left carrying a cartload of silence.

They didn't see any adders. They didn't see any other people. Even the skies were clear of birds, just this harsh blue glare staring down at them. The trees were beginning to drop leaves. Not because it was time, but more like because they couldn't be bothered to hold on any longer. All the seasons were mucked up, but when the friends got to the swimming hole, everyone cheered up a bit. The water was like this deep green colour. It was cold as hell but felt so good. Even the sound of it laughing over the rocks eased the soul. They swam and bathed and chatted, and it felt as if everything was almost back to normal.

Almost.

Though Becca never sat next to Finn, she'd always seem to end up close to Scratch, and there were no conversations for two going back and forth, not like it used to be. Whatever was going on, Scratch couldn't help himself. He felt on top of the world. His heart soared like a rocket. Things were shifting, shifting, and it could all work out, couldn't it? The girl wasn't just in love with Finn. She was in love with the three of them. The relationship. Take Finn out, and what did it leave you with? Scratch could come out of this with the girl on his arm and still have Finn as his best mate. It was fancy footwork at its best. This summer, everything was within Scratch's grasp.

Then Finn went off to have a leak, and when he came back, he found his lunch tin empty. It was the kind of joke Scratch did, only...this time, he hadn't done it. Finn must have believed him, which was good, but then this almighty argument kicked off. It was mainly Finn and Becca, but somehow Scratch ended up getting dragged in at the edges. Not what he wanted. He knew he needed to stay neutral, but it was proving hard.

All three of them stropped back through the wood. This time, no one was talking. He'd never seen Finn that mad. Normally, Finn was easy come, easy go, but not that day. Scratch figured it would all blow over after they'd got home, slept it off after the weather had shifted. Only when they got back to the road, no one would pick them up. They'd stood on the hot tarmac, thumbs out, spaced three feet between bodies as if they were bowling pins. It was going dark before someone saw fit to stop and pile them in the back of a pick-up. No seat belts. Air-con au naturel and this great bloody St Bernard's slobbering all over Scratch.

The next day, he'd woken up feeling like death. He could hardly breathe.

It was a week before Scratch came around fully. He'd been completely out of it. *At death's door* was the expression people liked to bandy about. They said he was lucky, and in fact—as it turned out—they were right. Because not long after, surprise, surprise, Finn disappeared off to sixth-form college, and then it was all history.

20

CROSSWORD

*(A rectangular grid of numbered white squares. The goal is to
fill the squares with words by solving clues.)*

Becca woke to Scratch laughing. A short burst, but
enough to yank her from the dreamless dark of her
head. The sound echoed briefly around the room,
the trail of it gone in an instant, hammering off like the tail-
lights of a train into the night. She sighed into the darkness.
Suddenly, she was wide awake, and that did her no good.
She needed sleep to hose her brain down every night. To
bathe its busy corners and crevices with the cool forgiving
void of nothing. Being awake set the bees active again. She
could hear them sparking like rock on flint at the base of her
skull, getting ready to fling recriminations. *'Why didn't you
tell? Why didn't you tell? Why didn't you...?'* She'd have to take
one of the other pills, the sleepy ones, to shut the
buggers up.

Scratch may have been laughing, but Becca failed to
see the funny side. She had to admit that even though the
laugh was nice enough, not a touch of a maniacal demon,

it was still more than a bit spooky. It felt as though maybe behind the bonhomie, there must be an evil maestro keeping cover, one she knew nothing about. Ryan walked sometimes. Meg would occasionally mumble a few words but laugh? No, Scratch was unique as they come on that. She rolled over and stared at his outline, the cheeks pulled down with gravity. The nose, a little snub if she were to be perfectly honest. Not chiselled straight like Finn's. Scratch was no oil painting. He'd be the first to confess that and tonight, his mouth was hanging wide, catching flies, not a care in the world. Maybe he wasn't the best looker on the planet, but she envied him. Life was easy for Scratch. He always had a smile he could muster, no matter what shit came his way, and it made her wonder, lying there in the dark of the night, if she could be anybody else (just slip into somebody else's skin), who would she go for? She didn't need to think for long because, no surprise, the thought was right there anyway, dancing front lobe. Daisy, she'd be Daisy. Even if the young woman couldn't string two sentences together or was fat as a house underneath that long slim neck in the photos: Becca had only seen a head and shoulders shot. It didn't matter. Becca would still trade her skin for Daisy's. Because that particular body, by luck or design or talent, had attached itself to the kind of life Becca had lost out on. She sighed again. Maybe she was overthinking. Maybe it wasn't luck, design or talent that had snookered Becca's chances. No. Maybe the big factor had been time. It was a different world for women these days. Becca had been born too early to stand a chance. She dug her nails into her hands, dug deep till her skin hurt, and the buzz sparked up again. *'Why didn't you tell? Why didn't you tell?'* But feeling sorry for herself was getting her nowhere apart from drowning deeper in a hole she'd already dug. Becca needed to sleep. She'd go take a tablet.

Suddenly her ears pricked. She was sure she could hear something. She listened hard. Yes, there it was again: the high-pitched sing of glass kicked and rolling, rolling over a stone step. *'When was the last time you saw a glass milk bottle?'*

She didn't need Scratch awake to hear his words. He was right. Of course, glass had gone out of fashion. Had Scratch really heard it? If he had, why hadn't he said anything to her? She stared at him once again through the darkness. Not an oil painting, true enough, but he was hers, and he was loyal. He'd have had his reasons for not mentioning the sound. He wouldn't have wanted to spook her. She was high-strung enough these days.

Becca peeled back the blankets, careful not to wake the hibernating man beside her, and went to the window. It was gusty outside. She could hear the low moans of the wind, intermittent as though the night was digesting things slowly. A little chew here, a little chew there. A rumble. Their room was sitting above the front door. You couldn't see the step; you were standing out over it, but the light was on, so she could see a small pool of house and yard. Everything was quiet inside. Yet still, the wind continued to chew, and the barns crouched in the shadows sitting at the edge of her vision like beasts slumbering. She didn't look for the tree. As long as it hadn't moved closer, which it hadn't because it didn't have legs and was dead, and besides, trees don't walk. As long as that tree stayed exactly where it was, she'd be safe. It was her witness, just like she was Finn's. If they all stayed in the exact same positions, nothing could change. The bees buzzed a little louder. In protest? Maybe that wasn't going to work anymore. Maybe change was what they all needed, a touch of the old musical chairs. She took the pill bottle, which she'd left on the top of the chest of drawers, opened the cap and shook one tiny white tablet out into her hand. Who would think something so small could help?

Suddenly she jumped, the pills scattering to the floor. There was a noise coming from downstairs: a brief tap. Becca waited, standing in the cold, silent room. She couldn't even hear Scratch anymore. Everything froze as she stood, listening into the silence. Nothing. Absolutely nothing.

Scratch spluttered from the bed, and she let her own breath start to flow. Becca bent, scooping the pills back into the container, putting the lid back on. Pausing for a moment to look again at the white dot in her palm. Then... There it was again; there was definitely some kind of movement downstairs.

'*It's coming for you,*' the bees said excitedly. '*They said it would.*'

She shook her head. They never said it would come for her. It was Byrde that the thing was supposed to come for. Only that hadn't happened. Nothing so nebula. It was people that chased him over the edge. It had been all too physical. All too real, and now those people, that person, was lying sleeping in Byrde's old bed like the Lord of the Manor. Becca folded her arms across her body, wrapping herself for warmth. She'd done nothing wrong.

'*Why didn't you tell?*' Byrde piped up from twenty-odd years under the ground.

The man might be dead, but he did make sense. She had done something wrong. The police would say she'd made herself a party to it. And why? Why carry around Finn's secret? Carry it close till it started eating her up from the inside? She'd read Finn's book now, cover to cover. She could see how he felt about her. Was he honestly worth protecting? A man that was so self-centred? He'd have thrown them all under the bus and driven over their bodies if it meant a ticket out of town for himself and his ego. Daisy could keep him.

Then Becca heard it again. This time there was no doubt: a door opening from somewhere below. There was somebody down there.

Bare feet on soft wool, Becca crept down the steps. Never mind the luxury, she wished she was home with threadbare carpet beneath her toes; with children sleeping soundly in all rooms, instead of this terrible hollow emptiness: the kind of emptiness that comes just before a disaster. Just before the hit over the head, the face at the window, the horror rising itself out of unlit corners.

Odd how you can tell when there's something else living in a house, something else moving. It's not just the noise. It's the way the currents in the air get pushed around, like water navigating its way around rocks. This wasn't her imagination. There was someone somewhere with a heart beating. Someone that was fully awake and stalking around Byrde's house as though they owned the place. She thought of Falham lying sleeping under the escarpment and of all those people out of work or struggling on minimum wage. Did they look up at the big white house towering high in the clouds, just like she'd done as a kid? Did they think it was partly theirs? Because when something's embedded that deep into your life every waking day, don't you feel ownership? Did they wonder about the re-fit: how much had been spent? How the out-of-towners flew in and out like seagulls grabbing what they wanted. The folks from London with their fancy sports cars and tech gear thrust carelessly into bags, toys and kits that amounted to a whole year of working at the checkout. More maybe. Did the people of Falham think: *We should go up to that big white house on the hill and take a look, see if there are easy pickings.* It wouldn't be a game anymore. Not knock three times and then scarper. When you were grown up and desperate, when the world had turned its back on you, the time for game playing was long gone.

Becca glanced into the games room. The door standing open. The pool table waiting. All the balls neatly laid out in their triangle, looking so inviting. The room was quiet. No lights on. Only shadows slinking. She glanced into the sunroom. She'd drawn the curtains earlier—keep the tree where it was, but some bright spark had pulled them open again. Becca could see the blackened form standing there in the moonlight, watching. It seemed far away. Where it should be. Maybe it was leaving her to whatever was inside the house. Maybe it was saying—*Tell you what, Becca love, I'll catch you on your way down.*

Something moved in the kitchen: hard material cut down on one of those shiny new surfaces. Someone was in there. Becca hesitated; she could go back upstairs, wake Scratch. He'd know what to do. She wouldn't have been able to take anyone on. If they saw her, they'd have the upper hand, the surprise would be gone.

Walking back to the staircase, she reached her hand out for the newel. Softly, softly, Becca thought to herself. Don't give the game away. Just like before, she needed to be quiet as a mouse.

'You're up?'

Her heart missed a beat. She looked towards the kitchen and saw Finn standing there, monographed dressing gown clinched tight at the waist, mug in hand. After what she'd read in that book, Finn was the last person she wanted to see. She'd have actually preferred to have men in masks about to turn the place over before streaking hightail across the moors with a full bag of booty. That would have been easier. But Finn? She had nothing to say to him.

'I didn't say goodnight,' he said, still lingering in the doorway.

'I had a headache. I just went up.'

He nodded. 'I couldn't sleep.'

'Looks like it.' She glanced at the book in his hand, Byrde's book. 'Bit of late-night bargaining with the Devil? Most people do their shopping on Amazon. You can get things delivered the next day you know, Finn, no soul required.'

He looked half-amused.

'Know what the real problem is?'

'Not sure I...'

But she didn't let him finish. 'The real problem is— guilty conscience. That'll be why you're not sleeping.' She pulled a weary hand through her hair. 'Seriously, Finn, how could you, of all people, want to come back to this place?'

He looked irritated, as though this conversation had worn thin, but she had no intention of letting him off the hook, not when it was just the two of them standing there. She glanced again at the book in his hand. Taking a step down the staircase towards him. 'You and Scratch...bloody games. That's all it is to you, isn't it? Life is just one big game.'

Finn shrugged, but he looked uncertain now. He'd somehow lost his footing, was unsure of the ground. 'Well, I guess a lot of life can be...could be described as a game: an agreement to play by a set of rules. When you think about it, any kind of agreement, any kind of transaction, it can be reduced to a game: rules, responsibilities, aims, outcomes. All human transactions are, in a sense, games.'

'Bollocks.'

He looked shocked by the word. Finn had got used to having stuff South-soaped.

'What was that? Bloody Mastermind.' She scoffed. 'Time for living in the real world, don't you think? I'd say we're well past spinning stories. So, according to you, nothing can be taken seriously. Everything is...is frivolous...without...'

She stuttered over her words. Finn was so sure of himself, so slick when he talked. Articulate. Bloody articulate, that was the word. Whilst Becca had been reading *The Tiger Who Came to Tea* and *The Gruffalo* for the past twenty-three years—sometimes the big words, the adult ones, those grown-up routes of expression, she found it difficult to kick-start her mouth, her brain, into gear. Irritatingly, Finn appeared to know that. The bugger shot her an indulgent smile, which sent her blood pressure through the roof. Bastard. She took a deep breath, marshalling her thoughts. Only when she spoke again, she hated herself even more because it came out not with anger but a pathetic sob. 'If what you're saying is true, can't you see where that gets you?' Tears pricked her eyes. Angrily, she brushed them away. 'It means everything. Everything is without true meaning.'

'I didn't say that.'

He did. She knew he did. The thing that hurt most, Becca realised, is that she was just a part of it—part of his game, and he doesn't give a toss.

'You see life as one overarching series of moves that makes everything alright in the end. Justified. Can't you see, Finn? Can't you see how bloody conceited that is? Because it's you at the centre. Isn't it? It's you making all the rules, winning all the prizes.'

There was a pause. Finn wasn't looking so sure of himself anymore. In fact, he was looking...embarrassed? Upset? When he spoke again, his voice seemed to have lost its smugness. 'Actually, Beccs, I can't say that I've won all the prizes.'

Hurt, he was trying for bloody hurt! 'No?'

'Look, we're both tired. We need some sleep. It's...maybe it is too emotional coming back. Maybe you're right. Maybe we shouldn't have done it. I'm sorry.'

'It's too late now, though, isn't it? Too late for everything. When you were playing pool, I had a quick look at that book of yours.'

Finn's face morphed to hard as granite. He wasn't finding things so funny anymore. 'Beccs, it's private!'

'You broke your end of the bargain. So, I figured me looking, I reckoned we were even. I have to say, I wish I hadn't. My view of you, it's...well, what do they call it these days? It's had one of those paradigm shifts.'

'What?'

'Wish three, Finn. My wish. Wish one: Scratch gets better. He gets his bloody heart's desire. Wish two: you move out and make yourself a fortune. Wish three, mine. My wish. What do I get? And just for nicking your bloody cheese and pickle sandwich when we went swimming. Punishment just for that! It was a prank.'

'It's just a book. It doesn't mean anything. It was a long time ago...forgotten.'

'Not by me,' she gasped.

'I was mad at you...you... That summer you were acting so...' Suddenly, Finn was struggling for words. 'Odd. It was like you hated me. I thought we had something.'

'Says the man who's getting married,' she scoffed.

'Says the woman who's been married for twenty-three years.'

'You left.'

Silence. Finn stared down at his tea, but he didn't take a sip. All bodily functions were on hold.

Eventually, he nodded. He had left. First opportunity to get shot of them, he'd taken it.

'I thought I could make things better.'

Becca snorted.

'You read any more of the book?'

She shook her head. 'Wish three, that was mine. That was the deal. You condemned me to love you forever. You wrote that.'

'Like I said.' He sighed, and she wasn't sure if it was from relief or exhaustion. It was emotional—digging up the past, trying to make sense of it. 'The book...it was just stories, just part of some kid's game. It didn't come true.'

'How would you know?' Her voice sounded hard in her own ears as if it could reach out and slash that pretty face of his. 'It was about me, Finn. Me and how I felt. No...wait...' she corrected herself. 'How I feel. How could you possibly know if it worked out or not?'

'I didn't...' he flustered.

'No, you didn't.' Becca stopped, letting the cold sink into her body for just a moment, pulling it in for strength as if the air was as solid as bricks. 'When we were young, really young, it was easy. We were just three sides of the same coin. That's what we used to say. Scratch used to say, those were his exact words. Remember?'

He nodded.

'Scratch started it. He must have got it muddled, the expression, and it kind of stuck, till we actually believed it. Three sides of the same coin. The same bloody person practically, you, me, Scratch, but coins don't have three sides. They only have two sides and an edge, and I was never sure which of us were the sides, which of us was the edge keeping the other two out of contact. Just one word...' She dropped her voice, suddenly aware of Scratch sleeping upstairs between laughs. 'I was waiting for just one word, one move, any kind of sign. I spent my teenage years willing you into action. If Uri bloody Geller could bend spoons with his mind, then surely, I could get you to stop seeing me as just one of the lads. Long before the bloody cheese sandwich and you off to college. Long before all of that...I wanted more. That night at your place when we lay on top of the covers, with my dad downstairs banging on the door, it almost...' She broke off. She couldn't go back there to that moment of absolute beauty. Beauty which never flowered.

Finn started to move towards her, but she held up her hand. *Why didn't you tell?* There was more than just Byrde's opinion that needed airing. 'I wanted to...' She sighed. 'To be taken inside of you, inside of your arms. Feel the edges of where I stopped blur so that there was nothing left outside, and I was yours. And it almost happened that once, but... But then...then Byrde died, and Scratch got sick, and everything fell to pieces. He's a good man, Scratch. I do love him... but he was second best, Finn. He was the scraps from your table, and that's what my life has been pieced together with, the rubbish you didn't want.'

'None of it was rubbish...and...'

Becca didn't let him finish. She knew she had to get all of it out because otherwise, it would carry on sitting there in her gut fermenting.

'I held off for years till that night upstairs at your mum's place. Of course, I loved Scratch, but not like I loved you, with every inch of my being, every inch. There wasn't a finger or edge of a toe, not a corner of my body, that you hadn't conquered, hadn't taken as yours. I knew Scratch had always carried a torch for me, but I kept him at arm's length.

I thought, deep down, I thought you had to feel the same way as I did. How could all this love, all this burning passion be one-sided?'

'But...' He moved towards her, but she held up one hand.

'For Christ's sake, Finn, just let me finish.' The bees were beginning to buzz louder. If they got much more excited, she'd have to ram her fingers inside her ears, and she didn't want to do that. She didn't want Finn to know how close she was to losing the *sanity fight*. 'It was after your party, that was when it happened. All those people polishing up your vowels, drip-feeding you a whole dictionary of new words and better ways of saying the old ones. Scratch and me, the rejects, crawling home, tails between our legs like emotional cripples. The uglies. That's how we felt.'

'No.'

'What gives you the right, Finn, to say *No*. Maybe if I hadn't got pregnant, but... You and me, I knew it was over. Me, you, and Scratch, that was dead too. Who we had been, it was lying like a dried-up snakeskin somewhere on the route home.'

'I didn't...'

'Don't tell me you didn't realise, Finn. Don't bother giving me any of that. Then there was Byrde.'

And as if on cue, she could hear him, *'Why didn't you tell?'*

'And coming back here. Here?'

'Becca, I'm sorry.'

'Aren't we all. Do you know what my life has been like without you? How empty?'

'Beccs, I...'

'Finn, please!' *Face the past*, isn't that what Phillips had said? Didn't she have to do that now? So she continued. 'When I found out I was pregnant, I thought about...I thought about getting rid of her. Our Ella...' A second tear pricked Becca's eyes, only this time, she didn't bother wiping it away. 'But whatever I did, I didn't need to marry Scratch. I could have walked away from everything. But...then it came to me...and it was a bloody revelation, you know, the type of thing they preach from the pulpit, a bright light and a sign-post saying, this is it, and I thought—why not? Out of this whole sorry mess, why not give one person everything they want. So, I decided I'd marry Scratch. Even got you to give me away because there was no going back. There is no going back. I made a vow to myself at that bloody altar that there were no might-have-beens. No hankering after what-ifs. That kind of thing destroys everyone.' She knew that much at least was true. 'He's a good man, Scratch. So, I've had to bury everything else deep down inside. Make sure it never got to see the light of day. Because...I do love him. How could anyone not love Scratch? And I swear I will never break his heart because I know how that feels. And you, Finn, you...' Her eyes suddenly shone hard as flint. 'You'd have damned me for a kids' tiff. So...try and sort that bloody mess out if you like. Put something about that in your stupid book.

Becca left Finn standing lost and alone downstairs. She went up to the bedroom and climbed in beside Scratch. Edged herself into his warm, yeasty body.

'I love you,' she whispered, kissing the side of his bristled face before slumping like a walrus into Scratch's bed of dreams.

21

CHESS

(A board game of strategic skill for two players. The object: to put your opponent's king under a direct attack.)

'Hey, hey, gorgeous.' Scratch kissed Becca gently on the forehead as she slouched past into the sunroom. Sadly, the kiss made her feel more reptile-crawled-from-under-a-stone than princess. Their personalities were a constant painful contrast. He'd set a table in the room, weighing it down with glasses, cutlery, mats, plates, everything all ready and waiting for the off. Becca couldn't be bothered with any of it. Her night-weary eyes felt eighty per cent sore and reluctant, with a little crusty thrown in for good measure. She'd been taking too many tablets, too much booze, not sleeping. It was a recipe for disaster. Becca felt as if her world was somehow lagging behind everyone else's. Her brain was going to have to play catch-up.

Meanwhile, the sun kept streaming in harsh and incinerating as a laser beam through those gawping-wide windows. Finn was already sitting at the table, yesterday's paper sprawled out in front of him, as if he was at some roadside café, waiting for Short-Order-Scratch to do his bidding. How the rich live, Becca thought bitterly, as her stomach contents settled momentarily, and she managed to squeeze a little more sense into her surroundings. She picked the chair with its back to the window, avoiding the harsh interrogative light of a new day.

'Thought it was a shame not to look out at that view,' Scratch said, staring out, king of the castle, full up to the brim with life-is-good.

Becca glanced behind her: out over the escarpment where it was all hard edges and frost-bitten grass. How could two people looking at the exact same thing see it all so differently?

'Just in time for a full English, my pet.' He let his hand linger gently on her shoulder, until they heard the ping of a timer from the kitchen, and he pulled himself away.

The room no longer smelt like a posh shop; the air hung thick with the fug of fried bacon. Becca felt her stomach lurch with the wash of too much liquid. It was going to be a long morning. Scratch bustled back in to the room carrying two full bottles, one of ketchup and the other, brown sauce. Her eyes began to settle a little, and she noticed he was wearing one of those daft aprons, the type that's emblazoned with the larger-than-life contours of a cartoon character. This one showed the torso of a muscle man. Becca hadn't seen it before. A frown cut through her forehead.

Bottles placed neatly on the table, Scratch caught her look. 'Finn bought it for me in town. You believe that? I was talking about them yesterday, and this morning, here it is. Like a fairy godmother, that boy. Hey Finn? Did you conjure it up in that book of yours?'

Finn raised his eyes wearily. 'There's a price tag on the back. Got it in town. Bealles.'

Bealles. Becca hadn't heard that name in years. It was a small department store selling everything from socks to sanitary towels. Maybe that's what you had to do to survive in a place like this, Becca thought, Jack of all trades, master of none.

Scratch flexed his muscles. 'What do you think, Beccs?' He was holding his right arm out in a bicep curl, left arm still clutching the condiments.

'You're perfect the way you are.' Her voice sounded dry and cracked, as though it was finding it difficult to surface from the dark hole of her thoughts.

Scratch remained blissfully unaware. He just laughed, joy lighting up his entire face. 'You see that, Finn. That is love. That is commitment.' Riding on his own personal cloud of smugness, Scratch disappeared back into the kitchen.

Finn watched him go, folding the newspaper, making the pages crackle and rush as he smoothed the edges before placing it to one side.

'Anything interesting?' Becca asked, but her voice sounded flat. She wasn't really asking, just filling the silence.

'World's still turning.' He looked up at her. Stared right down through her eyes as if he was daring her to what? She didn't know. Then again, it didn't matter because Scratch was back beside them, sliding a packed plate, awash with beans, in front of Finn.

'Know what, the only thing I'm hoping for,' Scratch continued as though he had never left the room. 'If you and your Daisy are just half as happy as me and Beccs, seriously, mate, your cup it would runneth over.'

Finn mustered up a half-smile, but he didn't look

pleased. If Scratch was acting like the good fairy fluttered in for the party and bestowing wishes, Finn wasn't impressed. 'Actually, Scratch, one bit of bacon's plenty.'

Becca felt her body tense. 'Then just leave it,' her voice snapped, taught as an elastic band pulled to breaking point and way too loud.

There was a solemn pause of pure-cut silence. It hung in the air for a moment longer than was comfortable, floating along with the smell of full-on fry up, like a volcanic dust cloud.

'Sorry,' she mumbled. 'I mean, if you don't want it all, just leave it on the side of the plate.' Her fingers rapped the white ceramic of her own plate. Rapped into the silence. Becca caught them before anyone else noticed, placing her free hand over the offending digits as though she was trying to pin them down. 'There's just...' She cleared her throat, dropped her voice a level. 'There's no need to draw attention to it. You could have just left what you didn't want. Scratch has been slaving away...'

Scratch laughed. 'Not quite slaving.'

'You know what I mean. It's just...there was no need to criticise.'

'I didn't...'

'To draw attention to the fact that not everything on your plate happens to be perfect.'

Despite the streaming sunshine, the air in the room cooled. There was another brief slug of silence before Finn nodded as though he was digesting her words, chewing them over instead of the food. 'I just thought... Well, if I take it off the plate now, we could save it for later.'

'There's a whole bloody pack left in the fridge.' Becca's voice sounded like acid, even in her own ears. She wanted to stop but couldn't shake the mood. She kept snapping at anything passing, just like that old dog on the end of her road, pulling on its chain.

'Sorry, Scratch,' Finn mumbled. 'I didn't mean to offend.'

Scratch glanced between the two of them, confused as hell. 'Me? Nah.' He ran his hand over Becc's shoulders. 'You alright, love? If you want to go back and have a sleep.'

'I'm fine.'

Scratch continued to look concerned.

'Got out the wrong side of the bed,' she sighed.

The mood in the sunroom appeared stuck in quicksand and was sinking fast.

'I'll have the bacon.' She sent a fork over the table towards Finn's plate, thrusting a couple of prongs into the meat and airlifting the bacon straight from his breakfast. If it was rude, no one appeared to give a fuck.

'Sorted.' Scratch nodded eagerly. He'd never been one for arguments.

Food, for Scratch, was the answer to everything, and in truth—it was beginning to show. He'd be going up another size soon.

'I'll get you a bap for it. Bacon sarnie coming right up. You want brown sauce or ketchup?'

She didn't care. Becca didn't give a damn. She wanted to scream. Inside her head, the bees were finding cracks and trying to get out. Any minute they would pour from every orifice, drown the whole bloody room in black, crawling, buzzing bodies. She didn't even bother answering the condiment question. Afraid that if she opened her mouth, maybe it wouldn't even be bees, but something nastier that would sure as hell spill out.

The silence left Scratch standing there like a lost dinghy in the middle of an ocean, unsure how to move forward.

'Maybe just butter then,' he said. 'It's that unsalted stuff you like.'

Shut up, shut up, shut up, she thought. But instead— 'That's great, Scratch, love.' Making sure to get the *love* in. Making sure to let Finn know that maybe he did have all the money in the world, but she and Scratch, they had something special, something Finn couldn't catch up on. Because even when Finn did tie the knot, she and Scratch were a good twenty years down the track ahead.

'So, the plan for today,' Scratch said, his voice light. Moods were all water off a duck's back to Scratch. Besides, he was used to her ups and downs. 'Finn, you're the stag. You got any ideas?'

It was out of her mouth before she had the chance to shut the hatch. 'He'll be fresh out of anything original then.'

Scratch's smile faded. 'Hmm. Someone really did get out of bed the wrong side, hey Beccs?'

'Just stating a fact.' She slipped the edge of one nail between her teeth and started tugging. Nail-biting? Something she hadn't done since she was a kid. Becca pulled the offending hand back out. 'Prove me wrong then, Finn. Go on, give us something inspired for the weekend jolly.'

'Becca!' Scratch laughed, but there wasn't a note of humour in it.

She sighed. 'It's just...I mean, this is a stag. I feel like extra baggage. Seriously, it's going to be difficult to rustle up an itinerary that hits all bases. If it was just the two of you... well, you'd be doing the strip clubs. Conjuring naked girls out of cakes.'

Scratch shrugged. 'Beats candles. Can I put an order in now for my next birthday?' He kissed Becca on the forehead, breathing her in at the same time as if she were a summer day, not a ball of angst. 'Becca, if you're tired, love, we'll stop at home. You can get some shut-eye.'

She didn't want that. She didn't want the exhaustion to win. To lose yet another day of her life under the blankets. 'I'm okay.' She sighed. 'Just tired. Just...being here, it brings things back.'

'Yeah!' Scratch smiled.

How enviable is a clean conscience? For Scratch, it was all one big adventure. Three kids go feral on the moors yet again. There was not a drop of bad blood in it.

'I just feel like I've cramped your style.'

'What?'

'No.'

'If I wasn't here, you two would be trying to find some nubile young girls to have a peek at. Instead, we're on for a day of National Trust properties and tearooms.'

'Beccs!' Scratch snorted. 'Who do you think we are! I've got all the nubile I need. Besides, not totally sure you're being PC there. It's a bit of a stereotype, wouldn't you say, Finn?'

But Finn wasn't playing. He had no intention of bringing out the steamroller to smooth everything over; the stings were beginning to hit home.

'We can do a strip club if you want. Why not?'

'I didn't say, I...'

Finn cut her dead. 'No, if that's what Becca thinks we should be doing, hey, I've got no problem.'

'I didn't say...'

'Having fun on all levels, isn't that the game? Why not fit into the stereotype? Not sure stags are supposed to be PC events. Got to make it memorable. You only have one.'

'Hopefully,' Scratch muttered, barely audible.

'So, let's go for the whole cliché. Strip clubs won't be

open until later, though.' Finn glanced at his watch. 'They'll think you're a bit keen if you turn up on the doorstep just after breakfast. So, tell you what...we can do tearooms first, then lovely young ladies.' He hit the *young*. 'Something for everyone. Textbook. How's that for a plan?'

'So, double the tarts.'

'Scratch!' Becca threw her husband an irritated look.

'Just following the joke through.' He shrugged. 'So, who's driving?'

She flicked her nails against her tea mug in a small trill as if heralding an announcement. 'Not me.'

'Skoda's still knackered.' Scratch yawned.

Finn shot Scratch an ironic look. 'Conveniently.'

'No flies on you.' Scratch smirked.

'Look, guys,' Becca pushed her chair back from the table, 'I can go home. Put me on the train. I'm missing the kids anyway.'

'Beccs?' Scratch looked serious. 'You haven't been phoning them?'

'Just once. I wanted to...'

Scratch pulled his large hands across his forehead. 'You said you wouldn't.'

'It was only our Meg.'

'Doesn't matter. You know what you're like. They'll be fine.'

'I know.' She dropped her gaze, uncomfortable under the scrutiny. 'And they were. But...'

'Look, love,' he reached over, taking her hand between his, his fingers so pudgy and soft, so familiar, 'this is good for us. We need some time away. You know that.' Scratch took her chin gently, tilting her head so her eyes stared into his. He could tell everything wasn't right, and he was so desperate to fix it. His green-flecked eyes said it all; he'd walk over red-hot lava if he could stop her hurting.

But the conversation dried as a thick acrid smell filled the room. 'Bloody Hell. Toast!' Scratch disappeared, and without him, she realised how futile it all was, this game playing. Backward, forward, my move, your move. The burnt smell was not the only thing filling the room. There was a silence as thick and heavy as a red-velvet curtain call.

Becca heard life going on somewhere else. Heard an alarm bleating, a window opening, the sound of someone, somewhere—Scratch, slashing through the air with something solid, trying to create a fresh waft of wind.

'It's not what you think,' Finn mumbled, failing to raise his eyes from his over-full plate, but not touching it either. 'You've no right to be pissed off. You married him, not me. No one was pushing you down the aisle. No one forced you into bed with him.'

As if on cue, they heard Scratch's muffled voice from the kitchen. 'Burnt it. Bloody burnt it.'

It was as though Scratch believed if he wasn't in the room, life would stop. As if he had to keep interjecting and jollying just to keep the whole world spinning.

'I love the way you do that,' she said, not taking her eyes off Finn, making him squirm under her gaze. 'Is that something you picked up at banking school—how to twist out of everything? Nothing's your problem. Useful for a stock-market crash, I'd say. Transferable life skill.'

Finn stared up at her, and for a moment, the energy between them was so strong it felt nuclear. But before their toxic chemistry had time to obliterate the world, Scratch wandered back in, burnt toast in hand.

'Sorry, guys. I put some more in. Managed to salvage

this, though.' He placed the charred slices of bread on the table.

She stared at it as if the carbon black markings were some kind of curious hieroglyphs, a code into another world. She stared at it because she couldn't lift her eyes to either of them—didn't want them to see what was going on in her brain. Because how could anyone miss it? The pain.

'Thanks, mate but...' Finn stood, pushing back his chair, wiping his mouth on a bit of paper towel. 'That was enough for me. I'm gonna grab some fresh air before we leave.'

'Sure.' Scratch smiled. 'And you're driving?'

Finn raised his hands, all out for surrender. 'Looks like I'm your monkey.'

'Bargain.' Scratch laughed, and Becca marvelled, not for the first time, at Scratch's thick skin. It truly was a blessing not to be perceptive. To keep life brushing over you rather than letting it sink down deep.

'You take as long as you like, mate, on your promenade.' Scratch drew out the last word making it sound like he was taking the piss, which of course he was. 'We'll be here. Beccs, pass me the butter.'

She did as she was told as they heard Finn shuffle-step neatly down the hallway and take his coat from the stand before the door opened, letting a brief audio snatch of howling wind into the house before silencing it, double-glazing style.

'That wind's up again,' Scratch said as a trapped blast of air rushed through the hallway, playing with the picture that was sitting on the wall.

'It's always up, Scratch.' Becca stared out towards the escarpment, watching as Finn came into view. 'You know that. It's twenty times worse up here.'

Scratch chewed his toast for a moment, like he was

thinking it over, before glancing out with her. Following Finn with his eyes as the small Lowry stick figure walked towards the edge. His cashmere coat turned up against the bite.

'God, I hope he doesn't jump.'

'Scratch!'

'Well, let's face it. The stag's not exactly turning out to be a barrel of laughs.'

'Are they ever?'

Scratch shrugged. 'They're normally more fun than a funeral. But I guess it takes all sorts. What's with you, anyway?'

'Just...' Becca had no idea where to start.

'Coming back here?' There was a hard edge to his voice, a weary tone. 'Look, Beccs love, you need to get over it. You can't talk to him like that.'

'What?' Instinctively, she was on the defence, wanting to deny that she had talked to their mutual friend in any way out of the ordinary. 'It's just banter.'

Scratch shot her a steady look. He wasn't buying it. He knew something was up. 'Know what surprises me? What I cannot bloody believe is that he didn't buy you a ticket home. Draft in a helicopter and get you out quick. It's his party, sweetheart.'

'Scratch, I didn't...'

Scratch held up one finger, dropping his voice down to quiet and serious. She hardly ever heard that tone from him. It made her listen. 'Finn's the one calling the shots here. It's his wedding. His stag. His move. He didn't even mention dancing girls and cakes, and there you are, taking umbrage. It's his party, love, bottom line—you've got to be nice to him.'

'I didn't sleep well.'

'Then you go back to bed or drop it. Listen...we're here

to have fun. That's it. When he goes back to London, you know what I want him to think? I want him to remember this as being one of the best few days he's had in years—golden days. Well...' Scratch stared out at the escarpment, which was blowing tumbleweed-style detritus across its edge. 'Golden days despite the weather. You know what I mean. The best few days spent with the only people Finn truly cares about. The only people he's got history with.'

Becca could understand all of this. Living one foot in the past rots everything from the inside out. She needed to confront Finn or let it drop. She glanced out of the windows. He was standing right on the edge.

'Like I said, this is his game. He's king. All of our moves have to support that. Did you talk to him about it?'

And her blood ran cold—what did Scratch know?

'About Daisy? Jeez, Beccs, are you okay? You've gone white.'

Becca felt her world expand once more, reaching into familiar corners. It was Daisy and Finn that Scratch was after. Scratch had no idea about Finn and Becca, about what she'd seen, about what she felt. 'I'm fine, just tired.' She toyed with the handle of her mug, lifted the thick china rim to her nose and inhaled the coffee, but she didn't drink. 'I asked him why he was getting married.'

'And? What did he say?'

'Oh, I don't know, Scratch.' Becca sighed. 'Some crap about being tired of standing at square one.'

'That what he said?'

'Yeah.'

'Nothing about love?'

'Scratch, why would he marry her if he didn't love her?'

'You tell me. People marry for all kinds of reasons. Chances are, Beccs, she's a gold digger. How old is she?'

'Scratch, you know this. Same as our Ella, early twenties.'

'I mean, that's just creepy. Our Ella!'

'People do it all the time. What about James Bond.'

Scratch laughed. 'He sheds his skin an' all.'

'It just seems odd because, because we've got a daughter the same age. That's all. Finn's a good-looking man.'

'He's a bloody good catch. That's what he is. Want to know what I think?' He didn't bother to leave her a gap so she could squeeze herself in and say *no*. 'She's a gold digger.'

'Scratch! You don't know that.'

'He's old; she's young. He's loaded; she's after it.' Scratch's words suddenly sounded hard. As if they carried an anger underneath them, a bitterness. The kind that takes years to ferment.

'Scratch, what's up with you?'

'Me!' He laughed. 'Now it's what's up with *me*! Beccs, use your brain. I'm being practical, babe. Didn't think he'd ever do it. Thought we were safe.'

She was feeling confused. 'Safe?'

'Think about it, Beccs. Finn's got no one, no family, no other close friends, just us. So, where do you think the dosh was going to go when he kicked it?'

For a moment, Becca was lost for words. How did Scratch even get himself into this position? 'Scratch! Finn's not going to *kick it*. He's the same age as us.'

'Yes but say he did. No one knows what's around the corner, and…I know it's odd, but I've always had this feeling.'

'Oh?'

'Yeah, like I'm going to be the last man standing.'

'What!'

'You know, he'll drop out first. It's as if Finn swallowed

all our luck, Beccs. Well, that can't last. Sometime the roundabout has to go the other way. Our luck. Our chances. He got all of them.'

'Life doesn't work like that.'

Scratch gave her a long hard look as though he was weighing her up. 'Sometimes you win. Sometimes you lose—rules of the game. You don't always lose. You don't always win. Sometimes you just get a streak. But our streaks have been down all the way, and Finn's, well, they've been the exact opposite. At some point that's gotta flip.'

'It doesn't mean he's going to die.'

'What about the book?'

'Oh, for Christ's sake, Scratch. That was just a story.'

'A story with one page left.'

'Two.'

'Two.' Scratch shrugged. 'Not much space for a lifetime.'

'Oh, come on. This is madness.' Becca stared outside at Finn, walking along the edge, breathing in the air as if it was his lifeblood. Standing right near that bloody tree.

Scratch followed her gaze. 'All I'm saying is, maybe things will change. We—you, me and the kids, if anything happened to him, we were down to get everything. But when Daisy gets her feet under the table, well, it's not such a sure thing anymore. You heard what he said about spending. The woman treats it like an Olympic sport.'

'You don't know that. Besides, it's none of our business.'

Scratch hit the side of his head in frustration. 'It was our business. He was our future. Now he's got a new missus lined up. Daisy pulls it off, isn't there some old musical with a song, Daisy pulls it off?'

Becca shook her head. She had no idea, but she'd had enough of this. 'Scratch, my head's spinning. Just leave it, love.' She couldn't follow his logic anymore.

But he grabbed her hand between his. He was agitated, his eyes full of fire. 'No way. No way am I leaving anything. We haven't lost yet.'

'Lost?'

Scratch didn't bother to reply. Instead, he stared out again at the escarpment, at that small thin figure walking the edge. 'He needs to remember how much he loves us. How much we mean to him. Looking after us, well, it's just being a good mate, Beccs. If the situation was reversed, we'd do the same. If Finn dies, I swear to you, he can have all our debt.'

Becca snorted. 'Scratch.' She reached out, gently running her hand across his chin, as he placed his hand over hers. They were so close now they could kiss. Not that they did much of that anymore. Maybe none of that mattered because his eyes were deep, sincere, solid. Scratch was her rock.

'All I'm saying, Becca love, is—be nice to him, hey. It's not going to hurt.'

She nodded sadly.

'It's just a long weekend. I mean, you never found it difficult before. You been taking your pills?'

'What?'

'Your happy pills.'

'Yeah, but last night I took something to help me sleep. They always make me feel...'

'Like a lead balloon?'

She smiled sadly.

'Well, leave off those. I'll give you something to help you sleep tonight, promise.' He ran his hand up her thighs under her short cord skirt. The one she got from eBay. It still felt like someone else's skirt, as if she could feel the other woman living with her under the green cord. She'd wash the thing again when she got home.

'It is difficult to take a guy seriously...' she stroked the lump that his hand made under the cord, gently easing it back down her leg, 'when he's wearing a muscle man apron.'

'It comes off. Everything comes off.' He smirked. 'And remember,' he gently eased the corners of her mouth up with his free hand, scaffolding a smile, 'remember, it's a stag, not a wake.'

Then he drew her gently towards him, hugging her to his chest as though he was trying to pass on some of his energy, some of his strength. 'Don't throw it all away, love. Finn's known us upside down and inside out. Every little detail of our lives he knows and likes. He likes us.' Scratch pulled away, straightening her hair with his hands as though she were a doll, and he was putting everything back in place. 'Know what, I'd go further; I'd say he loves us. Three parts of the same coin, that's what we are.'

'That expression...' She had to tell him. Had to say because keeping on saying it just made him sound stupid.

'What?'

'That expression...three sides of the same coin, you got it wrong.'

'What?'

'A coin doesn't have three sides. It has two.'

Scratch laughed, throwing back his head and roaring as if she'd just cracked the funniest joke ever, and suddenly she felt confused. 'How dense do you think I am, Becca? Two sides. Yup. That's it, babe. There's always only ever been just the two—you and me. That's why it's so important. Finn's just the bit left over on the outside. We've got to look after ourselves and the kids. Finn, he's been living it up in

London with his fancy cars and his shit-hot women. That's all fine by me…'cus you know what? I have the only woman on this planet that…' And for a moment, Scratch hesitated, stopping himself mid-flow as if he was about to speed over a precipice.

'Scratch?'

He smiled, just shook his head, and smiled. His lips tight, as if he were reining himself back in. 'The only woman that I could ever have wanted I have—you. And when Finn dies, we're in line for the rest.'

'Scratch!'

'Becca, love, be serious. He's not marrying this Daisy woman because he loves her.'

Becca pulled away slightly, reaching up for her face. Wondering if Scratch had seen the photo. If he had spotted the similarities. But she guessed not, because he seemed unaware of her awkwardness.

Instead, Scratch continued on as always, steaming merrily along the story he was carving out for them. 'He's marrying this Daisy because he's bored. He's fed up. Tired of standing at square one. He's had so many women over the years it's bloody hard to keep count, and every one a beauty. But that's alright. That's fine. Everyone deserves a beautiful woman, eh?'

Suddenly Becca didn't feel in the mood. This was all beginning to feel a little too much like yet another of Scratch's get-rich-quick schemes. She again glanced out the window at Finn. His ears must have been burning because he turned towards them and waved. She couldn't help herself, it was so stupid, but she waved back. So did Scratch, a great big smile on his face. They sat there in the sunroom, waving out like caged monkeys at a zoo. Finn on the outside, as if he'd just dropped by for feeding time.

'It's fine for him to screw around,' Scratch said before his smile had a chance to melt from his face. 'That's what Finn's best at. You look like Finn, it would be difficult to stop yourself, but him getting married, that changes things. All that lovely inheritance, the kids' uni fees...'

'He's helping us with our Ella.'

'We've got four more. Might even go for another.'

The thought made Becca queasy. 'Scratch...'

'Don't, Beccs...I know how you feel, love, but... They're our pieces of magic, those kids. Don't forget that. Not even for a minute and we need to protect them. Because you think once Daisy gets to hear he's spending a couple of grand a piece on our kids, she's going to be happy?'

'Scratch, you don't know...'

'Neither do you.' He parked the comment for a moment, letting it sink in. 'Point is, Becca, this woman that we don't know from Adam, she'll be frittering away all our money down the nail bar.'

'You're being so negative.'

'Me! No way, sweetheart. I'm a pragmatist, Beccs. Besides, do you think he's any better than us? Think on it. Do you seriously think he works any harder?'

'You work hard, love. And when our Ryan's at school, I can pull my weight.'

Scratch shook his head, long and slow. 'Not the point, Beccs. Is Finn better than us?'

'No, you know this. I...'

'Then do you think he deserves all that money any more than we do?'

'It's not about deserving.'

'Why not, Beccs? Because maybe it should be. Maybe we need a slice of the cake. We need more and we do deserve more.'

'He's not dying.' She glanced out at Finn, who had moved away from the edge and was walking slowly back towards the house. 'And he'll help with the kids. I know he will.'

Then suddenly, it dawned on her. Maybe that was why she'd sat on Byrde's death for so long. Maybe—the bees started to buzz again. Maybe she was going to have to use the information. Blackmail? Surely not. Not her. Not Finn. Only those bees were really cranking up a symphony now, almost as if they were egging her on. All through the years, Becca had thought of herself as a witness, maybe even a victim, but how about if she turned the tables, asked Finn to help her keep that all-important silence? Would that make Becca more complicit? Pragmatist, that was what Scratch had said of himself. Maybe Becca needed a bit more of that. Maybe instead of looking into the past, she needed to be planning a few future moves, putting the king in the corner.

'He'll pay for the kids' education.' She was surprised at how cold her voice sounded, how in control. 'I'll see to it that he does.'

Even Scratch looked taken aback. Then slowly, slowly, he nodded his head. 'Okay, but it starts off with you being nicer to him. Make him remember how close we are, all the things we've been through. What a laugh we had, we are having. Remember that kids' story about the wind and the sun? Remember how they're arguing about who's the strongest because the wind can blow whole buildings down, but the sun can dry up great lakes.'

Finn was cutting back across the grass towards the yard. He'd be with them soon.

'And then the wind and the sun...' He was staring straight out at their oldest friend. Scratch's eyes suddenly looked cold, calculating. 'They see this man walking down this long, lonely road. And the wind says to the sun, "Okay, let's see who can make that man take off his coat first." So, the wind goes up to the man, and he blows, and he blows till his cheeks crack with the strain. But the man, well, he just wraps that coat tighter around his body. Wraps it so tight he's almost shrouded in it. Not a chance of getting that coat off. Then up comes the sun, and the sun shines, and the earth grows warmer, and the birds, well, they all start to sing. And the man, he takes off his coat, just peels it off all on his own. So...' Scratch rested his hand gently back on Becca's shoulder. 'All I'm saying is, Beccs...put a bit of sunshine in that smile. It'll help us win.'

22

TRUTH, DARE OR PROMISE

(Spin the bottle. The person that the bottle lands facing has to decide whether they are going to choose Truth, Dare or Promise.)

The ruined abbey clawed over the landscape, cold and calloused as giant's fingers. *God's footprint*, that's what Scratch had said once. It was kind of how it felt; unfaltering evidence of belief cemented through stones and centuries. Even though Scratch had taken it on himself to give a verbal nod to the almighty, Becca couldn't help feeling that her husband actually saw it differently: carving out a perverse pleasure in the abbey's ruin; more *mighty have fallen*, as opposed to evidence of a higher being.

The three friends stood, cold in the sharp wind, at the end of the long nave. A tongue of green cut-grass, immaculate as the top of a pool table, led the eye straight down towards the east window, which was filled with a cut-out blue block of sky. Thick stone columns, humourless and straight as petrified soldiers, edged the nave. Since there was no roof to support, it seemed as though the columns had been left holding up the heavens. Which, by all accounts, had to be described as a big job.

Becca could almost taste the hard, mineral smell of Jenga-packed stone. Oddly enough, she had always found ruins more impressive than finished projects. They were filled with the tracks of past lives. Not sealed off with mundane functions: an office, a cloakroom, a café.

Her all-time favourite ruin had been the shell of the old hospital at the edge of Falham. As kids, they would play there for hours. To Becca, it had seemed like a storybook of possibility. All the things that had happened there: lives saved or lost. Love blooming between the emptying of bedpans. Card games going on late into the night.

They'd never known the hospital doors flung open or the windows set with glass. Right through their childhood, the place had been boarded up. Sitting there, planks over all orifices, rotting, but they'd got in anyway. There was always a loose board easily prised, and once inside, you could walk the rafters, one end of the building to the next, looking down into the patchwork of rooms below—a bird's eye view of what was left: an old filing cabinet, upturned plastic chairs. Unrolled bandages captured between reflected puddles filled with sky, and a girl, one single girl, standing high above, arms outstretched, walking the beam—Becca.

The lads didn't tread the rafters, at least not right the way along; there was a section where it had rotted down to a single plank; the edges chewed by damp; the floor below caved in, revealing a deep dark pit. The pit must have been the foundation of the building. Only the hole had always appeared to be even more ominous than simply the bowls of an empty building. They'd flung a rock down once and never heard it bottom out. One wrong step, and you'd be dead. Not even one wrong step; the plank could easily give beneath trainer-clad toes. Walking along that beam, you put your life on the drawing board of some higher plan. Becca hadn't cared, never sure if she walked the beam because she wanted to give God a poke: remind him she was still there. Challenge him to do his worst, or because she actually liked the activity: the feeling of standing tall on top of a thin mortal wire between heaven and deepest, empty nothing.

They'd taken a different route this morning when they drove out to the abbey, so she hadn't had the chance to see the old wreck of a hospital yet. Maybe on the way back, they could stop, peel back a few of those boards. Stick two fingers up to the *unsafe, keep out, trespassers prosecuted*, just for old times' sake. The place wouldn't be there forever. Time was ticking on the non-aesthetic ruins of the world. Scratch had already told her that some property developers were planning on putting up fancy flats. But Becca couldn't see the development thing happening. She couldn't envisage any person living in Falham and needing a "fancy" flat. Times may have changed, but the town's residents were still squeezed one-and-all out of the same no-hope mould. Something would happen. Eventually. Time marched on. Whatever it was, it would most likely be a pile of shit.

No one would be touching the abbey, though. Standing there, shoulder to shoulder with the lads, it felt to Becca as if time had stood still. You might not be able to climb through the stencilled-cut windows anymore, but maybe that wasn't a bad thing. The stillness of the place gave it an added sense of gravitas. Kids hanging off the rocks would call all that into question. A person needed to be still to appreciate gravitas.

If it had been all finished off, roofed and plastered,

would it have still contained the magic? A cathedral with a roof has limits and ends. This place had no boundaries. Everything belonged to it, the whole damn universe. There were pictures on info boards around the site, artist's impressions of how it might have looked, but Becca didn't want to see them. To her, she loved the mystery muscled to the abbey's awkward bones. It was as if some alien force had thrown the bricks down hard on the earth, and it had sprouted. God? Probably not.

'Reckon the grass is greener just the other side of the barrier.' Scratch dug his shoe into the immaculate green turf, making it buckle like a turd beneath his toes.

Motherhood made Becca feel awkward about willful destruction, forever the custodian, yet she said nothing. Besides, he had a point about the grass. The short furry tongue leading towards the east window appeared every inch high-definition: too green, too vibrant, painfully real, especially after a sleepless night that had left her eyes feeling bathed-in-bleach sore. Scratch raised one arm and lazy-arse pointed towards a small sign informing them that they shouldn't go strolling down the lush grass carpet. It wasn't for them. A thin rope barrier swayed in the breeze, seeming to Becca more like an invite than a *keep out*. Daring them to skip over.

What was that song they used to sing? *'One, two. One, two, three, I want someone in with me.'* She'd done it with her older kids, replacing *'someone'* with their names. From Ella all the way down, the children had stood, eyes of wonder, staring up at Becca's face as the wooden handles twisted in her palms and the rope slapped the tarmac. Slap, slap, slap. Cracking the air before a brief hesitation. Then all her children would be jumping. Jumping together, all bound up neatly within an invisible arc of air, cut by the swinging rope, keeping them close.

Sadly, her glory days of skipping had gone by the time she got to Ryan. She hadn't really wanted him in, couldn't be bothered with the added complication. He was too small, maybe? No. That wasn't it. Her skipping days were done. Poor Ryan had got the dreg-ends. No wonder he was difficult.

Becca stared at the rope barrier, swinging, swinging at the entrance to that long majestic walk. Knowing her luck, she'd probably trip on the blessed thing and break her neck. It made her sad to think some of the games of the past were lost; that lethargy was clamping its teeth down hard. Then again, she wondered, who would even call her in to skip these days? Next time, in another life, she'd keep the rope to herself. Maybe that was the answer. *One, two, three, four, five, skipping on my own feeling so alive.* That wasn't how she'd been brought up, though. That wasn't what all the stories told her. The game plan: two by two, that's how the world ran. One and three were silly numbers. Odd-ball digits. She could see that now more than ever. Becca had to pare everything back. Focus on what was important: the future, not the past.

'Ladies?' Scratch said, flipping the rope with his wrist, making it look flimsy and daft.

They all glanced at the DO NOT WALK sign, it's shouty white capital letters. Rules were made to be broken. That's what all kids thought, and when the three friends were together in one unit, somehow, somewhere, the years got rolled back. They were kids again. Living in that world where rules were for somebody else: all the faceless grey millions being processed through life. Not them though. For a rule to apply, a person has to "buy in" to the fabric of the game: the dos, the don'ts, the age-appropriates. You had to be a part of the rule-making machine; take comfort in the fact that rules are written by people like you, for people like you. It's all for your own good. As kids, they were never quite clear on how the rules related to them. Even now, even though Becca felt she'd been drowning for the past twenty-three years twenty-four-seven under other people's needs, she wasn't totally sure she was protected by the rule book.

Sometimes it felt to Becca that maybe it had been better being a kid, despite all the parent crap. She could remember a time which may not exactly have been happier, but it had something that she couldn't afford to lose—possibility. A sense of choice, a myriad of paths that could take her in so many different directions. If only she'd realised at the time. She'd thought life had been hemmed in by a crap start, but Finn had been right. It was she who had taken the staple gun and sealed herself into her future. If things had been different, she might have married Finn. If she hadn't been up at Byrde's house that night. If she hadn't seen. She'd have managed to keep the Finn she knew separate from the Finn she saw bullying an old man to death.

Then again, why did she think her pool of choices had to be so goldfish bowl small? What perverse life only offered up two options on the man front? There were around thirty-two million men in the UK. If Becca had been braver, she might have ditched what was an easy offer, gone off to college. She might have worked on a cruise liner as a croupier, seeing the world in an evening dress and a smile. She might have got a good job in an office with wide windows and some city sprawled under her feet. It didn't even have to be a northern city. It could have been anywhere.

Maybe she could have married someone different,

someone who didn't know the shit life she'd lived, who'd never seen the bruises and the tears. That might have worked out better. Because someone different could have helped her draw a line under the crap start. Not like Scratch, where every time they saw some idiot parent acting up, they'd shoot each other a knowing look, feeding the past slowly, slowly with morsels from the present, letting it live.

Becca hadn't realised all those years ago that instead of being sealed up in a coffin, given no room to grow, youth was not a cage but a platform. Everybody's future had endless possibilities. That's why the young needed good parents so that instead of clipping their wings, the next generation got the chance to fly free. Becca could do that for her own kids, but for her, now, there would be no second chances. Middle age would be sure to serve her up a hefty diet of more-of-the-same until it clogged her arteries and stopped her heart.

She filled her lungs with a deep slug of cold air, like drawing in a wish: if she could only muster up just a fraction of that openness she'd once felt. If she could just tap into just one of those parallel worlds and breathe a little life into it. Maybe when Ryan started school, Becca could start something for herself. A small corner of hope where she could mine away undisturbed while he grew in six-week slots into his own life catalyst.

'Good to be back?' Scratch mussed her hair like he used to when they were kids, and Becca found herself a small smile she could put on for the public.

'Yeah, kind of.'

He slipped his arm around her waist, kissing the side of her face. His chin gristling against her cheek. It could be worse. He was a good man, and now things were coming to an end. She could have a new beginning, come September. Real work and its germ of possibilities. September.

Scratch swung his arm in hers, and they stepped over the rope like they were kids out on an adventure. September. There would be no more kids. Becca didn't have the energy to turn anymore around. That all had to stop.

Sensing she was having a tough day, Scratch squeezed her hand, just a small touch, but enough. He'd stood by when she could barely get out of bed in the morning. That was a big ask. She'd been lucky to find someone who could do that. Her mum hadn't been so fortunate. It had probably been depression that had been her mum's downfall, too, undiagnosed. Had to be. The way she just disappeared off like that. You don't run that fast, dip under the radar that quick, unless there's no other choice.

'I'd forgotten how grand it was.' Finn pivoted around on his heels, taking it all in. His voice echoed briefly off the stone. They had the place pretty much to themselves. It wasn't the school holidays, and the weather had been uninspiring, but they'd needed to get out. The house was working on everyone's nervous systems, making them jittery. Or maybe it was the alcohol. Either way, fresh air was what they all needed.

Becca was double-wrapped: two coats, a scarf, gloves, and a hat. She hated the cold. She was glad Daisy wasn't there. No doubt Daisy would have some feather-light but super-insulated coat. Some fabric designed for city style and moonwalking or Martian windstorms. Becca couldn't be doing with competition on the fashion front. Only despite all the clothes and the bright sun, which had finally chosen to smile, she still found herself feeling ice-cold, and rubbed her hands together, trying to kick-start her circulation.

'Cold, love?' Scratch lifted her fingers gently between his, squeezing them tight.

'Just a bit.'

'We can go back to the café, get you a hot tea?'

Finn looked confused. 'We've only just got here.'

'Yeah, but if Becca's...'

She shook her head. 'I'm fine, Scratch. It's good to get out.'

He nodded, but he was worried about her. She could tell. Funny, he didn't worry about anything else: money, the kids and their school reports. It was only her that set that frown into Scratch's soft kind face. Yes, he'd put up with a lot. Becca stamped her feet, shaking out the frost.

'There you go, better,' she said, even managing a smile. She'd decided before they left the house that she was going to try harder. Let that deep sense of resentment she felt every time she glanced at Finn's car, or his expensive shoes, or smelt his pricier-than-gold aftershave—Becca was going to let all that go. She'd even managed to shoot him a smile when they met at the bottom of the stairs, getting their scarves, their hats, their coats into a pile for the trip. Scratch's words had had an impact on her. This was odd because normally everything Scratch said washed over Becca like an ocean pulling over a coral reef. Scratch talked a lot. You could afford to miss most of it. Only this time, she'd listened.

Scratch probably hadn't meant for her to draw the conclusions she'd drawn. How could he? He didn't know what she knew, but she'd seen straight off that there was a path through this mess. True, she would have to play the game carefully. Planning the future was not something Becca and Scratch had proved good at. Only now, it was crunch time. The support Finn could give the kids could even be worth all the distress she'd felt over the years. Finn had already put Ella through college. Becca hadn't even thought about the other four following on fast behind; they would all need something, and another woman in the mix at this late stage in the day wasn't exactly ideal. It wasn't even as if Becca and Daisy were ever going to become best buddies.

There was the age difference, the class difference, the geography, not to mention the fact that somewhere deep in Becca's marrow, she didn't really want Finn marrying anyone anyway. She'd been loyal to him, kept his secret. Boxed in her own life. So now she wanted just a little bit of loyalty back. Daisy could prove to be a spanner in the works. The young woman could turn Finn the full 360, with her fresh skin, her clear eyes, her look-to-the-future stride, which all those young women who have everything at their feet have. How about if Daisy suggested that maybe they get a little holiday place on the Costa Brava rather than stick four kids through college? Kids that weren't even their own. So yes, Scratch had a point; they needed to be nice to Finn, but most importantly, they needed to be sure Finn had their backs.

In short, Finn could have the haunting, have the guilt. She would hand it all over. Becca had done her time babysitting it. Phillips would be proud of her. Maybe his CBT really was working. She tilted her face up towards the sun, letting it seep in through her skin. Face that past. Wrap it up in some kind of sense, whatever sense might work for giving the future a foundation, then park it. No picking. Because it wasn't just Becca's future anymore, her kids were in the mix.

The three friends walked a little way down the green baize towards the east window. It was so peaceful. So grounded, despite the fact that Becca's mind kept buzzing with plans. Rushing in guns blazing wasn't going to work. Finn had no idea she'd seen it all. It was going to be a shock when she told him. She had to make the request easy to digest: some kind of trust for the kids. That wouldn't seem like blackmail, no. It was the kind of thing that good friends did for each other. Blackmail was an ugly word. This wasn't like that. She wasn't going to threaten him. She was just going to "suggest". She'd been a true friend, kept his secret safe. He had always said the kids would be alright. He'd always said that even when they kept having just that one more. Finn wouldn't have pulled out on the deal. The stumbling block was Daisy. Women don't like their men having unpaid emotional debts. For the first time in years, Becca felt a little life flowing back through her veins. She was taking control, and it felt good.

Would Byrde mind? Becca cocked an ear to the wind. He hadn't followed them out, thank God. She couldn't hear the *'Why didn't you tell?'* His ghost was probably mulling over all the twists and turns of the morning, trying to keep up. Could ghosts do that? She wasn't sure, and yet even the bees were silent now. Which was a surprise; those buggers hardly ever shut up. Maybe it was the place—God's footprint. It had chased them all out of the hive, left it empty. They couldn't compete with the reality of those solid stone arches and the green pathway to heaven. Although she couldn't help but feel that Byrde wasn't going to like this latest development. Then again, what could he do? He was dead. Whatever her decision, Byrde could stand on the sidelines and shout, but he couldn't step into the fray. And maybe...maybe now he would have his answer—Becca didn't tell because twenty-three years down the line, Finn was going to have to make it right.

'I reckon we were fifteen.' Scratch stared up at the sky, mouth open like he was a kid all over again.

'Not the first time.' Becca could remember it all too clearly. 'We were eight.'

'Eight!' Scratch did his best incredulous look, which had always been way over the top, but Becca knew she was right. She remembered the day as clearly as if it was edged in ink in her brain.

'It was after my mum went.'

'Shit.' Finn's voice echoed off the stones.

He was right; it was shit. Things had been bad at home since forever, but they'd been escalating. She couldn't remember much, but the shouting and the smell of alcohol, that was all somewhere in the mix. Her mum had been one of those women that everyone loved—Bella. Isabella, only no one ever called her that. Poor-Bella, that's what they said, as if it was one word, as though the *poor* was part of her name. Becca couldn't remember much of her, wasn't even sure if the memories she had were true or just wishful thinking. There had been a photo at her gran's, until her dad had smashed it.

'Yeah, we were eight. It was right after Mum left. You wanted to cheer me up, so you suggested this place. Took us two buses to get here.'

'And all our pocket money,' Finn said. 'Not that we cared.'

He added the last part a bit too quick. Becca wondered if he had cared after all. It was Scratch that had been tight with his money, but maybe the past had gotten everyone's motivation confused in its washing machine cycle.

'It did cheer me up,' she said, needing to lift the mood. If she stuck one foot into self-pity, Becca knew she'd never haul herself back out.

'She was a good woman, your mam,' Scratch said.

Becca just nodded.

'And there was never any trace?' Finn's forehead creased into concern. 'You never heard anything? I could pay for a...'

Scratch laughed. 'It's taken Finn this long to get his cheque book out!'

Becca sighed. 'Stop. Scratch, stop. I guess...' She'd rehearsed this through so many times in her head, wondering if she should try and find Bella. Rehearsing how she might go about it. But every time she talked herself out of it. Becca smiled kindly at Finn. 'Thanks Finn, I appreciate it. Only...I guess Mum didn't want to be found. If she did...' Becca shrugged, leaving the implication open. Because surely, by now, the woman would have got in touch.

'Maybe she just got right out,' Scratch said—always the optimist. 'She'll have been living it up in Australia, and sometime soon, she'll come knocking on our door with a koala for the kids.'

'Maybe.' Although Becca didn't want to think like that. It's way too painful to keep holding that door open so a person can return any time it takes their fancy. In truth, Becca had always imagined that her mum was dead. Maybe the man she met after Becca's dad was better with his fists and had managed to punch poor Isabella's lights out quicker. If not, why hadn't she come back? 'Anyway,' Becca shrugged, 'Mum made her choice. And this place does cheer me up, Scratch. You were right. Always.'

He blushed, so full-on flushed he looked like a schoolboy.

'Then we came back another time when we were...?' Finn glanced around as though trying to see his earlier self.

'Thirteen.' Becca remembered because she'd just started her period. In some ways, she was lucky, never had a day of pain. Instead, there was this kind of cold feeling all over her insides as if someone had deep-frozen her stomach. She hadn't been expecting it, thinking it probably wasn't going to happen to her; she was one of the lads. When they'd come up to the abbey, she'd nipped behind a bush to take a pee, and the blood had fallen on the grass, bright red and shining like a ruby. Becca had stared at the gleaming red dot, curious as hell, her pants still wrapped around her ankles. Then she'd realised. So, this was it! *It* had had such a major build-up. The other girls at school talked about it all the time; had some kind of mental league table set up in their brains—who had started when and what degrees of pain. Becca had seen the dispensers in the toilet, and most magazines had adverts. She'd been later than everyone else, but she'd never worried. After all, she was one of the lads. In truth, she hadn't really thought the bleeding would apply to her, but it did.

'You alright?' Scratch asked. 'You're kind of quiet.'

Becca had to stop that, nip that in the bud. 'Course.' Her smile was all bright and breezy. 'It's just odd being back. Not like the house odd, this is...different.' She moved forward towards the wide-open window.

'You remember that promise we made?' Finn asked.

It was winter now, but the place still smelt the same, the grass damp under her feet, the stone.

'I reckon it was about here...' Scratch lined his body between two arches. 'Middle of the nave, but about here.'

Becca glanced around, trying to get a sense of her bearings. 'I think it was closer to the altar.'

Scratch shook his head. 'I reckon it was this window here.' And without waiting for more debate, he dropped down to the ground, star-fishing his body over the cropped grass. 'Come on...' He wriggled his fingers as if they were asking to be held.

'It's damp.' Finn stood there awkwardly. Tall and thin in his fancy coat, not wanting to get it stained.

'Got to be done.' Becca sank down at an angle to Scratch. There was a short shuffle from above. She couldn't see Finn's face anymore, he was blocking out the sun, but damp or no, he was soon laying his body obliquely beside her own. It was as if they were three spokes in a wheel, all holding hands, just like in the old days. Becca was suddenly glad of the quiet; they must have looked daft.

'So, this was the place,' Scratch announced as if he was some kind of reality TV host. 'Where we decided that if there was an award for crappiest parent of the century...'

'Which century?' Finn asked.

'What?'

'We've straddled two.'

Scratch thought for a moment. 'I feel like I should say twentieth, but problem is, crappy parents kind of ripple through time.'

'The Harrises are still fostering,' Becca pointed out.

'Not very often, not anymore,' Scratch added.

Finn's eyes narrowed. 'She's looking after your kids, though, right?'

'More like they'll be looking after her. But yeah...kind of.'

Becca suddenly felt uncomfortable. 'It's not like we had a whole heap of choice.'

Finn turned his face towards her. 'Your Ella?'

'Not fair,' Becca snapped. 'I don't want her to be the default option. I want Ella to have a life.'

There was silence for a moment as they all stared up

into the sky, as though all life plans were laid up pasted to the clouds and on display.

'But Tod Harris is dead, right?'

'He is. Nan Harris married again. His cousin.'

Finn laughed. 'Say no more.'

'Exactly. So, I think we've got to link the two centuries, or even widen it out, possibly go for crappiest parent of all time.'

'Yeah.' Finn sounded resigned. He didn't have the energy to protest.

'Well,' Scratch continued, 'if there was, had been or is ever an award for it, I reckon all of our lot were running neck and neck; nothing to choose between them. 'Part from your mum, Beccs.'

'She ran off, didn't take me with her, believe me. You can throw her in as well.'

'Alright,' Scratch said, still staring towards the sky.

'And that was the reason for the pact.' Becca stared straight up, letting an awkward silence take hold.

'Okay, guys, you remember it?'

Finn laughed. 'You don't seriously want us to say it again? Now?'

Silence.

Finn drew in one long deep breath. The pact was maybe making him just a tad uncomfortable.

'I want all those gathered to swear,' Scratch began slowly, his voice sounding just that notch deeper. 'On these ancient stones that stand around us.'

'They're not even that old.'

'Finn!' Becca hissed.

'I mean not like Stonehenge old.'

'They'll do, brother.' Scratch's voice was still no-messing-low. 'As we lie before the gods in this place of great solemnity.'

Becca could hear a bird singing somewhere. It would be easy to be a bird. Just fly away if you felt like it.

'Eyes shut, please,' Scratch said, squeezing her hand.

'Girl's bloody blouse, this is…'

There was a yank on the circle, Becca figured Finn must have been going for a getaway, but Scratch had pulled him back down.

'Eyes shut.'

Again silence.

'Take this our oath—one out, all out.'

'One out, all out,' they mumbled behind him.

Somewhere, the bird called again, meeting with another song. The note so high, so clear and shrill that music filled the ruin.

Scratch pulled himself up so he was sitting on the damp ground. 'No hiding from promises, hey. They come find you.'

There was a moment's silence, but it was filled with electricity. Tension.

'You got something to say, Scratch?' Finn's voice had a hard edge; one Becca hadn't heard for years. A little too defensive.

'Me, mate?' Scratch laughed, holding up his hands like he'd been caught out. 'I've always got something to say. Verbal bloody diarrhoea.'

'This grass is wet.' Becca pulled herself to her feet. 'It's gone through to my thermals.'

'Had to be done, Beccs, history's a powerful thing, and our history, it's important. Don't you forget it.'

'Well…' Finn dusted the wet grass off his jeans. 'We all got out.'

'In our own fashion,' Scratch mumbled as Becca stared up again at the sky, that exact same colour as it was all those years ago. In her heart of hearts, she wasn't convinced that any of them really got out.

'Hey, what do you say? Hide and seek?'

Before they'd even had time to answer, Scratch was running off down the green baize.

'Scratch, no way. I'm cold and damp now.'

'It'll be a laugh, like old times.' He ducked behind a pillar.

Becca shook her head. She could do without this. 'We're too big to bloody hide.'

'He's your husband.'

She felt a twinge in her gut; it was okay for her to insult Scratch, but Finn, no, that would be all too easy. 'He's a good man, Finn.'

'I never said he wasn't.' Finn took a step backward as he spoke.

'We need to talk, Finn.' Becca wasn't sure this was the best place, wasn't sure she knew what she had to say, but if she didn't get it off her chest soon, it would explode out of her, uncontrolled and angry as hell.

'Sure.'

Only the slippery bugger was backing off.

She glanced down at his hand, to the band of white flesh where the ring used to be. 'I saw...'

'Oi, come on, Finn.' Scratch's voice appeared to come from everywhere, all around, ricocheting off the stone pillars. 'Becca, start counting.'

'He's right,' Finn said.

Becca looked at him, lost.

'You need to count.' Finn turned his back on her. 'You're it, Beccs.' And off he ran.

23

OLD MAID

(A game for two or more players. Requires a standard pack of cards with a joker added. Cards are divided equally. Pairs of cards are removed from each player's hand. Players attempt to get rid of all the cards in their hand by drawing from their opponent. The player left with the joker—the 'old maid'—loses.)

Sitting in the tearoom, sandwiched between tables, the clutter of cutlery, the steam fogging the windows, Finn was not looking happy. 'You didn't shuffle properly.'

'I shuffled fine,' Scratch said, a knowing twinkle in his eye. 'You've got her then, the lovely lady?'

Becca pulled a single card from Finn's hand. 'Well, looks like I'm out.' Relieved, she sat back in her chair, placing her cards down on the table.

Finn's lips settled into a narrow line. 'How come it's always just the two of us?'

Scratch shrugged, repositioning his three remaining

cards, pulling one so far up in the centre it was practically begging to be plucked.

Finn eyed it wearily, wondering if it was a double bluff. Impossible to tell with Scratch.

'Just do it.' Becca lifted the teapot and went to pour, but the stream of brown liquid ran dry. 'We need a refill.' She pushed her chair back.

'Wait, Beccs.' Scratch didn't even bother looking up. 'I like you to see me beat him. The luck's always on my side, at least where cards and love are concerned.' He reached out and patted her leg.

Finn's fingers extended, hovering out over the three cards, grabbing the central card in one clean sweep.

The tearoom echoed with Scratch's laughter. 'Double bluff there, and he sussed me. He's sharp, Beccs. You have to say that for those city boys—always one step ahead.'

Scratch took Finn's last card and abandoned the joker leaving it staring up from the table. 'I'll get that next round.'

'It's fine, Scratch, my treat.' Finn pulled out his wallet. Becca couldn't help noticing that it didn't bulge anymore, didn't need to. Those slim plastic cards were carrying all the weight.

'Think not, mate. Tea and cakes, I can support. Champagne at the strip joint, that's your ticket.'

'So, we're seriously going?' Finn looked amused.

'It's a stag,' Scratch stood, stretching out his legs, 'not a wake. So, yup, Champagne and lovely ladies are next on the itinerary. Only, I'm taking mine in with me.'

He kissed the top of Becca's head as if she were a kid, or property, or maybe even a pet.

Becca stared after him as he walked away, just like she would with any of the kids. Only this time, her motivation was different. She had private stuff she wanted to get off her chest. Becca wanted to be sure there was no doubling back with a wisecrack. But no, he was gone, and when she looked down at the table, she realised she'd picked up the card, got it clutched between her fingers: the joker or the old maid. Same difference. She placed it back on the table, turning the card, so its face was down, glancing at Finn's hands splayed out on the tabletop, at the white raw band of flesh on his finger.

'Daisy wanted your old ring?'

'Yeah.' He smiled fondly. 'So maybe she's not the gold digger you're making her out to be.'

'I didn't say...'

'No,' Finn drew out the word, nodding his head, taking his time, 'but you thought.'

Becca took a moment to sip her tea. It was cold, but she swallowed anyway. 'Well, she's a bit younger. People talk.'

When Becca was with Finn, the conversation, she noticed, spun out as if the words were hopelessly inadequate, resounding into a void. It was as though the whole time-space continuum thing had dropped into a different gear.

'What *people think*, Beccs? Like that bothered any of us.' Finn skirted the metal teaspoon around his cup as though he was a conductor waiting for an orchestra of sound to rush in. It didn't. There was just that high-pitched metal sweep.

'Becca, are you?'

'I was...'

Their voices clashed somewhere mid-table. They silent-smiled, lips caught on teeth, hearts pushing up hard through chests.

'You first...' She nodded, glancing at the door. Scratch must have taken a sidestep into the men's toilets; she was safe to say what she had to. Which was good because Scratch didn't need to know the details. Finn could make it look like another generous donation.

'I just,' Finn broke the silence, 'I wanted...to ask if you were happy?'

The comment hit her off-centre; Becca was no longer in the driving seat, not even sure where the pedals were or how to accelerate away to safer ground. She found herself blustering in with an answer before she'd even worked out where it was going. 'Course, well...'

'Only you don't seem it?'

'No, I've just... It's been tough recently. Money troubles.' It won't hurt, she thought, to get that part in—seed it so it could bloom later in the conversation.

Finn gave her a sympathetic look and a 'Sorry' before he shrugged his cashmere-clad shoulders as if money troubles were beyond his understanding.

'But you and Scratch, it's all working out?'

Maybe this was her way to approach it? 'Five kids, and you ask me that?'

'I wasn't asking about the kids, Becca. Not really. I was asking about you.'

God, this man! He really was on planet solo. 'I am the kids, Finn. Like it or not. We're all bound up in the same jumble sale. And...that's why...' she had to go for it now, 'the money problem, it's a...I mean, it is a real problem.'

'Ella's okay?'

'Yeah, sure. And we're grateful, I mean really grateful— you paying her fees. But...' Becca went for direct contact: holding his eyes fast with hers. And she was punched once again by that thought that was never far from her mind— why did he still have to be so bloody good-looking? Couldn't he have lost his hair, just a little from the front? Couldn't he have put on a few hard-to-shift tyres around his middle? Couldn't the years have cracked his forehead into crisscrossed spaghetti lines? No. She took in a deep breath. 'Only I've got four other kids. I was just thinking...'

'Beccs, you know I'll help if I can.'

'Yeah, yeah... But I thought maybe it might be an idea. I thought maybe you could set up a trust fund for the kids? Just so we all know what page we're on. If it's not too...'

Finn's body shifted awkwardly, and he glanced down at his hands. 'I mean...I'd like to... But...sometimes the financial market it's not always...'

No, she thought. This was not happening. She couldn't let him go down the *but* route. 'Sure,' she said, her voice sounding surprisingly breathless. 'But I mean compared to what Scratch earns. You know we made that vow—one out, all out.'

'Becca, we were kids. I mean...I'm strapped at the moment. We've just bought a new place in Islington. I even had to cut down on all my charity work.'

'Charity work.'

'A charity in Manchester, supporting kids with...'

'Crap parents?'

He smiled. 'Yes.'

She felt tears stinging her eyes.

'The house and having to support someone.'

'Daisy?'

'Daisy.'

The word stung.

'But when everything settles down...'

Settles down. She knew what that meant: a couple of new cars, a villa in the south of France.

'Finn, I saw what you did,' she blurted, the colour rising in her cheeks.

'Sorry?' He glanced over at the door. Scratch was filling it, grinning ear to ear as if he was the only creature on the planet that could start their party. Finn raised his hand and smiled.

'I saw,' Becca hissed. 'That night when Byrde died, Finn, I was there.'

His face dropped. Becca felt confused, unsure what it was showing, not fear, no, not that.

'Hey.' Scratch was standing over them, omnipresent as a magic genie conjured up through a trap door. 'The queue for tea is like sale time at Oxfam. You want to hit the road? We can grab something in town.'

They left the cards on the table, the joker sandwiched between teacups and crumbs. As they navigated out of the room, dancing around the tables, Becca made a mental note —they needed to keep Scratch out of this. If he was in the dark, he couldn't withhold evidence. If the shit did suddenly hit the fan about Byrde, at least there would be one person kept out of the clink; someone to look after the brood. Finn could free up some of those assets. He'd have to. She deserved that.

24

CONSEQUENCES

(A game for multiple players, similar to the Surrealist game Old Corpse. Each person takes a strip of paper and a pencil. They draw a hat, fold the paper down so the hat is covered, then hand the paper on. Players then draw a face, fold the paper down and pass the paper on. In this fashion, they continue working down through the body until an image is completed: a character made of many different parts.)

The room was dark: womb-like. The soft jazz beat appearing to seep out of the very walls smooth as a honey trap. Becca insisted they curl up in one of the high-backed booths. Scratch, being Scratch, had wanted to sit right by the stage. No doubt wanting a little spotlight for himself, but even Finn had said he'd prefer to keep a bit of distance, and it was his stag.

As the evening wore on and the drinks piled up, the women got younger and fresher. Until one pale, thin dancer appeared to be barely out of high school, with her long, white-blonde wavy hair and massive blue eyes. She looked a bit like Elsa from *Frozen*. Becca couldn't help feeling that the girl had been drafted in to the wrong story. Becca wasn't sure if there was a rule on how old you had to be to do this kind of thing, but whatever it was, it was too low.

'She's just a kid,' Becca whispered sadly over her champagne glass.

The drinks cost fifty quid for every thimble full. The lads had segued on to beers, but Becca had been curious when they wound up with the drinks menu; she wanted to see where Finn's line on the disposable cash front lay—what kind of price would make him baulk? The money tree didn't seem to be bottoming out any time soon. She'd had two glasses already, and it looked as though her brain would be pickled before Finn called a halt to the process. He was up at the bar again, ordering more, even though her glass was still half full.

'She's not that young.' Scratch gave the girl the once over, not paying much attention. 'It's just 'cus we're getting older. She's mid-twenties.'

Becca wasn't so sure.

'Can't hold a candle to you, my love,' taking her hand and pressing it to his lips. 'But...maybe Finn might fancy a little more than just two pot-bellied old codgers.'

'Speak for yourself.'

'What were you talking about?'

'What?'

'To Finn, in the café. What were you saying?'

Becca shook her head dismissively. 'Just asking him, you know, about Daisy.'

'He looked...odd.'

'Odd?'

'Kind of shocked.'

'I told him...' She scooted around her brain, looking for plausible stories she could throw into the mix. Suddenly the fruits of her eavesdropping came back to her. 'Told him not to have a kid.' The lie dried like arsenic on her tongue.

'So he says now,' Scratch said, swilling the liquid idly around in his glass before taking a slug.

Luckily Scratch had never been one for listening to details. He'd probably still been pissed out of his head when Finn had had his little heart-to-heart.

But the lie had served its purpose. 'Exactly.' She lay her hand gently across Scratch's. He was too easy to deceive. It made her love him more though, love him as she would a child. Surely that was wrong though. Her husband was not a child. He was her rock. The beat of the music pumped through Becca's eardrums, and she began to feel those familiar bees buzzing somewhere under the baseline, and with them, with the champagne, with the light feeling in her head and the womb-like confessional of the room, and the broken lie still sitting on her tongue, Becca had an itch to tell Scratch all. So what if he did know all the details? Scratch was no angel. They were in this together; that's what a marriage was.

'Scratch, that night...'

'Sorry love, I can't hear.' Amused, he shook his head, as if trying to dislodge a blockage.

She moved closer. 'I wanted to say, to tell you that...'

'Beccs,' he laughed, 'you're tickling my ear.'

'But I...'

'Later, love,' he shouted over the music, as two more drinks edged onto the table.

'Got two a piece.' Finn took another couple of glasses from the tray and propped them in front of Becca.

So...the man was nowhere near his financial pain threshold.

A cocktail waitress saw Finn struggling and came over to

clear the empties, but Scratch waved her away. 'These are our trophies, love, all our conquests.' He shot her a cheeky smile. 'You impressed?'

She nodded, widening her eyes, as if she seriously was, though, in truth, she probably saw a lot of *conquests*.

'Tell you what, we need a bigger table.' Finn glanced around the room.

'By the dance floor. By the dance floor,' Scratch started to chant. 'Long as you don't get up.' He ran one hand gently over Becca's body. 'My eyes only,' he said, standing and toppling towards the dancer. 'Close enough for ya?' he shouted back.

Finn just laughed. 'Sure. Why not.'

Becca looked down at the glasses. Was she supposed to ferry them over?

'Wait.' Finn grabbed his phone and took a snap of all the empties crowding the table before idling to their new banquette and propping his phone screen up, with its image of the empty glasses on full display. 'Absent friends,' he said, which started a whole new round of backslapping and guffaws.

'SEE FRIENDSHIP, FOR ME,' Scratch slurred, barely able to keep his head up, 'friendship is what underpins the whole of the social system.' He fumbled over the term. 'You, me, Beccs, what we have is something so...' He went to pour a bottle into his glass, but not one drop eased out: empty. 'What we have,' he repeated, looking surprised, 'is a serious drink problem. Lack of, not personal *drink problem* o'course...' He glanced around him. The waitresses were curiously absent. Scratch stood, looking for attention, but getting none, so he teetered forward a little, resting a hand on Finn's shoulder. 'Can I stick it on your tab, mate?'

Finn nodded. He hadn't been drinking as much: someone had to drive. He'd started off thinking they'd get a taxi home, but currently, he appeared to be stuck between bravado and moderately inebriated. The *bravado* meant he would drive. Becca knew he would. She should have complained. If it was Scratch, she wouldn't get in the car, but...just this once. Nothing bad could happen to them, not if it was only this once. She could see Scratch at the far end of the bar. He kind of missed it, waving as he passed. Stumbling a little and grabbing hold of the edge of the shiny walnut-style surface before laughing as though the stumble past was all part of his plan.

The dancers had changed so many times that Becca couldn't keep up anymore. The current woman on stage was a little older, although Becca would still only give her twenty-five. However old she was, it was still too young. Did they realise, Becca wondered, just how young they really were? This time the woman was dressed in red ribbons. The type that circus acrobats wear so they can wind themselves up and down from the ceiling like yo-yos.

'You wanted to know why, Finn?' Becca said, emboldened by the drink, the music, the woman dancing for their entertainment.

'Sorry?' Finn peeled his eyes away.

'Why I acted so...odd that time when we went swimming.'

Suddenly Finn was all bright eyes and attention, and she got the feeling he wasn't half as drunk as she'd thought.

'We had something, Becca. I seriously thought...'

'Water under the bridge now...' A ribbon flew out from

the stage towards her as though the woman was a spider keen to catch Becca neatly in its web.

'Because I know, Finn. I saw.'

'Beccs, I don't know what you...?'

But suddenly, he stopped. He was glancing over at the bar. She followed his gaze. Scratch was standing there asking for drinks, and this woman, this blonde, forty-five or thereabouts, was making a beeline for him. She was thin and angular in an animal print jacket that looked cheap, her body crumpled slightly inside it; as though she had no muscle to keep her clothes in shape.

'Can't keep their hands to themselves,' Becca said. She wasn't impressed, but she wasn't surprised either.

Finn's eyes narrowed. 'Do you know that woman?'

'Finn,' she shot him a mock-shock look before taking a swig of her champagne. 'It's not that kind of a place.' She looked around again just as the woman pulled Scratch into a hug.

'It just...' Finn turned back to Becca. 'It looks like she knows Scratch. She recognised him. And she does look kind of...'

'Finn. Stop changing the bloody subject. These women, they're all old bloody friends. We can find one for you if you fancy? Look, Finn.' Becca edged closer, wishing she wasn't so drunk. 'You need to listen to me. Finn!' She pulled his face back around to hers, away from the scrappy woman in the too cheap coat. Using his chin to angle his face into position. 'I was there,' she hissed, leaning forward into his space: all champagne breath and over sincere. 'I was in the house when Byrde died, and I saw...I saw who did it.'

Finn stared at her hard for a moment, neither of them saying a thing. Was it shock? Of course, it must be. She realised she had to bring it back around. In any discussion, you need to think of your end goal. Her end goal: family and kids. 'It was my dad who started it. He beat me up…'

'Becca, I…'

She shook her head, wobbling it a little too much on her neck, but the alcohol had loosened everything. 'Shhh. No sympathy, please. In fact, it was one of the last bloody times he really went for it. But the point is…I ran around to your house because…because that's what I always did. But surprise, surprise, you weren't there.'

'Look, I know your dad was a bastard, but I had a life too. You can't blame me for…I wasn't on call twenty-four-seven.'

'Yeah, I figured that.' Becca gave him a long hard woozy-at-the-edges stare. She hadn't felt like this for years, but at that very moment in time, she couldn't help it. She hated him. Hated him for buggering up just about everything. 'Anyways, Byrde found me. He'd driven into town for groceries, and there I was, skirt ripped, bruises down my legs, on my arm. He pulled into the kerb and said he'd take me to the hospital.'

'What did he do to you?' Finn's face was white as a sheet. If he'd been drunk earlier, there wasn't a trace of it now. The conversation was sobering him up.

'Byrde? Nothing.' She sighed melodramatically, remembering a time long gone and a quiet-spoken man who had helped her. 'He was nice. Byrde was alright. He knew me, my mum. He was… He wanted to take me to the hospital.'

'You said that.'

She stopped. Irritated with herself. God, those bees were buzzing. Even over the harsh baseline of the music system, she could hear them. 'I said no. Didn't want to go.' She let the thought flood her with bitterness. 'God, if only I'd said yes, hey?'

'I don't know, Beccs...'

'But you do, Finn. You do. Because I saw.' Another silence. She took her time now, stared up into his face, hard as a rock. 'And now I want something for it.'

'Know what, guys and gals.' Scratch was standing over them. 'Think I've had enough. Just realised the prices of those bloody drinks. Finn, my man, we need to move onwards and upwards.' He stared at the woman on the dance floor, her body disappearing behind a ribbon. 'You want a take-out?'

Finn said nothing, just shook his head.

If Scratch had been a more perceptive kind of a person, he'd have noticed that something was up. But the drink, and the day, and the excitement, it had all gone to his head. 'Pity.' Scratch smirked, lifting a beer bottle to his lips and draining it dry. 'What happens at Byrde's house stays at Byrde's house.' And he let out a laugh at his own joke.

25

OUIJA BOARD

(A game for multiple players. A flat board is marked with the letters of the alphabet and the words yes or no. Players place one finger on a heart-shaped counter, taking turns to ask questions as the counter spells out answers.)

'I've just had one of my brilliant ideas,' Scratch announced as they piled through the front door of Byrde's old house, ragged as leaves blown by the wind.

Why was it always whipping up a storm up on the escarpment? Becca's head felt as though it was splitting in two, but Scratch hadn't been able to stop grinning all the way home as if he had some massive secret that was burning a hole in his brain.

'Scratch, I'm dog-tired. Can whatever it is wait till tomorrow?'

'Beccs! It won't take a minute. Besides, listen to that...' He stopped, head cocked to one side. Even with the door shut firmly behind them, the wind was howling, excited as a four-year-old as it ran laps around the house. 'Perfect night for it. You get the kettle on.' And with that, he disappeared upstairs. Leaving Finn and Becca to stand for a moment in the hallway. Frozen momentarily like spikes of frost, before Finn broke the moment with a question.

'Does he ever get tired?'

Becca shrugged. 'You'd know as well as me.' She kicked off her shoes. The mud scrape of her boots, still there on the white wall, offered her a smidgen of comfort: a direct line to reality. 'That was me,' she said, easing her toe along the edge of the mark. 'You think you'll lose your deposit?'

'I don't care. What were you saying when we were in the club?'

Becca glanced up the stairs. Scratch would be back any minute and she didn't want her husband in on this. It was between her and Finn and maybe Byrde.

'Nothing. You want tea?'

'Nah.' Finn sauntered off into the sunroom, calling over his shoulder. 'Shall I light the fire?'

She wandered after him. 'It's late.'

'It's ten o'clock.'

Was that all? Christ, it felt later. She shrugged. 'Bit of a lightweight, I'm afraid. Know what I'd really like?' Purposefully, she walked over to where his case still sat. She couldn't help herself; she slipped her hand inside the soft leather pockets feeling for the book. Grasping it in her fingers.

Finn had her back to her, setting the burner, but he was on to it in an instant, pulling the book from her hands. His face looked hurt, betrayed, as though she'd picked his heart out from his chest and skewered it with her fingernail.

He eased his free hand over its cover, protectively. 'I should put this somewhere out of harm's reach.'

Despite her curiosity and the skinful of champagne, Becca couldn't agree more.

'I won't try and grab it again.' She indicated towards the cold log burner. 'Light the fire if you want. Scratch'll always stay up for a chinwag. Getting him to slow down's never been easy.'

'I take that as a compliment.' Scratch filled the doorway, big grin on his face, and a battered old game box clutched in his hand.

'Scratch,' she felt her shoulders sag. 'What is that?' Somehow she got the feeling whatever it was wouldn't be welcome. Not at this time of night.

He smiled, choosing to ignore her resistance. 'This...' Scratch waved the box in the air, 'just so happens to be the definitive answer to all your questions.'

They both stared at Scratch, feeling blank and exhausted, but Scratch had never been someone to be deterred by a lack of enthusiasm.

He pushed the rectangular box out into the room. 'A Ouija board.'

Becca felt a shiver of ice pass down her spine.

'Found it upstairs. It's dead fancy and all, real wood and everything.' He knocked on the box as if he had to prove just what a class bit of kit this thing was.

Becca sighed. There was no way she was going to play. Byrde needed no encouragement to start up a conversation. He was way too active as it was. 'Leave me out.' She pushed past Scratch. 'I'm off to bed.'

'Beccs! The night's only just started. It'll be a laugh. We can get hold of Old Man Byrde.'

'Scratch!'

'What do you think he'd have to say to us, hey?'

'Leave it, mate.' Finn's voice was quiet, barely audible, but sharp as an axe.

'Leave it!' Scratch laughed. 'I seriously doubt that's what the old guy would be saying. I reckon he'd have much more to say than *leave it. You Pesky Kids*.' Scratch laughed again, oblivious to the fact that, for Becca, the room had begun reeling like a whirlpool.

'Pesky kids.' Scratch laughed again. 'You remember that? Scooby-Doo. If it wasn't for you...'

Finn raised his eyes, and with a tired, ironic lilt said, 'We remember.'

'See what I mean. This...' he raised the Ouija board yet again, 'it's got to be done.'

'Scratch, drop it.' Becca's voice sounded hard and on edge.

'Aw, Beccs,' he gave her his puppy dog, all-innocence look. 'Why?'

'Because I asked you politely. Put the bloody thing back in the drawer. Don't go messing with stuff like that. It's bad luck.'

Scratch glanced at the board as though seeing it suddenly for the first time. 'Hmm. Good point. Had more than my fill on the bad luck front.'

'I'm done,' she said, walking off down the hallway, grabbing the banister for support. 'I'm going to have a bath. Hit the sack.'

No one bothered to call her back.

When Becca got safely upstairs, she didn't start the bath. Instead, she flopped down on the bed and stared up at the ceiling which was spinning slightly. She'd drank far too much. Becca could still hear the men from downstairs. The game had been put on the back burner, thank God. But they appeared to have no plans of curtailing the night. Scratch had headed for the kitchen. She could hear him humming as he paced around, opening draws, boiling the kettle. Then there was the click, click, click of the toaster.

'You want a slice, Finn?' He called out into the echoing house, mindless as to whether she was trying to sleep or not.

Tea and toast happened to be Scratch's answer to everything. It was about the extent of his culinary skills: buttered toast and a hard-boiled egg. Eggy toast, if you were really lucky.

Tomorrow was their last day. Becca let the thought flit through her head. She was going to have to get Finn on his own. She knew she needed to get their *agreement* signed off before they went home. The next time they met, it was going to be all confetti and roses. Leaving aside the Godfather franchise, that sort of thing didn't exactly mix well with bribery and corruption.

'Is she okay?' Becca heard Finn asking.

In her head, she could picture that dollhouse, the one she never got, the three figures moving in orchestrated jumps around the rooms, living out their lives.

'Just tired, I reckon.'

There was a brief silence, then Finn picked it up again. This time, his voice was coming from the kitchen. 'Only she was talking about Byrde?'

The bees in her head begin to buzz. They liked it when people talked about Byrde. Byrde was the "big picture". Becca slid herself off the bed and walked out to the landing. There was one of those chaise things out there. It was too narrow to lie on comfortably. A wash of textured vanilla with a perfect piping of dove grey around the edges. The kind of thing you see in magazines; looks great but isn't practical or comfortable. Becca perched on it anyway. She needed to hear, needed to know, needed to check that everyone in the house was in the right place.

'I guess it's being back here,' Scratch said, lightly. 'You sure you don't want toast?'

'I'm fine. Only...she said...Becca said she was here the night Byrde died?'

Absolute silence. Even the wind outside shut up at this latest revelation. The silence seemed to last forever. Finally Scratch cleared his throat. 'This house? Byrde's house?'

'Yeah.'

'You sure?'

'That's what she said.'

Scratch took in a deep breath, as though thinking it over. A deep breath then a small dismissive laugh. 'She was drunk, mate. I mean, look at this...'

Becca could hear stuff clattering out onto the table. If she had to hazard a guess, she'd say it was most likely the contents of her handbag.

'I mean, seriously?' Scratch's voice sounded taut. 'What is all this crap? Oxy bloody.' He sighed in frustration. 'Too many frigging letters. Pills and pills. Can you even drink when you're on this stuff? Becca hardly touches alcohol back home, and she was seriously putting it away tonight.'

'Shit.'

Sitting hunched up on the landing, tears stang at Becca's eyes. Yes, that was about the size of it; shake her hard, and she'd practically rattle.

'I didn't realise.'

'Hey. Not your fault. Like I said...you know, sometimes she's a bit fragile. Not your problem. You mate, you're a star. All of this,' Scratch paused as if giving himself time to gesticulate around the room, take it all in. 'It's been good for us, seriously. Today was a bloody good day.'

'And you knew that woman?'

Becca opened her eyes wide, not entirely sure what Finn was saying. From the sound of his reply, neither was Scratch.

'Sorry?'

'In the club. The woman in the club?'

Scratch laughed. 'Very friendly, those women. *Recognise* anyone, give them half a chance.'

'It was just.'

'Toast?' The sound of a plate slid across the wide breakfast bar.

'Thanks.'

That was the last thing she remembered. When she'd woken, cold and stiff, there was the shape of someone standing over her in the darkness. She gasped as though her heart had just been jump-started.

'Steady,' Scratch's voice came soft and clear out of the darkness.

Becca felt his hand reaching gently for her shoulder. She had no idea where she was. Her brain hadn't caught up with her body. Besides, it was so dark.

'You fell asleep, love.'

'I...where am I?'

'Finn's stag. We're at Byrde's place.' Scratch's voice was gentle as a night nurse.

Becca felt a soft blanket being draped around her shoulders; she'd caught him in the act of tucking her in, not wanting to disturb her. As gently as if he was sorting one of the kids.

'Couldn't have you catching cold.' He caught sight of her hand on the blanket. It was shaking. 'Are you alright, Beccs?'

His voice was full of concern. He knelt down beside her, staring into her eyes.

'I'm shattered, Scratch.'

Her husband ran one gentle hand through her hair and gazed long and hard into her eyes. 'Best get you to bed then.'

Becca stood, her limbs feeling sluggish and heavy as Scratch helped her back into their room.

'You can have a lie-in tomorrow,' he said, rubbing her shoulder gently. 'We don't have to be out till one.'

'Great.' She sank down heavily on the bed, making the headboard bounce for a moment as it knocked against the wall.

'Here.' He lifted her arms and pulled her sweater over her head.

Her body felt boneless and out of control. No longer hers. 'How can you drink so much,' she mumbled, 'without feeling out of it?'

'Always could. You, on the other hand...' He kissed the top of her head.

'Don't,' she groaned, the course sound of a killer hang-over already lacing her voice.

'We need you out of those trousers.'

Becca lifted her legs, and he yanked at the material at her ankles.

'God, Scratch, I'm such a bloody mess.'

'You've had too much to drink. I should have stopped you.'

'What would I do without you, hey?' A sob caught in her throat, and she looked up into his eyes.

He took her face in his hands. 'Doesn't bear thinking about.'

'It's the bees,' she mumbled, barely audible, as they started to buzz. Didn't the buggers ever go to sleep?

'What?'

She shook her head. 'In my brain.'

'Becca, there's nothing in your *brain*.' He smoothed his hand across her forehead. 'You're alright. You hear?'

She nodded. 'If I don't brush my teeth, it'll taste like someone's died in my mouth.'

He smiled. 'I won't kiss you.'

She sank back onto the springs. 'I ought to...' But she didn't have the energy.

'Tomorrow.' He threw back the blankets so she could ease herself under the sheets.

'Scratch, if anything was to happen to me...'

'Beccs, love, nothing's going to happen to you.'

'Yes, but if it did.' She eased her naked legs over the cool, crisp cotton of the bed.

'This is just silly talk.'

'But it's not, because sometimes, Scratch, even though I know, I've got everything—you, the kids, everything. Sometimes I'm so...so sad.' Her head crushed back on the pillow.

'Hey, let's talk about this tomorrow.'

She shook her head sadly. 'It's like this enormous weight. I feel like I'm dragging around...everything...my whole life, and it's all...it's all no good.'

'Becca!'

'No, not you...not the kids...not all of that. It's me...as though I'm diseased, useless, just wrong.'

'Never. You are... Love, you are the pillar of our world. You hold everything up. You're like the central pole in the big top. Without you, we're just this useless piece of canvas lying on the ground, all pretty colours but with no shape. No purpose.'

'But I'm...Scratch when I get in the shower...I take a shower, and I feel the water running over my body, but there's nothing. It's as though all my nerve endings are dead. The sun on my face...nothing. I feel nothing. I'm dead. I'm wandering around dead, and then... Then when I do start to feel, when I do start to finally feel again, I'm feeling all the wrong things and I'm scared.'

'Wrong things?' He stopped for a moment, and she could feel his eyes scanning her face. He was scared too, and she didn't want Scratch to be scared, but she couldn't help it.

'Not like...no...wrong. Crap, crap things, and loathing such deep loathing.'

'Tell you what, I'm going to get you one of your tablets...'

He magicked a little brown bottle into his hands. Had the pills been there in his hand all along? She wasn't sure.

Becca pushed the bottle away. 'No...I...'

'Just one, Beccs. So you're not low.'

'But I can sleep...'

'Not in this state. Just one. It'll be fine.' He went into the bathroom and grabbed a glass of water, returning with it and holding it out to her. Cupping the back of her neck to pull her up slightly. 'Here, just half a one. Just a bit.' Emptying a small white pill into his hand, he held it out towards her lips. 'Can't do any harm.'

She took the pill, chasing it down with a gulp of water.

'You've just got yourself in a state, Beccs. Tomorrow, guess what, last day I'm going to treat you—I've booked you into that beauty salon in the village.'

'Scratch!'

'No, I did. Fuck, know what? I hardly ever treat you, and I should. I really should because...you...I love you, Beccs, always have.'

Becca nodded sadly because the awful thing was, that part had never been in any doubt. Only what was truly heartbreaking was that Becca wasn't sure that Scratch's love made any difference. In fact, maybe it made everything so much worse.

'Hey, come on.' Scratch gently drew a finger below her eyes, and she realised she'd been crying. 'Dry these,' he said softly. 'Try to sleep. That's all you have to do. And tomorrow... Tomorrow well, my love, that's another day.'

26

MUSICAL CHAIRS

(A game of elimination for multiple players. When the music stops, all players must find a chair. There is always one less chair than there are players. When a player fails to find a chair, they are eliminated. After each round, a chair is removed. The process is repeated until only one player remains.)

Becca shouldn't have taken the tablet. Scratch's style of medical knowledge was one hundred per cent slapdash and take a guess. He had no idea what he'd given her. Three AM and Becca's eyes rolled open. It felt like her blood was dancing as opposed to flowing through her veins. She looked over to where he lay beside her, drinking in the night air, content as a walrus. It must be so easy being Scratch. They had money worries, but day to day, they got through. Something turned up. That was Scratch's mantra, and it always did. He always managed to scrape past the finish line, living life being just lucky enough.

Macbeth, Becca thought as she eased herself from the

acres of crisp cotton sheets and onto her feet. She seemed to remember from Ella's English GCSE Macbeth was the bright spark who murdered sleep. Well, Scratch appeared to have made his own half-arsed attempt, with his stab at medication coupled with his own personal hibernation night vocals. But at least the bees had stopped. At least the hopelessness had left. She pushed her nails into her skin. Now she had her answer. No pain. Yep—she was completely dead. The pill had been one too many. Thank the Lord for small mercies. Despite the hour, she knew Finn would be awake. Becca might have been dead inside, but she'd spent her life being so attuned to that man. She had known even before she'd pulled back the blankets and stepped out of bed into the cold room that somewhere in the house, Finn was waiting.

'Did you have fun tonight, then?' Becca leaned in through the doorway to the sunroom.

'Shit,' Finn started, turning sharply. 'You scared me. I thought you were in bed.'

He was in his pyjamas. A crisp striped cotton. Despite the hour, he looked so natural sitting there in the expensive chair, the expensive room, the expensive house.

'I couldn't sleep. Well...' She tied the dressing gown she'd bought from home tighter around her waist. 'I got off, but then...'

'Yeah.' He nodded, staring back into the grate.

'You got the fire going then?'

'I wasn't really cold, just...couldn't sleep either.'

In fact, despite the prowling wind outside, the room was warm, too warm, like a hot bath. Becca idled slowly in, pulled herself up a corner of the sofa and curled her feet up under her body. 'So, did you have fun?'

'Fun? No... No, I wouldn't say that.' Finn glanced over at

her, holding her inside those blue eyes. 'Becca, we need to talk.'

She raised one eyebrow. 'But where to start, hey?'

'I know exactly where to start.'

And for just a moment, it was as if the whole world stood still. *This is it*, Becca thought. This is where everything comes apart. Thank God.

'I sometimes think...' Finn sighed wearily, pulling one hand through his hair. 'I sometimes think that our lives got set on the wrong track.'

'Well, maybe that's...'

He held up a hand to stop her. 'You need to listen, Beccs. Because whatever we did wrong in the past, and believe me, there was plenty, but whatever it was, it can't keep rolling forward, polluting the present. We're running out of time.'

And for a moment, just a moment, Finn reminded Becca of Phillips with his CBT and sincere eyes and always living in the here and now. Only Becca had never been interested in living in the present with Mr Phillips. No, there was only one person Becca had ever truly wanted to be living *in the present with*, and there he was, sitting so close to her she could reach out and touch him. Looking so...so serious.

Finn glanced down at his hands, at that white mark where the ring should have been. 'In a few weeks, I'll be married to Daisy and don't get me wrong, because nothing's ever too late. But what I'll be doing is bringing one more person inside this sorry mess.'

'Scratch isn't a mess.'

'We all are, Beccs. All of us together, and none of it does anybody any good. D'you think Scratch doesn't know, deep down?' Finn got up and moved across the room to the sofa where she'd taken up residence, sat himself down, just a little too close, and yet she didn't move. 'Do you seriously think?' Finn continued, making a small choking noise, glancing up at the ceiling as if maybe all the answers were written up there. 'Becca, every time I'm with you, whenever you're close, it feels…'

'Then take some bloody pills. Take some pills to stop it *feeling*. This, what you're doing here, it doesn't help.'

She couldn't do this, didn't want to know, and those bees. She felt as if her entire head was going to split in two because part of what Finn was saying, most of what he was saying, was everything that Becca had been hiding from for most of her life.

Finn edged closer. So close he was barely sitting on the sofa anymore. He was leaning out towards her as if any minute he'd grab hold of her and carry her away. But it was all too late. Surely, it was too late?

'When I'm with you, Becca, I feel alive. The rest of my life, I'm sleepwalking. I'm like a zombie.'

'Finn, you have to stop this.' It was the trust funds she needed, financial security, something for the kids.

'Then tell me you don't feel the same way?'

'I have to go back to bed.' She couldn't handle this. It was like picking old wounds. Becca got to her feet, but Finn was quicker, grabbing her by the arm.

'We need to talk about this now.'

'Why?' Tears stung her eyes. 'So we save Daisy some pain?' The woman's name flew out of Becca's mouth, bitter as an insult. 'Daisy, bloody Daisy. You think I care? What about Scratch? Your best mate, my husband, the father of my five beautiful kids. You seriously think I could give a stuff about Daisy. This is all twenty years too late. You went away, Finn. You changed, not me.'

'No.'

'And then there were all those other women at university.'

His mouth opened wide in a gasp of indignation as he shook his head. 'There weren't any other women.'

'There were stacks of them. Pretty smiles in all the photos.'

'It didn't mean anything.'

Her fingers knotted in her lap, unable to sit still. 'Prince Charming all the fucking time.'

'Stop. Becca, every time you walk into a room, the world disappears for me.'

She snorted. 'Lucky you. I have mouths to feed and people to worry about.'

His voice rasped angrily in his throat as if stating the obvious. 'It's destroying you.'

'So, what's the alternative? Run off, like mother like daughter. That woman ruined my life. I have to stay. Can't you see that?'

'It cannot be too late, Becca. I've walked barefoot over hot coals for all these years. As long as the game was you and Scratch, as long as I thought you were happy, well... maybe I could put up with that. But you're not happy.'

'You're talking like a kid.'

'I don't care. Becca, I want to possess every inch of you. Touch you. I am so desperate to press my fingers into your skin.' His hands slipped onto her waist. Under his fingers, she felt alive, slim, beautiful. His face moved towards her, his lips at her ear. 'I want to drink you in. Every inch. We can do this, Becca, you and me. This is within our power. We can undo the mess. Put it all back together the way it should have been in the first place—with us at the centre.'

'I can't,' she mumbled. But she didn't move. Exhaustion

coursed through her veins. 'Don't you understand, Finn? I can't. Everything would be destroyed.'

'It was never right.'

'Really?' A sob caught in her throat. 'How do you tell a child...five children, that they're...their existence is built on regret?'

'It's not just about the kids. Becca, they've got their whole lives ahead of them. We...us...we have such a small time slot left, and we have to take it back.'

She felt a cry of frustration stick in her throat. 'Why didn't you tell me all of this years ago?'

'I tried.' He pressed his fingers into her waist a little tighter. 'Seriously, I did. Then you were pregnant, and... when you were, I mean the kids, how could I do that?'

'And now it's different?' None of it made sense. She beat her hands against her forehead, because it hadn't changed. It wasn't better. There wasn't a good time.

Finn peeled her balled fists away from her face and held them gently in her lap between his own hands, leaning in towards her so that their bodies seemed to be glued together. 'We need to put ourselves first, now Beccs. Just this once.'

Suddenly she didn't care about Byrde. She could hear the bees at the back of her brain, but this, what was happening here and now, this was so much more important.

Finn's voice was calm. His words deliberate, soft, barely audible. 'We need to do that, Becca—put ourselves first now.'

She shook her head, tears of frustration running unchecked down her cheeks. 'I don't do that.'

'No. But you can.'

'Don't you understand, Finn—through my infidelity, I would destroy lives?'

'No. No. Without it, you'll destroy yourself and me, destroy us both. The kids will get used to it, eventually.'

'Eventually!' she scoffed.

But his voice remained calm, quiet, rational. 'Don't you want to be happy? Don't we deserve just a little? I can't keep living this way, Becca, because it's not living.'

And suddenly there was only silence because Finn was right. Both his arms circled her, pulling her tightly into him; the smell of him, the clean, fresh, longed-for newness of him, and for one moment, one single moment of total bliss, Becca knew that she didn't care anymore.

Finn's bedroom might have been smaller, less pretentious than the master, but it felt more honest. Becca lay in his arms staring at the darkened room. Finn holding her so tight but so gently. She felt like a bird caged softly in his hands. They were both naked. There were no clothes on, and they were lying under the bed covers this time. This time they had gone for the full follow-through after the kiss. She could feel the hot trace of him still spilling down her legs. Becca had never felt happier, more complete.

'We'll tell him tomorrow.'

It sounded so easy when Finn said it like that. So logical, like it was just a statement of fact that they were planning on divulging, not some Tasmanian devil of meaning that could pull her whole world down in its wake. Although the funny thing was, lying there beside Finn, Becca knew it was the only thing they could do.

'Do you remember that story Scratch used to tell?' She gazed up at the ceiling, watching the light from outside dance across the plaster.

'So many stories.'

'It was about these demons. Rock babies that came out

of the cracks in the earth. Embedded themselves into families. Like cuckoos.'

Finn drew in a deep breath. 'No. Why?'

In truth, Becca didn't know why. She had read about them again in the visitors' book, yet she didn't know what would make her go thinking of that now. Perhaps it was the fact that her own family was breaking up around her. They didn't know yet, but tomorrow would see everything shattered as if they'd let one of the demons in themselves. And maybe it was the wind outside. It had started to prowl around the house, like a predator, something older and uglier than time.

'I'm going to marry you, Beccs,' Finn said, in a voice that she knew was talking nothing but truth. 'The kids...they can come live with us. The new house, it's big enough. You'll like Islington.'

She wasn't so sure, but anywhere Finn was going, Becca was going too.

'I'll have to give Daisy some kind of...something,' he said vaguely. 'Scratch too. I'll see them both alright. And the ring, I'll get that back for you.'

Her blood cooled. 'Finn, I don't want that bloody ring.'

'What?'

He paused for a moment, confused. Then decided not to ask.

'Then I'll get you another.' Finn's voice sounded sleepy. His words were trailing off at the ends, his eyes were closing. 'Funny, Scratch hated the ring too. Never wore his.'

Suddenly she was wide awake. Finn didn't notice. His body continued towards shutdown, getting ready for that whole future he had mapped out in his brain. 'Bought the rings with his winnings. One of his pacts. Never bleeding work.'

He nestled his face into her neck and was asleep just as quick as if someone had sprinkled sandman dust in his eyes. Not so for Becca. Her whole entire world had just come crashing down around her. The scaffolding had always been shoddy, but now she knew who it was that did such a lousy job of putting it up. It was her; Becca had put up her own scaffolding on life, tried to prop up her existence on what she believed was true, but she'd built everything in the exact wrong place.

27

PASS THE BOMB

(A game for multiple players. Participants must pass 'the bomb' before the timer ends. In order to pass the bomb, they must say a word that connects to a randomly turned card. The person left holding the bomb when it 'explodes' is out of the game.)

Not surprisingly, Becca couldn't sleep. Instead, she lay there thinking that she had never been so happy, yet so utterly miserable, in her entire life. There are no prizes for being a fool, only self-sickening realisations. When the first light of day started to pierce the room, making everything two tones of grey, she pulled Finn's arm from across her body and slid quietly to the end of the bed. It was done. Her entire life had been played out before her, and finally, she understood. She glanced at the clock on the mantelpiece: six o'clock. It would be a couple of hours before the house woke up, the shit hit the fan, and her life ended up crushed.

Becca stumbled towards the door, taking her dressing gown from the hook where she'd hung it.

Before she left the room, she looked back at the slumped

body in bed. It was this body that she should have been leaving every morning. This body that she should have been lying beside every night.

Becca walked through the quiet house, feeling like she could already hear the angry shouts that would be filling it in a couple of hours. She wasn't sure she was strong enough for that. She wanted to run. She wanted to pull open the door and dash screaming from the house, but no, she would wait. The whispers in her head were still quiet. They hadn't woken yet. When they did, she knew they'd be after blood. She wandered, heavy-footed, into the sunroom. It was just beginning to get light through the wide glass windows, the tree picking up the first rays of morning sun in its dead black branches.

Becca sat on the sofa, sighing as her body hit the cushions, sighing like a woman in her eighties with her life all behind her. It was then that she saw Finn's case in the corner of the room. You'd have thought he would have learnt: if it's private, best keep it locked in the boot of your car. Leaving it without a lock and key in a public space, well, that was just daft. Leaning her body across the sofa, she reached out one arm, waving her fingers in the air till they fixed around the black leather handle of the bag.

What harm could it do now? She drew the case towards her, holding it to her chest. The whispering was still quiet enough, only just beginning to mumble. Becca knew all the secrets now. There was nothing more to hurt her, but still, she wanted to look. She reached into the case, and her fingers clutched on the soft brushed leather of the book. Odd that it felt almost warm as if it were a living creature.

The writing inside was packed so tight. Becca wasn't sure if Finn believed he was seriously running out of time or if he just felt it was best to hedge his bets. She turned to the back page and felt a sickening wave of revulsion and emptiness. Some bugger had ripped it out. Becca knew immediately who that would be. Scratch should have one of those trademark logos so that he could stick them on all of his pranks: this was just his style. Slowly, carefully, she ran her finger down the cracked edge of the torn page. There was still one page left, though, just the one. Reaching back into Finn's bag, she drew out a pen. It looked expensive, felt heavy with a dark onyx stem and a lid rimmed with gold. But she wasn't interested in the pen. It was the book that held her attention with its one page left.

Well, Becca thought, seems like maybe she should get her story down as well. Get it inked for the record. Everyone else had fabricated their own version of events. And so, she began to write. Her script was larger than Finn's, the letters scrawled, untidy. The curves she used to take so much pleasure in when she was at school had all gone. Her alphabet now was sharp and boney as scratched, chalked men shouting out for justice. There was no need to cramp the letters, though. This page was hers, and she intended to fill it. In the very last half-inch at the bottom, she even scrawled THE END. Finishing it off with a full stop.

The book done, Becca replaced it carefully back in the case, but as she did, she leant on her pocket and felt the sharp edge of her phone. Taking it out, she stared at the thing as if it had been beamed down from another planet. Her last call had been to Meg. Becca looked at the clock on the wall. Six-thirty. Meg was an early bird. Did she dare? Becca glanced out towards the tree. It appeared closer now and looked as though it was holding that dull ball of morning light in its wide cracked arms. As though it was holding on to the day, never going to give it up. Outside, from the hallway, she was sure she could hear whispering:

kids. Someone standing on the doorstep with their wrist held high. *Knock, knock, knock—who's there?*

She pressed the home number into her mobile.

'Yeah!' a sleepy voice came over the phone.

'Megs?'

'Mum, is it late?'

'No babe, it's early, sweetheart. Half-six.'

'You okay?'

It was a simple question, but for a moment, Becca wasn't sure how to answer. 'Sure,' she managed after a gap that any adult would know was way too long. 'Yeah, everything's fine. I just...I wanted to hear your voice. I knew you'd answer. Miss you, love.'

'You too.' The voice came back flat, as though the words were spilling over the tongue but not touching the brain or the heart.

'I wanted to...I just wanted to tell you something.' Becca stopped, unsure how to continue. The silence was a little too long.

'Mum?'

'Yes. Sorry. Megs, you remember that book we had, the one that we got from the junk shop when you were little. It was a book of fairy tales, really beautiful ones?'

'With the crayon pictures?'

'That's the one. You loved it. Only, it was badly bound, you remember?'

'Pages fell out,' Meg said, her voice chipper, delighted at herself with being able to locate the memory.

'That's right, they came unstuck. I tried sticking a few back in with Sellotape, but in the end, we had to throw it out.' She hesitated.

'Yes?' came the small voice from the end of the phone.

'Well...what I wanted to say was...the fact that the book

was badly bound, it didn't affect the story inside. The story was beautiful anyway. We still had that, the story, Megs. We kind of had it in us, internalised it. So even when the whole thing fell to pieces, we had the…the story, the memories.'

'I guess…?'

'Sorry. I just…just started thinking about that book.'

'How's Dad? Uncle Finn? Is he all excited?'

'Everyone's over the moon,' Becca said, in a voice so flat it could have been automated.

The whispering from the hallway was getting louder now. It sounded as if the pesky kids from the past had finally got in. *Knock. Knock. Knock. 'Why didn't you tell?'*

Becca dug the nails of her free hand into her thigh. 'Will you say to everyone that I love them?' Her voice was perfectly level.

'Yeah, okay.' There was a brief pause before Megs continued. 'They do know.'

'Of course,' Becca felt her voice fluster. 'But…don't forget, Megs. Promise? Tell them I love them, whatever.'

'You too.'

And the phone went dead in Becca's hand, leaving an unbearable silence. Becca pushed her mobile onto the coffee table. She wouldn't be needing it anymore. Besides, the silence was soon broken—the whispering was in the room, actually in the sunroom with her; the three kids and Byrde, all of them telling her there was only one way to get out of this.

She stood at the window, looking out at the tree. It was so much closer, and still holding that ball of sunshine, that dull new day. Becca blinked, and the tree was only a few feet away. She blinked again, and The Watcher was closer still. Again, once more, Becca blinked, and the blackness of the dead tree engulfed her.

28

ROUND UP FIFTY-TWO

(A joke, rather than a game, involving a regular pack of playing cards. The player asks the innocent if they would like to play a game—Round Up Fifty-Two. When the innocent says 'yes', the player flicks the cards all around the room, for the innocent to gather.)

Scratch stared anxiously through the kitchen window. Where the hell was Becca? It was ten-thirty. She could have gone into town. He'd made her that appointment, but both cars were still standing outside in the yard. She'd been a mother for twenty-three years. There was no "freedom of movement". Becca was used to being accountable: telling everyone where she was going, when and how long for. She even announced when she was going to the toilet. Something wasn't right. Bullets of rain hit the window. If Becca had decided to walk, she'd be in one hell of a mess by the time she got down to the town, and why leave her phone?

Nothing was making sense this morning. Scratch could

see Finn struggling across the yard; he'd been out to check the barns.

Scratch heard the front door rattle open, letting a cool ghost of air into the house. 'Well?' he called out, still not taking his eyes from the yard, scanning, scanning every inch.

'Nothing.'

'You checked the barns?'

Finn came into the kitchen, bringing the smell of wet moors with him. 'Checked them all. What would she be doing out there anyway?'

Scratch shrugged.

'What about home? Any news of her there?'

'Meg had a phone call early this morning.' Instinctively Scratch glanced at his own mobile. Still nothing.

'What time, early?'

'Six-ish.' Scratch rapped his phone, as if the motion might help some long-lost message surface.

'What did she say?'

'I don't know...some crap, stories.' He stashed the phone in his pocket, pulling one agitated thick hand across his chin. 'I didn't push too hard. I don't want to worry them.'

'No. Course.' But Finn was worried, his face was so pale it looked as though he might just throw up.

'I mean, she'll be here somewhere.' Scratch glanced around the room, as if expecting Becca to appear out of the walls.

'Yeah.'

'I booked her an appointment, one of those beauty places in town. She's probably there.'

For just one moment, Finn's features relaxed. 'Did you ring and ask?'

'How stupid do you think I am?' Scratch shot Finn a gormless look.

'I didn't...'

'Course I rang,' Scratch said, his voice short. 'She's not there. Yet.'

'Maybe she's on her way. Ring them again.'

'I asked them to call us when she arrives.' There was a clear thread of irritation in Scratch's voice.

Finn gave a quick nod as though *that was sorted then*, not wanting to push more, but his lithe body normally so calm and collected was all jittery, boundless energy. He barely looked like himself anymore.

Leaning against the counter, Scratch shot him a curious look. 'Mate, what's up with you?'

Finn stopped dead; his legs had been walking him in circles. He slowed himself down, suddenly aware of his body language. 'It was cold outside. I was just getting warm. I could go down to the village and wait for her?'

'What, my wife? *You* go down to the village and wait for my wife?'

'I just thought...'

'If there's any waiting to be done, Finn, my friend, it's going to be me doing it.'

The word *'friend'* sounded bitter in the air.

'What were you two talking about last night anyway?'

'What?'

'I heard you downstairs.'

'Oh, nothing.' Finn appeared to be avoiding eye contact. Glancing aimlessly at his hands. 'Just...you know, talking.'

'She'll call when she gets there.'

'Yeah, course.'

'And I'll go pick her up.'

There was a brief pause before Finn offered up a strained, 'Sure.'

Scratch gave himself a stretch that any cat would be proud of. 'So, that's it then. I'll get the kettle on. Maybe we should play a game?'

Finn didn't answer. He'd started pacing again.

'Help pass the time.'

'Yeah.'

'Cheat.' The word came low out of Scratch's mouth like a rumble, like an accusation.

'What?'

Scratch fixed Finn with eyes that were no longer twinkling, no longer full of fun. 'Cheat. It's a card game.'

'Course.' Finn sighed, trying hard not to look relieved.

'Oh, damn.' Scratch took two mugs out of the cupboard. He stared at the mugs for a moment, not bothering to put anything in.

'Scratch?'

'Yeah, yeah. Cheat, it's for three players. We'll have to wait till Becca comes back. Till I go and get her.' The last sentence came out as hard as knives.

Finn squirmed, looking about as comfortable as a fish on the end of a line.

Suddenly there was a buzz. The phone on the units was vibrating—Scratch's phone. Both men stared at it jittering, moving like the planchet on a Ouija board.

'Well, pick it up,' Finn said a bit too quick.

Scratch took it in his hand, swiping the green phone icon, before standing there, head cocked, listening.

'Well?' Finn couldn't help himself.

Scratch placed the phone back on the units.

'Not there, hasn't turned up yet for her appointment. There's time. She probably underestimated the walk down.'

'Why wouldn't she take her phone?' Finn dragged his hand through his hair. 'If she was going out, why leave it in the sunroom?'

They stood for a moment, still as salt pillars, unsure what they should do next. It was Finn that finally broke the silence. 'I think we should call the police.'

'What did you say to her, Finn?' Scratch's eyes flashed hard as stone.

'Nothing. We should call the police.'

Scratch drew in his bottom lip, mulling it over. He'd got no love for the police, never had. 'We search the house first. Every room upstairs, I'll take downstairs and the cellar.'

Finn was already out of the door, taking the staircase two steps at a time.

Scratch unhooked the latch on the cellar door, switching on the light and staring into the pit below him. Why, he wondered, would she be in the cellar? Becca was right. It was creepy down there, one of those places that seemed to absorb the cold straight out of the rock face, and there was no sign of her.

The pool room was empty. The balls all set out on the table. Scratch cracked the triangle, rolling the white down the green baize. It took a long time to glide all the way down, and the impact, when it came, was disappointing— just a dull thud and a few balls scuttling away.

The sunroom was just the same as it had been when he'd come in around eight that morning, the wide curtains had been partially closed. It was so wet outside that he hadn't bothered to pull them open. But there was something odd about the room. He tilted his head and sniffed at the air —a thick smell of musk. Suddenly, he knew what it was— sex. He could always tell when a woman had had sex. They carried it around with them from room to room, that unmistakable rotten citrus odour.

'She's not there.' Finn burst through the door, unaware. 'I'm going to go down into town.'

'No mate, stay. You stay here with me.' Scratch sat down on the pale blue sofa, planting his feet firm as though he meant business.

'I won't be long.'

'My car's parked up behind you. You'll have to move the Skoda first.'

Finn was fidgety, a regular pent-up ball of energy. Every move he made had five smaller ones balled into it. 'Okay.' His voice sounded breathless, unnerved. 'Where's your keys?'

'In my pocket. Hanging up by the door.'

Finn dashed out of the room quick as a whippet. Scratch sat there watching him go. Scratch knew that with a lot of things in life, you just have to wait. People are always tiring themselves out, rushing here, rushing there, when in actual fact, if they just stopped still for a moment, everything would end up landing in the right place, or near enough. Suddenly all the footsteps, all the breathing, all the million and one barely perceptible noises that Finn kept letting out into the universe, they all stopped. Replaced by a silence so loud it could give a sane person tinnitus.

Then in walked Finn, his face white and drawn. A single scrap of paper in his hand. 'What is this?'

Scratch smiled. 'My joke. Slipped it into your pocket.'

'You tore a blank page out of the book?'

'You know me.' Scratch shrugged. 'Just a bit of harmless fun.'

'It's not funny.'

'It wouldn't stand up at a comedy club, maybe, but in context…I don't think it's too shabby.'

'Did you…' Finn shuffled into the room.

'What, read it, read your book?'

Scratch got to his feet and grabbed Finn's case and pulled the book out of the bag. 'All your secrets.'

'Give it back.'

But Scratch had leapt onto the sofa and was standing on the wide cushions book held high. 'Piggy in the middle. Need Becca for this one, really. You ever noticed that, Finn, my boy? Everything's more fun in threes.'

'Scratch.' A twitch started to pulse uncontrollably in Finn's chiselled jaw, and his cheeks had flushed beetroot red. He was trying oh-so-hard not to feed Scratch's fun. Slowly, Finn extended one arm out towards Scratch, palm stretched upwards.

'Look at you. Model of restraint.' Scratch flicked the pages with his thumb before putting on a high-pitched girly voice. '*Dear Diary. I am going to hatch a cunning plan and screw my best mate's wife.*'

Finn's lower jaw clamped. He was mad as hell but trying to keep it all in. 'I didn't write that.'

'No, worse, mate. You fucked your best mate's wife!' Scratch sniffed the air. 'I can smell you. You sleazy bastard. So, what did you say to her? Where did she go?'

'Give me the book back.'

'What the fuck for?'

'It's mine.'

'Know what, mate, you have a sadly deluded idea on the ownership front. You bastard.'

Finn's shoulders drooped, exhausted. 'Scratch, I'm sorry.'

'Like that makes it any better.'

'This is hard for all of us.'

'No, mate.' Scratch stepped off the sofa, his large heavy body sinking into the floor. 'Honestly, seriously. You have not got a clue on this one.'

'I wouldn't have had it turn out like this for...'

'Don't come that with me, Finnbow. This was exactly how you wanted it to turn out. It's all written here in this frigging book.' Scratch waved the book into the air, the pages flapping like crocodile teeth. A crazed glint flicking through his eyes. 'But you're running out of time, matey-boy, aren't you? Not many pages left, all of them disappearing off and your luck with it. You're scared shitless because you're on the last page. Not much of a story left to write now that I've got rid of one of those blank pages for you.'

'It's just a stupid kid's story.'

'Maybe, but you take my wife, and I swear to you on the life of every single one of my kids that you will rot in Hell. Know what—I will push you there myself. Suggestion. It's a powerful thing.' Scratch waved the book again, but this time sweeping it through the air in random arches as though it was some kind of wand. 'People who can't see, well, they begin to see. The lame walk, and the damned...'

'Crap.'

'If you ask me, things have a funny way of working out. I shouldn't tell you, really, but...know what...I'm feeling a bit pissed off this morning. A bit down in the dumps. Something's been kind of eating me up from the inside. And hey, what's the good of a joke if it's only the joker that's laughing?'

Finn's face folded into a question mark. He had no idea what Scratch was on about. 'Scratch, what are you...?'

'It was just a game, the book. It was just a bit of a prank, a lark. When it started, after Old Man Byrde died, I'd only come up here to see if the old guy had anything worth nicking.'

'Scratch!'

'Oh, don't come the innocent corporate banker with me. You've always had light fingers, only difference is now the amounts you lift are way bigger than you can stick in your pockets from the corner shop.'

Finn sank down onto the sofa; the insults, the jibes, didn't matter. What mattered now was the truth. 'So, you were here?'

'Oh yeah, very familiar with this old place. I just came up to see if we'd left anything. I already did a once over, but the day of the funeral, I reckoned most of the town would be tied up. Thought I was safe. But surprise, surprise, in walks you. So, I thought to myself: hello, hello? There was all this stuff lying around: electronics, alcohol, Byrde's wallet. But you, Finn mate, you didn't touch any of that. You just went straight for the book. Promises, promises.'

Finn's eyes glazed over, resigned and hollow. 'All this time, you knew I had it?'

'All-seeing, all-knowing, that's yours truly. See, you might be the games master, but me...I'm the storyteller, the spinner of dreams, the teller of tales. And believe me... whatever you might think, this story we're standing in right now, this story here, is not a love story. Nah. This is something in a whole different league. A new genre. It was just a laugh: Byrde's book, but then it got...interesting. I knew everything that was going on in that oh-so-tiny little head of yours because I could read it all in the bloody book. The beauty of it? I was always two steps ahead. And do you know what was even better—all the time you were scribbling away, tiny little writing, I could see the pages turning, the ink eking out, and the life...the life running right out of you sure as sand slipping through an egg timer.'

Finn sunk his head into his hands. 'It's over now, Scratch. All of it. We all need to talk, figure this one out. She'll be back soon.'

'Not if she does manage to turn up at that salon. Not for a while. I booked her in for the full treatment. Leg wax, bikini, they'll be finding hair on the woman that she never knew she had. Now it's just us, and you, my friend, have been drooling over my wife for far too long.'

'I love her, Scratch. I always have.'

Scratch threw back his head and laughed. Laughed so loud it was a wonder they couldn't hear him in town. 'Oh, come on! What sort of a revelation is that! What am I supposed to do with it, hey? Love! How old are you?'

'It should have been us—me and Beccs.'

'But it wasn't, you daft pillock. You know how easy you are to read? I don't even need the sodding book.'

'Becca feels the same.'

A flash of anger sparked across Scratch's eyes. 'Leave Becca out of this. I can't believe how frigging wet you are, Finn-boy. Look at you, sitting there on your big posh sofa with your simpering hurt face. *"I love Becca."* Know what? It's me you screwed really, not Beccs. How does that feel? Only see, I don't let people get away with things like that, never have.'

Finn's voice, when he spoke again, sounded quiet but steady; the emotions flatlined out of it. He knew how the land lay between him and Becca. Of that, Finn was in no doubt. 'She's going to leave you, Scratch.'

'No.' The word whipped around the room, hard as a slap. 'Becca will do what I tell Becca to do. That's the wonderful thing about women. Piece of advice, Finn, since we're having this cosy little heart-to-heart—never put your faith in a woman. Why? Oh, it's not their fault, the fairer sex. You can't really blame them. Their little minds get all muddled up. Specially when there's love and kindness in the mix. Women, Finn-boy, my mate, are easy to play. All a woman needs is a bit of careful handling. One thing you were right about—it's all a game.'

Suddenly Finn's face dropped three shades lighter. 'That woman in the club, she did know you.'

Scratch laughed. 'Two and two together making four? I always thought you were supposed to be the math genius, but it's sure as hell taking you long enough to figure it all out. That was the elusive Freya Hennings. Blast from the past. It wasn't scratch cards that made me rich as a kid. No. Cards were just the cover story. There are easier ways to make a penny. Find a pretty girl, buy her a few presents, a few gifts, doesn't have to be expensive stuff. Be nice to her. It's amazing what a young girl will do for a pleasant enough guy with a good sense of humour when his cash flow's not running in the right direction.'

'Fuck!' Finn stared up at Scratch in horror.

'Got it in one. That's the name of the game. Easy. And once the drugs start getting to be a habit, you've got them for as long as you like. Unless they O.D. Silly bitches, that can be a problem.'

'You're a...'

'No...was.' Scratch drew the word out as though he was setting Finn straight on some small domestic trifle. 'Not anymore. Gave it up years ago. Pimping, it didn't really fit in with the family man image. *"What does your dad do for work, Ella dear?" "He sells young women for sex, miss. Like me to draw you a picture?"'*

'Oh my God.' Finn's jaw dropped, and he grabbed the sides of his head, as if wanting to shut it all out.

'There you go again, Finnbow,' Scratch's eyes sparkled, 'making connections.' He smiled. 'I can see it. The way your little face keeps going that lime green colour, as though you're going to spew for England.'

Finn looked up again. His jaw clenched. His eyes wild. 'The money for sixth form college and then for uni?'

'Exactly.' Scratch prodded a Bingo-style finger triumphantly towards his oldest friend. 'That is the connection. I mean, a university education, like all the politicians on the box say, it does not come cheap.'

'You pimped women so I could...'

'All for the greater good.' Scratch shrugged. 'Well, not theirs, maybe. There are some nasty STDs around, specially then.'

Finn shrank into his body, seeming to grow smaller in the wide sofa, as if losing surface space might make his faults smaller, his footprint on the earth less. 'Young women were paying...'

'Well, no, Finn, be realistic here. Not just young women. I mean, the whole cutting you loose thing was very pricey. You needed books, a place to live. It cost a fortune getting you out of the picture. Course Old Man Byrde, he helped a bit too, inadvertently.'

'You bastard.' Finn stood suddenly, lurching towards Scratch but then stopping suddenly in the middle of the room as though lost, as though not wanting to actually touch.

Scratch smiled, though there was no joy in it. 'Well, Finn, you are right on that point. Nah. The whole pimping thing was short-lived in the end. Mrs Hennings and her daughter never forgave me, but...' he shrugged nonchalantly. 'You can't please all of the people all of the time and it was a lot of fun while it lasted. Anyway...' Scratch crinkled his nose, stepping carefully down from the sofa, evening out their heights. 'Money didn't impress Becca much, didn't turn her on at all. Had to think of something different to press her buttons.' Scratch smiled, pumping the back cushion on the couch before sitting down, leaning back in the soft cushions. 'Do you know how long I've been planning this?'

'Sorry?'

'Me and Becca, have you got any idea how long the whole scheme's taken to get all the balls lined up and in place: planting suggestions, the book, the party.'

'Party?' Finn stared at Scratch, lost.

'Your college bash, mate. Only one we went to. You must remember? And didn't it all just play right into my hands. If you don't mind me saying, Finnbow, you were a first-class tosser that night—all your big words and your new friends. Becca was so down after that party. One small act of kindness would have reeled her in, and who was waiting in the shadows? The shoulder to cry on? Course, I needed more than tears. I spiked her drink, cut the condom.'

'What!' Finn gasped, the horror of Scratch's revelations proving too much.

'Small details, mate.' Scratch waved his large hand through the air dismissively. 'Only, see it's those small details that are oh so important. And the rest...well, let's just say, the gods, they must have been smiling down on me.'

'You bastard.'

At last, Finn stood, lurching forward, fists flying, but Scratch was too quick, rolling away from Finn's lunge and standing in front of the wall, a big leering grin plastered over his face. Again, Finn lunged. Again Scratch dipped, letting Finn's punch land hard against the wall.

'Nice one.' Scratch laughed. 'We used to fight when we were younger, remember? It was just for a laugh then. I like it better now—when there's a bit of feeling behind it.'

Finn shook the pain out of his fist, glaring at Scratch in a look of pure hate.

'Oh come on, mate,' Scratch said, amiably. 'Know what I think? Call me old-fashioned, but sometimes the only way to settle things is with fis....'

The last word got cut in half as Finn's knuckles made contact with the side of Scratch's smirking face.

The joker fell back, but not for long. He was soon on his feet, sinking back behind the couch, using it as a barrier between them. Shuffling like a tennis player foot to foot. 'That the best you got?' He rubbed his jaw. 'I think you can do better. Some really nice big bruises, that wouldn't go amiss. Great big shiners. Come on, mate. Best shot.'

Finn dived towards the sofa. Scratch turned slightly, but he was too slow. Finn managed to catch him on the shoulder, flattening him back against the wall. Scratch didn't stop. He was off again, moving faster than a dancer.

'Better, mate. Now you're getting the hang of it. Not sure it's justified, though. Not really. I mean, it is you that's been drooling over my wife. She is mine, Finn. By hook or by crook.'

Finn's face was red, contorted in anger as he prodded an angry finger towards Scratch. 'Not when she hears what you did.'

Scratch continued to smile. Never losing his calm, taking all of Finn's energy and turning it into something to fuel the irony, the Divine Comedy. 'Well,' he smirked knowingly, 'the future's a tricky bugger, and you,' he snorted, 'look at you, dancing around with those lily-white bloody banker's hands. Do you think I'm just going to roll over, say some white-collar worker crap about the best man winning, then let you and Beccs go waltzing off into the sunshine, Sunshine?'

Scratch's eyes were flint now, hard as laser beams of hate. 'You are fucked, mate.'

Finn drew back his arm, letting his fist fly towards Scratch's nose. It hit with a resounding crack. Scratch clutched hold of it in both hands, a trickle of blood oozing from between his fingers as he fell back onto the floor.

'I thought you were my friend.'

'Friend!' Scratch laughed, despite all. 'You say that! It's me taking the beating here. Reckon you broke my fucking nose.'

There was a moment's quiet, a second of stillness. The world, with all its rational elements, appeared to come rushing back. Finn hesitated, letting his fist drop to his side.

'Sorry. Shit.' He sighed. 'This is bad enough already without...'

But Scratch wasn't there anymore, not cowering on the floor. He was up, a raised vase held high over Finn's head. It came crashing down in a shower of plaster and sharp china pieces. Finn sprawled across the floor.

'Bloody idiot. For a bright guy, Finnbow, you're not exactly smart.'

Finn's head felt like it was split in two. Raw as if it still had a few fragments of china slicing out of the skin. He could hardly see straight. Scratch didn't miss a beat. He was working, working away—moving Finn's hands, Finn's feet.

'Nice and loose, mate. Don't want to mark that lovely soft Money Man skin. When they find you dead, mate... because mark my words, they will find you dead. That is the next chapter. When they find you dead, I'm going to tell them about that-there book of yours. Beccs will back me up.

We'll say...' he continued, winding the tape tighter around Finn's ankles. 'We'll tell them how you felt your time was running out. The Devil's book. The power of suggestion. Did I ever mention what a powerful thing that is? And I'll say to them that you fought me.' Scratch let his fingers run gently across his nose. 'You did a bloody good job on that, mate. Credit where credit's due. You see, I'll say that it was all too much for you, Finnbow. You want to know how the story goes, what happens next? You see, in the story...she says no. She rejects you. Yet again. And that, my friend, is what pushes you over the edge.'

Scratch took a little time to catch his breath and admire his handiwork. Finn's hands and feet were bound neatly with tape, his head was showered in streams of blood. It was a long time since Scratch had done anything quite so physical, and he was surprised how, when the chips were down, all that strength, it just came back. He glanced quickly around the scene, realising he was going to need more.

'Just. You just hang on there, mate. Won't be a tick.'

In the kitchen, Scratch found a pair of marigolds and a little barbeque oil.

'I've got a ready can in the boot of the Skoda,' he shouted back over his shoulder. 'If this doesn't get the party going, I'll nip out and get that, but...' He shook the bottle. 'This may well do the trick.'

Back in the sunroom, Scratch gave Finn a little kick, just for good measure. Finn groaned. So he was still conscious, just. Scratch couldn't help feeling pleased with himself: that smash over the head had been exactly what was needed. Still smiling, Scratch started to douse Finn with the oil.

'Very dramatic this,' he said, giving the bottle an extra

squeeze. 'Nice touch if you ask me, a little bit Middle Eastern.'

Scratch wiped Finn's hands across the bottle, then stood back to admire.

'Who would have thought,' he said, gazing proudly over the carnage, 'that the man had it in him—this final gesture of undying love?'

Scratch took the matches from the mantelpiece, struck one, and held it close to Finn's trouser leg till it caught.

'So long then, Romeo.'

He picked up the book—it was his evidence. Scratch was going to have to take it with him. He flicked through to the end, and then his heart stopped. He stopped breathing, stopped thinking, stopped scheming for just one moment because the last blank page, it wasn't there anymore. Instead, it was his wife's handwriting jamming every inch of the paper. It was Becca who had decided to go bargaining with her soul.

Leaving Finn burning in the background, Scratch made a dash to the windows, pulling the curtains open frantically as if he was late for a concert at the Royal Albert Hall. There were no smiles on his face now, not even the hint of one, because now he saw it, toppling out there through the wind and rain towards the escarpment edge was the small, huddled figure of a woman—Scratch's woman.

29

KERPLUNK

(A game for multiple players. A series of marbles are suspended in a plastic tube on a bed of straws. Players take turns removing the straws. If a marble falls when a player draws a straw, the player is out.)

Exhausted, Becca dragged herself through the bitter horizontal rain towards the escarpment. The voices in her head pushing her forward. Every single limb ached. She just wanted to sit down and stop, only the voices wouldn't shut up. The bees, Byrde, and even her own mother had chosen to pipe up. Everyone was getting in on the blame game. How could anyone live like this? Wrecking the lives of everyone she came into contact with. She was an abomination, utterly loathsome and should not be allowed to exist. It would have been better for everyone if she'd never been born.

She wasn't sure how long she stood there, teetering on the edge, letting the wind wrap around her, waiting and waiting, scared to take that final step. Initially, when she heard another voice, Becca wasn't sure if it was in her head or something fixed to the real world. Then it came again, a single voice. Was this what she was waiting for?

'Becca, Becca.'

She knew it wouldn't be much longer now. There was one more thing she had to do.

'Becca.'

Turning slowly back towards the house, she saw Scratch struggling towards her through the rain. Head down and thrust forward. Only behind him, there was something odd: a bright orange halo. It looked as if he was an angel shrouded in a warm glow. Her angel? God, if that man knew what she'd done!

'Becca, stop, love.' He pushed forward.

She smiled sadly. This was it. It was all over. 'The voices,' she explained. 'The book. I wrote the last page, Scratch. It's coming for me. You and Finn, you're fine. One soul is enough.'

'No, no, no.' Scratch shook his head. Water poured over his features as if he was melting, but he didn't come closer: scared to rush forward in case she startled and fell. 'It's stories, Becca love,' he shouted over the roar of the wind. 'It's just stories. There's no ghost. No devils. No one's lost their soul. Get back from the edge, sweetheart.'

'I saw you,' she said, her words sounding pathetically small and cracked. But there was no accusation in her voice. It was simply that the game was finally up. 'You killed Byrde.'

'No, love. Byrde fell.'

'You were with him.'

'Me, no.' Violently, insistently, he shook his head.

'I saw you.'

'I didn't kill Byrde, Beccs.' Scratch shook his head

dismissively. 'He ran. Come on, babe. I wouldn't have pushed him over. You know that.'

Behind Scratch's shoulder, Becca saw the glimpse of something glowing brighter. The wood burner must be on. The house would be warm, only there was a problem: it was his house—Byrde's house. She'd written in his book. There was no going back now. 'No more games, Scratch. I'm tired.'

'Course, yeah. Look, Byrde was an accident. We can talk about this...it wasn't...'

'I filled up the last page.'

'I saw,' he said dismissively. 'But it's just a book, just a story.'

Becca toppled slightly.

Scratch gasped. 'Becca, come away. Please, princess, just step...'

Suddenly, the whispering was so much louder than Scratch's voice. Amplified as though in an echo chamber. Clawing at her brain. '*Why didn't you tell?*' and '*Run, Run, Run,*' said the kids playing knock-out-ginger. And then her mother. '*It's all for the best. Join me.*'

'Can you hear that?' she sobbed.

Scratch's ears were red-raw with the wind. 'There's nothing, Becca.'

'There are voices,' she said.

'No, Beccs. There's no one here. It's just us. It's the wind, love, playing tricks. That's all it is. The voices, sweetheart, they're in your head.'

Becca's eyes shot up for a moment staring heavenward as if she was thinking this over. Then she smiled. Just a little. 'You think it's important where the voices are?'

He didn't know. 'It's cold, love. We need to get you in.' He thought of the fire. How was he going to explain the fire?

'The problem isn't where the voices are, Scratch. The problem is that there are voices.'

'We can get help. More help. There will be someone, Becca. Something that we can do.'

She was so close to the edge. One step from oblivion.

'Please. Becca. Please. The kids. Think about the kids.'

She dropped her gaze, looking down for the first time towards the hard ground below. The magic word. Scratch had used the magic word: the children. Conjuring up images of their small, innocent faces. Out of the corner of her eye, she could feel the shadow of a hand. He was holding it out towards her.

Slowly, Becca raised her own hand towards his, her body about to turn.

'See, love...'

She could hear the smile in his voice which for some strange reason sounded odd. Too earthy. Gravelly.

'...It's easy, Becca, sweetheart.'

Of course it was. She couldn't leave her family. She knew how cruel that was. 'Okay.' Becca turned back to him, a small smile haunting her lips. It would be okay. Only, the smile froze; it wasn't Scratch standing there beside the old tree. No. This was something different. The true horror of the frenzy he'd had to conjure up in the house still haunted his features. This thing wasn't human. Its face slate and grey like shafts of rock. A hideous creature. Something cold and inhuman had crawled out from the earth, slipped out from a nightmare. Becca faltered, stepping back. In the distance, she could see it now, the house blazing, a burning pit from Hell. The reptilian mouth, Scratch's mouth, pulled itself into a fixed grin. His teeth bared behind his lips. His eyes shining wild, hard and merciless. Hungry for her, for her soul. Again, Becca stumbled back. Her body toppling as the monster that was Scratch reached out towards her. That joker's face leering. Those eyes as sharp as flint. Instinctively she backed away, toppled, was about to keel over when something caught her at the knees, some dark creature rushing up behind her. An enormous black cloud. No, that was wrong, a black hairy ball knocking her to the side, to safety, as the angry giant coming up over the escarpment, all fur and teeth and jowls, flew at Scratch. The dog—Trouble.

Scratch's body swayed. His eyes lost that granite look. The rock-like skin appeared to crack and flake as his large body fell forward, clawing hands out in a desperate attempt to fix on something, someone, only to meet thin air. Two hundred feet of air and counting. There were no screams. Not even a heavy thud when he landed, and when Becca searched around for the dog, she realised it had gone. The only movement she could see was that of the flames, leaping greedily up into the cold moorland air, as though they had been waiting for this for far too long.

30

END GAME

(*Chess*: (End Game): the phase of the game after most of
the pieces have been exchanged)

They found Scratch's twisted broken body at the bottom of the escarpment. Mrs Hennings had called the police when she spotted the smoke. There were flames and sirens, and men in blue running towards Becca as she wandered back towards the burning house. A paramedic wrapped her in a blanket, its coarse hair bristling under her chin, and Becca realised she was shaking uncontrollably; her teeth clashing together sending jolts of pain into her head. Despite the shock, a police-woman bundled her into the back of an open car, trying all the time to take Becca's statement. To discover what had gone wrong.

Scanning the forecourt, Becca couldn't help but think that the ambulance was a waste of public resources. Despite this, the ambulance waited patiently. They couldn't get Finn's body out of the house, not until the blaze had died down. Becca said nothing. All words appeared to have been robbed from her body, scuttled away over the escarpment with the wind. She managed to tell the policewoman their names, but that was it. The true horror of the situation didn't sink in at first. She had been a few steps away, and had missed the action unfolding at the house. There was also that other nagging thought circling her brain; that it could easily have been her twisted and broken at the base of the escarpment. So she felt curiously outside of the drama, numb. Although, she noted, it was a different kind of *numb* than she used to get from the pills. Now there was a vast emptiness inside her. She had been living the wrong life. A life someone else had carved out for her, and suddenly with all the people, the police, the activity and sirens, there was so little time to think.

Thankfully, they didn't hold her long for questioning at the station. In all truth, she didn't know how to explain what had happened; the way her husband's face had twisted into something older and nastier than time itself. Thinking about it, Scratch, or whatever it was she had seen looming towards her, made her experience a gut-wrenching sense of vertigo. As though if she looked too long at that face, at that portrait of evil, she would be dragged down with it. So, when she gave her full statement to the police, she had left out the bit about her husband's skin; how it had seemed to fuse into granite scales in front of her. Besides, Becca had to get home. There were five children waiting and bad news to deliver.

It was only later, ensconced in the warmth and everyday chaos of her family, that Becca began to form some kind of story in her mind. The reports in the newspaper helped. She just needed a truth and anybody's truth was better than her own. Having said this, even the reporters struggled. They claimed the events were unclear. The two men, old childhood friends, appeared to have fallen out. There had been a fight which ended in a fire. The blaze had been started deliberately. There was evidence of fuel being poured over one man's body. The woman, Becca Harris, had not been on the scene during the fight or when the fire started. Although she had subsequently witnessed her husband being attacked by a large Irish wolfhound. The man, Scratch Harris, and the dog had fallen together from the escarpment to their deaths.

Becca had caught sight of Daisy at Finn's funeral. She was being supported by an older guy and a woman, her parents, perhaps? She looked out of it, drugged up to the eyeballs. Becca knew that look all too well. There had been no wake. These were the kind of deaths people just wanted to forget about. Because of the circumstances, the date for the funeral had been dragged out. The will had already been read. Finn's small fortune had been left in its entirety to Becca, Scratch and the kids. Scratch, of course, had no use for any of it. There had been no mention of Daisy in the will. Despite the impending marriage, Daisy and Finn had not been together that long, or perhaps Finn had forgotten to update all the details. When Becca rang Daisy, she thought the young woman would put the phone down on her. Instead, Daisy agreed to meet.

Becca took the train to London. She travelled first class. Arriving at the restaurant just outside of St Katherine's docks, with its wide glass windows looking out on Tower Bridge, Becca instantly recognised Daisy. She was sitting alone in the window, looking at, but not really taking in the menu. She still had the air of someone who has had reality whipped out from underneath them. Despite all, Becca couldn't help smiling to herself as she walked towards the table; it could have been her younger self sitting there. The woman was better dressed, slightly slimmer, her hair cut with precision and art, but the similarities were obvious.

'Daisy?' Becca asked, as she pulled out the chair opposite.

The younger woman looked up, a frown creasing her face, but Becca didn't give her time to judge. There had been too many games played over the years. Instead, Becca slipped her slim olive hand gently over Daisy's in an act of reassurance. 'I wanted to say sorry.'

With her free hand, Daisy pulled a clean tissue from her handbag and dabbed it at her nose.

'You got tangled up in a mess. It was unfair.' Becca eased the seat opposite Daisy out from the table, so that she could sink down to the younger woman's eye level. 'I know it's been difficult. I know you've had your dreams smashed. Finn should have altered his will.'

Daisy's mouth opened a little, the lower lip flapping idly, as though she had so much to say, but Becca simply held up one hand. The poor girl was out of her league. No amount of explanation could set things straight. 'I've instructed my lawyer.' Words which would have, only recently, sounded alien in Becca's mouth, had over the past few months suddenly become so familiar. 'You're to keep the flat.'

As the two women talked and cried, and held hands over their barely touched food, Becca would have liked to think she had done the decent thing through a sense of common humanity, but deep down she knew it had something else at its root. Becca felt a gnawing all-consuming sense of guilt. Finn had never loved Daisy, and second best only ever got people into trouble. Hadn't it all ended badly for Scratch? Maybe the monster that he had become had been brought out because deep down he was always on the outside.

Maybe Finn and Becca had a hand in creating the creature that Scratch had become.

When they parted outside the restaurant, Tower Bridge glittering in the background, the two women hugged. There were promises to meet up again, but Becca had to press on; Daisy hadn't been the only reason for Becca's visit to London. She still had the book. Byrde's cursed book had been rescued from the fire. Surprisingly not one page of it had been burnt. Even so, parts of it were barely legible. The police had scoured it, but found nothing of interest. Only, Becca still had so many questions. London proved the perfect place to find an expert in handwriting, one who could untangle Byrde's words from the book. Someone— Scratch?—may have charcoaled angrily over some of the entries. Yet, as Becca began to realise, nothing stays hidden forever. Within an hour, the expert had unlocked the scrawl.

On the train home Becca had time to mull over those missing words Byrde had written in his book, and the words filled her heart with sadness. All that time, she had thought Byrde had been angry with her when, if anything, his ghost had been trying to protect her; to encourage her to tell the authorities and get to the bottom of the mystery. The lines in Byrde's handwriting read simply: *Keep Rebecca Nilsen out of harm's way.*

Back at home, Becca tried to put everything behind her. Tried desperately to erase what she had seen that day. Monsters didn't exist. The drugs and the high emotional state she had been in must have caused some kind of warped hallucination. But six months later, the parts of her husband that she had been trying to salvage were well and truly destroyed. Another phone call from the police. The voice dry and serious. She knew from the moment she picked up it wasn't good news. Initially they were asking questions, wanting to get to the bottom of yet another mystery that they felt might be connected to the three *friends*. Only now, they were dipping way back into the past. When the developers had taken out the foundations of the old hospital, they had found a pit with a woman's body buried deep down inside. At the other end of the phone, Becca felt her heart falter. She knew what this meant.

Leaving the handset in the hallway, Becca tore up the stairs. Frantic, she pulled down Scratch's childhood journals from the hideous wall cupboard that sat above their large double bed. Grabbing them all down so they cascaded over her head as she sobbed. Ella found her mother later in the evening. The light had faded from the room. Becca was kneeling distraught in a sea of paper. It was obvious. Scratch had always known where her mother was. One day just after school finished, Scratch had called round at their house in a state. He'd told Becca's mother that young Becca was stuck in the old wreck. Everyone knew it was a death trap, just itching to open its jaws and snap. It was no place for kids to play, but back then, nobody cared enough to stop them. Nobody but Becca's mum. She would have been better off not caring in the long run. When Scratch had heard the rumours that Bella Nilsen was planning on getting out, leaving town and taking her daughter with her, he had walked Becca's mum up the hill to the old wreck. Telling her stories of the broken beam, of poor Becca falling, of the need to get there urgently. It's oh so easy to push someone when they are standing above a pit looking down into its depths.

Years would pass, and seasons fall. In the back of the Skoda, an old leather notebook lay beneath homework bags, winter coats, and crayoned school pictures. Its pages full. Becca had no idea what to do with it. She just knew she didn't want the thing in the house. There was another book in the car boot as well—*Moor's Myths Uncovered*. Becca wanted there to be a trail. She wasn't sure what happened to creatures like Scratch: Rock Babies that came crawling out of the centre of the earth looking for families or people foolish enough to take them in. It was only Ella, Becca's eldest, who knew there had been something off about their dad. Becca kept the others in blissful ignorance. What good would it do? How could you even explain? Although, despite all, there was one blessing. One thing Becca was sure of was that if evil did rear its ugly head again, this time she would be strong enough to fight it because despite all the trauma, and even though she missed Finn, Becca felt lifted somehow: her mother hadn't abandoned her. Old Man Byrde had wanted to protect her. Finn had never wanted anything for her but happiness, and so she felt sure, deep down, good will always find a way.

A NOTE FROM THE PUBLISHER

Thank you for reading this book. If you enjoyed it please do consider leaving a review on Amazon.

We hate typos. If you find any, let the team know and we can get it amended. publishedwithpassion@aol.com

MORE BY THIS AUTHOR

The Insect House - Bloodhound Books

Helen and Gareth grew up in a world where absolute freedom was the norm, but the arrival of a predatory priest saw their childhood paradise turn rotten. A murder was committed. Gareth went A.W.O.L, and Helen put her life on hold. Twenty-five years later, Gareth is back.

"An Outstanding piece of new writing." James Holloway.
The Cut.

"Loved this. Well constructed plot with a twist at the end."
(amazon uk review)

"Fresh Original writing. A gripping tale with great characters,
and a twist." Rob Backhouse. Mustard.

"From start to finish, not a word wasted." Alan Huckle. Eyes
Write.

ALSO AVAILABLE:

Reap What You Sow - Bloodhound Books

Struggling journalist Sophie can't believe her luck when she lands the job of a lifetime—writing the personal history of renowned geneticist Tim Henderson, from his idyllic Greek island. But the island, and Henderson, turn out to be hiding much more than Sophie bargained for.
5 out of 5 stars

"A compelling psychological thriller that is always one step ahead of the reader, a great read." (Amazon Review.)

"Totally gripping. I loved this book. Couldn't put it down and read it more or less in one sitting." (Amazon Review.)

"Greek mythology expertly woven into a creepy psychological thriller... what's not to love!" (Amazon Review)

ACKNOWLEDGEMENTS

With special thanks to Eileen Ryan, who told me to rewrite it. Breck, who helped me do just that with their expert Beta-Read. Paige Lawson and Isla. Maryssa for editing, Louise McGuinness for proofreading and Axy Pater for cover design.